MW01132937

A Tempting Arrangement

Twisted Vows

J. Wilder

Join Jessa Wilder's Readers' Group

JOIN THE WILD ONES READERS' group if you love giveaways, polls, teasers, quotes, early access to covers, blurbs and all kinds of other things.

Wilder Ones - Jessa Wilder Reader Group

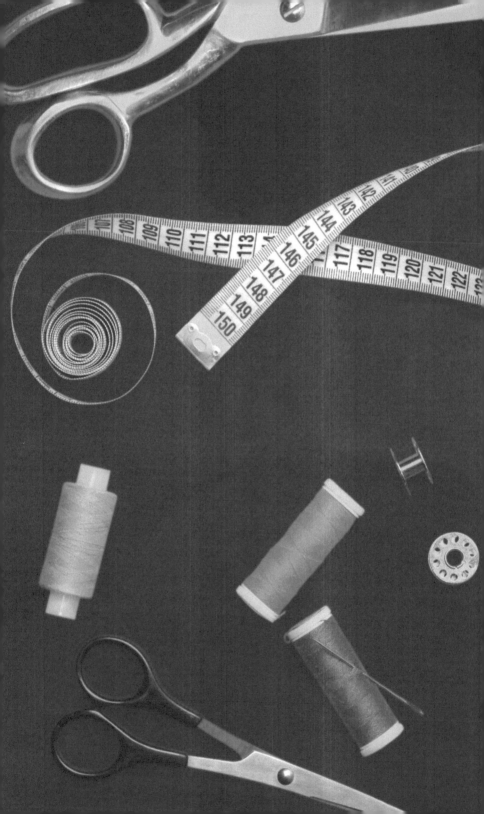

Dedication

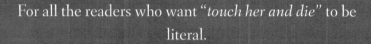
For all the readers who want *"touch her and die"* to be literal.

Dear Reader

The Twisted Vows series is a spinoff from the Rule Breakers series. In this book you'll get to see the full cast again, but I want to be **extra** clear. This is not the same kind of book.

If you are hesitant at all I highly suggest you check the trigger/content warnings. Damon and Misty's story covers tough topics that will make your heart ache. There's also a considerable amount of graphic on page violence that can be hard for some to read.

READ ME! CONTENT/ TRIGGERS:
- Gourmet phallus Torture
- Stalking
- Kidnapping
- Touch her and die for real
- Somnophilia
- Cock warming

- Overall violence (against others and the MMC/FMC)
- Reference to past SA (not by MMC)
- Reference to miscarriage.

Flashback of past SA (not by MMC) that can be skipped: marked in chapter heading, also indicated in italics.

Chapter 1

Damon

THE FEEL of Selena's pretty pink lips swallowing my cock barely registers. It's not that she's not talented—her fist is wrapped around my base while her palm cups my sack, working me simultaneously. She's one of the best in the industry and knows what I want. A quick, uncomplicated release, then to be left alone, but no matter how deep she takes me, my body refuses to respond.

I have no shame in paying for what I want, which is anonymity. I'd tried casual hookups in the past, made it clear that it was a simple matter of physical needs, but they never failed to ask for more. I'm the heir to the Everette fortune—I can't blame them for trying. The only motivator stronger than greed is revenge.

Which is why I switched to a service. No feelings, no awkward goodbyes, purely transactional. It had been the perfect solution and one I desperately needed today after Miss Hart brushed back her pale pink hair, leaned

9

over the conference room table, pinned me with her fierce gaze, and demanded I pay attention to her.

As if I wasn't already.

As if she wasn't the entire reason I was in that meeting to begin with.

Yes, I'm the owner of the Boston Bruins, but I'm the owner of a lot of companies, and I do not sit in PR meetings.

I have people to do that. When I'd told my brother I was attending today, he gave me a knowing look. I told him to fuck off before he could get a single word out.

Men in my position do not attend day-to-day meetings, but other men in my position aren't obsessed with their pixie-like employees.

She's young and fresh with a spark of life I have no business coveting. I would ruin her the second I touched her. The blood that permanently stains my hands would coat her, slowly dirtying her every inch until it snuffed out her light.

But fuck me, I wanted to reach over the table and capture her mouth when she'd hissed out, *"Yes, Sir,"* with one raised eyebrow.

I'm not bothering to pretend that it wasn't why I chose this spot for tonight's activities.

Selena pulls back with a pop, looking up at me with warm brown eyes I wished were pale green. "You okay? Am I doing something wrong?"

"You're fine." I fist her hair and guide her back to my cock, determined to find my release.

I focus on where Misty sat at the conference table. I picture the scene from this morning, only this time, I don't wall off my emotions.

This time, I stand, stalking around the table, and press Misty's chest into its hard surface.

Her flower-covered skirt slides easily over her hips as my palms wrap around her thighs, revealing her perfect ass.

A groan rumbles in my chest, and Selena sucks me harder, knowing that it's working.

I can almost feel the sting of my palm as my hand lands hard on Misty's round ass, leaving a perfect red print. I've wanted to mark her since the first day we met.

She stood in the hall with both hands on her hips, her head cocked to the side. Her eyes were round, her chest rising and falling too fast to be normal, but she'd played it off and walked around me without a word.

Fuck, it had taken willpower not to pull her back and slam her into the wall. I'd never responded to anyone the way I do her.

I crave knowing the sounds she'll make as I drive my cock hard inside her. I'd make her beg for more until she screams out my name as I sear myself into her soul.

I moan through clenched teeth, hips pounding harder into Selena's mouth, tension shooting down my spine. Every muscle tightens as my release builds painfully. I rock harder, and she takes me down masterfully, but it's not enough.

It's not what my body craves.

I grunt out in frustration, ready to pull her off my dick and give up on tonight, when the conference room door opens, and a gasp rings through the space.

Misty stands in the doorway, the light from the hall illuminating half her face. She's twisted her hair up, revealing the smooth column of her neck, and I follow it down to where her breasts puddle above the neckline of her dress like they can no longer be contained.

I want to rip it down and feel how perfectly they'd fit around my cock, hear the sounds she'd make as I fucked her tits.

She breaks my control, turning me primal.

I shouldn't want her. I should sell the team and stay the fuck away, but instead, like the bastard I am, my eyes drift to her mouth.

Dropped open in shock.

Suddenly, the lips expertly wrapped around my shaft are hers. She's making the needy sounds as she sucks me deeper. It's pale pink hair clenched in my fist and pretty green eyes watering as I hit the back of her throat.

I groan low in my throat, balls tightening as image after image of my girl on her knees barrages my thoughts.

Misty closes her lips, breaking the illusion, and I rip myself away from the warm mouth, instantly fisting my cock in full view of this mystical pixie who captures all of my attention.

Misty's eyes are locked around my fist stroking from

base to tip. The light catches on her hardened nipples, and a flush crawls up her chest, pinkening her cheeks as she takes me in. She should be disgusted, but my girl's captivated.

Her teeth sink into her bottom lip as she takes in every stroke. My hips jerk forward, and a pained whimper escapes her throat, sending me over the edge.

My orgasm slams into me, shivers rippling down my spine as my cum coats my hand.

Her eyes track my movement as I grab a handkerchief from my pocket and wipe myself clean. She doesn't look away when I tuck myself back in but leave the button undone.

I take a step forward, closing the distance between us with sure strides. Her eyes widen as I step into her space, but she doesn't move. Caught like a rabbit, frozen in place while I stalk toward her until the toes of her shoes meet mine.

She has to tip her head all the way back to continue looking at me, and I bend toward her, close enough that our breaths mingle together.

I can't stop myself from touching her, and I rub my thumb along her bottom lip, freeing it from her abuse, then dip the tip inside. Her soft tongue runs along the rough pad, sending a blistering heat rushing through me, the taste of my cum filling her mouth.

She startles back, eyes wide with shock, and she stumbles. I catch her arm, steadying her. "Welcome back." I breathe the words in a whisper.

Shock turns to fear, turns to mortification, and she practically squeaks, "I'm sorry."

Then turns and flees.

I tense against the need to chase her, to press her into the wall and slide my fingers into her pretty panties to see if she's as wet for me as I think she is. I swallow hard, breathing through my nose. My little mouse isn't ready for me yet, but it's far too late for me to stop now.

A feminine cough comes from behind me.

"She's the reason you called?" Selena inquires. She's fully dressed, silk shirt tucked into a perfectly tailored pencil skirt. She looks like she belongs in board meetings; she's everything that Misty isn't.

Making her everything I don't want.

"It won't happen again."

She nods, then looks at the ground where my cum is staining the carpet. "You go. I'll clean up."

I swipe my fob for the elevator. It's coded to come directly to me, skipping all floors. If I'm lucky, it'll bring her right back to me.

Frustration licks at my skin when the car's empty, and I have to wait for it to reach the bottom floor. By the time I'm out the front doors, her bright hair is disappearing into an Uber. I run my tongue along my top teeth, pressing hard enough to feel the sharp edges, and roll my neck. I don't like her getting into cars with strangers, and that will be the last time.

"Fernando," I say to our security guard. He's been here for the last ten years, and I know I can trust him.

"There's a Miss Selena on my floor. She won't be a problem, but make sure she leaves."

"Will do, boss."

The valet pulls up my car without being requested. I weave in and out of traffic, following the faint silhouette of the navy blue car she's in until I'm tailing a few lengths back.

I know better than to follow this closely. I'd been trained to stay invisible, but I can't stand the idea of losing sight of her.

This way, if her driver veers off from the quickest path, I'll know immediately. I know where she lives, and I know the best way to get there.

This woman's been haunting my dreams, gasping my name, and has quickly become my obsession.

I pull up to her apartment moments after her and watch as she steps out of the car and makes her way to the door. It takes several precious seconds for her to unlock it, more than enough time for someone to come up, and a muscle ticks in my jaw.

I pull up my brother Matthias on the dash and hit Call.

"What's up?" He sounds tired, and I realize it's almost 1:00 a.m. What was my girl doing at the office so late?

"I've got a job," I reply, eyes still glued on the door. He doesn't question it. "Personal or business?"

"Personal."

"Oh, who is he?" He sounds interested.

"She." I huff, already knowing I'm going to get shit for this.

He hums, and I can hear his sigh. "You know we used to use our skills to control the Society. Now you're stalking a girl? Talk about using your power for evil."

"It was always evil," I say, voice low. Dangerous. There's a stillness in the car that transcends down the line to my brother. We'd both learned young the cruelty of being the Lords of the Order of Saints. I'd nearly lost him, and I turned into Satan himself, giving up a piece of my soul to get him back.

My brother clears his throat. "So who are we stalking?"

"My future wife."

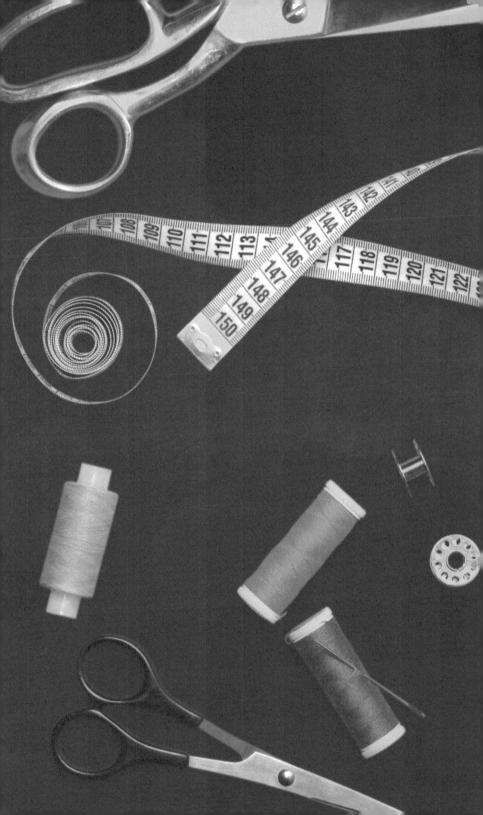

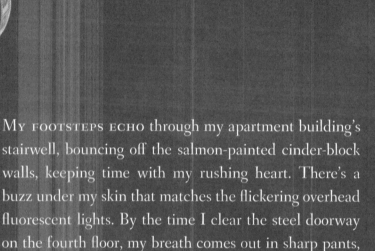

Chapter 2

Misty

MY FOOTSTEPS ECHO through my apartment building's stairwell, bouncing off the salmon-painted cinder-block walls, keeping time with my rushing heart. There's a buzz under my skin that matches the flickering overhead fluorescent lights. By the time I clear the steel doorway on the fourth floor, my breath comes out in sharp pants, and I have to take deep lungfuls of air to keep myself from hyperventilating.

Every second of what happened in the conference room has played on repeat in my head.

I'd just stood there, frozen in place, watching his hand, the way his tip glistened, until he parted my lips and the taste of him filled my mouth. It snapped me out of my daze and doused the rapidly building heat between my thighs with ice-cold water.

I spent the entire ride here trying to justify what happened, like maybe it was some weird hallucination and I'm just having a psychological breakdown. Or I'll wake up from a month-long coma only to find out all of this is just in my head. Because there is no possible way I stared at my boss getting head from another woman and got wet off it.

On top of that, we don't even like each other. The first day as the PR rep for the Boston Bruins, I'd walked into the office, all bright-eyed and bushy-tailed with an overwhelming sense of pride that I'd landed the job. There had to be hundreds of applicants, but I'd gotten it.

Only to be completely deflated by Damon Everette. He didn't miss the opportunity to let me know three of my closest friends, who play on the team, had influenced me being hired. He'd taken one look at me, his eyes narrowing on the green, blue, and purple block pattern of my dress, then my pink, shoulder-length hair, and made a snap decision. Clearly not a positive one since the only thing he said to me was a clear shutdown.

Then, he'd disappeared for months.

So why was he at our meeting, today of all days? The day I was presenting my new plan for the season's advertising schedule, the pitch I'd painstakingly practiced for hours.

I was prepared, notes in hand, perfect PowerPoint loaded, and then I walked into that conference room, and my stomach plummeted at the sight of him.

Head down, flicking through his phone looking like he would love to be anywhere else but there. Good. I didn't want him there either, but sure enough, his gaze met mine, and he gestured to the front.

He proceeded to pick apart every aspect of my plan. I swear he was doing it to antagonize me. At one point, the corner of his lip curved up into the hint of a smirk, and I thought I was going to lose it.

I take pride in my ability to keep control over my emotions, to push anything negative down and present the world with a positive face. So, tell me why he had my fist clenched at my sides and the muscles in my neck straining so hard I swore it would give me a migraine. Pure rage tingled under my skin as he watched me, enjoying every second of my misery.

That's why it's so hard to understand what just happened because there is no possible way that it was Damon Everette the Third—the king of condescension— who has my clit throbbing and my core aching like this. Not a chance that I just stood there and let him run his damp thumb over my bottom lip and across my tongue.

No, I'd have called for security, so... I'm circling back to hallucination.

"You okay? You're looking a little flushed." Gorie's familiar voice comes from beside me.

I meet the warm gaze of my neighbor. I hadn't even heard the stairwell door open. She must be on her way back from the late shift at the restaurant. It takes me a moment to realize I'm standing in front of my door, key in hand, but I haven't moved to unlock it yet.

"A...all good here." My voice sounds off, and she definitely notices.

She searches my face, then looks me over a little longer before placing both hands on her hips and smirking at me knowingly. "Who is he?"

"I have no idea what you're talking about," I lie. We've been neighbors for the better part of a year now, and as two women living alone, we look out for each other.

"Uh-huh." Disbelief is clear in her voice. "Please tell me it's one of those hockey players. Girl, you know they're loaded."

If she only knew just how loaded he really was, she'd lose her absolute mind. "Sorry. No hockey players here."

She raises a brow, unlocking her door. "Fine, don't tell me, but just make sure you take care of yourself."

"Always." I give her a wave, but she stops me.

"Hey, thank you for watching Charlie the other night. I know he can be a bit much."

Charlie's her overexcited puppy, who is the absolute sweetest, even if he peed on my floor. "Anytime."

The puppy in question comes rushing toward me the second she pushes her door open, and I lift him up into my arms, speaking in my best doggie voice. "How's my little troublemaker doing?"

He licks my chin in response. From the size of his paws, he's going to be massive, so I take every opportunity I can to hold him in my arms before he's too heavy.

I gently place him on the ground. "Sorry, boy, I don't have treats tonight."

As if he understands, he lets out a little whimper, and Gorie chuckles.

"Charlie, come, I've brought a treat for you." With that, he dashes back into his place.

They disappear into her apartment, and I finally twist my key, letting myself into mine.

Now that I'm not distracted by Charlie's wrinkly adorableness, tonight hits me in the chest. I swiftly lock the door, collapsing against it, my back sliding down the wood until my butt hits the floor. I drop my head into my hands, letting the night run through my mind. The way he watched me with darkened eyes, tracked my every move while he brought himself to release, would be seared into my brain forever. I should be absolutely mortified, but there was a glint in his gaze, an intensity that wouldn't let me be.

I'm one hundred percent certain he'd wanted me. Wanted me to watch, wanted it to be me on my knees in front of him.

A shiver rolls down my neck, and my thighs press together, searching for the pressure I desperately crave. There's no way I'm going to get off to that man. No matter how hot it is.

I peel myself off the floor and head to my room, kick off my heels, and unzip my dress before hanging it up. I've been making or modifying my own clothes since I was a teenager. Nothing had ever felt right until I'd gotten my hands on a needle and thread and I was able to weave color into my world. Now, my wardrobe is a sea of greens, purples, and pinks. My twelve-year-old self would be in heaven.

Unsnapping my bra, I dress in my coziest oversized shirt, then crawl into bed, too exhausted to do anything else.

Relaxing seems out of the question as my heart pounds in my chest. I'd seen my boss—the freaking billionaire—getting head at work. Can I blackmail him with this? Maybe get a few million and live the best life from now on?

Who am I kidding? Even if I could, I'd never do that. No matter how much he deserved it. It wouldn't feel right.

Deep brown hair falling over smoky gray eyes, hooded with heat, flash across my mind, and I bury my head into my pillow, doing everything I can to drown out my thoughts. I bring my knees together and bite my fist before sliding the tip of my tongue over my lip, tasting the remnants of him.

My panties are already soaked, and I'm so tired of resisting the temptation. My hand slides down my stomach and up my thigh before cupping my core. A soft moan escapes me as my hand turns to his.

Him pushing the thin fabric to the side.

His fingers the ones buried deep.

His palm massaging my clit.

My breath catches when my imagination has my

mouth wrapping around his cock, but instead of pulling out and coming on the floor, I swallow down every ounce of his release. My orgasm crashes over me, wave after wave pulling me under with his name on my lips.

Tomorrow, I'll pretend none of this happened. Tomorrow, it'll all be a dream.

It's not like I'll see him again anytime soon.

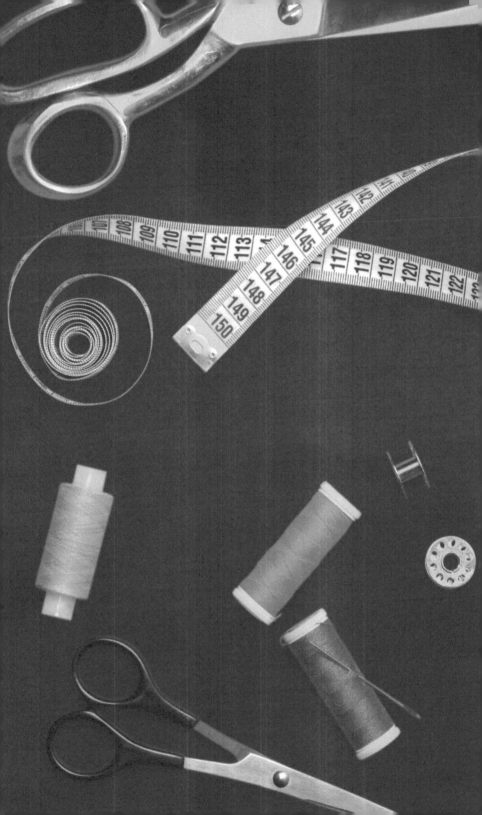

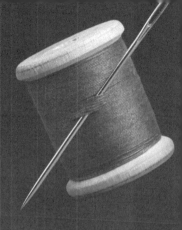

Chapter 3

Misty

I STARE BLANKLY at my laptop screen, the soft glow illuminating my cubicle in the otherwise dim, empty office. It's late, and I'm just putting the finishing touches on my proposal when an email pops up.

There is no flipping way this is happening. But there, clear as day, is a summons to the black-tie event held by the Everette family every year to celebrate the patriarch's birthday.

The email gives some shallow reason for needing a PR representative present, but this screams of Damon. Is this some sort of twisted game? Did he not play with me enough the other night? Unlike what I told myself, I didn't for a single second forget what happened. I swear the memory is burned at the back of my eyelids. Every time I shut them, I see the way the muscles in his arms flexed with each downward stroke of his fist.

I shake the thoughts from my head and hit Reply on the email.

MistyHart@Bostonbruins.com   **to** **Events@Bostonbruins.com**

I'm sorry to inform you I am unavailable to attend the gala.

Best wishes,

Misty Hart

Junior PR for the Boston Bruins

Perfect. I smile, cool and professional. Moments later, a message pops up in the company's messenger app. My cursor hovers over the red dot notification. Something tells me I know exactly who it is.

Damon Everette - *CEO of Everette Industries:* *Mandatory attendance. See you there.*

Black tie, dress appropriately.

He didn't even bother to say hello. There is no rational reason I need to be there. I had nothing to do with the planning since it's an Everette family event and not a Boston Bruins event. My back teeth grind as my fingers hover over the keys, awaiting my reply.

Misty Hart - Junior PR representative: *My apologies. I've previously booked the weekend off and have a prior engagement.*

I've barely hit Send when his reply comes through.

Damon Everette - CEO of Everette Industries: *Not a request.*

Gah. I snap my laptop shut, frustration burning in my chest. I couldn't just say no, no matter how badly I wanted to skip it out of spite. A slow, mischievous smile pulls at my lips. He can insist I show up all he wants, but he has no control over how I dress. If he wants to boss me around, I'll show him exactly what happens.

The driver, Nicholas, comes around to open my door when we pull up to the Everette hotel. He's an older gentleman, likely late fifties, with a soft smile and warm eyes. It took him a bit to open up, but by the time we arrived, I'd learned he has a beautiful wife, Sarah, and two kids. Once we got to the topic of his kids, he'd rambled on freely about the youngest entering her first year in law school and the eldest being the top of her class in med school.

I'd gotten a text before he arrived at my apartment, letting me know the company was sending a car.

Probably didn't want me showing up in an Uber.

I chuckle internally at the thought of the look of horror on all of these rich people's faces being forced to witness my lowly commoner state.

The building's architecture is full of art deco

elements, making it feel like it's from a different time, but there's no mistaking the luxury details of the marble exterior or the stained glass windows in white and black.

I take Nicholas's hand as he helps me out of the car. "Thank you."

He gives me a nod and stands with his hands behind his back. There's a rigidness to his posture that screams of years of training. "Of course, miss. I'll wait out front for you when you're ready to leave."

I adjust the strap of my dress so it lies flat against my shoulder. "You don't have to do that. I'm sure I can grab a cab at the end."

"I assure you, Miss Hart, I do have to do this. I'll see you in a few hours."

I'm still puzzling through what he means when a man in a black suit ushers me toward the entrance. "Right this way, Miss Hart."

I don't recognize him, and he must notice the confusion on my face because he answers. "We've studied the guest list thoroughly. You'll find all members of the staff will know who you are."

I scrunch up my nose. "Weird."

He laughs, a glint in his eyes. "Not used to this?"

"Is anyone?"

"Oh, definitely." His eyes dip lower and slowly rise. "Come find me before you go. We can grab a drink."

"Are you hitting on me?" I ask incredulously. The guy doesn't look old enough to get into a bar.

"Maybe? Are you open to that?"

"No." I laugh. "Nice try though."

My heels click against the marble floor as I make my way to the grand staircase. Soft velvet underfoot, my hand glides over the intricately carved railing.

My carefully styled hair is tousled by a gentle breeze as I follow the elegantly dressed crowd through the towering double doors into the lobby. The interior is even more impressive than the exterior; trees adorned in vibrant red flowers and twinkling lights fill the space, while the delicate scent of jasmine and honey saturates my senses.

"Holy crap," Mia, one of my closest friends, says, followed by a long wolf whistle as her eyes travel down my dress. Her pale blonde hair is styled in a french twist, and she's wearing a deep purple gown that looks amazing on her. "Who pissed you off?"

"How do you know someone pissed me off?" I mean, someone *did* piss me off, but I didn't think it would be so apparent.

"Because that's a Princess Diana–level revenge dress." She gestures to me, indicating it's obvious.

The dress in question is a deep navy, fading into a pale blue. It has a square neckline that I designed to sit barely an inch above my nipples. The satin fabric is perfectly tailored to me, skimming over my curves. It's so tight I opted for two layers of Spanx so I don't get light-headed sucking in the entire night.

I do a spin. "You think it'll work?"

"Definitely," Mia's boyfriend Alex says, stepping up to us and handing her a champagne flute.

River comes up behind Mia and kisses her temple while cupping the back of Alex's neck, giving a gentle squeeze. The two men make a striking pair in black tuxes and crisp white shirts. Where Alex is blond and playful, River's dark and broody.

He lifts a brow at me, a slight smirk on his face. "Who's the lucky guy?" He'd never smiled like this until the three of them got together.

I've grown pretty familiar with Alex and River since they're both forwards on the Bruins. River had been known for being standoffish, which is just so completely different from who he is today. Which is basically a teddy bear, at least when it comes to the two of them.

A weariness settles around my shoulders. What exactly was I thinking showing up like this? Am I really this transparent?

Mia must see my thoughts on my face because she grabs my hand. "You look stunning. Whoever this mystery guy is, he'll eat his heart out. Might even beg on his knees."

"I don't think I want him to beg on his knees." *Do I?*

She turns, pulling me deeper into the room, and tosses over her shoulder, "Even better, leave him wanting."

Even with the grand size of the ballroom and the exclusivity of the event, the room is overfilled with impeccably dressed people. Working in the NHL has made me fairly used to being around wealth, but this is something else. This is old money, daddy owns an island type of wealth.

Lucas and Piper spot us through the crowd and head our way. Her hair is down around her shoulders in golden waves like something you'd see in an old-time movie.

She and I grew close as roommates in university, and I had front-row seats to the whirlwind romance that brought them together. It was touch and go for a bit, but Lucas finally got it together.

"Hey, Misty. How did you get roped into coming to this?" Lucas asks, looking stunning in his deep navy suit, which pairs perfectly with his warm brown skin.

"Same way you did. Work." I scrunch my nose, knowing none of them want to be here.

"Don't you normally get out of this stuff?" Alex asks.

"Yup. Boss's orders." I sigh.

Alex and River stiffen. It wasn't too long ago that Damon tried to block Alex from becoming the captain. According to him, the owner of the team had some kind of weird vendetta against him.

"We've got to do our rounds. Don't get into too much trouble," River says, eyeing his girlfriend.

Mia crosses heart. "Double promise."

River lifts a brow. "Why don't I believe you?"

"It's the grin. Who could believe that grin," Alex adds with a wink.

"Okay, bye," Mia cuts in, and River leans close, whispering something into her ear that has a pink blush painting her cheeks.

The second the guys are out of earshot, Mia spins on me, still flushed. "So, who is he?"

"Who is who?" Piper asks.

"Whoever Misty wore this dress for," Mia responds, taking a sip of her drink. "He must be here."

Piper scans me head to toe with wide eyes.

"Why don't you ever dress like this for me?" she says playfully.

"I just wanted to look good, okay. No hidden agenda."

Both girls smirk. "Fine, don't tell us."

My shoulders relax when they drop it. Honestly, I don't even know what I'm doing. I'm not lying to myself that I didn't pick this dress to see Damon's reaction, but I didn't get far enough to anticipate what would happen after that.

He forced me into coming here for no reason, and I want him to regret it.

There's a hum in the crowd filled with excited whispers. I strain to overhear the group of women behind us. I don't dare turn around to see who they are. Instead, I do my best to make out their whispers.

"*Did you see them?*"

"*Not yet.*"

"*I heard they just got back from their place in Monaco.*"

"*By place, you mean mansion?*"

"*Doesn't one of them race cars?*"

"*Which one? I could learn about cars if it means I can get closer to one of them.*"

"*You wish. Plus, we all know they go through women like it's a game.*"

"*Not Damon. Only the younger two.*" The girl sounds wistful, and I tense, leaning a little closer to listen.

"*That's because he doesn't date at all. I hear no one's ever stayed over. Brittany hooked up with him and said he wouldn't even kiss her when they hooked up. That it was like having sex with a robot.*"

I roll my eyes. There goes my theory that he'd be good in bed. There's nothing worse than a selfish lay.

"*Wait, you mean she didn't...you know...finish?*"

"*Oh, she did. Said he insisted, but there was nothing personal about it. Like it was just a part of the transaction. Honestly, he hasn't been seen with anyone in years.*"

"*His mother must be furious. He's thirty now?*"

That makes him a five years older than me. A little thrill trickles down my spine, and I ignore it. Just because I think older guys are hot doesn't mean anything.

"What are they saying?" Piper whispers in my ear, and I jump, startled. I press my hand to my chest, not realizing I'd spaced out that much.

I lean closer to her so our shoulders touch and whisper so the girls can't hear me. "Gossip."

"Juicy gossip?"

"Everette family stuff. The usual. I have no idea why people are so interested in them."

"No idea, huh?" Piper raises one brow. "Let me see, handsome, influential, and unimaginably rich. What's not to like?"

"Alex and River don't like them," Mia adds.

"See?" I say to Piper.

"That's because he tried to break them apart. He already fixed that, and you know it."

"Why does it even matter?"

"You tell me," Piper replies. There's a suspicious gleam in her eyes.

The ballroom lights dim, drawing our attention to the large stage set up to the right of the dance floor.

The girls behind us provide an entertaining running commentary as, one by one, each Everette brother climbs the stairs and stands in a row at the back.

"That's Sebastian. He's the youngest."

"I heard he has a death wish."

"From the rumors I've heard, I don't doubt it."

His sandy-blond hair is disheveled, falling loosely over his eyes. There's a sharpness to his smile, one that warns he's not quite as he seems.

The next brother's slightly older. His hair is brushed back from his face, revealing his bored expression.

"Xander. God damn, that boy is fine."

The room grows eerily silent as the next brother takes his place. There's a dark presence that wafts off him that I can practically feel from here. His near-black hair covers his face, casting his eyes in shadows.

"*Matthias,*" one of the girls whispers, but they don't gossip about him, not willing to risk anyone overhearing. Which is a shame because I'd love to know what makes him glare like that.

Damon is the last to walk up, and I don't need any introduction. I know exactly what kind of arrogant, cocky, overdemanding boss he is. That doesn't mean I can't appreciate him in his suit. Tailored flawlessly, it shows off his wide shoulders while simultaneously cutting into his narrow waist. The man is all sharp lines and perfection. I hate him a little for it. No one *that* annoying should be allowed to be that good-looking.

He unbuttons his tux, and I can see the contours of his abs beneath his shirt from here. Why did I think it was a good idea to stand so close to the stage? My mouth waters, and I have to remind myself that this man spent an entire hour tearing apart my presentation for Mia's charity event. From the smirk on his face, I swear he enjoyed every second of it.

A perfectly styled woman climbs the stairs with poise on the arm of an elderly man. Even with his age, the man manages to look regal. I recognize him easily as the patriarch of the Everette family conglomerate and the grandfather to the four men standing behind him. He's old, at least eighty, and frail. Why hadn't the patriarch stepped down years ago?

The answer comes from whispers behind me. "*His*

son was mysteriously killed. Not even the news covered it."

The woman releases his arm, placing a kiss on his cheek before moving to his right. The resemblance between her and the brothers is undeniable, even with her hair being a light silver color.

The grandfather approaches the microphone, and the room is completely silent, no one daring to speak over him.

"Thank you all for gathering here tonight for the annual Everette ball. I'll admit I have an ulterior motive for being here."

Tension weighs the air as the anticipation settles over us. The man certainly knows how to command a crowd.

He continues, a slight curve to his mouth. "As I'm sure you can see, I've grown old."

There's chatter around the room, and the grandfather waits until he regains their attention. "I'd planned on passing down my title of head of the Everette family to my son, but after his tragic passing, I've been waiting for his eldest son to be ready."

I can't stop my gaze from traveling to Damon, who stands completely still, his face in a neutral position. You'd never know he was being announced as the next head of his family.

"As a part of the Everette tradition, my replacement is required to be married, which will be my grandson Damon's final hurdle prior to taking the family helm."

This time, the whispers grow louder, the attendees unable to suppress their excitement.

"Did you know about this?"

"No, but I wasn't even alive the last time this happened, and the previous heir was obviously very much married." A picture pops in my head of the girl behind me pointing at the four brothers.

The old man's voice grows crisp, demanding their attention. "As I'm close to my demise, my eldest grandson will be required to wed as soon as possible. Which is why I've tasked him to find his wife this summer. If he fails to do so, the role will be passed down to his next brother."

The man steps away from the microphone and immediately leaves the stage. He disappears from sight, clearly wanting even less to do with this event than I do.

The whispers pick back up in the room. The girls behind me are filled with bubbly excitement.

"Did you know they're a part of the Order Of The Saints?"

"Not just that, I heard they're the Lords."

That catches my interest. *"Please don't tell me you believe in that? It's just an old wives' tale."*

I huff out a breath. It doesn't surprise me that the ultrarich play at secret society. Aren't there secret societies in basically all fraternities? But I somehow can't picture Damon *playing* at anything.

"You've just never been invited."

"Oh, and you have?"

"Do I look like a billionaire? I dated a guy in it. He would go on for hours about him being Unsainted and how he'd soon be made a Saint. Whatever that means. I had to promise to keep it a secret. I only told a few people, but word must've gotten out because he showed up at my place one day, accusing me of ruining his life and how I cost him his 'Sainthood.' Apparently, they even did some kind of severing ritual so he can never get back in. He was furious. It was to the point I thought he was going to kill me.

"Then, out of freaking nowhere, Matthias showed up. I swear it was like he was following him or something. Never saw the guy again."

"Have you noticed the way the men in here look at him? With a mix of envy and fear."

"All I know for sure is out of the five most influential families, the Everettes are at the top."

From my experience with Damon, this isn't exactly a surprise. Something tells me he'd never settle for anything below being the king.

"Do you think this whole forced marriage thing is to gain more power through a merger with another family?"

"Probably. You know how the ultrarich are. There's no end to their greed."

"The only thing I know for sure is there's never been an unmarried Everette patriarch."

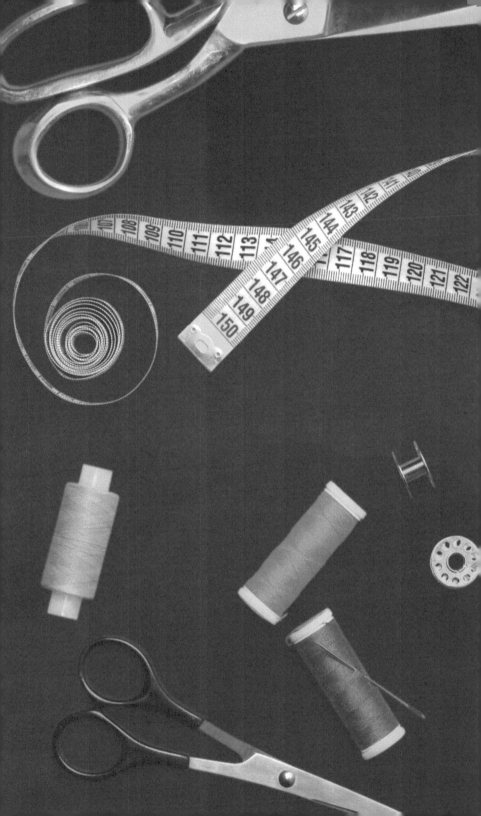

Chapter 4

Misty

MARRIED. *Married.*

A sinking feeling settles deep in my gut, and the rush of noise with the announcement blurs to meaningless words as Damon looks toward his grandfather. I expect him to scowl. No one tells a man like Damon what to do. No one has that type of control, but instead, he smiles wide, taking the microphone.

"My grandfather honored me with the opportunity to bring in someone new to the Everette family. As he mentioned, I've been a bachelor far too long. It's time for me to settle down and start a family of my own." He scans the crowd in a sweeping motion as he speaks, as if looking for someone specific.

I tamp down any delusions that it might be me. Whatever happened the other night was clearly a mistake. Maybe he's just that intense with everyone?

"The future Mrs. Everette cannot be just anyone. She'll be courageous and fierce while simultaneously kind and giving." His eyes slide over me, then double back until they lock on mine. "She'll walk with pride and confidence knowing she has the support of the Everette family."

My heartbeat rings in my ears, and my breath turns shallow as I fight against the confines of my dress to inhale.

Slender fingers wrap around my wrist, and Mia asks worriedly, "Are you okay?"

"Yes, of course." My voice sounds weak even to myself.

She eyes me like she doesn't believe me.

"Just a little too much champagne." I shift, and the stage enters my view, but the men are gone.

The world is narrowing in on me, and my vision goes fuzzy at the sides, feeling like the walls are pressing in.

I give her and Piper a faint smile. "Just going to run to the ladies' room. Be right back."

"We can go with you," Mia says, but her gaze has already caught on Alex, River, and Lucas's approach.

I use their temporary distraction to sneak away. The restroom is down a long hallway, with at least fifteen women waiting. Figures, even in an expensive place like this, they can't figure out women need more stalls.

There's a glowing exit sign at the other end, and I make the snap decision to head out. I need the space to breathe and to escape the crush of people.

The women speak openly about the new turn of events as I walk by.

"I heard it's going to be Anastasia Volkov. They've been seen together before, and her father's company would make a valuable partnership."

"Not a chance with Aubrey interested in him. No family can pass up royal lineage. Not even the Everettes."

"She just needs the money."

"And? Do you think Damon's looking for a love match? Do you think any of the Everette men will be able to?"

A sadness wraps around me at the thought. Damon might be a jerk, but does that mean he can't have love? All I have to do is look at my friends to know it's real. To know it's worth fighting for, which just makes me all the more disappointed that none of those men will get a chance.

Talk about money can't buy happiness.

I push the steel horizontal bar, and the exit door swings open with a click onto an alleyway. It's narrow, no wider than ten feet, with a brick wall flanking the opposite side.

I step out fully, letting the cool night air fill my lungs and chill my exposed skin.

The sweet scent of tobacco has me turning my head, and I spot a man stepping out of the shadows like he was made from them, the crisp red cherry of his cigar lighting his face. He looks like the devil standing there half in shadows, eyes lazily taking me in.

"Are you following me, Miss Hart?" Damon asks in a low, deep rasp that has heat washing through me.

I can't escape his gaze as I breathe out the word "Hardly."

My body eases a little when he props his back against the wall opposite me and takes a long pull on his cigar, never looking away.

My skin tingles where his gaze trails over me.

"Torture," he says, so low I'm not sure I heard him correctly.

"What?"

He tilts his head to the side, his body turning rigid. "What are you doing back here?"

"I can ask you the same thing." Anyone else, I'd have answered easily, but he just lights something in me, a recklessness that comes forward when he calls.

He exhales, smoke surrounding him. "I needed air. Had to get away from a perfect distraction."

What could I even say to that? "Shouldn't you be in there finding your future wife? Isn't that what these parties are all about, after all." My voice is a little too edged to be polite.

He runs his tongue along his top teeth before taking another drag of his cigar. "Who do you think I should marry?"

I shrug. "I'm sure you could marry any of them."

"What if I don't want them?" he asks.

"From what I heard, you don't have a choice."

He seems to be processing that for several moments, and then he pushes off the wall and closes the distance between us.

My chest squeezes at his approach. He moves like a predator. Like someone who gets everything he wants.

"What if I've already made my choice?"

My gut twists, and I struggle to keep it off my face. I have no business reacting to that.

Instead of answering, I glance at his cigar. "You know those are bad for you."

The corner of his lips lifts, revealing straight white teeth. It makes him look sinister.

Damon takes another drag and blows it out against my chest, sending shivers over my suddenly heated skin.

When I don't move, he sucks on the cigar again, this time leaning down until his lips nearly brush mine.

My mouth falls open, and he exhales the smoke as I gasp, filling my lungs with his breath. The tobacco burns my throat, and I struggle to suppress my cough. But within seconds, it hits me, softening the world around us as it floats to my head. He repeats the process, and I suck in each of his breaths.

He pulls back slowly, looking down at the neckline of my dress, and runs his finger over the edge of the fabric. "Absolute torture."

His gray eyes meet mine. "It's time for you to go inside."

"What if I don't want to go inside?" I can't help the small whine of my words.

He gives me that same chilling smile. "It's not safe out here. You never know who you'll meet."

Chapter 5

Damon

I TAKE a second to adjust my rock-hard cock before following after Misty. She's already slipping through the crowd toward her friends by the time I reach the main room.

River says something, and she's laughing, that full-body, head-thrown-back laugh she does, exuding a freedom I've never felt. When I first saw how Alex interacted with Misty, I'd been livid. They had an easy, relaxed, almost intimate relationship that I mistook for something more than it was. I was jealous enough. I went as far as blocking him from becoming captain until I'd realized he'd been in a secret relationship with River and Mia.

Misty had been nervous when she told me about them, assuming I'd be pissed if it created a scandal. But I'd been thrilled.

Now, I can see the almost sibling-like way they tease

each other. She has a playfulness to her that she never shows to me.

The air caught in my lungs, and I fought to keep my carefully shielded expression when I finally spotted her in the crowd earlier.

She's fucking effervescent in her low-cut dress, pale pink hair pulled up, with curls framing her sun-kissed skin. A goddess of temptation. I had to flex every single muscle to stop myself from closing the distance between our mouths in the alleyway.

She is captivating me with her clear green eyes, pulling me in like I'm a planet and she's my sun.

I'll gladly spend my days orbiting around her.

The only thing stopping me from owning her body is knowing that the second I break the kiss, she'll flee.

I need her to be tied to me, irrevocably mine.

I'm not a patient man, but I'll wait for her. Show her that we're meant to be. That she's the piece of my soul that's missing and I'm the armor she desperately needs.

Her words are lost to the sea of voices, but her friends light up around her. Even from here, I can see the way she teases them and how fondly they look back at my girl.

I don't like sharing what's mine. And there's no doubt she will be, but I would never deny her this. For whatever reason, these people are her family.

But after months of watching her, it's clear she hides parts of herself. They don't spot the tiredness or the fear that flashes in her eyes when someone moves too fast. But I do.

She conceals a part of herself from everyone but not from me.

For me, she's brilliant in her anger.

For me, she doesn't mask her emotions under pretty smiles.

For me, she lets herself shine through.

I wonder if she's aware that she only reveals herself to the most dangerous man she knows. The one that's been irrevocably changed by his past. Blackened into something darker than the people around them. That something deep inside her recognizes I'm the one who can understand her.

A low growl vibrates silently in my chest as Anthony Ricci, heir to the Ricci family, approaches them. He's a Saint but knows his place in the hierarchy, which is below the Lords.

The Ricci family made their fortune in the lower crime rings, anything from drug running to car theft. We would have left them as Unsainted if they didn't also provide an uncontested aptitude for technology.

It's tempting to play with them, but it's simpler to just let them be.

Anthony is wearing a charming smile on his face as he lifts Misty's hand and brings it to his lips, sending rage burning through my gut.

I stop my forward momentum when she snaps her hand back and tilts her head, taking him in. My smart girl recognizes something's off with him and crosses her arms over her chest when his gaze dips there.

Soon-to-be-dead fucking heir.

"Dam, we're heading out," Xander, my second youngest brother, says as he approaches my side.

I don't look away from Misty as she moves away to stand between Lucas and River, creating space between her and the Ricci heir.

I've had enough of this. I step forward, but Matthias's strong grip on my arm holds me in place.

"Relax. There's too many eyes in here."

My eyes flash his way, but his fingers don't loosen. He knows I won't come after him.

I shrug him off. "I'm not leaving until she does."

"She's fine, brother," Matthias says. Our shared history allows him to read me better than my other two siblings.

"You've got to chill, man. You're looking stressed."

I ignore my youngest brother, Bash, and bore my gaze into Matthias.

"Shut it down."

His head snaps back, knowing exactly what I'm asking. "Seriously? You know that'll be the entire building, right?"

I don't give a shit. I'm not leaving here while that asshole is still within speaking distance of my future wife.

"Fuck. Okay...okay." Matthias pulls out his phone,

hitting several buttons before the emergency alarm goes off.

The staff ushers the guests out in an orderly fashion, and I track Misty's movements.

"I'll meet you out back," I tell my brothers before following after her.

The night air is crisp as I step out of the building. I stay in the shadows, watching as Nicholas guides her to the car.

Misty looks over her shoulder, scanning where I'm standing hidden like she can feel the weight of my gaze. Feel the invisible chain that ties us together and can't help but turn toward me. She tilts her head, then climbs into the back seat when she doesn't spot anyone.

Nicholas takes out his phone, sending a quick message that immediately pings my phone.

> Nicholas: I have Miss Hart. Proceeding to her home.

> Me: Drive carefully.

Nicholas smiles.

> Nicholas: Of course.

Matthias is the only one waiting for me when I exit the back of the hotel.

"Where's Nicholas?" he asks.

"I gave him a special assignment."

The corner of his lips twitches. "So he's with your girl?"

The construction of the Elysium club took years. Xander led the project, pitching his concept, then following it through to completion.

The space is designed with revelry in mind. A complete loss of inhibitions. There's fabric panels hanging from the ceiling, creating private areas that encourage guests to push the limits of their comfort zone.

Electric music fills the space, the underlying bass controlling their bodies.

Xander created a club where we're gods controlling the peons' every emotion.

Tobias, the security guard responsible for limiting access to the upper floors, gives me a nod and shifts out of the way of the spiral staircase leading up to our level.

I swipe my key fob at the door, and it swings open to our private area. There's floor-to-ceiling windows that overlook the chaos below, tinted to only see out.

Matthias comes in behind me. The noise from the club silences as the door shuts, and he sits in a deep green leather club chair facing our brothers.

Xander paces on the side, his expression void while he speaks on the phone.

Bash is laid out over the other club chair, one wrist

over the arm while he leans all the way back. As the youngest, he has an almost sinister playfulness that's become the bane of Matthias's and my existence.

We've all but given up, switching to the strategy of reducing the fallout of his actions.

I pour a glass of whiskey, swirling it around my tumbler before sitting on the long leather sofa, facing the rest of them. "What's the update?"

Matthias leans forward, a darkness taking over his face. "Someone's taking out the Unsainted."

The Unsainted are men who haven't gone through their trials to be initiated as Saints yet. The Order of Saints has a clear hierarchy, and the Unsainted are at the bottom. That doesn't mean we're going to let people go around killing them.

As the Lords, controlling The Order is our responsibility, and someone's fucking with it.

"How many?" I ask.

"Five," Matthias answers, and the serious look on his face has my muscles straining.

Bash whistles under his breath and tips his head back. "Sounds like someone's goading us into war." His toothy sneer makes it clear he likes that idea.

Xander sits beside me, raking his hand through his hair. "Fuck that."

Matthias agrees. "We watch for now. I've got eyes on all the Unsainted. If something happens to them, we'll know."

I lean forward, resting my forearms on my knees. "Who is it?"

"Unknown. There's no benefit to anyone to challenge our authority," Matthias responds seriously.

I drum my fingers. "Set up guards, then we'll use one as bait and see who bites."

"That's just cruel, brother," Bash adds, not looking disappointed at all. He and Xander were just kids when everything went down. We'd hoped they were young enough to forget, but there's a twisted side to Bash. One that shows glimpses of the damage it caused him. He's not just an adrenaline junkie; he walks on the cusp of death every chance he gets.

My phone vibrates in my pocket, and I pull it out.

> Nicholas: Miss Hart has been dropped off. Do you want me to stay here?

Nicholas's always been able to anticipate my needs before I can ask. It's one of the many reasons he's my personal driver.

> Me: Yes. I'll send someone to relieve you.

I switch to my monitoring app and watch as Misty kicks off her heels in the building's entryway before picking them up and making her way up the stairs. I tense when a large, burly man appears on the steps, looking her over.

I'm about to text Nicholas to get the fuck in there

when she waves at the stranger, and even through the feed, I can see the wide smile she gives him.

The man relaxes, completely disarmed by my little nymph. They say a few words, and I make a note to have Matthias add microphones into the system. Misty pauses to open her door, and I switch the cameras to see her apartment. She drops her shoes in the now familiar living room. I've been watching her movements since the system was installed and have mapped out every possible weak spot. There are only two entry points, a balcony and the front door, both of which I made sure are firmly secured.

I'd prefer a better system on the patio but haven't figured out a way to get it installed.

The apartment super could be bribed into doing it, but I don't like the idea of him being in her place.

Misty disappears into her room, and I curse under my breath there isn't a camera in there. She's left the door open, giving me a sliver view of her space. When she appears, her dress is undone, revealing the side of her back, but she steps out of sight before I can examine her.

I clench around the phone, trying to mentally encourage her to come back, when Bash slaps me on the back.

"You're looking pretty hard at that phone."

I meet his gaze until he looks away.

He clears his throat. "What was all of that 'it's a tradition for the heir to get married' shit about?" He grabs my arm. "And for that matter, why weren't you freaking the fuck out?"

"I created it," I deadpan and shrug him off. He steps back, hands up in surrender. Even my family knows not to touch me.

Xander leans forward. "Why would you do that?"

"Because the girl I'm going to marry needs some extra motivation."

"Who is it?" Bash asks, curiosity filling his voice. Now that we've gotten onto the topic, he's not going to drop it.

"The Bruins' PR rep."

Bash laughs. "Fuck, I've seen her. She's hot."

I glare, and he shuts up. "You're not too old for me to beat you."

Xander cuts in, pulling my attention from Bash. "And...you think this random girl's just going to marry you?"

"She will. She won't have a choice by the time I'm done."

"Fuck, brother. That's scary. You know, you could always ask her," Xander adds.

"I like my deals to be secured before moving forward," I respond coldly, making it clear I'm not open to their suggestions.

"Is that why you had me monitor her building?" Matthias asks like he doesn't already know the answer but is happy to fuck with me.

"Oh shit. This is getting good." Bash collapses onto the sofa, rubbing his hands together.

Xander, the most reserved out of all of us, shoots Matthias a look.

"Don't worry. I refused the bathroom and bedroom. Let's just hope she's not the type to walk around naked."

"Watch it," I warn.

"You know, this whole desperate stalker thing is a good look for you."

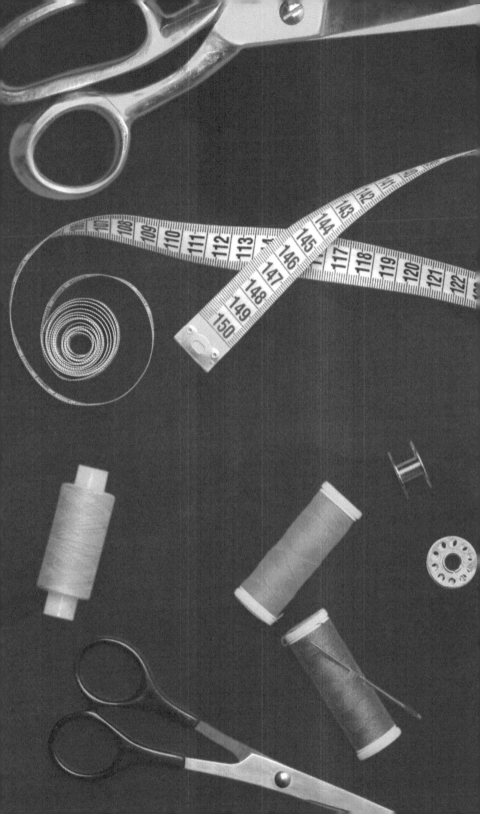

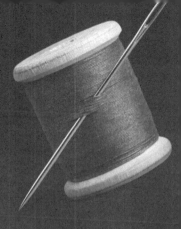

Chapter 6

Misty

I LOOSELY CURL my chin-length hair, giving it some texture, then twist it back and away from my face. The rope braid result looks way more complicated than it is to do it.

I've dressed in a high-waisted, deep emerald skirt that hits mid-calf with a two-foot slit up the side and paired it with a pink, yellow, and green striped sweater.

Clothes have become my creative outlet, a way to let my true self shine through while being a silent protest of my past.

I'd been raised in a well-off family, but we never fit in with the rich Canadian community, no matter how desperately my parents tried. They'd enrolled me into Baskerville Hall when I was three years old, always reminding me of the status they expected me to reach. My wardrobe had been a sea of muted pastels that looked lifeless with their lack of personality. My parents dressed me up to fit in with the people they desperately wanted to be.

Until...after the "incident," as my parents like to call it. When I woke up in the hospital with stitches along my back and a soreness between my legs, I'd expected my parents to be angry, furious.

Instead, they cautioned me to be quiet. That it would only come back on me. That he was from a good family and I'd been dating him for several weeks. It didn't take long for their words to turn accusatory, wanting to know what I had done to bring it on and letting me know they would never be on my side. They made me promise to not tell anyone. That this was the type of secret that would ruin me and not him if it came out. Finally, they told me if I loved them, I wouldn't ruin this for them.

From the moment my parents said that, I knew I would escape them and everything they represented.

And I did. I filled my life with color. Even went a little overboard with my obsession with college hockey. I allowed myself to do whatever I wanted. Whatever made me feel happy. But I never forgot the lesson I'd learned that day. Even the closest people to you can turn their backs if the situation inconveniences them.

So I let my light shine through, presenting the world with my perfectly happy demeanor, and pushed that darkness deep inside. I locked the helpless rage into a box and tucked it into the corner of my mind, never to think of again.

Then last night, I stood in a room full of pastel dresses, of carefully constructed faces, and that box shook in my soul, reminding me that I do not belong.

I slip on my favorite patent leather Doc Martens that always manage to make me feel stronger. Like I can stomp out any of my problems and lock the door behind me.

The app says my Uber is waiting, but when I exit my building, it's Nicholas standing there with a wide, welcoming smile as he opens the back door of a black sedan for me.

Alarm bells ring in my head as I take in the strange sight. "What are you doing here?"

He shifts on his feet and loosens his perfectly tied tie. "Mr. Everette has requested that I remain your driver for the foreseeable future."

"What?" The word snaps out, and my mouth opens in shock. I stare at Nicholas for several seconds, but when he doesn't correct himself, I pull up the Uber app again.

"Not happening," I say without looking up. "You can tell your boss thank you, but I'm not interested."

"Understandable, Miss Hart. It would be a great favor to me if you let me drive you until you can speak of this with Mr. Everette himself."

He looks so agitated that all the air pushes from my lungs. I'm not angry with him.

"Just this once."

The corner of his lip lifts, and he bows his head slightly. "Of course, miss."

We're quiet on the ride. The tension of the situation makes it hard for me to put on my usual happy persona. When we arrive, I make sure I thank him genuinely and apologize for any inconvenience.

"No inconvenience at all. It's an honor to drive someone so important to Mr. Everette."

He makes absolutely no sense. I'm a lowly PR rep, and I might be good at my job, but this entire situation has me trying to sort out any rational reason, and I come up empty.

I'll give it an hour to get myself under control before calling Damon. His name conjures up images of him standing in front of me, his breath filling my lungs with each inhale. I shake my head. Better make it a few hours.

Thank God he's almost never here, so at least I don't have to worry about running into him.

I go to my cubicle first, dropping off my things and checking my emails before heading down two floors to the fitness center. Since the building houses an NHL team, it's stocked with the finest equipment. There's a lap pool, a weight room, and even a running track that circles the entire floor.

Directly in the center of the space is the juice bar that enticed me down here.

"Hey, Mike. The usual, please."

The attendant waves in acknowledgment. "One orangesicle smoothie coming up."

It's the least healthy item on the menu, but hey...I'm not the one trying to be on the top of my game, and a little sugar rush never hurt anyone.

"Misty," Lucas says and rubs a cloth over his face as he approaches. He rests it around his neck, the white fabric bright against his deep brown skin. "How's it going? You took off pretty fast after the fire alarm. Piper wanted you to come over for drinks."

I take a long sip from my smoothie. What am I supposed to say? That the owner of his team turned me on in the alleyway and I'd been desperate to escape from that point on? I'm not ready to face that, let alone speak it aloud, so I go with, "Headache. I texted the group chat when I got home."

"I know, I got it." He searches my features like he's not sure if he should believe me or not. "So long as you're all good?"

"Yup, yes...perfectly good," I stammer, and his brows pull together. Desperate to change the subject, I bring up the one thing I know will work. "I've been working on the fundraiser with Mia. We're going to do an auction. I know how well that worked out for you and Piper."

Lucas huffs a laugh through his nose and grabs one of the bottles of water from the small fridge under the counter, full of grab-and-go snacks for the guys. "This is going to cost me thousands."

I shrug. "Probably, but it's for a good cause. You should bid on Alex. River will lose it. You can see how high you can make him bid."

"You're evil, you know that?"

"I prefer clever."

"That too."

"Hey, what are you two laughing about?" I startle when Carter, one of the second-line D-men, comes up from behind me.

"Just that Misty's an evil genius and I'm glad she's on our side," Lucas replies, then takes a long drink from his water.

Carter smirks, showing off his dimples. I'm sure that smile worked for him in the past. "Is that true?" He brushes a strand of hair behind my shoulders. "I don't think that's right. No one as bright as you could have a dark side."

I stiffen. This guy's nice and all, but we're definitely not close enough for him to touch me. That being said, neither are Damon and I, and I let him get way closer than this. The thought of Damon just makes it all the more apparent that I'm not into Carter. It's too bad. I could definitely use a release.

Hoping he doesn't notice, I shift, putting a little more distance between us.

"You should have more faith in my mastermind abilities. Do you really think you'd know if I don't want you to?" I punctuate my words with a wink.

Lucas laughs. "I told you, man. Keep an eye on this one."

Carter's gaze meets mine. "I plan on it. Want to grab lunch sometime?"

It would be so much simpler if I was attracted to him. But nope, not even a heart flutter at his obvious flirting. "I...I don't—"

Angry, clear gray eyes meet mine from across the floor, and my chest constricts like I've just been caught doing something wrong. By the way Damon's glaring at me, it looks like he thinks so too.

I place my hands on my hips and glare right back at him.

He lifts one brow in challenge. This man is absolutely infuriating. There's something about Damon that has me losing my grip on my carefully constructed cheerful facade, and I find myself wanting to push him.

"Sure, give me your phone." Carter hands it to me, and I punch my number in, ignoring the way the back of my neck is being branded by Damon's piercing gaze.

I don't look back. Instead, I smile up at Carter. Evil indeed.

Chapter 7

Damon

EVER SINCE MATTHIAS installed the cameras in Misty's apartment, I've been addicted to watching her. She floats around her apartment this morning, captivating me until I can't look away. I cuss out Matthias for a good five minutes because of my inability to zoom in. It damn near kills me when she steps out of her washroom in just a small pink towel, her skin flushed from her shower.

My hand's already fisting my cock, and I know I'd be late, but I'm too entranced to give a single fuck, letting all my carefully laid plans go to shit.

This girl has me forgetting who I am, and she's not even here.

I watch her move around her room, the terry cloth barely covering her ass while she makes toast. With every step she takes, the fabric shifts, giving me brief flashes of her thighs beneath. By the time the bread pops, my hand is fully stroking my length as I imagine her perfect fingers in its place.

She bites into her toast, and jam spills over her lip, dribbling on her chin. I tighten my fist over my tip, the precum lubricating my thrusts, and groan when her tongue slides out to swipe off the excess jelly with a pure blissed-out look on her face. I stroke myself harder, picturing her on her knees looking at me that way, licking my release from her mouth. My dick jerks, coating my hand with my cum.

Fuck me. Just watching her got me off.

I clean myself up but don't leave until I watch her exit her building and go all the way to where Nicholas waits with the car. She briefly looks like she won't get in, but whatever Nicholas says has her climbing into the back seat.

I run my thumb over the screen. I'll have to give Nicholas an even bigger bonus this year. A hundred grand should suffice, but I'd give him more if he keeps my future wife safe.

I'm not released from the trap she's unknowingly entranced me in until my phone beeps with Nicholas's message, letting me know he's picked her up.

Already late, I press the gas pedal to the floor, my Audi R8 going forty over the limit. I switch lanes to get around a slow-moving car. I'm expected in my office for an investors meeting, one I can't miss, but every mile pulls me further from her. I grip my steering wheel, keeping my eyes focused on the road ahead of me. I'm driving brutally fast, but I need it to keep my mind off the flashes of her pretty bare skin that have infiltrated my mind.

I crave finding her and living out my fantasies, but I know she's not ready yet, which is why I'm white-knuckling the steering wheel and heading to the furthest building I have away from her.

My phone rings, and I hit the Receive Call button, slowing down minimally. "What?"

"Dropped Miss Hart off, sir." Nicholas's voice comes through the speaker.

"Were there any issues?"

He huffs. "If you want her to ride with me in the future, you'll likely have to speak to her yourself, but I'll be here whenever she's ready to leave."

"I'll speak to her now." Even the barest of reasoning has me caving. I yank the wheel to the right, crossing three lanes.

Nicholas clears his throat. He's worked for me for years, but he knows not to push my limits. "I wouldn't expect a warm welcome."

I laugh. "I'm looking forward to it."

I end the call, take the next off-ramp, and jump onto the highway, heading in the reverse direction. The pounding in my chest settles, knowing I'm finally closing the distance between me and who I want most. I'm lucky my Little Nymph doesn't know the power she has, or I'd be fucked.

I make my way directly to her floor, and the cubicle partition groans under the force of my grip. Her bag and laptop are here, but that's it. Frustration courses through me, but there's an underlying sensation of something else. Disappointment? I pull out my phone and send off a quick text.

> **Me:** Where is she?

> **Matthias:** You know I don't have a tracker on her.

> **Me:** Good idea.

> **Matthias:** Fuck man, that wasn't a suggestion.

I ignore him, not giving a single fuck about what he thinks about all of this. There's nothing healthy about how I feel right now, but I have no desire to fix it.

> **Me:** She's at the Bruins facility. Check security for what floor.

I grind my teeth, waiting several minutes for him to message me back.

> **Matthias:** Gym floor. You're not going to be happy.

My back tenses at his warning. I watch the elevator

light change, indicating each floor, and I spot her the moment the doors open. Matthias is right, I'm not happy. She doesn't notice me walk in, too focused on a player. I recognize him as one of the Bruins' second-line D-men, and if he keeps crowding her like that, he'll be looking for a different team to play for.

My feet eat the space between us. If he doesn't back off, I'm going to claim her right here, then marvel at how sexy she is when she's pissed.

A primal part of me is screaming to do just that. To press her against the counter and make her moan for me. Show her she wants me just as badly because I know she does. I can see it in the way her breath catches and her pupils dilate whenever I'm near her.

Pale green eyes finally meet mine and go wide. I enjoy the second of her surprise before her face hardens and she turns a false smile on Zach? Chad? Whatever the fuck his name is. All that matters right now is that he moves away from her.

A muscle in my cheek twitches when she glances at me, a smirk curving her lips. Fuck. My teeth grind together as she gives him her number. She's going to pay for that.

It's painful to turn away from her, but for what I have planned, I need to find her direct supervisor. If she wants to play games, I'll show her I always win.

There are several workers gawking at me when I stride through Misty's floor. "Who here is Miss Hart's supervisor?"

A rail-thin woman in a straight-lined dress steps forward. Her face is pinched together when she asks. "What did she do?"

I raise a brow at her accusatory tone, and she takes a hesitant step back.

"From now on, Miss Hart will report directly to me as my personal PR representative. I want her removed from all current projects and focused solely on me."

"She...she's got quite the workload currently. Can I offer you a different employee?"

"Did I ask for your opinion? Miss. Hart. Now."

I don't pause for a response, instead heading directly to my office, pulling out a cigar, relaxing in my chair, and waiting for her to come to me.

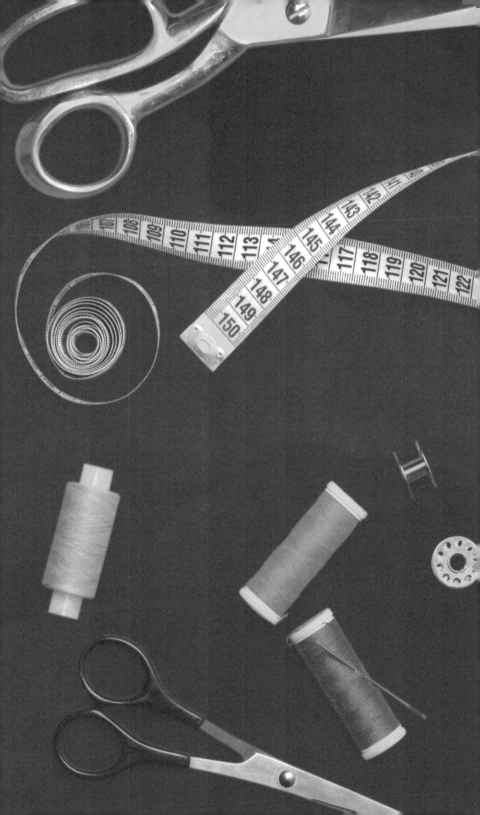

Chapter 8

Misty

I PULL Damon's office door open so hard it clangs off the wall, and the glass rattles so hard it's dangerously close to shattering.

He raises one perfectly arched brow, his gaze traveling down my outfit, stopping on the slit up the side of my skirt. His eyes darken, and I fight against the shiver threatening to roll through me and the growing heat between my thighs.

Why does he have to be so hot?

"You have no right to do this." I straighten and pin my shoulders back, refusing to cower to him.

He leans forward, pinning me with his stare, and takes a long, slow toke of his cigar, releasing the smoke between us. The action has my brain spiraling back to the alley, and I struggle to take my next breath.

My heart pounds in my chest, heat flooding my lower abdomen when he runs his thumb over his bottom lip. I can feel the ghost of his touch from that night in the conference room, and I shiver at the memory of his taste. Damon's mouth tugs up in a dangerous smirk. He knows exactly what he's doing.

Hands and teeth clenched, I let out a huff of exasperation. I'm this freaking close to stomping my foot.

I shouldn't be doing this. He's my boss...he's more than my boss. He owns the company. The company I depend on to be able to stay here. The company where my contract is already almost up.

But he's just so infuriating I can't stop myself.

Damon's deep brown hair falls into his eyes, and his crisp black shirt pulls when he leans back, revealing muscles you wouldn't expect on someone who works in an office setting. He watches me with stormy gray eyes, a slight curve tipping up his lip. He looks entirely too satisfied with everything that's happening.

He puffs out smoke before he commands, leaving no room for misunderstanding. "As my personal PR representative, I expect your complete attention. I may call on you at any time. Nicholas will be your personal driver, and I expect you to use this service wherever you go."

"Why would I do that?"

"Because you want this job, and I'm the boss."

"I already have a job." My shoulders collapse. "I have a lot of important things I'm working on."

"The quicker you help me with this, the quicker you can get back to them." He shrugs like none of this matters, when it means so much to me.

"Help you with what?" I fight to keep the curiosity from my tone. I constantly need to remind myself that I do not care what this man is up to.

"I need a wife. And you're the only person to make that happen."

It's been hours, and I'm still fuming at Damon. I pull the pins out of my hair, letting it swish around my shoulders, gently brushing my collarbones. Massaging my scalp, I try to relieve the tension headache that's been plaguing me all day, and I click through yet another email. It's an hour past the end of my shift, and for once, I can't wait to get out of here.

It took all day to transfer over my projects to Melissa. She'd promised profusely that she could handle them and wouldn't let anything fall through the cracks.

The only one I don't let go of is the auction because there's no way anyone is planning Mia's event but me. Damon is just going to have to deal with it.

I open my unread emails, filing them into folders labeled "action" or "information required" or deleting them altogether. It's mostly just a million back-and-forth emails that could've been said in a five-minute conversation.

I click on the next one, ready to trash it, when my heart plummets.

Sender: U.S. Citizenship and Immigration Service

Subject: H-1B visa renewal.

Miss Hart,

There was an issue found in your H-1B renewal request.

You will have 31 days from receiving this message to reply with the appropriate documentation to validate your employment.

If you fail to provide the requested prerequisite, your H-1B visa will be revoked.

Please see attachment for more information.

Sincerely,

Joseph Cole

Sr. Administration U.S. Citizenship and Immigration Service

Revoke. Revoke. Revoke. My breath comes out in fast, shallow pants, and the world goes blurry around me.

Overwhelmed, I slide my chair back and rest my forehead against my desk to help ease the nausea.

I'm fine. This is fine. Everything is fine.

It's just some paperwork. No big deal. I can fix this.

My sweater lifts easily from my skirt, and I run my thumb over the scar across my back, the raised line a stark reminder of the past.

I need to fix this because I can't go home. Not when Thomas can find me. Not when even my own parents would be happy to hand me over to him.

I blow out a breath and force myself to stand. I wouldn't give that man the satisfaction of me freaking out for a single second over him.

Krista, my supervisor and currently my second-least favorite person, is in her office. She'd been the one to fill out the paperwork before, so it shouldn't be too hard to submit it again.

"Yes?" she asks, not bothering to look up from her laptop.

I cut to the chase, no use wasting either of our time. "There was an issue with the paperwork you filled out for me for my visa renewal. They're asking for it again."

She leans back in her seat, her fingers dancing on the arms of her chair, taking several seconds before answering. "I'm sorry, Misty."

I hate the way she says my name. She's disliked me from my first day and has never given me a hint of the reason as to why.

"As you know, I'm no longer your boss. You'll have to put this request to Mr. Everette."

Shit.

"It's just resubmitting it. You must still have the file. I can give it a quick look over." I'm practically begging by the time she cuts me off.

"There's nothing I can do. You'll have to speak with

your *new* boss." She gives me a vicious smile. "I'm sure you'll have no trouble sorting that out."

Dread forms a pit in my stomach. Something tells me I don't want to hand over any leverage on me to Damon, but the other part knows I don't have a choice.

"Thank you for your time." I turn and walk out of her office before she can see my tears.

I'll do whatever it takes to never go back there.

I grab my stuff from my desk, needing to get the hell out of here.

My phone vibrates just as I'm walking out the door.

Carter: Teams heading to Elysium. You coming?

Normally, I wouldn't. Besides Lucas, River, and Alex, I don't make a habit of spending time outside of work with the members of the team. I liked to keep clear lines between us.

But I'm in the mood to do something reckless. Anything that can take my mind off today's events. There's a tingling feeling that Damon wouldn't like it, which just makes it all the more enticing. He changed my job without asking, like he thinks he owns me as more than just an employee. I'm grinning when I reply.

Me: I'm in. See you there.

Chapter 9

Damon

DECIDING to give my girl a little time to cool off, I spend my evening working from my home office. I designed it specifically to my needs during the renovations a few years back. The walls are flanked with built-in storage and open shelving displaying first editions I've been collecting. It's been painted a deep, moody shade of green that is inherently masculine while simultaneously making the space feel more relaxed.

My eyes burn from staring at my screens for the last four hours, and my head feels like it's about to crack apart. I take a long drink of my whiskey and welcome the smooth burn. Fighting the urge to watch her, I have several more hours of this torture to go before I can call it a night. Not that I sleep anyway.

A loud buzzing denotes a text coming in, and I check my phone.

Matthias: Your girl isn't where she's supposed to be.

Me: What the fuck is that supposed to mean?

Matthias: You should really keep better track of her.

Me: That's what I have you for. Now, where the fuck is she?

Matthias: Looks like she snuck out, better call Nicholas. He's going to lose his shit when he realizes he's lost her.

Lost. Fuck, I don't care how long the old man's worked for me, if something happens to her, I'll strangle the life out of him myself.

Matthias: Relax. She's at Elysium. I'm looking at her right now.

Matthias: You better hurry though.

Me: Stop fucking around and tell me.

Instead of replying, an image pops up on the screen. Blood beats like a drum in my ears at the sight of my future wife throwing back a shot with the same asshole hockey player from the office, who has his fucking hand on her hip.

Me: I'll be there in ten.

Matthias: You live twenty minutes away.

Me: Don't let her leave with any of them.

Matthias: I like you like this, brother.

Me: Like what?

Matthias: Desperate. It's cute.

Me: Fuck you.

Any other time, I'd be happy Matthias is joking around. He's been closed off since the incident. But right now, all I can focus on are the fingers wrapped around Misty's waist.

Matthias: You better hurry or someone's going to fuck your girl.

My teeth clack together and I grip my phone tight enough to break.

Me: Do you have a death wish?

Bubbles come and go several times before his message comes through.

Matthias: Sometimes.

Fuck. I'm such an asshole.

Me: Just remember she's my wife.

Matthias: Not yet.

Me: She's MINE.

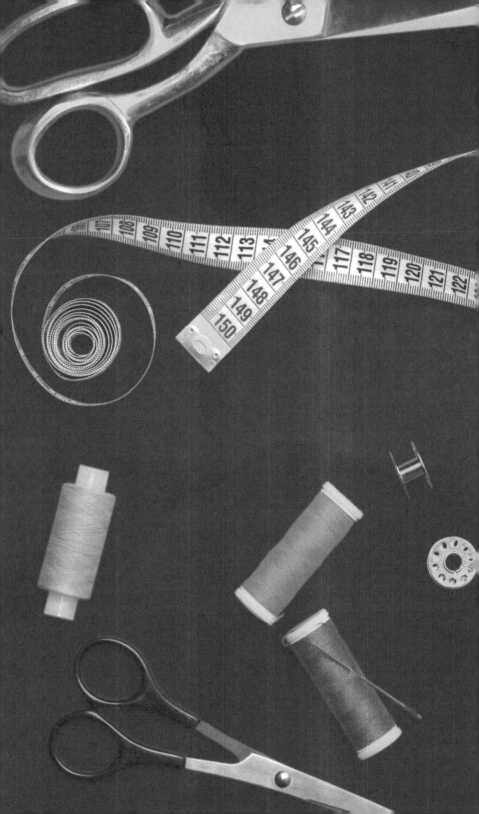

Chapter 10

Misty

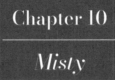

I TOSS BACK the shot Ethan hands me and cringe as it burns my throat.

Nicholas had been waiting to take me home from the office after work. He raised both hands in surrender when I stomped up to him and just laughed when I said I'd find my own way.

He told me to take it up with the boss, but if I didn't want him to get fired, I needed to get in the car.

Nicholas was still outside my front door when it was time to head to the club, so I snuck out the side exit and walked a block down the street before calling for an Uber. Something tells me I don't want Damon to know what I'm doing. That he'd put an end to all my fun.

"Easy there. That's your third one," Carter warns, giving me a worried look.

When he said come out with the team, I expected more than him and his two friends, but after the first couple of shots, I stopped caring. I didn't need a bunch of people for my plans tonight. Relax, let myself forget about everything, and maybe even let Carter take me home.

"I'm fine. Just needed to take the edge off," I reply, proud that I didn't slur.

I've never been to Elysium before. The sleek seating and floor-to-ceiling drapery caught my attention the second I walked in. This place practically dares you to be depraved.

The bar's lit by strobe lights, casting us in alternating shadows and muted colors, giving the same feeling as the cover of night, when everyone feels just a little more reckless.

The deep bass of the music vibrates through my body, calling to something inside me, and the rhythm lulls me into a dance.

The shots go to my head, lowering my inhibitions, and I finally feel free from overdemanding bosses and visa applications.

Fear threatens to take over with the fact that after everything, I could lose it all. I close my eyes and let the thoughts slide off me, drift into nothingness, and vanish into the beat of the music.

I grab Carter's hand, and he follows eagerly as I make my way toward the dance floor. Large, warm fingers settle on my waist as I move in time with the music, and I don't pull away when his chest meets my back. He's tall, several inches over six feet, and he has no trouble keeping up with me. I lean into him and suck in a breath as the length of him presses into my lower back. He grinds his cock against me, holding me in place with an arm banded around my middle.

This is what I wanted. Needed. Fun, release, to let go. But there's something wrong. Something is missing.

He smells like pine, and the way he says my name isn't quite right.

Any chance of Carter and me is crushed as images of Damon's broad shoulders, stormy eyes, and sweet, smoky scent flood my mind.

I push Carter back, taking a step forward and breaking the contact between us. He lets me go easily but tilts his head as he takes me in. "Did I read you wrong?"

Did he? "No, it's fine. Just the shots going to my head. I'm going to freshen up, and I'll be right back."

"You sure you're okay?" His concern is sweet, but there's no warmth in my stomach. No shivers raising goose bumps down my neck.

"Yup. Totally good. I'll be right back."

He gestures his thumb toward his friends. "I'll be at the table."

I rush out, suddenly needing to put distance between us. Turning, I stumble on my heels and smack into a wall. A warm...hard...breathing wall.

My gaze slowly travels up, following the buttons on a crisp black dress shirt and pausing where he's left a few open, revealing a hint of his olive-toned chest and intricate black lines of a tattoo impossible to make out.

I touch the tip of my tongue to my top lip and lift onto my toes to get a better look.

Damon drops his mouth to my ear, his breath fanning over me. "Eyes up here, Nymph."

Goose bumps explode in the wake of the shivers traveling down my neck.

Narrowed, hooded gray eyes meet mine. He looks pissed. "How did you get here?"

"Uber." Hic. "Snuck out the side exit." Hic. "Please don't blame Nicholas."

Damon searches my face for a moment before groaning, "Fuck," under his breath. "We're going."

"Hey, Mr. Everette. She's with me," Carter says.

"Uh-oh. Not a good idea." I whisper it like a secret.

Damon's fingers twitch where they're wrapped around the curve of my hip.

"Is that right?" Damon looks at me. "Are you with him?"

A muscle ticks in his jaw. It's more of a warning than a question.

I reach up and brush my fingers over it. His skin is hot and rough with evening scruff. I'm momentarily mesmerized by the sharp cut of his cheekbone. He's hard and soft, warm and cold, every opposite smashed together, and suddenly, all I want is to figure him out.

He reaches down, bands his arm right below my

butt, and lifts me over his shoulder, snapping me out of my daze.

"Put me down!" I squeal and try to pinch his back. He shuffles me higher, shoulder landing into my stomach.

"I hope I puke on you," I groan.

He vibrates beneath me. If he was anyone else, I'd think he was laughing.

"Man...I mean Mr. Everette. I can take her home. She came here with me," Carter protests.

"And now she's with me. She needs to sober up. We have things to go over," Damon says firmly.

Things?

Damon turns us and moves effortlessly through the dancing crowd, seemingly unaffected by my weight.

I wave at Carter and mouth, "Sorry."

He's just standing there, mouth open, gaping at me.

"I'll call you tomorrow!" I shout it over the music, but I'm cut off with a crisp smack against my ass.

"Ow!" I whine, even as heat pools between my legs. My panties should not be getting wet over him. "You can't do that!"

"Don't move." He squeezes my ass, the sting changing to a tingling ache, sending shock waves to my clit.

I squirm, and my thighs rub together, searching for friction. If I didn't need a release before, I do now. I twist to see where we're going, giving up on being embarrassed. I'll leave that for tomorrow.

Damon stops to speak to a huge guy with one of those TV spy earpieces in.

I can just make out a few of Damon's words. "Three guys...out...banned...now."

The man doesn't even look at me. Like it's completely normal for Damon to go all caveman and throw women over his shoulder.

I ignore the way that thought sours my stomach and try to push myself up. "I can walk."

Damon doesn't respond. He jerks when I pinch his back hard enough it'll bruise, but he only tightens his grip around my thighs.

I pinch him again. "Where are you taking me?"

He grunts and spins me in the air, so now one arm is below my knees, and the other one is wrapped around my back, pressing me into his chest while gripping my wrist.

"I'm bringing you somewhere to sober up," he says darkly, his hold tightening on my wrist, just shy of hurting.

"Oh...thanks." I snap my face forward, hoping he doesn't see the flush that crosses my cheeks.

He juggles me in his arms and unlocks the door with a cool little key pass thingy.

"What were you thinking?" he murmurs under his breath.

I'm not exactly sure if he's asking me or himself, but my answer just sort of pops out.

"That I needed to get laid." Oops.

He inhales sharply, dropping my feet to the ground, and grips both of my shoulders. Which is good because the look on his face has me feeling dizzy. "You came to *my* club to hook up with some guy?"

Alarm bells go off in my head. Warning. Danger. Proceed with caution.

I suck air through my teeth and shrug. "Well, technically, I didn't know it was *your* club until right now... It's nice... And it was more of a let-myself-loose situation than a booty call."

"Jesus Christ." He pinches the bridge of his nose and takes several deep breaths. His entire body is rigid, pulled taut with tension.

Should I ask him if he's okay?

"Fuck it," Damon growls and crowds me, forcing me to take several steps backward until my back connects with glass. I barely register that we're in a private room overlooking the dance floor before Damon's mouth is claiming mine.

He takes control, tongue rough as he punishes me with his kiss. It's sharp, fast, all teeth and demand. I struggle to pull back, but he holds me still. I shouldn't be doing this—he's my freaking boss—but he's lit my body on fire, and I can't seem to care.

I kiss him just as hard, fighting for my own control. He grips the back of my neck and groans when I nip his bottom lip, sucking on it.

We kiss until my lungs burn and I'm forced to break away to gasp for breath.

Releasing my mouth, Damon turns his abuse toward my neck, sucking and biting the tender skin.

My head smacks against the glass, and I go to reach back, but his hand is already there, rubbing the sore spot and creating a buffer between me and the hard surface.

His fingers bury in my hair, then tighten, forcing my head back and to the side, making more room for him.

Sharp teeth sink into my neck, and I moan, fisting his shirt at the feel of his bite.

"What are you doing?" I practically gasp the question.

"Marking you," Damon declares, then swirls his tongue over the raw spot he left behind, drawing a whimper from the back of my throat. He grips my jaw between his thumb and forefinger and forces my head back to meet his gaze. "If you need to come, you come to me."

I freeze, in too much of a daze to fully understand what's happening. "What? Why—"

He cuts me off with an earth-shattering kiss and lifts me so my legs wrap around his waist and his hips sink between my thighs. My eyes roll back, and my mouth drops open when the shape of his hard cock lines up perfectly against me, applying a delicious pressure I desperately need.

Any self-preservation I've been holding on to evaporates at the feel of his hot length, and my hips tilt into him on their own.

We groan simultaneously at the much-needed friction. He lets go of my mouth and whispers into my ear. "That's my girl. Rock your pretty pussy against me."

"I'm not yours." I try to pull back and drop my legs, but he grips my thighs, holding them open, and presses his cock into me.

His breath fans over the spot he just abused, and he whispers dangerously. "That so?"

He slides one hand up my thigh, easily supporting my weight with the other. It grazes the hem of my shirt before pushing under and branding a trail of white-hot heat up my side. All of my focus is on its path, and I quiver when his thumb brushes the bottom curve of my breast.

"This is mine." He twists my nipple, sending shards of electricity tumbling through me, and I buck against him, lust completely taking over all my senses.

"Yes," I gasp and roll my hips, willing to say anything he wants to get him to continue touching me, searching for the right position to hit my clit with the head of his cock, desperate for more.

His chuckles tickle the sensitive shell of my ear, and a shiver runs through me as the sharp ridges of his teeth gently close on the soft earlobe. "Such a good girl."

He drags his hand down my body, exploring it like he's mapping every inch of me by touch alone. I quiver in his arms when his firm palm meets the bare skin of my thigh and slowly travels up under my skirt.

His thumb grazes my clit overtop my underwear, and a pained cry escapes my lips.

"Do you know what good girls get, Little Nymph?" He slides under the thin fabric and circles the spot I need him the most. "Good girls get to come."

"Please," I beg. Every molecule of my being is focused on his fingers. The weight of the air around us compresses until it's hard to suck in my next breath. Tension radiates as I wait for what happens next. His touch is the only thing that matters.

He shifts us so he can reach lower, sliding wet fingers through my slit, then circling my entrance. I whimper his name as he sinks two fingers inside me.

"Look at you, soaked for me. Ready. This pussy knows she's mine." His voice is a dark rumble as he pumps his fingers in and out in a slow, torturous rhythm.

"I need more," I grind out through my teeth.

"Take it. Fuck my fingers," he encourages against my ear and loosens his hold to allow me to take control.

I wrap my arm around his neck, leveraging myself, and grip his hair as I work myself on his fingers.

Damon's breath comes out in hot pants against my jaw, and he bites down on the edge at the same time his palm massages my clit. I forget to breathe as I rock against him, my head buzzing with the lack of oxygen.

"That's my pretty little pussy, fucking herself so well." He adds another finger, and my world goes blank. All that's left is his command. "Come for me."

Tingles shoot up my spine as my entire body pulls tight, and then my orgasm crashes over me in shuddering waves. "Damon."

He pumps every last ounce of my release. "That's it. Say my name."

"Damon," I say, barely a whisper, and collapse, my cheek against his shoulder, too lost in the warm afterglow to worry about the consequences of what we just did.

He carefully lowers me to the floor and bands an arm around my back for support. "You're fucking stunning when you come."

I can feel the blush heat my cheeks. Even after what we just did, I can't get over the brazenness of his words.

He brushes my hair from my face, tucking it behind my ear, and trails his thumb tenderly down the column of my neck. My chest fills with a warm, fuzzy feeling, and I lean back to grin at him. Whatever I was expecting tonight, it wasn't this.

He doesn't smile back, his gaze intense. "Say you're mine."

I startle, and I'm surprised by just how much I want to say it. Even if it's just to see his reaction. "I'm no one's."

His grip tightens before letting me go. "We'll see."

The serenity of the moment's broken, and the reason why I ended up at the club settles back into the forefront of my mind. But this time, the man who can fix it is standing directly in front of me. Relief and hope crash through me. He can fix it. I don't have to go back. Nothing needs to change.

"I need to renew my H-1B visa, and as my new boss,

you're the only one that can fill out the paperwork. It's a rush, so if I get it to you tonight, could you have it signed and back to me on Monday?" My words tumble out of me in a rush.

His head cocks to the side, studying me like a predator would his prey. "No."

"What do you mean no?"

He huffs out a breath. "I'm not signing the document."

Confusion seeps in as I try to understand. "But we just..."

"We just what?" he deadpans, voice completely void of emotion.

Embarrassment flashes through me, leaving me cold in its wake. I rip myself away from him, already heading toward the exit. "You're an asshole."

"Never said I wasn't."

He closes the distance between us and drags me toward a different door.

Chapter 11

Damon

"You ARE SUCH AN ASSHOLE!" Misty shouts the second I release her arm out the back of the club. She's all fire and damnation right now. Pink hair wild around her shoulders, eyes flashing. If it wasn't for the hint of hurt in her eyes, I'd enjoy pissing her off all the time.

I open my passenger door and gesture to her. "It's time to go."

"Are you kidding me right now? I'm not going anywhere with you." Her arms are crossed in front of her, and she's practically levitating with agitation. She's stunning when she's raring for a fight, and I only have so much willpower.

I close the distance between us and lean in so only she can hear me. "You can either get in the car, or I'm going to drag you back into my private room and fuck the fight out of you." I lean back, smirking when her pupils dilate, but there's nothing sweet about it. I mean every fucking word. "Your choice."

"You can't do that."

"Can't I? Do you really think if I get you alone, you wouldn't beg for my cock? Just like you did earlier."

Her hand smacks into my face with a loud crack, and the sting has my dick twitching and me closing the distance between us. I grab her wrists and pin them behind her back in one hand. If she keeps this up, I'm going to forget all of my carefully crafted plans and lock her in my room until she agrees to marry me. My dick grows harder at the thought, and I give her hands a sharp tug, drawing a gasp from her perfect lips, swollen from our kiss. I tilt my head and warn, "I'm dead serious, Nymph. What's it going to be?"

She scans my face, eyes darkening, and her tongue slips out to wet her bottom lip. I wonder if she knows her expression gives her thoughts away.

I run my thumb along the curve of her jaw, stopping just below her ear. She tilts her head back, opening herself to me, and I have to restrain myself from capturing her mouth in a kiss.

I repeat softer. "What is it going to be?"

She snaps out of it, seeming to process her current situation. Hands pinned behind her back, chest pressed up against mine, and me towering over her. She looks around frantically and spots a familiar car pulling up.

Nicholas steps out. "I'm sorry, boss."

He's lucky he has years of loyalty behind him. He

had one job, and he fucked it up. By the way he's looking at me, he knows exactly what's coming for him, but before I can say anything, Misty cuts in.

"I'll go with him."

I rear back. "What?"

"Listen to me, Damon. Unless you're going to physically restrain me, I am not getting in your car." She pauses and watches as I tilt my head, running my tongue along my top teeth. Does she know how appealing that sounds?

"But you'll get in Nicholas's car?"

"Yes."

I look at the man in question, who's smart enough to take a step back. I'm known for my cool, impenetrable exterior, but there's nothing rational about my thoughts now. She's triggered something inside me that doesn't seem to give a shit that his literal job is driver.

"Damon." My attention snaps to Matthias, who's leaning against the brick wall beside the exit door. "Let Nicholas take her home. We've got things to do."

Reality seeps back in, and some of the charge leaves the air. I expect Misty to be scared, but she's watching me with attention. I loosen my grip finger by finger, in no hurry to let her go, but she stays in place, even when I'm no longer holding her there.

"Mr. Everette, I resign." She startles at her own words, fear lancing her face. Her mouth drops open in shock at what she's said.

I breathe through the need to demand to know what

scared her because I don't think it's me. "Not until I'm married, Miss Hart. That's your job. Then you can do whatever you want to."

Her head tilts, and her brows pinch together as if she's trying to read between my words. *Come on, Nymph. Figure it out.*

"You can't do that!" Her brows pull together. "I'll get another job."

Anger flashes through me. "Not in my city."

"Why?" she pleads, confused desperation filling her voice.

I step back, hating the distance between us, but if I don't let her go now, I won't be able to stop. "Nicholas, take her home. *Don't lose her again.*"

"I won't, boss. I swear," Nicholas replies, remorse in his tone. Misty doesn't waste any time climbing into the back seat.

I don't say it's okay because it's not.

"One last chance," I warn.

"Yes, sir." He closes the door, Misty disappearing behind it.

Matthias stands silently until they disappear around the corner and follows me into my car. He's known me long enough to know I need time to calm down. I trail Nicholas, not bothering to hide it. I doubt Misty's paying attention, and I'm not ready to have her out of my sight.

We pull up to her place, and my eyes trail after her as she struggles to unlock the apartment door. "Fix that."

"Oh, so you're talking to me now?" Matthias responds.

"Can you fix the door or not?"

"Yes I can fix the fucking door." He doesn't look up from where he's typing on his phone. "I'll have someone manning it before the morning."

"Good."

I pull up the camera feed and watch Misty make her way up the stairs. She looks exhausted, all the fight seeped out of her, and I hate that I can't go to her yet.

"So, let me get this straight. Your girl comes to your club to hook up with somebody else." Matthias ignores my growl and keeps going. "Then you pick her up, throw her over your shoulder, and carry her through the bar. I wiped our cameras and everyone's phones. You're welcome."

I nod. The press would have a field day if that got out. It would have been an appealing way to force her hand, but I'd probably kill someone if they printed anything negative about her.

Matthias continues. "Then you get jealous of your driver, who's been with you the last fifteen years and is happily married. And now you're sitting outside her front door fucking watching her on your personal feed?"

I settle into my seat, ready to spend all night here, just in case my little vixen decides she's going to take another late-night trip. "Do you have a point?"

"Only that I find it absolutely hilarious to see you like this. Please continue."

My eyes dart to him, but any anger I'm going to lash out with dies at the smirk on his face. I should have found him sooner. It's the happiest I've seen him in a while, and since I have no plans on stopping myself, there's no reason he can't enjoy it.

"She'll come around," I say.

"I don't know, Dam. She looked pretty pissed. Didn't you learn you aren't supposed to have to restrain them? Hell, girls should be begging for your cock right now after Grandfather's announcement."

He's not wrong, but the answer is simple. "They aren't her."

He huffs out a breath and leans his head back on the headrest. "Fine. What did you do to piss her off?"

"Refused to extend her visa."

His head snaps up. "Why the fuck would you do that?"

"Because now I have the leverage to make her marry me. It'll at least give the semblance she had a choice."

"Poor girl's going to be pissed."

"Wife. My *wife* is going to be pissed at me." I smirk, loving the way that sounds.

Chapter 12

Damon

WE DON'T LEAVE until the lights go dark in Misty's apartment.

I would've stayed here all night, but there's something we need to oversee at The Vaults, and we're already late. Not that anyone would dare say something to us.

I stretch out my neck and reach into the glove compartment, my fingers brushing against the two cool, weighty masks tucked inside. Each one is shaped like a snarling wolf's head, its mouth gaping open as if ready to devour.

I hand one to Matthias, twisting the other one in my hand.

The gold wolf is the symbol for the Lords. It denotes power without a word. The Everette family has been the keepers of these masks for the last century, and we don't plan on that ending.

I pull up to the Everette hotel, the valet taking my keys as we get out. There's a wedding happening in the ballroom, but that's not why we're here. We take the spiraling staircase that leads to the basement. The grooves worn into the marble make each step uneven; mixed with the dim light coming from the sconces, the entire place feels medieval. The Order of Saints came over from London in the 1800s and built The Vaults to resemble their own chambers.

The hotel above has been continuously renovated, but other than updating the electricity, The Vaults have remained unchanged.

A reminder that the Order of Saints is steeped in centuries of tradition.

Bash and Xander are waiting for us at the bottom, their gold wolf masks already in place, as Matthias and I slip ours on.

"Fucking took you long enough," Bash complains.

I cut him a sharp glance, and he looks at the floor. This is not the place.

They push through the door, and the crowd goes quiet. The men wearing cloaks with hoods covering their heads disperse to line each side of the aisle, heads bowed low as we pass. Their silver fox masks denote them as Saints.

My brothers and I take our spot at the head of the dais.

"You may rise."

The men stand at once, facing us.

"Tonight, we witness the Unsainted become Saints," I say, already dreading tonight's events. It's hours of pure ceremony that I'd rather spend watching the live feed of my Little Nymph. Even if I can't see into her room.

It's comforting just knowing she's in there...safe.

"Bring forth your initiates, and let's begin."

My brothers and I sit on large, delicately carved wood thrones, knowing this will likely take all night.

Men without masks, dressed in white flowing dress shirts that look like they're from a different time, line up next to their Saints sponsors.

There are three main tiers to the Order of Saints, although those tiers are unofficially divided and sliced several more times.

The Lords.

Matthias, Xander, Bash, and I make up the head members of the Order, a position granted to all Everette direct descendants. We are the leaders, the kings. Our power in a room full of the most influential men in the world is insurmountable. They are at our mercy.

The Saints.

All Order of Saints members who have been initiated are called Saints. They wear silver fox masks to denote their station. They're able to lean on the power of the Order to influence the world around them. They are the men who rule the world, who sway the tides of war, policies, and politics.

They create the laws so that none can hinder them.

The Unsainted.

These are the uninitiated members of the Order of Saints. Generally, they are the younger siblings of the families, waiting for their turn once they are twenty-one. They have power through proximity but can't rely on the Order of Saints' full influence until they've gone through their ceremony and become Saints.

"Proceed," I command, keeping my words clipped and to the point. As a Lord, I stand above and leave no room for argument.

The first two men approach us.

Even with the mask, the head of the Volkov family is easily recognizable. The Unsainted beside him is his eldest son.

The Saint, his face hidden behind a silver mask, grasps a sharp knife from the antique table placed at the front of the room. A dark and ancient scroll bearing hundreds of names written in blood sits alongside a quill and a glimmering silver bowl.

"With this knife, I pledge my unwavering responsibility to you," the Saint utters in a low, menacing voice. "Your actions will determine my respect." He reaches out and tightly clasps the hand of the trembling young Unsainted.

Only those escorted by their sponsor are allowed into the Vaults, but never for ceremonies like this.

With a quick jerk, the Saint pries open the Unsainted's fist, drawing a sharp gasp as the tip of the knife makes an incision into his skin and a thin trail of blood drips into the bowl below. He then cuts his own hand and allows their blood to mix together in the vessel.

All is silent as the Saint dips the quill into their mingled blood and scrawls the name of the Unsainted onto the scroll.

I rise from my seat and approach the two men, holding out a silver fox mask between them. "Welcome to The Order of Saints," I intone coldly. As I place the mask over the man's head, he bows deeply in submission. I call out to everyone gathered in The Vaults. "May the power of Saints forever reign."

The resounding reply echoes through the dark halls, sending shivers down my spine.

I return to my seat as the next two men approach and suppress a groan at the fact that we still have at least another two hours of this.

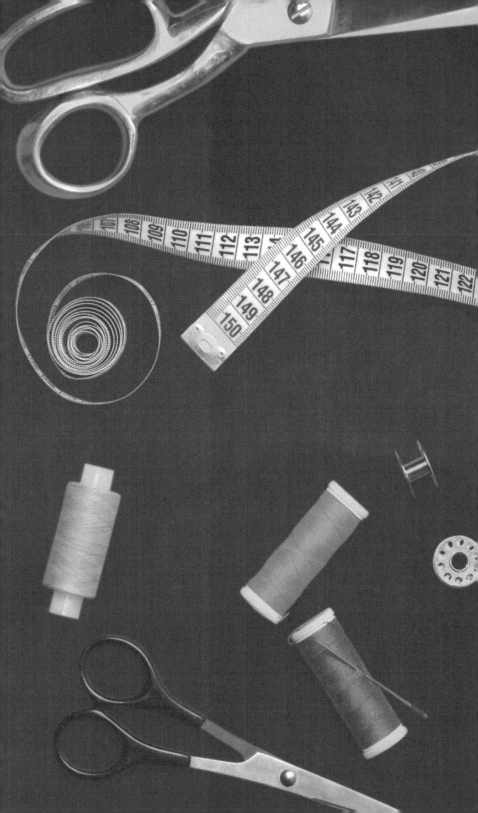

Chapter 13

Misty

THE FAMILIAR BUZZ of the serger is the only thing that calms my nerves. My living room is a disaster of vibrant-colored fabrics, strewn across every surface. I'd woken up this morning with a wicked pounding in my head, like a tiny man moved in and was determined to tear down the walls with his tiny hammer.

I straighten from my hunched-over position and pull my hair off the back of my neck. It's too short to pull up into a full ponytail, but I manage to peel the damp strands from my heated skin. My apartment is sweltering in the summer heat. It's cute, and I've made it my own, but it's lacking a lot of the luxury amenities, like air-conditioning.

I reposition myself with two hands on the deep mulberry-purple fabric of my new project and press down on the pedal. It's going to be an A-line skirt that hits just above the knees. It's the third piece I've

121

attempted today, the last two left abandoned in a pile on the floor.

Anything to keep my mind off last night. A world-altering, mind-shattering mistake. Because there is no world that I, Misty Hart, fooled around with Damon Ares Everette the freaking Third. Even his name sets us worlds apart.

But somehow, in my oh-so-drunken state, my mind convinced me that he'd wanted me. No, needed me. And I needed him. That his touch had become essential to my very existence, and nothing could stop what was happening. Certainly not me.

Which in the light of day is epically stupid. I can't even blame it on being drunk because the second that man lifted me over his shoulder, I was light-headed for a completely different reason.

Which is why, with one simple word, *No*, it was like he'd dumped an ice bath down my shirt, snapping me painfully back to reality. He's fully capable of fixing my problem with my H-1B visa, and he said *no*.

The worst part is it hurt. It had no business hurting, but the way he'd dismissed what we'd just done...his touch, feel, taste had pushed me over the best orgasm of my life, and he treated it like it was nothing.

Like *I* was nothing. Because of course I am. I'm only as good as my happy exterior, and I'd asked for some-thing more. Had the audacity to be vulnerable for a single second, only for the world to slam reality back into my face. I hadn't been able to rebuild my cheerful exterior, that easygoing, likable facade. No, he'd stolen that from me in a few warm touches and a single denial.

Nothing explains why he showed up there and ripped me away from Carter like that. The way he'd hauled me over his shoulder, like he'd had some sort of claim on me. I knew better than to believe in things like that.

Hell, I have firsthand experience with what happens when a rich boy doesn't get what he wants.

I curse when my hand jerks, wrecking my stitching, and I stop the machine, pulling the fabric out and grabbing my seam ripper.

That's when I notice that my normally precisely crisp line, one I'd mastered in high school, now looks like the path of a guy that's three sheets to the wind.

It's all Damon's fault. With his perfect eyes. Perfect hair. Perfect freaking voice.

I never should have gotten close to him. I definitely shouldn't have let him touch me.

My phone buzzes on the table, and I swipe it, noticing the dozen missed texts.

> Piper: Misty Lynn Hart. What the hell did you get up to last night? You're on the freaking news.

> Mia: Damon is H.O.T. Good for you.

> Piper: Girl, you better respond or Mia and I are coming to find you.

The news. Oh no, no, no. Please freaking no.

I flip through my phone to a popular news site, and my stomach plummets.

Damon Everette, caught in a passionate discussion, leaving the Elysium club with a mystery girl. Could this be the new potential Mrs. Everette?

I close my eyes and take three heaping breaths. At least it wasn't me hung over his shoulder. At least we can spin this as a meeting once it's announced I'm his personal PR. A simmer of frustration boils under my skin.

I've spent the last several years keeping my head out of the media as much as possible. Which isn't the easiest thing to do as the PR rep for the Bruins. And in one fell swoop, Damon has all eyes on me.

> Me: Damon Everette the Third is a cocky, egotistical asshole who thinks the world revolves around him and doesn't care who has to deal with the fallout.

My phone vibrates, but instead of another text, a group video call comes through. I hit Accept, and all the anger, helplessness, and frustration boil over at the sight of my best friends. Like I'd been holding back a dam, and seeing them gives me permission to let it all out.

Piper searches my face through the screen. "Oh, Misty, are you sewing? Tell us what's wrong."

"Details now." Mia pops a piece of popcorn into her mouth.

My words pour out of me like a flood I can't dam. "First, I caught him getting head in the conference room, and I freaking froze in place like some petrified animal. Then, he cornered me in the back alley, looking way too hot for someone who just announced he was being forced to get married."

Both girls' eyes are wide on me, mouths slightly open, but I can't stop the words from tumbling out.

"He went to my boss and switched me to his personal PR person. He took me off all of his projects. And because of that, my old boss refuses to sign the visa renewal papers that *she* messed up. Then, he showed up at the club, out of freaking *nowhere*, looking way too hot. Why does he always have to look so hot? It's not fair," I whine and continue.

"He literally picked me up and hauled me up the stairs to some private suite—because of course he has a suite—only to give me the best orgasm of my life. *Then* says he won't sign the visa papers! No reason, no sorry. No explanation! Just a simple *I never said I wasn't an asshole.* Like *seriously*, what the actual fuck. Don't even get me started on the whole car thing. Like, who hires a personal chauffeur for their PR person?" I inhale deeply, and my lungs heave, sucking desperately for air as the last sentence leaves my mouth and the girls are caught up.

They're both stunned silent. Mia's piece of popcorn is suspended in the air halfway to her mouth.

"Well, aren't you going to say anything?" I ask, maybe a little too high-pitched.

"He's a total dickwad," Piper responds immediately.

"Yup, grade A asshole," Mia adds. "A superhot, ridiculously mind-boggling rich asshole."

"Which is exactly why he thinks he can get away with absolutely anything he wants," I practically scream.

"Do you think so?" Piper hesitates. "Just that...you mentioned a particularly good orgasm."

My cheeks heat, but she ignores it and goes on gently. "That just maybe, you like him? A little bit?"

"Or I hate him, and he's just hot," I respond.

"You know, I bet the hate sex between the two of you is absolutely insane," Mia adds, finally popping the popcorn into her mouth.

"I am not having sex with him," I screech.

"Uh-huh, because he's a cocky, egotistical asshole who thinks the world revolves around him. Who you are also super attracted to."

"Yes...no...wait." Both girls smile as I stumble over my words. "I never said I'm attracted to him."

"Yes, you did," Piper laughs.

"Several times," Mia adds with a mouth full of popcorn.

Piper raises a brow. "Did he or did he not get you off in the club?"

"That means nothing," I protest.

They simultaneously laugh.

"Hey, you're supposed to be on my side, and we're supposed to be hating on him together."

"Okay, sorry, you're totally right. We'll leave out the fact that you're obviously into him"—Mia ignores me when I try to cut her off—"and go back to talking shit. I can't believe the audacity that man had to switch your jobs to work directly for him. Like, what does he think he owns, the company?"

"Not funny."

Piper smirks. "Oh, come on, it's a little funny."

"If you aren't going to be helpful, I'm hanging up," I threaten.

"Wait!" Piper's face turns serious. "The visa paperwork stuff is complete bullshit, and for that alone, we hate him. You should have told us. Maybe the boys can help."

I deflate. Her agreeing that he's an asshole doesn't invigorate me like I thought it would. What is wrong with me? "It really shouldn't have been a big deal. It's just a quick change and a new signature. He's doing this on purpose."

"Why though?" Mia leans back and tightens her pale blonde ponytail. "I don't get it."

"That's because it makes absolutely no sense!" I drop my head into my hands. "I just need to convince him to sign it."

"Clearly, something was up last night. Maybe he'll be better at work?" Piper replies calmly.

"Right...right...okay." I inhale, count to three, then let

it out. "I just need to show him exactly what kind of asset I am to the company and how stupid he is not to sign the paperwork."

"He'd be a total fool not to," Mia agrees.

I already feel better with a plan. "Okay, I just need to go to work, kick ass, and no matter how hot he is: don't kiss him."

Both girls smirk at me.

Shit.

Chapter 14

Damon

"ANY NEW INFORMATION regarding the missing Unsainted?" I question Matthias, holding the phone to my ear as I push the button to the fifth floor. I'd been surprised when Misty's meeting popped up on my calendar. I thought I'd have to chase her, that she would try to ignore me going forward, not that I would let that happen.

Whatever it is, it's the perfect opportunity to speak with her. I know she's pissed about the other night, but now I'm going to make all of her problems disappear. A thrill shoots down my spine at the thought of tying her to me forever. Not that she'll know that. Baby steps.

"Damon." Matthias's voice rings loudly in my ear, catching my attention back from my favorite distraction.

"What?" The elevator door chimes, and I step out, proceeding down the hall.

He huffs out an amused breath. "Welcome back, brother. It's not my fault you space out."

I don't bother lying. He'd just call me on it anyway. "Tell me."

"We've lost another three Unsainted. These ones are a big hit..." He's quiet for several seconds. "Someone's coming after us."

My feet pause, and the full force of his words slam into my chest. The last time a family challenged us, it didn't end well for them. Every member was erased and the kids pushed out of the Order. Their name is only brought up in whispers to remind people what happens if you fuck with the Lords of the Order of Saints.

What people don't know is it almost ripped us apart. Up until then, we'd lived pampered, if not hard, lives. Our father was a strict, powerful man who demanded perfection. When they killed him and came for my siblings, the world fell apart. Everything I thought mattered was pointless, trivial bullshit.

I scorched the earth to get my brothers back, rooted out the ones who took them, preying on their weaknesses until they broke and their plan shattered. By the time I was through with them, the walls dripped with their blood, my hands permanently stained red.

To the outside world, I'm the billionaire prince, heir to the family fortune.

To our world, I'm the Lord they fear.

Darkness settles over me as malice flows through my veins, and my heart kicks at my ribs. I sold my soul to get my brothers back, killing anything decent inside me. There's no telling what will happen if someone's stupid enough to try again. A slick, dangerous rage burns in my chest, threatening to take over.

"Let's send a reminder." My voice is cold, ice licking up my tongue.

"Consider it done," Matthias responds, and then the line goes dead.

Pink flashes in my peripheral vision as I approach my office. The swirl of purples, greens, and navy pulls me out of the sea of gray I've fallen into. With each step, my chest loosens, and my heart pounds for a new reason.

She's practically glowing where she stands inside the door, straightening a folder on my desk. She's wearing a green skirt that hugs her hips and ass and a crisp dress shirt that's tailored perfectly. A stray dark pink strand untucks itself from her bun, and my fingers itch to tuck it back behind her ear. My mouth waters, and I stop myself from pushing her into the desk and running my hands up her thighs to see what color she's wearing underneath.

Clear green eyes meet mine, going wide for a heartbeat before narrowing.

Misty crosses her arms. "You're late."

Fuck. My cock swells as she glares at me, chin held high, shoulders back, and her eyes glued on my face. Tension is taut between us, and I'm instantly pulled toward her. I take slow, calculating steps and watch as a warm flush darkens the tops of her breasts and climbs up her neck before covering her cheeks. Her mouth is cracked open, and for a brief moment, I forget to breathe.

"Don't look at me like that." She places her hands on her hips.

"Like what?" I ask, amused.

"Like you're some kind of scary Big Bad Wolf."

I raise a brow, and the corner of my lip tilts up. I shouldn't press her, but I can't stop. "Why? Does it make you nervous? Uncomfortable? Or is it that it makes you wet, like it did the other night? I think I crack your perfectly constructed shell. I like you like this. So no, Miss Hart. I will not stop. Not when you look at me the same way."

She rolls her eyes. "Hardly. I think you think you're scary."

My voice is dark, and a low rumble grows deep in my throat. "That's where you're wrong, Miss Hart. Most people would say there is every reason to be afraid of me. That I've earned their fear." Her breath hitches as I close the distance between us. I lift my hand and capture the loose strand of hair, wrapping it around my finger. Her gaze is locked on mine, pupils taking over the green. Her chest rises and falls rapidly with her breaths the closer I move toward her, but she doesn't back away, feet firmly planted on the floor, chin held high, showing just how little she fears me. Fuck, she's perfect. I tuck the strand behind her ear.

"But not you, Nymph. You've got nothing to fear from me."

Her exhale is a soft hiss between her teeth, and then her cheerful mask closes over her features, and she takes a step back. "Good, because we have work to do. I spoke with your mother, and she and I went through a list of potential..." Her eyes dart to the side, breaking from mine. "...brides for you. We can go over the list, then I'll book the restaurants accordingly." Each of her words comes out faster than the last, as if she's practiced them over and over and can't wait to get them out. "I can call the woman to set it up, but I think even you can see the merit of reaching out yourself. This may be a marriage of convenience, but no reason to skip all formalities."

"Did you now?" A darkness licks up my veins and heats my skin, and I barely suppress the growl from emerging from my chest. Despite the fact that she's doing what I asked, it pisses me off that she's able to set me up with other women. I want her to feel the same jealousy as I do. I want it to climb up her chest and eat her alive. I want her to squirm with the idea of me with anyone else. Soon, she'll know this is all pointless, that she belongs to me.

The only thing that's saving her is the way her body has angled itself away from mine and the fact that her head tilts down, like she doesn't want to meet my eyes. No sight of the fierce presence she was before.

Silently, I walk to my cabinet, open a drawer, and pull out a cigar, ignoring the look she's giving me. I light it, sucking the sweet smoke down my lungs and letting it numb the anger burning there. My Little Nymph has no idea what she's set off in me. I take a seat, legs splayed wide, and lean back in one of the large club chairs located in the corner of my office. I take another drag and pierce her with my gaze, happy to see the shiver that runs over her arms, leaving goose bumps in its wake.

"Show me." I dare her to proceed.

She clears her throat, giving her head a gentle shake, and reads from her notes. "There's Miss Davenport."

"Pretty," I say and fight the smile at the way her teeth clench together. "Unfortunately, I prefer my women to be able to think for themselves. Next?"

She visibly relaxes, then says the next name. "Evelyn Menard."

I blow out a long stream of smoke. "You can do better than that."

She rambles off several more names, frustration building in her as I shoot them all down easily.

"You can't say no to everyone," she says sharply, exasperation getting the best of her. I'm pleased to see how uncomfortable she's getting, that she keeps turning to the door like she'd rather be doing anything but pitching me potential bride ideas.

I don't respond because that's exactly what I plan to do.

Something inside her finally snaps, sending a thrill through me. She stalks up to me and leans in close, having no idea the danger she's put herself in. How easily I could pull her onto my lap and make her pliable to my touch. Her delicate fingers pull the cigar from my mouth, and she puts it out in the ashtray. "You asked me to do this. Why are you being so difficult?"

"Because you haven't named anyone I want. I told you, I need someone who can stand beside me in this family, who will lead with grace and confidence. There's only one woman who can do that, and she's not on your ridiculous list."

She stands tall, hands on her hips, like an adorable, pissed-off pixie, and lets out a sharp breath. "If you already have someone, why didn't you just say that?" Her voice drops lower, almost strained, and my heart twitches in my chest. "Who is she so I can book some public dates for you."

"You," I say and marvel at the way her eyes go wide.

"W-What?" She shakes her head. "We don't have time for these games. Just tell me who she is so I can do my job."

I lean forward, practically looming over her, even in my seated position. "There's no joke, Miss Hart. It will be you."

"And if I say no?" she scoffs, some of her spirit shining through.

"You won't."

"So confident. Well, I'm saying no. I wouldn't marry you in a million freaking years. Remember, I think you're a heartless asshole, or do you go through so many girls you've already forgotten?"

I ignore her words, knowing I've already won. That there is no other option for her before this conversation even started. "There are rules that come along with this. I need to be married for at least a year, we will live together, and you will sleep in my bed."

Her cheeks flush a pretty shade of pink. "Why would I do that?"

"Because I'll sign your visa papers."

The breath wooshes out of her, and she stumbles back, the reality of the situation hitting her. I smirk, knowing it's an offer she can't afford to turn down.

"I...I...have to go." She turns abruptly and scurries from my office. I let her go, knowing she'll come back to me. Knowing that I'll get exactly what I want.

I light another cigar. Misty Hart will be my wife. Whether she wants to or not.

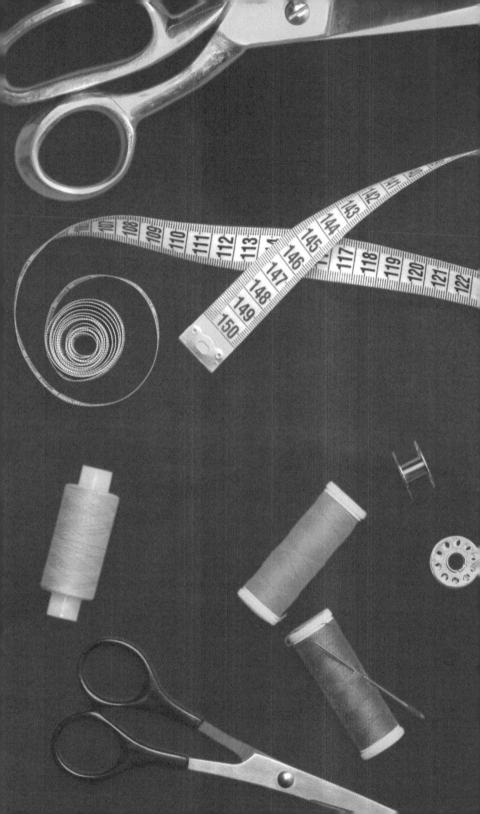

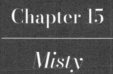
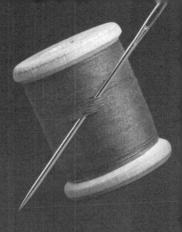

Chapter 15

Misty

NICHOLAS IS smart enough to not speak to me during the short ride to my apartment. I hop out of the car the second we roll to a stop, not bothering to let him open my door. There's a man dressed in all black standing in the doorway. I freeze until I see the security badge on his vest. Since when did my crappy apartment have a doorman? My mind is swirling too fast for me to process the fact that he calls me by my name as he opens the door for me. All I can think about is Damon's audacity to ask me to marry him. No...to blackmailing me. How dare he take the one thing I need the most and hold it over my head. And why? Why me? What could I possibly give him that the countless more suitable women on his mother's list can't? My back tingles the entire way to my place, a heavy sense of being watched branding the back of my neck, but when I turn, there's no one there.

Get it together.

I stomp directly to the kitchen, heels clicking loudly on the vinyl floor. I need a drink, and I need it now. I don't bother with a glass, instead taking a swig of tequila straight from the bottle. I cough at the burn in my throat, but it doesn't stop me from taking another.

He thinks he can do whatever he wants. Well, screw him, screw his proposal, screw his blackmail. Images of him pushing me against the glass at his club, hand buried between my legs, flash through my mind, and I have to rub my thighs together. I ignore it. This isn't about attraction. It's about control, and I'm going to take it back.

I pull out my phone and search through my contacts and text Carter before I can talk myself out of it.

> **Me:** Come over tonight?

> **Carter:** Fuck yes. What time?

> **Me:** Now.

I need to do this before my courage runs out. I just have to prove to myself that I choose what comes next. I punch in my address.

> **Carter:** I'll be there in fifteen. Can't wait to see you.

I throw my phone down on the counter and brace my elbows on the cool surface, supporting my head in my palms. I ignore the voice screaming at me in the back of my head that this isn't what I want at all. That a twisted, broken part of me is thrilled at the idea of marrying Damon. That's why I have to do this. I need to stamp it out so I never give in. Not to someone who will ruin me. Because that's exactly what he plans. He doesn't want a wife. He wants a doll to stand perfectly on his arm. I learned that I don't belong in his world years ago, and it's not a mistake I'll repeat again. No matter the fact that my breath catches with a single look or my panties grow wet the longer he watches me.

I've learned to survive. And something tells me I won't survive Damon.

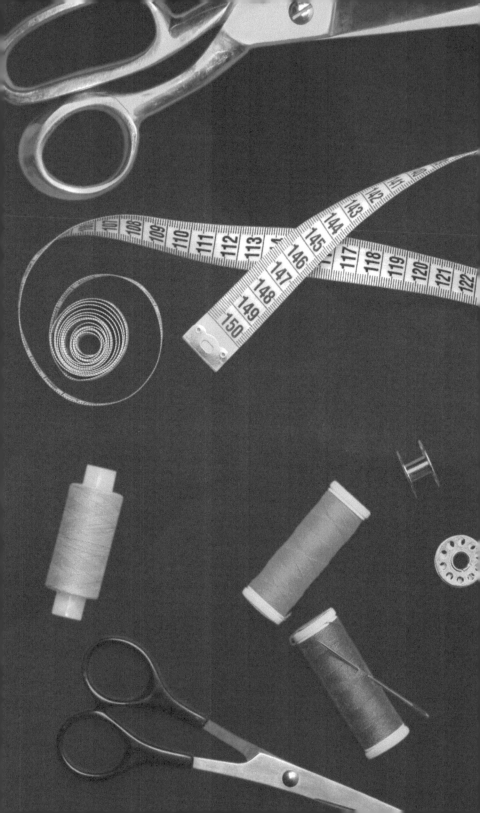

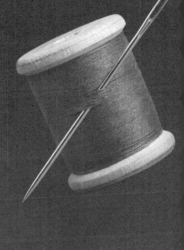

Chapter 16

Misty

DREAD FORMS in my stomach at the sound of Carter's knock, knowing this is a mistake before I even open the door. Every fiber in my being screams at me that this is wrong. That no matter how many times I tell myself Damon has no hold on me, I know that's a lie. That even though he's a controlling, egotistical asshole who was born with a silver spoon in his mouth, some part of me has latched onto him. Wants exactly what he's offering and is more than willing to pay the cost. There's this cord that draws me to him, pulls me right back to his side whenever I dare to walk away. A part of me craves to know what it's like to be his, to let him own a piece of me.

"Misty?" Carter knocks again.

I twist the door open. There's nothing left to do. I'll just let him in and explain that I'm not feeling well, apologize for wasting his time and never speak of this again.

I open the door, revealing the over six-feet-tall hockey player. He's dressed casually but nice. Polo collared shirt, dark-washed jeans. I can't help but compare him to Damon, and he comes up lacking. Accepting the inevitable awkwardness, I invite him in.

Carter's gaze trails up my legs, over the short hem of my deep purple dress, and finally to my face. His eyes are hooded, and his tongue skates over his lips. I shudder, revulsion turning my stomach. I've made a lot of stupid mistakes, but this is near the top.

I have to get rid of him, but I can't break my carefully crafted persona. I'm the chipper, happy girl, not the complaining, teasing you on a date girl. I fire off a quick text to Mia, telling her to call me in five. She hits thumbs-up on my message.

Carter's looking at me, his head tilted. Crap. I've totally been ignoring him. I clear my throat. "Want a beer?"

A slow smile pulls at his lips. "Yeah, I could use something to loosen up a bit."

That's the last thing I want to do, but I just need to stall for the next few minutes, and this mistake will be over. Plus, I doubt he thinks we were just going to bang the second he got here. I grab his beer from the fridge, the steel can cool against my palm, and pass it to him.

"Aren't you going to have one?" he asks.

The whole atmosphere is off, and it's obvious even to him. He's no doubt wondering why I invited him here.

He steps toward me, closing the distance until his toes reach mine.

"You don't need to be nervous. Forget about the hockey stuff. I'm just a regular guy." He says it so sure of himself that I have to fight the urge to roll my eyes.

Of course he thinks I'm intimidated by his "greatness." I swear, it's a miracle my friends ended up with the guys they did. He tries to move in closer, and I shift back. This can't wait until Mia calls. I need him to go now.

The loud bang of my door slamming open has me jumping out of my skin. A cold chill runs through me at the sight of Damon standing in the doorway, eyes narrowed on where Carter's hand is on my waist. He's so livid it's wafting off him in waves. I finally see the darkness people talk about. His features are cut in cold, vicious lines as he stalks toward us.

"Have you grown tired of living, Carter? I can fix that for you," Damon asks him, his voice barely above a whisper, somehow making it worse.

Carter rocks back on his heels and lifts his hands. He still seems too casual for this situation, and I briefly wonder if he didn't catch on to Damon's meaning. Because watching Damon approach us like we're his prey makes it really apparent that he's not joking.

"You should go," I tell Carter and nudge him toward the door.

He looks back at me, confused. "Really?"

Idiot... "Yes...sorry. I'll text you later."

"No." Damon's voice is a firm demand. "You won't."

He grabs Carter by the collar, and his eyes finally flash with the fear I'd expected to see. Damon drags him through my apartment like Carter's not an over two-hundred-pound NHL player. Carter struggles against his hold until Damon has him bent over my balcony railing, and then he's begging him not to let go.

I should be scared, terrified, but seeing Damon like this has my thighs rubbing together and my pulse racing in my ears. There's something sick and broken inside me that loves the way he's handling my date.

Carter yells, and my mind snaps back in place. "Don't kill him!"

Damon looks back at me, head tilted. "Only because you asked."

He slams the patio door shut and locks Carter outside. All of Damon's attention is focused on me. His shoulders rigid, dark eyes narrowed, as he eats the space between us. Rationally, I know I should run. That nothing in this scenario is right. So why is my blood heating, my heart racing, and every fiber of my being coming alive at the way he stalks toward me?

I take a tentative step back, and he shakes his head, clicking his tongue. I freeze in place, not daring to disobey him.

A realization lands on me like a rock. I wanted him to show up. I wanted him to be jealous, and now I'm thrilled that he's here. He wants to marry me, and I want him to prove it's not just a game. He says I'm the one he wants, but I need him to prove it.

There's a wildness inside of him as he closes the distance between us. His fingers aren't gentle as they wrap around my chin and direct my gaze to his.

"This is a dangerous game, Little Nymph," he warns, voice low, and a tremble runs through me.

My instincts are on high alert, but I don't try to pull away. I swallow hard. "What game?"

"The one where you act like you're free of me. That you don't already know who you belong to. Or do you need a reminder?" He shifts his grip and circles my neck with his fingers, resting them on my collarbone as a warning.

Heat pours into my core, and my clit throbs. A low moan escapes me, and his smile turns dark.

He pushes closer, bent so his breath fans against my mouth. "I'm going to spin you around and fuck your pretty pussy against this counter. This is your last chance to tell me to stop."

My ears ring, and all my thoughts vanish with his words. I lift on my toes, closing the distance between our mouths. He groans deep and takes over the kiss, running his tongue against mine until I'm consumed by him. My head feels light from the lack of oxygen, but I don't pull away, letting him do whatever he wants to me.

There's a power that surges inside me, giving in to his control. No matter his threats, I know if I told him to stop, he would. He's not gentle when he tears my dress up the side seam, revealing my side. He seems pleased that I'm wearing a control-top underwear instead of something sexy underneath. He yanks the fabric down, letting it fall to my feet, and twists me so my hips press almost painfully into the counter.

"Are you on birth control?"

I nod my head yes, and he pushes a palm into my shoulder blades. "Good. Bend forward."

The solid surface is hard against my front, and my ass is fully displayed for his view. With my dress split and pushed up around my hips, underwear around one foot, I don't hesitate to move when his foot meets mine and spreads my legs further apart.

He grunts his approval and runs his fingers up my slit, sending ripples of pleasure through me before sinking two fingers deep inside.

Fuck. I suck in a breath against the stretch. Nothing about this is gentle. His touch is a clear signal that I'm his. He can do whatever he wants to me, and I'm going to let him. I don't bother to fight it. I want him.

I moan again when he dives another finger deep inside me.

His teeth graze my ear. "You're going to come all over my cock."

I don't bother correcting him because at this moment, that's all I want.

The thick head of his cock replaces his fingers at my entrance, and my eyes roll back in my head. "Yes. Please, Damon."

"Please what?"

"Please, fuck me."

"You're so pretty when you beg for my cock." He slams himself all the way in until his hips slap against my ass. He doesn't give me time to adjust before withdrawing and slamming in again, his thrust doling out punishment and pleasure. I rock back, and he grips my hip, holding me in place. His grip is hard enough to leave bruises. He's ruthless in his movements, drawing out my orgasm without mercy. This isn't love; it's possession, and I'm falling into it willingly.

"*Fuck*," he hisses when I squeeze around him, and a sharp slap lands on my ass. "You're so tight."

The quick pain sends me over the cliff of my release. He quickens his pace, groaning his own release, and hot spurts fill my core.

Damon slides out of me, and his cum leaks down my leg. He grazes his teeth along the curve of my neck before sinking his teeth into my skin. I cry out at the sharp pain but don't pull away.

He licks the mark he left, fingers gathering his cum and pushing it back inside me. "Don't make me remind you again."

He tugs my dress back into place, and cool air hits my heated skin when he pulls away. My mind finally clears just in time to see Damon slide the patio door open. Holy shit. Shit. *Shit*. How did I forget about Carter? Oh my God. I just let Damon fuck me in front of Carter. I look around frantically, but Damon chose his spot carefully. Carter had a front-row seat to Damon taking me, but everything below my waist was blocked by the island.

The hockey player doesn't look at me while Damon walks him out of my apartment, hand grasped to the back of his neck.

Damon turns to me where I'm still standing frozen in the kitchen and commands, "Never pull that shit again."

The door closes with a click, and the clear sound of the door locking catches my ears.

Damon Ares Everette the Third has a key to my apartment.

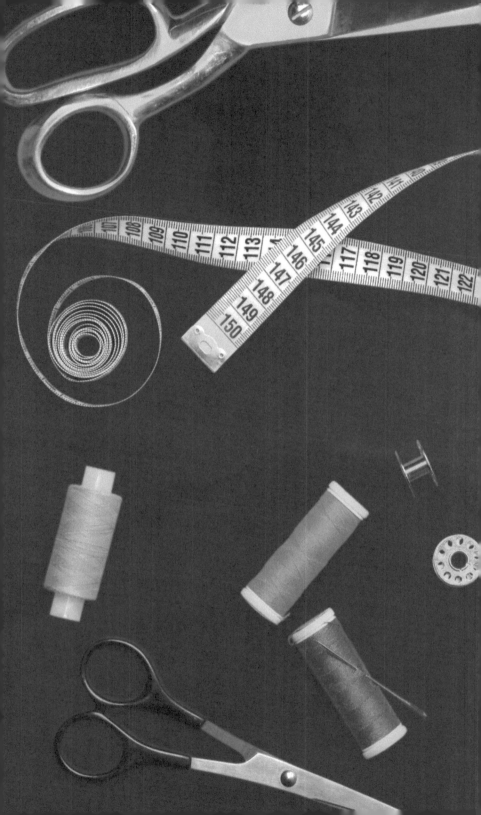

Chapter 17

Misty

THE MORNING SUN shines through the slit in my blinds, shining directly into my eyes. For a second, I let myself believe it was all just a messed-up dream, but the soreness between my thighs tells me the truth. I let Damon fuck me in front of someone else.

No, I'd begged him to do it.

Heat flushes my body, and I bury my head into my pillow. I've lost my freaking mind.

I pull myself out of bed and drag myself into the shower. I stay under the heated water, letting it sink into my muscles until my fingers prune.

Towel wrapped around me, I make my way to the kitchen and hit the On button on the coffee machine, checking my phone while I wait for it to heat. There are several missed calls from Mia.

> Mia: I guess you didn't need to be saved after all.

> Mia: Text me and let me know you're okay.

> Mia: I'm not kidding. I need you to message me back.

> Me: I'm fine. He left. I fell asleep.

Nothing was technically a lie, just a lot missing.

> Mia: Lunch date this week?

> Me: Sure.

> Mia: Perfect, I'll set it up with Piper.

There's another missed text message from an unknown number. My thumb hovers over it before I hit Open. Ice coats my skin, and my stomach drops to the floor.

> Unknown: Misty, it's your father. You clearly have us blocked. We saw the pictures with you and Damon Everette at the club. Come home so we can discuss it. You belong here with us.

I block the number instantly, fighting to breathe. I won't go back there. I can't.

A low sob escapes me, and I fight back the second one. I'm done crying over my family. I should've known they'd see the picture of Damon and me fighting outside his club. The news has gotten a hold of it and acted like it was the juiciest story of the year. It's not surprising that they reached out. They'd always wanted to climb the social ladder, and no one is higher than Damon.

So long as the angle I spun of us just working together stays at the forefront, there's no reason for my parents to come after me. They want me home so they can hand me over to Thomas like some kind of bribe. And there's nothing I won't do to stop that.

I never told Piper, Mia, and Sidney about my past. I didn't want them to know this dark side of my life. I wanted them to see me as the happy, free girl I am now.

Guilt pricks at my sternum, knowing that I'm not being fair to them. That my friends would support me, no matter what. Hell, my biggest problem would be stopping them from flying over there and doing something that got us all in jail. I chuckle and look at my phone again, not letting my dad control me anymore.

There's only one way I can fix this. Marry Damon.

I smile, tingling filling my chest at the thought of how pissed he'll be when I tell him my own set of rules.

Chapter 18

Damon

"Isn't it a bit early to be drinking?" Bash asks, snickering. I glare at my brothers through my computer screen. Apparently, Matthias had enough of my shit and put together a little intervention after last night's stunt.

"No." I take another sip, not even feeling the burn anymore. I returned to my office after leaving Misty's, knowing there was no chance I'd be able to sleep.

I'd tried to be a decent man and give Misty the space she needed to process the fact we're getting married. I love that my Little Nymph's charming to everyone else but has no problem showing me all the fire she buries deep inside. That's how I want her—open, free, *real*.

She's been burying her feelings, but not with me. Never with me.

Which is why I thought I'd give her some space to come to the only possible solution on her own.

She will be my wife.

When the alarm I had set up on her door beeped last night, I said fuck it and pulled up my surveillance app.

I know I shouldn't have gone over there, but the second I saw that asshole walk into her building, my mind had whited out in rage. I don't remember leaving the office or getting into the car. I'd been overcome with the overwhelming need to show her that even if she doesn't admit it to herself, her body already knows she's mine.

"What's with the family meeting, Matthias? News on who's been picking off the Unsainted?" Xander cuts in and runs his hand through his hair.

"Fuck, I wish that's why I called you here." Even through the screen, I can tell my brother is looking right at me. "Seems our older brother has lost his fucking mind over his girl, and I can't believe I'm going to say this, but we need to rein him in before he fucks it up."

I hate that he's right. I have no idea how Misty will react to what happened in her kitchen. She'd been wet and pliable, the air filled with her moans, but that didn't mean she didn't turn to pure fire the second I locked that door.

Bash chuckles and leans forward, his chin propped up on his knuckles. "Oh, this is going to be good."

Matthias shared his screen and played the video of me crashing through her building, storming up the stairs, then nearly taking her door off the hinges with how hard I slammed it open. Fear took over Carter's face as he took in my rigid stance, veins popping out of my neck, fist clenched at my sides. He's not a small guy, several inches over six feet tall, shoulders meant for checking opponents into the boards.

But he looked at me like I came straight out of his nightmares as I closed the distance between us.

I turn my attention to Misty, suddenly hating the idea of her looking at me with that same fear, but when my eyes land on hers, a slow satisfaction heats my abdomen. She's watching me with flushed cheeks and dark eyes. It's not fear but interest in her expression. Fuck, my cock's growing hard just watching her reaction.

My brothers are completely silent as they watch until the video cuts off right before I pin Misty to the counter.

"Fuck, man," Xander says on an exhale. "I thought you wanted to marry her, not make her hate you."

I look right at Matthias, and I know he knows my attention is on him. "Fuck you."

He shakes his head. "No, don't take your shit out on me. Someone's got to step in before you screw everything up. No one wants to deal with your grumpy ass when this all blows up in your face."

"No wonder you're drinking whiskey at 9:00 a.m. You just went all caveman in front of the first girl I've ever seen you actually interested in." Bash is smiling ear to ear, fucking loving every second of this. "Does that video finish the way I think it does?"

"It does," Matthias responds.

Anger curls in my chest. "You watched?"

"No, I didn't fucking watch. Not that you weren't putting on a show. Pretty sure that pretty-boy hockey player had the show of his life."

My skin prickles at the idea of anyone seeing Misty's bare skin. It was one thing for someone to know I'm fucking her. It's another to let them lay eyes on her. "He didn't see anything. I made sure of that."

Bash whistles low. "Can we just roll this back a second? Are you telling me you had her date watch you fuck her?"

"Watch how you talk about her," I warn.

I finish my whiskey and pour another one before speaking. "I told her we're getting married, and she took off from my office. I was just waiting for her to come around. Then she invites that asshole over."

"You *told* her you're getting married? Jesus Christ, Dam." Xander's voice is full of disappointment. "To think I looked up to you."

I rub my hand over my face. My brothers are the only people I'm willing to show weakness in front of, and even then, it's rare. "I fucked up."

"You think?" Xander sighs, collapsing back into the couch he's sitting on. "You're going to be fucking unbearable when she tells you to fuck yourself."

"Maybe we can convince her it was temporary insanity?" Bash adds.

Matthias shakes his head. He looks fed up with this entire conversation. "He tried to manipulate her into marrying him, then proceeded to break into her home and fuck her in front of her own date. Yeah, I'm not sure there's any fixing this."

"Send her flowers?" Xander winces, knowing that's not an actual solution.

"I'm sorry, brother, but I think you may actually be fucked on this one. Cut your losses."

My muscles stiffen as a darkness crawls up my veins. "Not an option."

"Well, unless you plan on drugging her before marrying her—" Xander's mouth falls open. "No, that wasn't a suggestion."

"If you want this girl to be anything but terrified of you, you need to back off," Matthias hisses. "She's never going to agree—"

He cuts off when my door slams open, and a whirlwind of color flies through it. Misty's looking down at where I'm sitting at my desk. Her chest rises and falls in rapid succession, and her hair is a wild storm of colorful curls.

"I'll marry you. But I have my own conditions."

Fuck. She's beautifully terrifying. I raise a solitary brow. "Is that so?"

"First, we keep this private. I don't want it splashed all over the news. You can tell your lawyers and your family to meet whatever requirements you need to."

"People will notice if I'm not actively looking for a wife."

"Which is why you're going to keep going on dates."

The muscles in the back of my neck leading into my hairline clench, hating the idea she'd be okay with me dating other women. I'm not fucking okay with it. I rein myself in. "What other requests do you have?"

"They aren't requests. If you want me to marry you, this is the way it will be."

I unclench my teeth. "Alright. What's your second one?"

She straightens, lifting her chin, but I don't miss the way her hands fidget in the pleats of her skirt. "No sex."

I let out an exasperated sigh. "Nymph, that's not possible—"

"Do you want to marry me?"

"Yes," I answer immediately.

"Then make it possible." She crosses her arms over her chest, and I wonder if she realizes how fucking adorable it makes her.

"As you wish," I respond, standing from behind my desk and stepping toward her.

She doesn't move as I eat the distance between us, not stopping until the leather of my shoes touches hers. "I agree not to fuck you until you beg for it."

She sucks in an audible breath, a pretty pink flush covering the tops of her breasts.

"That's not going to happen." There's a tremble to her voice, and I don't believe it has anything to do with fear.

I run my thumb along her cheek and lift her chin with my fingers until she looks at me. "We'll see."

"My last condition is that it's over in one year. That's long enough to meet your grandfather's condition. Not a minute longer."

I bite the tip of my thumb, watching as her ears turn red. I want to fight her on this, but it's not like she can get away from me anyway. "Fine. Anything else?"

She leans into my palm for a millisecond before snapping herself out of it and taking a step back, breaking the contact. "Can you make it happen this afternoon?"

"I'll see you then, *wife*." I nod and let her flee.

I return to my desk and throw back the remainder of my whiskey. I can't help my smile.

"Fuck, man. How blue are your balls going to be?" Bash breaks the silence.

I'd forgotten about my three brothers, who are now all smirking at me.

"Are we invited to the nuptials?" Xander adds playfully.

"No, thanks. He probably wants to bond her in blood."

I end the call with them and lean back in my chair, a thrill glowing in my chest.

A few more hours and she'll be mine.

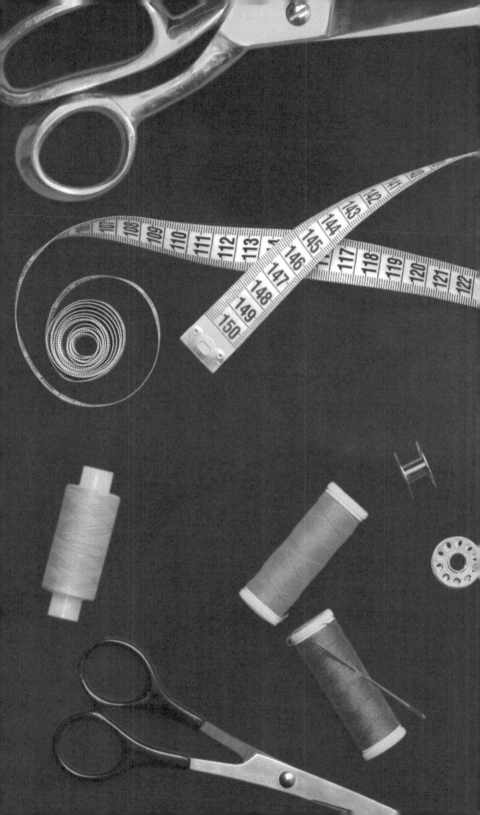

Chapter 19

Misty

THE TIRES RUMBLE OVER INTRICATELY LAID bricks as Nicholas pulls into the mansion's roundabout. Oh my dear God, there's a freaking ten-foot-tall marble fountain depicting a horse in the middle of it. I swallow hard as I look through the back-seat window at the home that could be called a castle. It has marble pillars and stone and mortar walls. There's even ivy growing up the walls. It's something out of a movie.

Everything is perfectly manicured, not a single leaf out of place, and I suddenly can't get out of the car. I don't belong here. I don't belong in this world with its perfect lines and white walls. I tug at the skirt of my silk slip dress.

I'd dip-dyed the bottom a brilliant shade of green that I thought played nicely with my eyes, but all I can see now is how inappropriate it is for a place like this.

My door opens, and where I expect to see Nicholas,

Damon stands, his hand extended to me. My breath catches in my throat as I take him in. His hair's been styled back off his face, and he's wearing a perfectly tailored tuxedo. There's no doubt in my mind he belongs here, that this place is meant for him.

When I don't take his hand, he crouches and meets me at eye level.

He looks apprehensive when he asks, "Are you okay?" His tone is so soft, tinged with worry that has some of the bands tightening around my chest loosening.

"I don't belong here, Damon," I say honestly. I'll just have to find another solution for my visa.

He reaches in and cups the side of my jaw, drawing my attention. "Listen to me. There isn't a place where I am that you don't belong beside me."

I huff, ignoring the tingles running down my neck left over from his words. "I'm not even dressed appropriately."

His dark eyes roam over where the dress cowls low on my chest, revealing the top of my cleavage, and travel to the colorful hem. He looks back to me. "You look divine."

I bite my lip and peer around him at the house. It looms above us. It's perfection, and I have to steel myself to get out.

"Do you not like my house?" Damon asks, a lightness to his voice.

"No! Of course not. It's...it's stunning. Anyone would love to live here."

He searches my face. "But not you?"

I wince, knowing my expression betrayed me.

"Stay here," he commands, then stands up, disappearing through the grand entrance. My throat grows thick, and there's an annoying burning at the back of my eyes, knowing he agrees with me. How could I let myself get into this mess? I knew this was stupid. When did I let him get into my head? And why does it feel like my ribs are tightening around my heart?

I'm struggling to get myself together when Damon emerges with an older man in a black suit. It's not tailored perfectly, and the wrinkles tell me he's also not from here.

Damon approaches me and holds out his hand. "He's agreed to wed us out here so you don't need to come inside."

My mouth falls open on a gasp. "I don't have to go inside?"

"No one's ever going to make you do anything you don't want to do, Misty. Never again. I promise you that."

His words wrap around me like a security blanket that I want to clutch and never let go.

I place my hand in his and let him guide me out of the car. "Aren't you making me do something right now?"

He turns to me, his expression serious. "You chose this. I gave you the motivation, but no one forced you to say yes." He takes a deep breath, and a muscle ticks in his jaw before he says, "Do you want out of our arrangement?"

There's an unexpected vulnerability to him, one I'm sure he didn't intend for me to see. Bubbles form in my stomach and float up in my chest. I shouldn't be feeling like this about him. I can't deny that my body responds to him, but it's not safe to open my heart. I take a deep breath and let it out. "I still want to follow through with our deal."

He nods once. "Let's go make you Mrs. Everette."

"You may kiss the bride."

Damon's hot mouth is on mine, stealing my breath away. My fingers bury into his shirt, anchoring myself to him. Everything is happening so fast, but right here, in this moment, with his mouth on mine and his arms wrapped around me, he makes me feel grounded. Like he's anchoring me to his shore. His hand slides down my back and grips my ass, giving it a tight squeeze.

I break the kiss. "There are people here."

He drops his mouth to just below my ear and places a delicate kiss there. "They're paid to look away."

"Damon." I laugh and push at his chest. "Don't forget my rule."

He groans and nips my neck. "Stupid fucking rule."

"I don't have a ring for you yet," he says, a look of pure annoyance on his face.

I huff out a laugh. "I wouldn't wear it anyway." I lower my voice to a fake whisper. "It's a secret."

His dark gaze bores into me as he adjusts his pants, then points at the car. "Let's go."

I look at the entry to the house. "We're not going in?"

"No," he replies simply and takes my hand, leading me into the car and following after me.

Nicholas climbs into the front seat. "Where are we headed, boss."

"Back to her apartment," he replies absentmindedly, like this is a totally normal situation.

"My...my apartment?"

"Ours now, Nymph." He smirks, then brings his phone to his ear. I can only hear half the conversation, but it's quickly apparent that he's having all of his things brought to my place.

I grab his arm and tug the phone from his ear. He raises one brow in question. "Yes?"

"You can't move in with me. My apartment is tiny. You're a freaking billionaire!" My voice rises with each word.

"I'm aware of the state of your apartment. I was there."

My cheeks flame red at the memory, and I push it to the back of my mind. There are other things I need to worry about right now.

"You don't have to live with me," I say.

He snaps his attention to me, no longer paying attention to whoever's on the other end of your line. "It's one of the requirements you agreed to."

"Yeah, but we could just pretend. You don't have to stay in my shitty apartment."

"Is it that you don't want me to stay with you, or you're embarrassed?"

It should be both, but right now, I'm still overwhelmed by how different our worlds feel. He must read it on my face because he leans in and kisses my temple, his mouth brushing my ear.

"It would be inconvenient for you to sleep in my bed each night if we don't live together. Or did you forget that's one of my requirements?"

His breath tickles my skin and sends shivers down my neck. I swallow hard. "I didn't forget."

He pulls away and goes back to ordering his employee to move all of his things. I have no idea how he expects to fit it all in my small space.

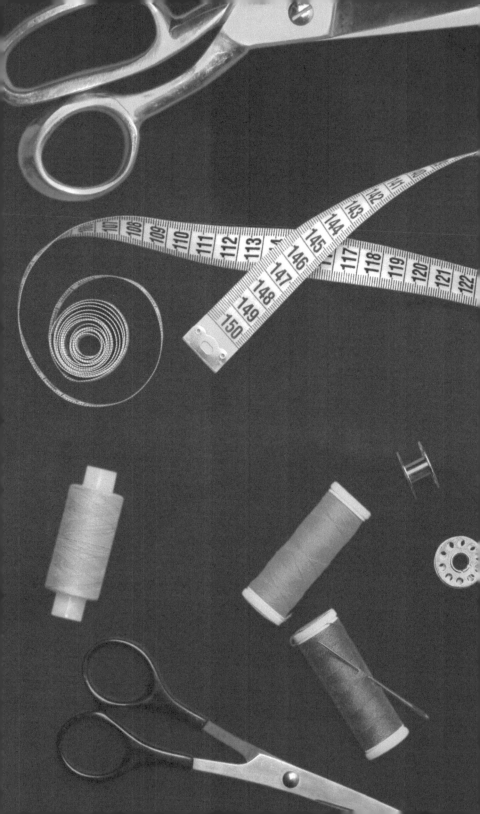

Chapter 20

Misty

By the time Damon's people have finished moving his belongings into my apartment, it's after eight at night. He looks ridiculous at my tiny dining table with his laptop, his large frame overwhelming the chair.

I thought for sure he'd walk in here, realize what a horrible idea this is, and head back to his place. Instead, he surprised me by asking questions about my sewing. Commenting about how cozy the bedroom is. The smirk he wore when he said it had heat licking up my thighs.

Damon's still in his tux, but he's removed his coat and rested it on the back of his chair. His sleeves are rolled to his elbows, and I find myself captivated by the intricate designs he has etched into it. Who knew he had a canvas of art painted on his skin under his stuffy outfits.

I move around to get a better look in the pretense of

grabbing a glass of water. His eyes follow me, taking in my teddy bear pink flannel pajamas with a smirk.

"I'd be happy to take my shirt off if you want a better look."

"No...no, sorry. I just didn't..." I stammer.

"Didn't expect me to have tattoos?" he questions.

"They're just...they're just so colorful." Flowers, fish, skulls, an array of designs.

He turns sideways in his chair to face me, his legs spread wide enough I could step between them. I fist my hands in the soft fabric of my pants to keep myself from doing anything stupid as I watch him meticulously pop his shirt buttons through their holes one by one, slowly revealing inch by inch of his chest.

My breath catches in my lungs as he shrugs the fabric from his shoulders, revealing himself to me. It's one thing to guess what he'd look like underneath; it's a whole other thing to come face-to-face with Damon's naked chest. The world seems to tilt on its side as I take in the seemingly endless rows of abdominal muscles. My mouth waters, and I teeter on my feet a little, only for him to reach out and brace me.

Embarrassment rises in my throat. "Sorry."

He shakes his head. "It's okay. You can look."

I can't help myself. There's a lavender lotus flower taking up his forearm that fades into a pond motif filled with fish and lilies. The colors deepen the further up they go, black, smokelike swirls blending in with the design until they wrap around his collarbone.

I gaze up at his face. "What does that symbolize?"

"In darkness, there is light."

I bite the corner of my lip and let myself admire the art. "The black really makes the colors stand out. Almost like it's there to make them shine brighter?" I look up to meet his eyes, and he's wearing an odd smile that I can't make out.

"I'm glad you like it," he says. There's a glint in his expression that makes me feel like he's teasing me, but I'm not sure about what.

My gaze catches on raised scars along his chest and shoulder. My hand rises involuntarily to touch it, but my stomach rumbles loudly, breaking the moment.

"When's the last time you ate?" He looks displeased.

I have a feeling he's not going to like the answer. "Last night."

"What? Why didn't you tell me?"

"Well, it's not like it came up or anything, and I was...too nervous to eat today."

He runs his thumb and forefinger over his mouth, thinking. "Do you like sushi?"

Eight pieces of sushi later, I'm tucked into the side of my couch. I still haven't processed the speed at which everything's happened. I went from being royally pissed at Damon to being married so fast my brain can't catch up.

I didn't even have time to tell the girls. If I'm being honest, I don't know how to explain why I did it without revealing parts of my past.

The parts I've buried deep inside and never wanted them to know. There's a beauty in starting over, a freedom to create whatever world you want. However, there's a guilt that comes along with hiding a part of yourself from the people closest to you.

Damon's sitting at my tiny table again, his head bowed down to the laptop, where his long fingers fly over the keys. The only thing more distracting than the flex and shift of his forearms is that he didn't put his shirt back on, using the excuse of being hot in here. Nothing in the way his clothes fit him gives away the muscles on muscles stacked along his abdomen and sides.

My mouth waters as I trace the contour of his oblique to where it disappears into the waistband of his black slacks.

"You're drooling," Damon says, his voice low but playful.

My mouth snaps shut, no doubt a rose blush covering my cheeks at getting caught.

"No need to be embarrassed. Wives are supposed to check out their husbands."

Husband... I swallow hard as the word rocks through me, momentarily distracting me from the look on his face. His mouth is quirked up at the side as he stands from the too-small chair and stretches his arms above his head before entwining his fingers behind his neck. He's taunting me, daring me to cave and break my own rule. The worst part is I want to. I'm already growing wet between my thighs, and if my top was any thinner, he'd be able to see exactly what he's doing to me.

My fingers grip the worn fabric of my sofa, holding me in place. "We don't have that kind of marriage."

He raises one singular brow. "Don't we? You begged me to touch you, to fill your pussy last night. What makes you think you can resist doing it again? I own you, Nymph. It's only a matter of time before you accept that."

I bristle at his challenge. He wants me begging, but I know just how to drive him insane.

I look at my shabby pajamas, the corner of my lip curling into a smile. Two can play this game.

"You're right. It is hot in here." I stand from the couch and slide the top button of my shirt through the hole. His whole body tenses, and his gaze is pinned to where my hands work the next button, revealing the top of my breast.

He takes a step toward me, but I skirt away from him, making my way toward the bedroom. I close the door behind me and drop my head against the hollow wood surface, taking several breaths. Am I really going to do this?

The rational part of me screams no, but there's a darker part of me that pushes me forward, that wants to break his control.

I slide my dresser drawer open and dig toward the

back, pulling out an emerald-green silk nighty. It's cut high in the back and devastatingly low in the front. Quickly divesting my flannel, I slide the cool fabric of the dress over my head, letting it fall to just below the crease where my butt meets the back of my thighs. Any attempt at bending over would reveal the vibrant pink lace beneath.

My reflection in the mirror is someone who barely looks like me, and my smile grows, knowing he's about to get a taste of his own medicine. With any luck, he'll be the one begging. Preferably on his knees.

The loud click of his water glass hitting the counter fills my tiny apartment the second I walk out. I make my way to the kitchen, ignoring the hot brand of his gaze on my bare skin, and move behind him to grab a glass from the cupboard.

They're a little out of reach, and I lift on my toes. He lets out a guttural groan when the hem rises several inches. The sound coats my insides, pebbling my nipples instantly. I gasp when his chest meets my back, caging me against the counter. My heart pounds in my ears until it blocks out all sounds, and the only thing that matters is where his body touches mine.

All reason vanishes from my mind, and I press back into him, wanting nothing more than to have his hands on me.

His mouth grazes my ear, sending shivers down my spine, and his breath is warm on my skin, setting me on fire when he says, "Be careful or you'll lose this game, and I'm not done playing with you."

He reaches up, hands me a glass, and steps back, putting several feet between us. The air's cold with the sudden loss of his heat. An overwhelming feeling of being dismissed curdles in my stomach, and a sick wave of embarrassment takes over. I spin and glare at him. "You're awfully sure of yourself."

He runs his thumb along his bottom lip. "Your nipples are hard."

Dammit. I cross my arms over my chest. "It's cold in here."

"Sure it is." He chuckles low in his throat, giving me a knowing look. He doesn't bother to hide when he reaches down and adjusts his pants. The outline of his hard cock. Shit, even through the fabric, it's clear that he's massive. He wants me to see what I do to him.

I hurry from the kitchen, needing to put space between us before I do something epically stupid, like jumping him. He glances at my empty glass, then back to me. I don't bother going back for it. I'm not sure what I'll do if I have to be that close to him again.

"I'm tired. I'm going to bed." The excuse is lame, but I can barely think.

"It's ten." His smirk grows into a smile.

"It's been a long day." I don't even care that he knows I'm hiding when I escape into my room, thanking God that the bathroom has double access from both the living room and my bedroom. I lock the connecting door and place my hands on the counter, letting it take my weight. My pupils are blown wide, leaving only a sliver of green, and my cheeks are flushed pink. I look wild, untamed, and the feeling is addicting.

I pull my hair back into a clip and wash my face. The water is the only thing cooling me down. I don't hear Damon walk in until his arm touches mine.

I startle, splashing water over the counter.

"You're jumpy tonight. Does something have you anxious?" He says it entirely too casually as he grabs his toothbrush from my counter.

I'm momentarily shocked at the normality of the motion. Like he's been in my bathroom a thousand times before and there's nothing unusual about this whole thing.

"Of course not." Determined to not let him see just how much he is getting to me, I grab my own toothbrush and brush my teeth. He watches me in the mirror with dark eyes as he bends over to spit in the sink. I'm completely unprepared for how hot that simple action is.

It's not hot. It's disgusting.

I rinse my mouth out, glad that this whole thing is nearly done. "Okay, well, good night."

Why does he look so freaking amused by that?

"Good night."

I crawl into bed and pull the covers over my head. "Shut the light off when you go out, please."

See, I can be normal. He hits the lights, but instead

of leaving, he walks to the opposite side of the bed. The sound of his zipper has me spinning to see him.

"What are you doing?" I screech.

One brow rises. "Going to sleep."

Pure panic fills my chest, and I squeak, "In here?"

"Yes." He drags out the syllable. "As per our agreement."

"But...we don't actually have to do that. No one is going to know you didn't sleep with me." I immediately regret my choice of words. If he caught it, he doesn't let on.

"I'll know." He pushes his pants down his legs, revealing gray boxer briefs.

What could I possibly have done in a past life to deserve this? "You're not getting in here like that...where are your pajamas?"

"I don't have any. I never wear them."

"Never?" I squeak.

He pulls back the covers and gets in behind me. The double-size bed makes it impossible to leave any space, and his breath fans over the back of my neck. "Never. It's entirely too hot."

A shudder runs through me, and I can only pray he doesn't see it. Every inhale is a struggle. He shifts, his chest grazing my back. I try to muffle my whimper into my pillow as heat floods my core, and my clit throbs, begging to be touched.

Traitor.

He shifts again, this time his hand landing on my hip.

"What are you doing?" My voice comes out breathy.

"Your bed's tiny. There's no room."

"Wouldn't...wouldn't you be more comfortable sleeping somewhere else until we can get a bigger bed?" I fight not to stutter.

His grip tightens on my hip and tugs me closer. "No. This is perfect."

My back arches against my will, my body completely ignoring my brain. When I don't pull away like I should, he slides his hand down the curve of my hip, and his fingers brush the inside of my thigh, millimeters from where I need him most.

A moan escapes my lips, and he takes it as permission to move further. He doesn't turn his hand to meet my core, instead driving me crazy with the barely there caress of the back of his knuckles against my clit.

"You think you're in control, but your body is mine." His lips meet the back of my neck in a kiss so soft it feels imagined. "Beg for it and I'll give you whatever you want."

I've stopped breathing altogether, willing him to grasp me where I need him but refusing to beg. I rub my thighs together, bringing his fingers closer so they press firmer against me. I moan when it's not enough to soothe the aching in my core.

"See how much your pussy wants me. How much

she needs me." Cool metal slides over my wrist. I'm too lost to him to question what it is.

"Yes." My hips shift, and my ass grinds against his hard cock.

He growls, a pained, primal sound. His hands tighten on my hips almost bruisingly, and the air shifts as whatever's been holding him back cracks around us.

Pleasure rocks through me as he thrusts his cock against my ass, the sensation mixed with the barely there touch of his hand has my mind blanking as my clit throbs for his attention.

A low groan rips from his chest, and he pulls back, breaking all contact with me.

I whimper, and my body shakes with the loss. Damon chuckles, but it's a dark, warning sound. He rests his chin on my shoulder, his evening stubble scraping the side of my face. Heat flashes through me as he runs a single finger along my slit, and my body shakes with need.

"That wasn't very nice. You almost made me lose control," he rasps against my ear.

I shiver, even though I'm anything but cold, as I try to process what's happening through the spell he's put me under.

"You will crawl to me and beg me to fuck this little pussy." His teeth scrape across the sensitive curve of my neck, and all reason disappears from my brain. I don't care that I'll hate myself tomorrow. I'm more than willing to beg for him tonight.

Before I can form words, Damon stands from the bed and walks out of the room, leaving me panting with burning lust.

"Damon?" Confusion is clear in my voice. "Damon!" I call out louder.

He doesn't respond, and shock rolls through me, unable to process what just happened. Several agonizing seconds later, I hear the front door shut and the lock click into place.

"You've got to be kidding me." I groan and roll over.

My clit throbs with my pulse. *Dammit.* He's left me desperate for release. I give in to my need and slip my panties off, my fingers immediately stroking my clit. I shift my hand lower and imagine it's his fingers burying themself deep inside me. It takes seconds to make myself come, his name a whisper on my lips.

Panting, I roll onto my stomach, and the glimmer of silver catches my eye in the moonlight. He's put a thin bracelet on me. I twist it, trying to get it off, but it's too tight to go over my hand. I stop when the pressure bruises the bones in my wrist.

A shiver runs down my spine. What the hell is this?

Chapter 21

Damon

"Fuck." I dig my fingers in my hair, tightening them until my scalp hurts. Anything to cut through the consuming need to go back into her apartment, flip her over, and sink my cock into her pretty pussy. Even without removing her panties, my fingers are wet from where I touched her. I groan as I suck each one, licking off her taste.

She's temptation incarnate. I smile, satisfaction burning in my chest at knowing she's mine. She doesn't know it yet, but she's locked to me forever, right where she belongs. My Little Nymph is the only thing keeping me from sinking into the darkness, and I will not let her go.

I adjust my pants, which I grabbed off the floor on my way out, and tuck the head of my cock beneath the waistband, pinning it in place. There's no chance it's going down anytime soon, especially now that her taste is in my mouth.

Thankfully, I have other things to do to take my mind off it. I grab a spare shirt from my bag, a cigar, and my favorite pen before heading to the building's front door.

As expected, there's a man guarding the door, holding a folder in his hand.

"That for me?" I ask, the air heavy and humid when I open the door.

"Yes, sir." He startles momentarily before handing it over. "Lawyer dropped it off a few minutes ago."

I head down the hall to where the owner lives. Part of Matthias's research of the building was to provide me with all the information on the owner. The man lived here his entire life, the building passed down by his father. Even in its crumbling state, it's turned a profit year after year, only increasing in value with the higher property cost. Which complicates things, but I do love a challenge.

The door rattles on its hinges as I pound the side of my fist into it, not giving a shit that it's past eleven.

"Who the fuck is it." The owner's voice is muffled through the door.

"You can open it, or I can break it. Your choice." I keep my voice emotionless, letting him know I don't care what he chooses. I'm getting to him no matter what.

It takes several moments before the door cracks open, a thin chain link holding it closed. I hit my palm next to its connection point and meet his gaze when it snaps. "Are you done fucking around?"

The door swings open, and the middle-aged man stands in front of me with a gun pointed directly at my chest. His hands shake as he cocks it. "Don't move. I don't have any money. There's nothing for you in here."

"That's where you're wrong." His eyes widen as I step into the gun, letting the muzzle touch my sternum, calling his bluff. In one swift move, I grasp the barrel while simultaneously connecting with his palm, taking control of the gun.

"Oh fuck. Please don't hurt me. I'll do whatever you want. There's money in the safe," he pleads, his voice cracking.

"No need for that." I engage the safety and place the gun on a small entry table. "I'm here to make you an offer."

His brows pull together. "Listen, whatever you're selling, I'm not buying."

"You're mistaken. I'm the one who's buying. Your building."

"What? It's not for sale," he scoffs.

"You turn a profit of three hundred thousand a year, correct?" I ask, but I already know the answer.

He shifts his jaw from side to side, trying to figure me out. "Around that."

"You expect to continue making that or more over the next ten years," I state, then pull out the paperwork I brought with me. "I'll pay you ten million dollars if you sell it to me now. I already have the documentation ready. All you have to do is sign, and the money will transfer directly into your account."

His mouth falls open, closes, then opens again. "I don't understand? That's way above market value."

"Do you accept the deal or not?" I'm prepared to offer him double, but I don't tell him that. Instead, I wait, keeping my face impassive.

"Don't I know you? You're that Everette heir, aren't you?" A spark grows, dissolving his apprehension.

"Good, you've heard of me." I pass the papers over. "Do we have a deal?"

"I have to have my lawyers look over it." He grasps them in his hand, unable to hide his excitement.

"No." I shake my head. "It's now or never."

"Fuck, man."

"Take it or leave it, but I'm growing tired." I take a step back, and panic takes over his features.

"Wait! Okay, I'll do it."

"Good. My lawyers tabbed everywhere you need to sign it." I hand him a pen, and he flips through the pages, putting his name down in rapid succession. He thrusts them all at me, and I sort through the top few and hand them back to him.

"These are your copies. You'll see I've already signed them."

"You were that sure of yourself?"

"I'm always sure before I head into a deal." I hit dial

on my phone, connecting with my accountant. "He accepted my first offer. Send the money."

"First offer? What do you mean? Would you have given more?" he says incredulously.

"Life lesson. Always negotiate."

"Don't you need my bank information?"

"I already have it. I suggest you change your passwords to something other than your mother's name and birthday."

He goes ghostly white.

"Relax. You're a millionaire." I cut him a sharp smile. "I expect you out by morning."

"Morning! I can't do that."

"I'm afraid it's in the contract, or you will owe me one hundred thousand for every day you're late. I've arranged a moving company to pick up your things and put them into storage until you find a new place." I check my watch. "In exactly eight hours. I suggest you start packing. Goodbye, Mr. Williams." I shut the door behind me and head outside.

It's cool, the clawing humidity of the day finally releasing its hold. I pull out a cigar and pass it between my teeth before lighting it and taking a long drag in. Even the gun to my chest did nothing for my aching erection. The only thing that's going to work is her.

> Me: Do a background check on all residents. Evict anyone that seems suspicious.

She'll be pissed if her friends are thrown out, so I make sure my brother knows who they are.

> Matthias: I can't believe you bought the building.

> Matthias: Scratch that. When it comes to this girl, I totally believe it.

> Me: You've always been smart.

> Matthias: Don't flatter me or it'll go to my head.

> Matthias: I'll have the eviction notices out by tomorrow. Some of them might create trouble.

> Me: Nothing a bribe won't fix.

> Matthias: You're so fucked up about her.

> Me: One day you'll understand.

> Matthias: Never going to happen.

> Me: We'll see.

When he doesn't respond, I pocket my phone, finish my cigar, and head back up to our place. I'm quiet as I make my way toward her room, and just as I expected, she's passed out on her bed just where I left her. Pink panties on the floor catch my eye.

I close the distance so I'm looming over her mattress and bend down to pick the scrap of lace up, bringing it to my nose and inhaling deeply. My lungs fill with the sweet scent of her, and the limited amount of control I had remaining snaps.

I snap the button on my pants and pull out my throbbing cock, wrapping the delicate fabric around it. With each stroke, the lace scrapes against my skin, making my dick twitch. I watch her sleep as I fuck my hand roughly. Her lips are parted, and I picture painting them, then thrusting deep into her throat. I picture her with tears in her eyes as I thrust in the back of her throat, and she takes every inch I give her.

My orgasm starts in my balls, tightening, sending a nearly painful pressure until my cum explodes from my tip. I wipe it with her panties, internally smirking at the mess I've made of them. I strip out of my clothes and climb in beside her, hating the distance between us, no matter how small. I pull her small frame over my chest until her leg drapes around me and her breasts press into my chest. She lets out a soft moan and cuddles further into me, her mouth brushing my skin as she sighs out my name.

She might be fighting it, but her body and subconscious have already accepted their fate.

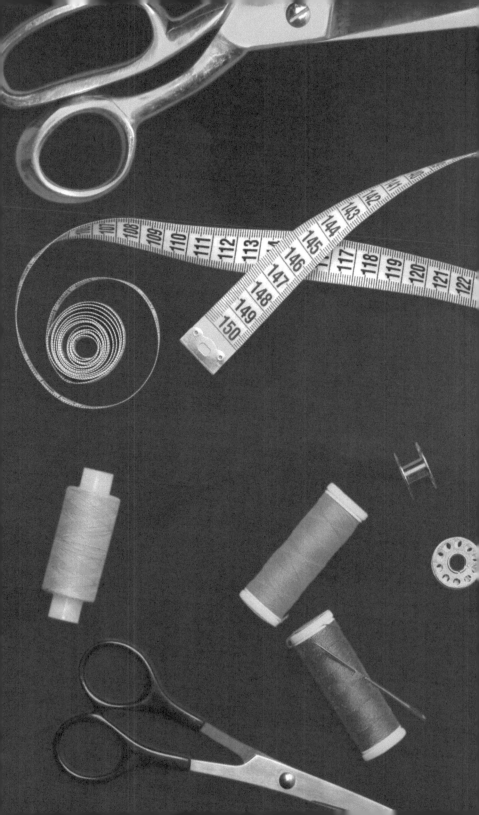

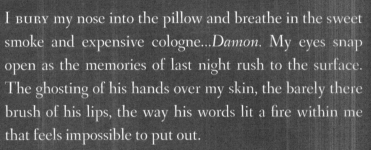

Chapter 22

Misty

I BURY my nose into the pillow and breathe in the sweet smoke and expensive cologne...*Damon*. My eyes snap open as the memories of last night rush to the surface. The ghosting of his hands over my skin, the barely there brush of his lips, the way his words lit a fire within me that feels impossible to put out.

I groan, flipping onto my back, and rub the sleep out of my eyes, frustration building inside me. He just left. Like we weren't in the middle of the hottest thing that's ever happened to me, like he didn't have control over every fiber of my being. Maybe it's good he left because I would have done anything he wanted to get him to touch me.

I'd think he left for the night if it wasn't for the vague memories of him pulling me into his arms sometime later last night and his fingers stroking my hair, so faint they could've been a dream.

Knowing there's no way I'm going back to sleep, I roll out of bed and grab my giant unicorn robe, hoping he's already left.

Nothing could have prepared me for the sight of a shirtless Damon leaning against my counter, casually drinking coffee from a neon pink cup while staring at his phone. My heart skips in my chest at just how domestic he looks, like he's done this every day.

Meanwhile, I'm about to swallow my tongue to stop myself from drooling over the way his gray sweatpants mold around his curves. I can't stop staring at the way his long, slim fingers dwarf his phone. Tingles scatter over my skin of the memory of how they felt against my skin.

"Morning, Nymph," Damon says, his voice filled with amusement. "I like the unicorns. Cute."

Suddenly feeling completely exposed, I pull the corners of my robe tighter. The realization of just how bad I look in the morning, hair a wild mess, half sticking to my face, sinks in and has me fidgeting with my hair.

"I like your sweatpants." I go for sarcasm but fail miserably. I'm never like this. I've spent years mastering the art of hiding my irritation, but one look from Damon has me bristling like a defensive cat.

He chuckles. "I can tell."

Dammit. My cheeks heat, only bringing him more amusement.

"Whatever," I grumble and make my way to my coffee maker, only to stop dead in my tracks. My little box-store-bought pot is nowhere to be seen. Instead, it's been replaced with a stainless steel, state-of-the-art espresso machine. I go to turn it on, but my fingers hover over the dials. I don't even know where to start. An underlying frustration builds within me, sparking a fire in my chest. "Who said you could bring your coffee maker?"

"Grumpy in the morning, I see?" Damon's voice is right next to my ear, and a shivery heat tracks down my back.

I scoff. "I've been told I'm a joy in the morning."

"Mm-hmmm," he hums in mock agreement before grabbing a cup from the top shelf. It's a pale blue mug printed with the words "Oh" and "It" and a cute fox in between them. He moves to the machine and turns a few dials. He hits a button, and it comes to life with a loud rumble. I stand, mouth dropped open, as he uses the machine, effortlessly frothing milk. He dumps several scoops of sugar into my cup, and his arm moves in tightly controlled gestures as he combines the frothed milk with the espresso.

My mind is so monumentally surprised at the scene that's playing out for me it takes a second to catch up and realize he made it exactly how I order them at a fancy coffee shop. "How did you know—"

Damon thrusts the warm mug into my hand, cutting me off. "You have half an hour to get ready. I thought it would be better to let you sleep in as long as possible."

"I'm not coming with you." I hum as the perfectly made cappuccino passes my lips.

"Yes, you are." His eyes flash with hidden meaning. I wish I could read him better. "Now, go get ready. I have a meeting first thing."

"Can't do that." I shake my head, enjoying the way his mask cracks, revealing his growing annoyance.

When I don't elaborate, he asks, "Why not?"

I raise one brow in a mock portrayal of his favorite expression. "Well, I'm pretty sure that would ruin the whole *keeping our marriage a secret* thing, don't you think? Or do you want the whole office to just jump to the conclusion that I'm sleeping with you to get a promotion? Because I can promise you they won't guess we're married."

His teeth clack together, and a muscle ticks in his jaw. "That's why we should announce it."

"No, we...we can't." Coldness freezes in my lungs, preventing me from taking in a breath. The last thing I need is for news of our marriage to get out and my parents to see. "You agreed."

I expect to see anger, but it's concern creasing his brow. "Why is that one of your rules, *wife?*"

A shiver rolls through me, and I try to suppress my reaction to the title. I swallow hard. "Telling you isn't a part of our agreement."

"Fine." He cracks his jaw from side to side. "Nicholas will drive you."

I smile at his attempt to stay calm and can't resist giving his control a little shove. "Actually, I have the morning booked off."

"Who approved that?" He practically growls out the word.

"My husband." I smirk.

He visibly softens in front of me and rests a hand on the counter, a slow smirk curving his mouth. "Why would he do that?"

"Because I asked him to." I meet his gaze, playfulness evaporating. "I need the morning to speak with my friends."

He watches me for several moments before nodding. "Nicholas will be waiting for you when you leave. We'll have lunch at the office."

"Oh, that's not going to happen. You're really bad at this whole *covert* thing."

He tilts his head and bites his lips. "Apparently, only when it comes to you. I expect to see you this afternoon."

"Yes, boss." I roll my eyes.

He crowds me, my coffee pressed between our chests. "What happened to *husband*?"

Heat builds in my lower stomach. I need to get away from him before I do something stupid, like kiss him.

"It's a secret," I stage-whisper.

He leans in and brushes his lips over my forehead, his words a caress. "Not when we're alone."

He shifts so his dark gaze meets mine, and time stops with the intensity of the moment. The air grows thick with the tension surrounding us, making it hard to breathe. He doesn't look away, instead scanning my face for any reaction. My carefully protected heart starts to crack open, and fear seeps in. I can't do this.

His brows pull together, eyes scanning rapidly between mine.

"What's wrong?" His voice comes like he's speaking to a scared animal.

"I...I have to get ready." He's still in front of me and doesn't move when I try to skirt around him. "Please, let me go."

The plea in my voice startles him, and he steps back so fast his back bangs into the counter.

The glint of my silver bracelet catches my eye. "What the hell is this?"

"You said no ring. You didn't think I'd marry you and let you walk around without something that marks you as mine?"

"I can't take it off." It's not so tight that it imprints my skin, but it can't be removed.

He smirks. "You're not supposed to."

"You're very frustrating, you know that?"

"I could say the same for you."

Warmth fills my stomach, expanding throughout my limbs at the way he's looking at me.

Ugh. I turn away from him and his perfect smile, escaping into my bedroom. Stripping out of my clothes, I bury my head under the shower. I stay like that for what feels like forever before finally peeling myself out of the room, my unicorn robe firmly back in place.

There's a coffee on the counter and a handwritten note.

You look cute in the morning, wife. I'll see you for lunch.

--Your husband.

I ignore the fact that Damon has, once again, suggested we have lunch together and run my fingers along the thick textured paper. I subconsciously raise it to my nose and take a deep breath of his scent.

Husband, husband, *husband.* The word both thrills and terrifies me. Everything feels like it's barreling down a freeway at a million miles a minute, so fast that I can't make out the passing buildings. So fast the world blurs.

I spin the silver bracelet around my wrist as I look around, the cool metal now warm against my skin.

Damon's things are all around my place. There are a few bottles of whiskey that look more expensive than my rent sitting on a new table tucked against the wall. The smooth oak looks out of place with the cheap laminate of everything I own. His suit jacket is still hanging over the back of the chair from last night.

My cheeks flush at the memory of his barely there touch, and I shake off the shiver traveling over my skin. A bubbly feeling grows in my chest, spreading warmth through my body.

The plan seemed so simple yesterday. Get married, get my visa reinstated, get divorced in a year, and forget all about this.

Then he had to go and be so freaking observant. He

was understanding when I didn't want to go into his house. Now, he's moved into my place, and he's leaving little reminders of his presence everywhere I look. There was a softness to him that I didn't anticipate. An understanding, like only he could see what I've buried deep within me.

He didn't ask questions or try to pressure me. Instead, he bent to my level and gave me a choice in what we did. He gave me a say in his life and had no trouble adjusting. If I'm not careful, I could get used to this, and that's not the plan at all.

My chest tenses. One year, and this will be over.

I have one year to survive with my heart intact.

First, I have to face the inevitable chaos that's about to ensue when I tell my friends what I've done. I bring my coffee to the couch and collapse against it, pulling up the group chat with Piper and Mia, and take a deep breath, steeling myself for what comes next.

> Me: I did a thing.

Piper: Why does that sound so ominous?

> Me: I got married. Surprise.

Piper: No seriously. What's up.

> Me: Yesterday, I got married to keep my working status in the US.

Mia: YOU DID WHAT?

Piper: Explain.

Mia: To who?

My thumb twitches above the keys, and I bite the corner of my lip. It's one thing to marry Damon. It's an entirely different thing to admit it. I pull the Band-Aid off and type out my reply.

Me: Damon Everette

Piper: WHAT?

Mia: I KNEW IT!

Me: I can explain. Kind of...

Explaining means opening up my past and letting them see me for who I am. It means owning up to hiding a part of myself from my closest friends, which is considerably easier to not feel bad about when you're the only one who knows.

Piper: Girls meeting. Now.

I sigh, resigning myself to the disaster that's going to be the rest of the morning, and get up to pick out the perfect outfit.

If I'm going to the gallows, I might as well look pretty doing it.

"So let me get this straight. He wouldn't sign your visa papers, so you...married him?" Mia asks from across the small bistro table.

We'd chosen a cute cafe down the street to meet. I thought it was better to have this conversation with witnesses in case they decide I've gone insane and my only hope is for them to kidnap me.

When I'd told Nicholas it was ridiculous to drive somewhere so close, he opted to trail me as I walked the entire way. I rolled my eyes at him, but he just smiled.

I shrug. "Pretty much."

"Okay, not to be insulting, but why you?" Piper lays her chin in her palm, leaning forward with rapt attention.

Excellent freaking question, unfortunately one that I'd also love to know the answer to. "He didn't say. Just that he has to get married and he wants it to be me."

Mia grins into her coffee. "That's actually kind of sweet."

"He coerced me into marriage," I scoff.

She shrugs. "Still sweet."

"Why did you do it?" Piper cuts in.

Confusion tumbles through me. "What do you mean? You know I needed to do something, or I'd have to move back."

"Yes, but don't you think getting married is extreme? You could have moved home, then had everything sorted and come back. *Or*, now that you have experience, you could have found a Canadian team to work for." She twists a strand of her hair. "So, what's the real reason?"

I've been avoiding telling them for so long I have no idea how they'll react when I do, but I owe them at least some of the truth.

"I can't move back there because my ex will find me and won't leave me alone."

I explain everything I can about my past, holding only the most painful parts back. My manipulative ex. The rape, how my parents chose his side over mine. Chose their reputation over my sanity.

Piper's brows pull together, hurt clear in her expression. "Why didn't you tell us?"

Ah, there's the question I've been expecting. I take a deep breath. "When I met you, I'd just restarted my life. I'd cut all ties with Thomas and didn't want anything from that time seeping into the new me. I wanted to forget everything that happened and let myself recreate my life. Don't get me wrong, there were countless times I *wanted* to tell you, but in the end, I just wasn't ready." Tears slip down my cheeks. "I really am sorry. Eventually, it just felt too late to bring it up."

Piper reaches across the table and gives my hand a gentle squeeze. "Misty, there is nothing to be sorry about. You went through something traumatic, and you chose how you would recover from it. What kind of friends would we be if we centered our own feelings over yours?"

"Thank you." I sigh.

"Of course."

"You know, the guys are good at threatening exes," Mia adds, a playfulness to her tone, but it's cold dread that fills my stomach.

"Not him." For a second, I debate explaining he's a part of some rich people's secret society, the same that people speculate Damon's in. It basically makes them untouchable. I drop it. Some things are meant to stay secret, and the knowledge that a bunch of asshole men are basically controlling everything is one of them. No need to feel like a helpless ant if you don't need to.

I subconsciously spin the silver bracelet. It's providing way more comfort in this conversation than it should. Despite the fact that my dear husband coerced me into this marriage, he's never made me feel like I should be anything but what I am. The thin band should freak me out, but there must be something wrong with me because I'm eating up the fact that he wants me to wear it. I can't even begin to process how I feel about him. I know how my body responds, like he's set it on fire, and it somehow was meant to be that way. Like, it's just been waiting for him this entire time. But my brain? It's split in two, and the sane, rational part tells me I need to get away from him as soon as possible.

The instinctive, selfish part of me, however, wants to believe he wants me. That I'm more than his latest obsession. I quickly squash that part because in one year, he'll be gone, and if I'm not careful, there will be nothing of me left.

Chapter 23

Damon

I LEAN FORWARD, elbows braced on my desk as I rake my fingers through my hair. The clock's been ticking on the wall, slowly driving me insane, as I watch Misty speak to her friends on my phone. Nicholas's videoing from the car, so the angle's bad, and there's no sound, but I can still make out her expressions. Every time she looks unsure of herself, I have to press down the urge to go to her. To make her see that even though I'd coerced her into marrying me, it was to hurry along the inevitable.

She's always been mine.

The second she tied herself to me, my world clicked into place. Like everything I've lived through brought me to her. I'd endure the pain all over again if it meant making me what she needs.

Because she doesn't need someone soft. She needs someone to see the darkness she tries to hide and worship her because of it. She needs someone who she isn't afraid to show herself to because she knows I'll never reject her. She instinctively knows that already. It's why she shows me her fire and no one else. It's why she's comfortable pushing my boundaries every chance she gets. And I fucking love her for it.

I love the joyfulness she shows her friends, making everyone feel lighter, but it's the sharp edge to her wit that has me willing to drop to my knees to give her what she wants.

There's no feeling like tying the person you are meant to be with to you permanently. Because we are permanent.

I let her believe it's only for a year, but that's never been the plan. She's about to learn what it means to be mine.

Fate has always been something people told themselves to justify their shitty lives, but I can see it now. Fate brought her to my team, pulled her from a different country to work for me. Now, I'm just waiting for her to admit it because I know she knows we're meant for each other, even if she's lying to herself.

I turn off my phone and stare blankly at my computer. Her wanting to keep us a secret itches under my skin. The way she looked away from me when she laid down that rule had suspicion growing in my gut. A nagging feeling I can't ignore tells me there's more than just losing credit at work. That there's something deeper behind my Nymph's lies.

My phone dings with a text from Nicholas, letting me know they're on the way to the office.

I smile. She may be keeping secrets, but I'm going to do everything in my power to figure it out. I tried to give her at least some privacy, but now all her secrets will be mine.

***

Misty walks into my office, all sharp lines and determination. Her heels click against the tile floor as she eats the space between us. But she's not looking at me. Instead, her head's bowed, attention focused on her tablet while she comes toward me.

"Wife," I say, and her head snaps up, her pale green eyes meeting mine. My lips curl in satisfaction, and I lean back into my chair.

"Husband." Her voice is smooth, professional, and it's grating against my skin. We may be at work, but there's nothing professional between us. Still, the word sounds sweet on her tongue.

I want to push her, crack the cool shell she's wrapped herself in. "So, wife, how do you suppose we go about our marriage when I'm supposed to be shopping for a wife?"

Adorable wrinkles form at the top of her nose, but she clears her expression before responding, nothing but the perfect employee showing through. "Simple. We're going to stick to the plan, and you'll appear to still be looking for a *suitable* wife. Your mother and I have put a lot of work into making this list, after all."

Bitterness fills my mouth, and my teeth grit hard enough to break, the muscles in my jaw aching in an effort to bite back my reactive response. A slight growl forms in the back of my throat as I try to figure her out. She's watching me just as hard, head held rigidly high, arms crossed over her chest as she waits for my response.

It's her clenched fist and the tight tendons leading up her neck that give her away. My girl thinks she can act unaffected, that I can't tell that jealousy is eating at her. She wants me to refuse, but it's the perfect opportunity to find out why she's doing this in the first place. It's her rule that got us here, and she needs to be the one that breaks it.

My lips curl into a smirk as I relax into the back of my chair, and I give her a little push. "When do we start?"

She visibly flinches, nostrils flaring as she takes a deep breath before drawing herself up to her full height, her chin held high as she maintains eye contact with me. There's a defiance in her gaze, a cunning willingness to play this game with me. My cock starts to harden. She's meant for this, meant for me.

It's her mischievous smile that lets me know I fucked up.

"Perfect, so we're agreed. We're not exclusive."

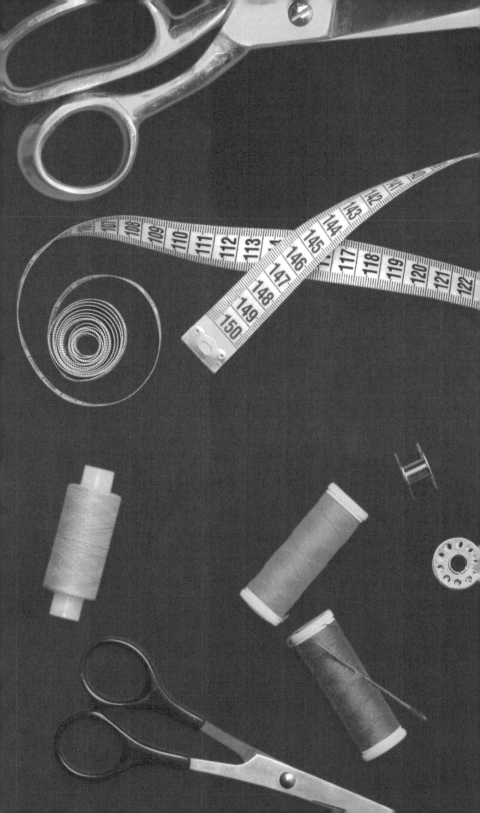

Chapter 24

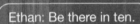

Misty

Ethan: Be there in ten.

MY HEART BEATS WILDLY in my chest as I swoop
eyeliner over my right lid. I cuss under my breath when,
once again, the wing jerks at the end, and I have to wipe
it off for the third time. I've been attempting to do my
makeup in my tiny bathroom mirror for the last twenty
minutes, avoiding my entirely too-casual husband. His
gaze tracked my movements when I got home, but he
stayed silent as he watched me move about the small
apartment.

Taunting Damon is like taunting a wild animal. I'd
declared we weren't exclusive, then quite literally scur-
ried out of his office.

I found the first single hockey player I saw and asked
him on a date tonight. Then, I hid in an unused office for

the rest of the day, praying that my bracelet really isn't a tracker.

Damon didn't come for me though. Instead, Nicholas was waiting for me at the exit, as usual. It was his low brow and quietness that let me know he was disappointed.

What I didn't tell Nicholas, and I can barely admit to myself, is that I'm jealous. I shouldn't have expected him to fight against *pretend* dating. After all, I'm the one requesting it, but I did. Against my better judgment, when he'd asked when we'd start the charade of him dating, something snapped inside of me.

A bone-deep feeling that made my stomach turn and my chest burn with the need to deny him. To scream at him that he's married to *me* and how dare he even pretend to date other women. But the slight curve of his lip had my carefully controlled emotions shredding apart, and all rational thought disappeared.

I wanted him to feel like I did. I wanted him to taste the nausea on his tongue the way I was.

So I declared us nonexclusive and then hid.

The thing is, I want him to find me. I want him to prove there's nothing that will come between us. It might be sick, twisted, and wrong. But after what happened to me in the past, I want someone who's obsessed with me in the best way. Who's happy to prove it time and time again.

A man who will enjoy the game as much as I do.

I don't know when it happened, but Damon's made

me feel daring, like I can be as defiant as I want and he'll still never let me go.

The doorbell rings, and I take a deep breath, suddenly worried that Damon's left and I misread this game between us.

A sigh escapes me when I find him waiting for me, leaning on the wall directly beside the front door. His arms are crossed over his chest, his crisp white dress shirt rolled up at the sleeves, revealing the bright colors of his tattoo.

I take my time, scanning up the column of his neck, finally daring to meet his gaze. A thrill goes through me when it's a burning heat in his expression. His jaw is tight, one brow slightly lifted as he runs a thumb over his lower lip.

"You look beautiful, wife," he says in a low, raspy warning.

My skin erupts in goose bumps as his attention settles over me.

He uncrosses his arms and gestures to the door beside him. "Aren't you going to open the door for our guest?"

I swallow hard. "Maybe you should wait in the other room? Don't you think it'll look weird that you're here?"

He cuts me a sharp look, and his head tilts to the side like a predator.

"Open the door, Nymph. Let's see who you invited to replace me," he dares.

Damon looks dangerous, unhinged, but it's not fear

running through my veins. There's a certainty locked in place within me that he'd never hurt me. That he'd protect me at all costs. Which just makes this game all the more powerful because I've trapped a dragon and forced him to play it with me.

When I don't move toward the door, he smirks. "Good girl." Then, he opens the door himself. Damon's shoulders are so wide I can barely make out Ethan, but his words carry over to me easily.

"I'm here to pick up Misty."

I wince, feeling a little bad that I dragged him into it. At least I'd picked one of the guys that had a reputation for being a dick to the girls he dates.

"Your date is canceled," Damon replies.

"I just talked to her. I know you're her boss, man, but you can't monopolize all of her time."

Damon's posture grows supple as he leans against the door, but there's nothing casual in his stance. "It's you who can't go out. You'll want to call your agent. I'll let Misty know you're sorry you had to cancel your...evening."

"What's that supposed to mean?" Ethan asks, confusion clear in his voice.

"Just that I hope you like the cold. Now, leave." Damon shuts the door, locking it before turning on me.

"What did you do?" My voice comes out barely above a whisper.

He stalks toward me, eating up the space in a few long strides. He reaches up to grasp my jaw, his fingers too gentle for the motion. "This is what you wanted, right? To have me in your control?" His thumb dips into my mouth and runs along my bottom teeth. "Did you have fun making me jealous?"

"I...that's not what I was doing," I lie badly.

His lips replace his thumb, grazing against mine. "Sure it isn't." He nips my bottom lip. "I'm always happy to play with you, but I told you that you're mine. I don't share what's mine. Now, what's your punishment?"

"W...what?" I gasp.

"I told you not to pull that shit again, and here you are, pushing me. You obviously want to be punished."

Heat floods between my thighs, and I stagger, unable to support my weight. He catches me around my waist, providing support, but he's standing with a blank expression, wanting my answer. My brain is screaming that hell no I don't want to be punished, but my body's lit up with the idea. There's something in the way he asked it, like he would be doing it *for me* and not to me, that has my heart skipping in my chest. I started this game, and now it's up to me to decide to follow through.

I trail my nails up the firm lines of his chest, struggling to take controlled breaths in preparation for what I'm about to do. "I..." My fingers clench in his shirt as I fight against the tremble in my voice.

Stormy gray eyes meet mine. "You don't need to be afraid of me. I'll never do anything that you don't want. I will never hurt you, Misty. Let me make you feel good."

"Okay." The air rushes from my lungs, and there's a dampness pooling between my thighs.

A low purr forms in his chest. "That's a good girl." His fingers dig themself into my hair and tilt my chin up. "Now, kneel."

A shiver rolls through me in anticipation of what comes next. I lower myself to the floor, the smooth linoleum cool on the bare skin of my knees. The outline of Damon's hard cock is directly in front of me, and I internally celebrate when it jerks with my attention.

"Take it out," Damon says in a low command.

I pull at the belt, the smooth leather cool on my overheated skin. The small silver prong refuses to let go, and I have to lean closer to gain better leverage. My neck grows warm with embarrassment when it's clear I'm struggling with the simple task.

Damon strokes his thumb below my hairline, and I look up at him. I let out a long exhale. He's not judging me or disappointed; he's staring down at me with pure lust written into his black gaze. I'm still watching him when the belt finally slips free, and I make quick work of getting him out.

His cock is heavy in my hand, and when I try to wrap my fingers around it, the tips barely graze around his width. My mouth waters as I take in the swollen tip, precum dripping from the slit. I can't help myself from running my tongue over it, filling my mouth with his salty taste before taking the head between my lips.

He groans low in his throat but doesn't guide me.

Instead, he lets me play with him how I want. A power rocks through me as he staggers when I swirl my tongue around him, taking him deeper with each pass. His hips jerk forward, causing me to moan around him.

"Fuck..." He pulls his length out of my mouth, his large hand tightening around the base. "You have no idea what you do to me."

I whimper at the loss and dig my fingers into his thighs. I want this...more desperately than I should be willing to admit. He runs the tip of his cock along my bottom lip, painting it.

"Open your mouth."

I swiftly follow his command.

"Stick out your tongue." I don't have time to question this position because he slides over my tongue. My lips immediately close around him, and I groan when he pulls out.

"I said open," he commands in a low, raspy voice that has me trembling.

I open wider, giving him full access, and he doesn't hesitate to thrust deep into my mouth. I gag when he hits my throat, tears pooling in my eyes. He doesn't stop, stroking in and out, using me like a toy. My jaw starts to ache from keeping my mouth open, but he doesn't stop his punishing, delicious movements. His cock grows larger, causing my teeth to scrape across his soft skin, and he buries his hand in my hair, pushing me further down his length. The tip bruises my throat as my mouth waters in anticipation. I've never taken anyone this far, and with each thrust, he demands more.

He doesn't pull out when I gag again. If anything, he pushes in deeper. "That's it, wife. You look so perfect, mouth filled with my cock." He bends and strokes a finger along my jaw and down the side of my throat. "Swallow it."

My gaze snaps to his, unsure I can do what he asks.

"You can. Relax." He runs his thumb over my neck in a calming motion, and I try to swallow. "That's it. Just like that." A thrill goes through me, and I swallow again, moaning as his cock breaches the barrier and I take him deeper.

"Fuck," His movements grow jerky. My head is dizzy from the lack of oxygen, but all I want is more. I want him deeper. I want to see him break control until he's wild. I grip his hips and yank him forward. That's all the encouragement he needs, his cock slipping out and slamming back with each thrust.

He groans and fills my mouth with his cum, bracing himself as he slips out of my mouth. "So fucking perfect."

His eyes track my tongue as I lick his taste off my lips.

"Is that my punishment?"

A slow, sinister smile curls his lips, and he rubs the corner of my smudged eyeliner. "Not even close."

He steps back, leaving me on my sore knees, and walks the short distance to the couch. "Come here, lay your stomach over my knee, and take your punishment like the good girl I know you are."

A thrill mixed with fear tumbles through me. His dark eyes dare me to go through with it. To push myself past my boundaries.

I go to lift myself from the ground, but he stops me.

"Crawl to me," he demands.

I rear back on my heels, the world swirling with my shock. "I...I can't."

"Did you purposely set out to make me jealous?"

I should deny it, but my head's fuzzy, and I can't help but do as he wants. "Yes."

"Do you think that deserves punishment?"

My panties are soaked through. "Yes."

"Then crawl to me. Show me how good you can be."

Every ounce of feminism evaporates from my mind. I'll be a feminist tomorrow. I crawl on my hands and knees as he watches me with pitch-black eyes, the silver completely taken over by his pupils. His hands clench the sofa so hard his knuckles are white, and a muscle ticks in his jaw. Power trickles down my spine, knowing that I'm the one doing this to him. That even though he's giving the commands, I'm the one making the decisions.

I close the distance between us with more confidence and kneel between his spread legs, eyes wide as I look up at him. The air is thick around us with anticipation.

He pats his thigh. "On your stomach, wife."

My body trembles as I lift up and lay myself over him, the hard muscle digging into my stomach.

He flips my skirt over my back, revealing my pink lace panties. A low groan escapes his throat, and he rips them off, balling them in his fist. "You're going to pay for wearing these for him."

He brings the fabric up to my closed mouth, and I refuse to open. His free hand smacks hard against my exposed ass, and I gasp with the shock.

He fills my mouth with my panties that taste like me, and he closes my jaw when I go to spit them out.

"Keep them in, or you'll just prolong this."

There's a frustrated anger wrapped around my lust that has every nerve standing on its end. I wiggle on his lap. He pins me down with one arm as his other hand trails over my ass, already sore. Tension builds in my stomach, a desperation for more burning through my anger. I can't stop myself from rocking against him, searching for the friction I desperately need.

His fingers dig into my hip. "Beg for it, wife."

I glare at him and spread my mouth wider, revealing the panties he'd stuffed it with. How am I supposed to beg?

He chuckles low, but it's the slow motion of his fingers up my thighs that has me moaning for more.

"Please." My words are muffled from the fabric in my mouth, and he takes them out.

"Please, what?"

I let out a frustrated whimper. "Spank me."

He pulls my legs further apart, leaving me completely exposed. Vulnerable, I attempt to close them, but he stops me, and I stay perfectly still.

A low chuckle rolls from him. "That's my good girl." It's punctuated by the sharp sting of his palm. My entire body comes alive, the pain quickly morphing into pleasure, causing my clit to throb. He spanks me again, and I moan.

His fingers dig into my hair, tilting my head back so he can look into my eyes. "You like that, don't you, wife? You like to be punished."

I can't speak. I'm breathing so hard, but he must read the answer in my eyes because he spanks me again, this time landing right over my core. My senses shatter with the new sensation, and I struggle to inhale before he does it again. My clit pulses with the tempo of my heart that he sets with each touch. I'm completely lost to him, brain short-firing through the fog. He shifts lower and lands his slap directly against my clit.

My orgasm slams into me, my entire body quaking as it rushes through my limbs. Damon doesn't stop, instead alternating between my clit and spanking me hard, building a pressure inside me I've never felt before. He guides me higher and higher until I explode, my cum gushing out of me. *Holy shit. What was that?*

"Fuck yes," he hisses. "Such a good girl. So perfect for me, wife."

I collapse against him, too exhausted to be embarrassed, trying to concentrate on my breathing before I pass out. He doesn't give me time to come down, instead flipping me stomach down on the sofa. He straddles my ass, pinning me down, and tears the seam of my dress up the side.

My veins freeze at the memories of another time, a different man pinning me from behind. My muscles seize, cutting off my breaths. *No, no, no. Please, no.* I grip the sofa, trying to hold on to the here and now.

I'm safe, I'm safe, I'm safe.

I repeat the words in my head, trying to surface from the fear, but I can still feel Thomas's clammy hands holding me in place, the sharp edge of his blade cutting through my skin.

I'm in Boston. He can't get me. I'm in Boston. Boston. Boston. Boston.

The chant in my head slowly grounds me enough that my surroundings trickle back into my consciousness. My face is buried into something warm and hard, and the scent of cigars and cologne fills my lungs with each breath. Strong arms are wrapped around my middle, holding me up, but the terrifying feeling of being trapped is gone.

Damon.

"It's okay. Shhhh, Misty. It's okay. I promise nothing can touch you now." He splays his fingers over my back, spanning from my ribs to shoulders, and strokes up and down over the thin fabric of my dress, murmuring reassurances in my ear. "I have you. I won't let anything happen to you. You're safe with me."

I let out a shuddering breath as his strength slowly infiltrates my mind, burning away any memory of Thomas. He's gone, and Damon will never let him get me back. The realization that I feel completely safe with Damon rattles me. I'd purposely set out to make one of the most dangerous men in the city jealous, and I didn't worry about the consequences. I knew, whatever it was, he'd make me like it. Somehow, this man has become safe to me, and my heart doesn't know how to handle it.

I pull back just enough to meet his gaze, no doubt looking like a complete disaster, nose red, tears streaking down my face. "Sorry."

"How very Canadian of you," he murmurs as he trails a thumb along my cheek, catching a stray tear. He's being gentle with me, but there's an underlying coldness in his gaze, a rigidness to his body that gives away the rage building within him.

"Tell me what happened, and I'll fix it." His stormy gray eyes glint silver as he studies me.

"It's...it's fine." I relish the idea of Damon tracking Thomas down and ruining his life, but that would come with the need to face everything.

Cool air hits my back when he moves his arm, and I flinch, scrambling to grab the ripped seam of my dress. Suddenly, even the idea of him seeing my scars, of how broken I've been, makes me want to throw up. I grab the seams of my dress, holding them together in a fierce grip.

"I can't."

His head rears back, hurt written in his eyes.

"Just...just leave my dress on." My voice is almost a cry, and I can see his face drain of color.

Damon stares at me for several seconds before nodding and pulling me against his chest. I can feel his heart pounding against mine as he sucks in air. His body's trembling, as if he's using every ounce of his willpower. His arms bind me to him, squeezing once, then letting go. He kisses the top of my head before getting up and leaving me to go to the bathroom without a word.

I collapse back on the couch. I've upset him, but I don't know what to say to make it better. I care what he thinks more than I want to admit.

I want him to see me as he does right now. Not as the broken girl I was.

Chapter 25

Damon

THE BEDROOM DOOR clicks behind me, and I collapse back against it. Every instinct in me screams to go in there and demand to know who it was so I can cut them up, inch by inch, while they watch. Someone hurt my girl. Some sick bastard dared to lay his hands on her, and I'm going to hurt them back.

It's the fear in her eyes and her trembling body in my arms that keeps me in place. She needs me here, and she doesn't need the sick, twisted version of me.

I'd nearly puked when she'd flinched back and gripped her dress together. The small motion told me everything I needed to know about what happened to her. I want to rage, but it's not what *I* want that matters; it's what she needs.

And right now, the last thing she needs is me stomping around her place, intimidating her.

I grab my phone and text Matthias.

> Me: Pull up her past.

> Matthias: I know you're new to this whole husband thing, but even I know you should just ask her.

My jaw clenches together, and I breathe through my nose, trying to keep my shit together.

> Me: Someone hurt her.

> Matthias: Oh fuck.

> Matthias: Give me a few hours.

I take several deep breaths, pushing down my anger until it's a quiet simmer, and place my phone on the dresser. Grabbing one of my gray gym hoodies from the bag, I head back into the living room.

My heart stills at the sight of her. She's tucked herself into the corner of the sofa, pink hair wild around her temples, and her knees are pulled into her chest. Her vulnerability has me wanting to drop to my knees in front of her and beg her to let me erase it. Instead, I approach her and hold up the sweater between us.

"Arms up."

It's a testament to how unsettled she is that she lifts her arms and allows me to lower the hoodie over her head without a word of protest. It falls around her, engulfing her entire body, and I rock back on my heels, taking her in. She looks good in my clothes.

Before I can do anything idiotic, I go to the kitchen

and grab her a glass of water, hauling her over my lap with one hand. "Drink this."

Apparently, I've been reduced to monosyllabic grunts.

She takes a small sip. "I'm okay, really."

I raise a brow at her lie.

"I just...I'm okay, *now*."

I search her face for any lingering fear and drop my forehead to hers when I don't find any. "You can tell me."

"I know," she answers but doesn't elaborate.

Finally, I pull back and grab the remote, and a sewing show appears on the screen. It's some kind of competition to see who can make the best dress. I reverse our positions so I'm pressed against the sofa and she's tucked into my side.

"We don't have to watch this." She hesitates.

"You like it, right?" I murmur.

She looks at me sideways, an adorable line pinched between her brows. "Uh...yeah."

"Then it's what we're watching."

She looks like she's going to argue again, but I give her a quick shake of my head.

"Okay, but it's not my fault if you hate it," she says, blowing out a breath, and I'm pleased to see her shoulders relax.

I hold her close to me and watch her as she watches the show. It takes less than fifteen minutes for her eyes to close and her breathing to slow as sleep takes her under.

My phone beeps, and I answer Matthias's call.

"What did you find?" I'm careful to speak low enough not to wake her.

"Someone's wiped her blueprint. The most I can find is that she went to the hospital and stayed there for twenty-four hours when she was in high school."

"Why?"

"That's the thing. It doesn't say why. Her files are blank, no notes from nurses, no reason for her going in. It takes power to make this shit go away."

I stroke my thumb along the back of her neck, reminding myself that I have her forever. There's an unease crawling under my skin, knowing there are only a select few families who are connected enough to hide something from my brother.

"Keep digging," I command.

"You know I will, but...you should *ask* her."

I hang up the phone, having nothing left to say to my brother. I will not push her on this. She'll tell me when she trusts me. My teeth grind together at the memory of the fear that flashed through her eyes, and my blood grows cold.

I'm going to catch whoever's responsible for touching my wife. I breathe through the rage burning through my veins and kiss the back of her neck, promising, "I'm going to take my time killing them."

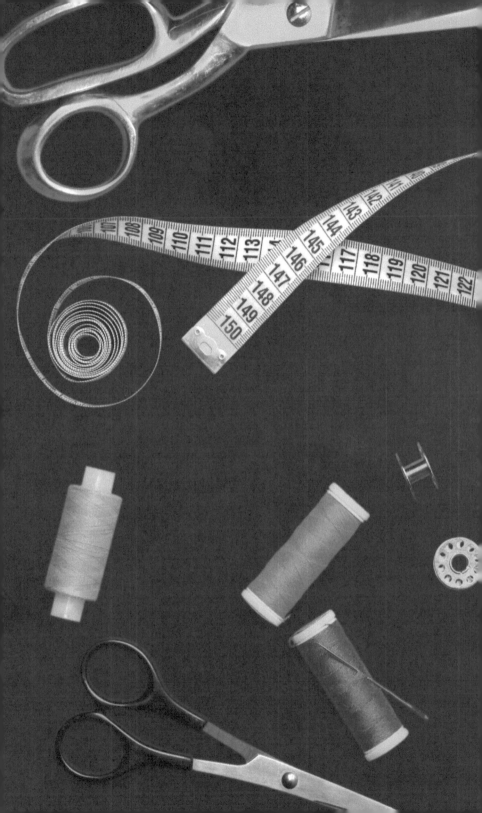

Chapter 26

Misty

I TWIST MY HAIR, doing my best to capture the stray strands in my pale pink claw clip. Damon's oversized gray sweatshirt engulfs me, leaving only the bottom four inches of my dress exposed around my thighs. It's hard to picture him wearing something so casual, even though the thick, structured fabric screams expensive.

Taking a deep breath, I open the door. I can't avoid what happened last night forever. I'm sure he has a million freaking questions that I don't want to answer, but I owe him some kind of explanation. Something tells me he'll see right through me if I try to lie.

His back is to me when I come out of my room, giving me a few extra seconds to take him in. Damon's dressed in an expertly tailored black suit, the long sleeves concealing the evidence of his vibrant tattoos beneath. He's pinned his phone between his shoulder and speaking to someone low enough I can't quite make out what he's saying.

"The man is practically a work of art at this point," I grumble under my breath.

He spins and spots me, and I can feel the heat rush to my cheeks. There's no way he heard that.

"I'll call you back," Damon says into his phone before disconnecting so fast I doubt the person on the other end had time to respond.

"How are you?" he asks me, voice low and soft like he's afraid I'll startle if he pushes too much.

I hate it. I hate that he's already looking at me like I'm breakable.

"Fine. Shouldn't you be gone?" I bite out a little too harshly and instantly regret it.

His head cocks to the side as his eyes roam over me, assessing.

The worry in his expression vanishes, and he gives me a cocky smile. "Now, now, wife. Don't tell me you want to get rid of me?"

He's standing there wolfishly, daring me to respond.

"Not for another..." I pretend to look at a watch on my wrist. "Roughly another three hundred and sixty days, give or take."

There's a pang in my chest at the reminder this all has an end date. When did I grow so attached?

A muscle in his jaw ticks, and I don't think he'll respond until he says, "You are surprisingly unfunny, dear wife."

I huff out a laugh, happy the moment's broken, but he cuts in before I can respond.

"I wanted to see you before I head to work since you'll be starting at the Everette Tower today."

He's oblivious to my confusion as he explains my new office location while simultaneously making a latte. It's only when he turns to hand me the drink that he spots my expression.

"What?"

I robotically take the coffee. "But I already have an office."

"Yes," he responds slowly as if looking for the catch. "But you'll need to be there since that's where I'll be."

"Can't I just email you?"

"You are my personal PR person. I'm planning PR things. You'll need to be close by."

"You know that's not true, right? I can just stay at the Bruins building."

His brows pull low over his eyes. "Unless you want me to trade half the team, you'll be coming with me today."

"That doesn't make any sense."

"Exactly. So, we're agreed. You'll be coming to my office."

"That's not—"

"I took the liberty of checking your schedule. I noticed you have a morning meeting with my mother. I've already messaged her to be on her best behavior. She has a tendency to be...less than pleasant with people she deems below her."

My muscles unintentionally stiffen. I don't miss this world at all. One where people think they're better than the other. "I can take care of myself."

"Of course you can. You're an Everette now."

Damon Everette - *CEO of Everette Industries:* *How was your morning?*

Damon's message pops up on my computer screen. *Less than great*, considering I'd spent it with his mother, who landed several backhanded comments about my appearance while simultaneously exulting the pedigree of the young women she was setting up for her son. Like they were dogs and not people.

At least now, I'm doing pretty good. I have an extra-large coffee, and I'm currently scrolling Amazon instead of getting any work done.

Dealing with Mrs. Everette had to count for a week's worth of work at least.

The temptation to yell that I'm her son's wife, me, in all my messy, wild imperfection, had crawled under my skin and pushed at my throat, begging to come out. If only to see the shock, quickly followed by despair, register in her eyes.

It's not lost on me that the girl my parents tried to

groom me to be is the exact type of woman Damon's mother is looking for:

Pastel

Polite

Pliable

Someone she can twist and mold to be Damon's perfect society wife.

Well, she'll have to wait a year because I'm none of those things.

Misty Hart - Junior PR representative: *Fine. We found lots of potential wives for you. You could even start a harem.*

I drum my fingers against my oak desk. The office they set me up in is across the hall from Damon's. If it wasn't for his privacy blinds, he'd be looking right into my cubicle all day.

Damon Everette - CEO of Everette Industries: *Speaking of wives. Your last name is wrong.*

I roll my eyes at the ridiculousness of the comment.

Misty Hart - Junior PR representative: *Oh, yeah sure. Because changing my last name wouldn't raise suspicions at all. At best, people would think I'm some kind of stalker freak.*

Damon Everette - CEO of Everette Industries: *If only I were that lucky.*

Damon Everette - CEO of Everette Industries: *Tell me. Was she nice?*

Misty Hart - Junior PR representative: *As nice as someone like that can be.*

Damon Everette - CEO of Everette Industries: *I don't like that answer.*

Misty Hart - Junior PR representative: *That's nice. I didn't like it either. I've set up a calendar with all of the events you'll need to make appearances at.*

I pause before writing the next part, not willing to say "date."

Misty Hart - Junior PR representative: *And a list of potential women to accompany you.*

Damon Everette - CEO of Everette Industries: *Cancel them.*

Misty Hart - Junior PR representative: *What? I just spent all morning scheduling all of these.*

Damon Everette - CEO of Everette Industries: *That's unfortunate since I won't be going.*

Misty Hart - Junior PR representative: *You have to!*

Damon Everette - CEO of Everette Industries: *Do I?*

Misty Hart - Junior PR representative: *I did not spend all morning with your mother just to have you bail. You're the one that's supposed to be finding a wife!*

Damon Everette - CEO of Everette Industries: *You're the one who refuses to admit to everyone YOU are my wife.*

Misty Hart - Junior PR representative: *Temporary wife.*

Damon Everette - CEO of Everette Industries: *You keep saying that.*

Misty Hart - Junior PR representative: *That's because you seem to keep forgetting.*

Damon Everette - CEO of Everette Industries: *Is that what I'm doing?*

Ugh! This man is impossible.

Misty Hart - Junior PR representative: *Fine. But you need to go to the Primrose.*

My fingers shook when I saw the event in the list Mrs. Everette provided me. This is a level of exclusivity I never thought I'd get a window into. I'm not talking about movie stars and influencers. I'm talking about being born into it. But it's the secrecy that really catches people's attention.

Every year, my social media feed is filled with people's conspiracy theories.

My favorite is that the attendees are actually a bunch of vampires who attend for their yearly blood-drinking celebration, and we never hear anything from the waitstaff because they're all dead.

Damon Everette - CEO of Everette Industries: *The only gala I'll be attending is the one for Prosthetics For Kids.*

Warmth fills my chest, but I temper it. It may be my friend's charity, but he's not going because of me. He made the commitment to participate prior to our arrangement. Honestly, I was shocked when he volunteered himself and his brothers for the auction.

Misty Hart - Junior PR representative: *Your mother is insisting I get you there.*

Damon Everette - CEO of Everette Industries: *Since when has my mother been your boss?*

Misty Hart - Junior PR representative: *Since you told me to work with her.*

Damon Everette - CEO of Everette Industries: *There's a simple solution.*

Misty Hart - Junior PR representative: *Please, do tell.*

I twirl a sleek black pen between my fingers, hoping he can hear the sarcasm with which I wrote that.

Damon Everette - CEO of Everette Industries: *Go with me.*

The pen stalls mid-twirl as shock registers through me, and I'm momentarily stunned. I don't want to admit just how appealing that sounds. I'm not going to even bother denying how curious I've been to know what goes on in there.

Oh yeah, Misty...*that's* the reason you want to go. It has nothing to do with the shivers that trickle down your spine at the idea of going with *him.*

Misty Hart - Junior PR representative: *CEOs don't go to galas with their employees.*

Damon Everette - CEO of Everette Industries: *Are you asking to be fired?*

Misty Hart - Junior PR representative: *Do you want to be murdered in your sleep?*

Damon Everette - CEO of Everette Industries: *Be careful, Wife. I like it when you're all murdery.*

I ignore the flush in my cheeks, thanking God we aren't having this conversation face-to-face.

Misty Hart - Junior PR representative: *You would like that.*

Damon Everette - CEO of Everette Industries: *I will speak to my mother. Don't bother planning anything else. I won't be attending.*

Misty Hart - Junior PR representative: *But you need to appear to be looking for a wife.*

Damon Everette - CEO of Everette Industries: *I found one. And everyone who needs to know, knows.*

I swallow hard.

Misty Hart - Junior PR representative: *You're really not going to go?*

Damon Everette - CEO of Everette Industries: *You seem to be under the impression I'm willing to give you up.*

Misty Hart - Junior PR representative: *Ok, well I guess that means you don't need me here since I don't have any work.*

Damon Everette - CEO of Everette Industries: *I'll get back to you with the details.*

Chapter 27

Damon

"Sign here." My lawyer hands me a piece of paper, and I sign it without reading. I may have overpaid, but my contracts are solid.

He places another paper on my desk. "Here and here."

My pen flies over the sheet, blue ink marking the swirls of my signature. Misty's little *I guess you don't need me* text has been a gnawing pain that needled into my side until I found a solution. Sure, I could force her to stay in my building, but I didn't want her being near me to be a punishment. And something tells me I shouldn't waste her time.

I considered letting her go back to her old responsibilities, but I didn't fucking like that idea. So I bought the airline. It was the closest deal we had in negotiations. Sure, we could have negotiated down, but I needed something immediately.

My lawyer gathers the papers from the desk, straightening them before tucking them into a file. "You are all done, sir."

"Thank you for your help, Mathew. You'll see your compensation on your next check."

"That's too kind of you, Mr. Everette." He tossed the words out, then disappeared like I'd take his bonus away. He'd earned it. It's 3:00 a.m., which means he's been working the last twenty-four hours to get this deal done.

Sleeping next to Misty without touching her is damn near killing me, and my desperation is getting pathetic. But I'd do damn near anything to keep her happy. What's one company acquisition?

I send her a text, the corner of my lips curling in anticipation of her reaction. Some kind of adorable annoyance mixed with disbelief. Fucking perfect.

> Damon Everette: Better hurry and get a press conference planned.

A cackling laugh from across the room has me setting my phone down. I know she's asleep. I've checked.

I lift my glass of whiskey, drain it in one swallow, and ask Bash, "Why are you still here?"

He leans forward, practically peeling himself off the couch. He'd shown up an hour ago, drunk, collapsed on his seat, and passed out.

His smile is mischievous as he drapes both arms over

the back of the sofa. "Please tell me you just bought an airline so your wife will hang out with you?"

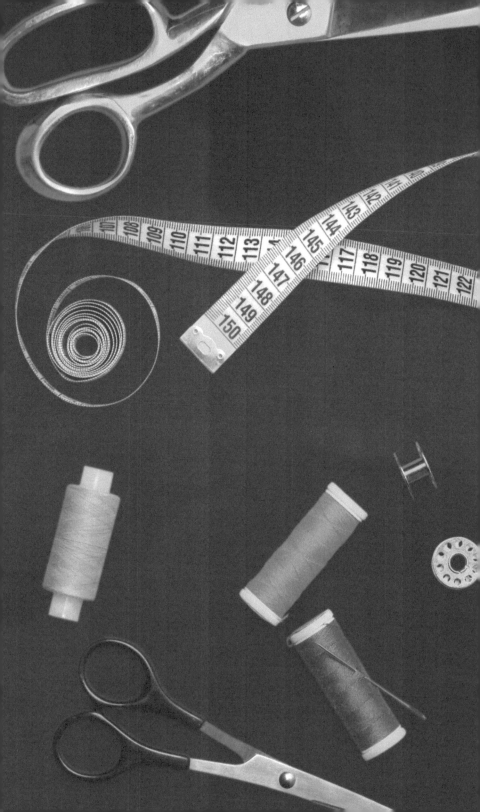

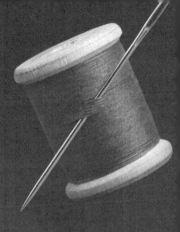

Chapter 28

Misty

I STARE at the text for what must be the twentieth time and rub my fingers into my temple.

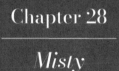

> Damon Everette: Better hurry and get
> a press conference planned.

I groan, my head feeling fuzzy. He bought a freaking airline. An *airline*! When I said I didn't have work, I didn't think he'd actually go out and do something crazy. Because this is definitely next-level insane. He probably had this purchase set up in advance because there is no world he went through all of that just to get me to hang out with him. Right? *Right*?

If I wanted more work, I definitely succeeded. I'm now down to three days to get this planned.

Of course, the rich don't just put an announcement in the papers like normal people. Nooo...they put on a six-course meal with all of their billionaire buddies. That way, they can all join hands and congratulate themselves on their success.

I pull open my contacts list and start sending off emails. At least the Everettes owned several buildings nice enough to pull this off. It would be impossible to book something like that with such short notice. I put in a favor with one of my best event planners and pray it all turns out.

> Me: You don't acquire new companies often enough to keep me busy.

> Damon: You'd be surprised what I would do to keep you with me.

Tingles roll down my neck, raising goose bumps along their path. I have no idea what to say to that.

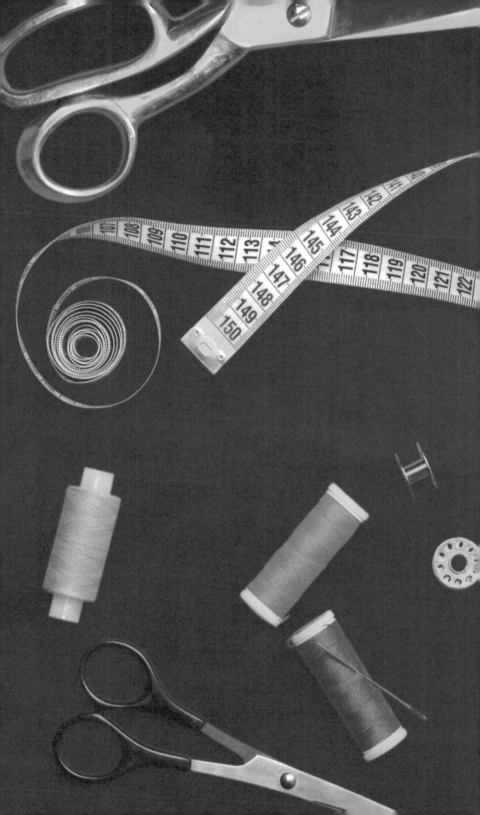

Chapter 29

Misty

THERE'S an eeriness to the hall while Damon stands in front of the podium and makes his speech. He'd let me read it in advance, after I insisted as his PR manager it is something I need to review. He'd handed it over with a knowing smile that had the hair rising on the back of my neck. It didn't take long to realize why he'd looked so smug. There wasn't a single word out of place in his document. It was the perfect level of serious and light-hearted to capture anyone's attention. Because of course he knows how to write his own speeches. He's probably been giving them since he was a kid.

There's an older gentleman watching him with rapt attention, tall and lanky but impeccably dressed, without a single hair out of place. I can just make out a silver pin attached to his lapel under where his palm is resting. Come to think of it, it's a super-odd position to be in.

He's standing ramrod straight, at perfect attention, as he listens to Damon go on about airplanes and the future.

I swear, if I were anywhere else, I'd think he was in the military, listening to his commanders or whatever they're called. Definitely not a member of society's elite. A quick scan of the room reveals every man is in a nearly identical stance—back straight, chin forward, and one arm crossed over their chest.

Chills roll through me. It's like I've stepped into the Twilight Zone or, better yet, some kind of yuppie cult. If I didn't know better, I'd say they were treating Damon like a leader instead of a peer.

The loud smack of clapping snaps me out of my rambling thoughts as Damon closes off his speech. His eyes dance over the crowd until they meet mine, and he lifts one brow at me in question.

I can't even begin to process my thoughts right now. I clearly need some sleep because the idea of some underground world where people worship my husband is freaking ridiculous.

"It's lovely to finally meet you."

I turn sharply to face an older gentleman. I instantly recognize him from the event Mia, Piper, and their guys went to weeks ago. The one where I'd somehow found myself face-to-face with Damon in an alley. I ignore the knot in my stomach at the raised memory.

"It's an honor, Mr. Everette."

"The honor's all mine," Damon's grandfather says with a warm smile. "You look lovely this evening."

"You are way nicer than I thought you'd be." The words are out before I can stop them, and I instantly wish I could reverse time and take them back.

His smile widens. "Oh? And how did you think I would be?"

Freaking shit. I twitch uncomfortably, but he just stands there calmly, waiting for my answer.

I blow out a slow breath, praying that this doesn't somehow get back to Damon. "Sorry...I just meant...well...after your speech at the last event, you didn't seem like you wanted to be around people much."

He tilts his head slightly, and I swear a dimple appears in his cheek. It's clear he's exactly who Damon gets his looks from.

"You, my dear, are different though. You are part of our family, aren't you?"

Of course he knows—that was the entire point—but something in the way he asks the question has me wanting to apologize for God knows what.

I lower my voice to barely above a whisper. "Yes, of course."

He looks at Damon, who's now staring at us.

The old man returns his attention to me and raises one brow in an identical look to his grandson. "So tell me, why the secrecy?"

Freezing, I take a shallow breath and try to gather my thoughts as his question tries to scramble them. I can't very well tell him we're keeping it a secret because

I don't want people to judge me when Damon and I get divorced.

"I work for him. I don't want our relationship to sway people's opinions of me. It's already hard enough to be a woman in sports." I push the words out at rapid speed. They feel hollow at best, like a story I removed every other line out of.

He gives me a disbelieving look, and I cut him off, asking him the question I've been dying to know.

"Why force your grandsons to get married? Isn't that a bit antiquated?"

He's kind enough to ignore my rudeness completely. "Family is rooted in tradition. It's there for a reason. Without it, everything would be chaos." He points toward several men standing in a semicircle around Damon, who keeps glancing our way, concern growing in his features.

"Each one of those men is the head of their multi-generational household, but look closer."

I examine them more. Each one of them is wearing the identical silver pin I saw earlier on their lapel. I bite my lip as I concentrate on them more. I jolt at the realization that their heads are slightly lowered to Damon. As if they're bowing.

"What do you see?" he asks.

"I think...are they bowing?"

"Smart girl. Our society is old, and our customs are deeply ingrained. Each one of these families is part of the hierarchy. A different rung on a ladder." He points toward the group again, and that's when I see another row standing behind the men speaking with Damon. Then another row behind them. They're concealed by their chatting wives, but once I spot them, I can't unsee it.

"When you say society...you don't mean just the social construct, do you?"

He doesn't bother to answer. "Tradition fosters power. If you want to lead, you must first prove yourself as someone to respect. Now, there are many ways in which that can be accomplished. Many have tried to earn it with bloodshed."

Mr. Everette turns to me with cold eyes. "They did not walk away from the attempt."

My skin prickles. Did he just allude to people killing each other?

"And Damon getting married solves that issue?"

He gives me a long look. "We'll have to see."

"Okay, but sleeping in the same bed rule. Is that really a necessary part of your tradition?" I ask.

His mouth twitches up in the corner. "I can't say much about that rule, to be honest."

I give up on that line of questioning and ask what I really want to know. "And your grandsons just do whatever you ask?"

That's the part that never sat well with me. Even the idea of Damon following blind orders is laughable.

"The Everette family has been at the top of society for generations, and my boys will do what it takes to keep it that way. They just needed a little push in the right direction."

"And *I'm* the right direction?"

"Of course. You've obviously enraptured my grandson."

"Oh...no. It's not like that... You told him to get married, and I was...convenient." I snap my mouth closed because it's not like I can tell him I was coerced because I need a visa.

His eyes glitter in the dim light, and he chuckles softly. "That's interesting."

"What is?"

He glances up at someone before looking back at me. "That you haven't realized that everything Damon does is intentional. I assure you, Mrs. Everette, it is not because it was convenient."

Reeling at his words, I try to sort through them. Damon married me because he needed to and I was easily manipulated into the terms he wanted. Right?

"I'm sorry to cut this short, but there's a man I need to speak with. Please, stay here until my grandson comes and finds you." He's gone before I can tell him that I'm working and not here as Damon's date.

I'm still reeling from my conversation with the patriarch of the Everette family when two men approach me, who I recognize instantly.

"Hello, sister." Sebastian Everette gives me a lopsided grin and winks while throwing his arm around my shoulder, pulling me closer, as if we really are family.

"Be quiet," I warn, eyes darting around to see if anyone heard him. "I *work* for your brother. Remember?"

"Ah, yes. You're his employee only. Our mistake. I guess we'll need to bring you into the family another way." Bash lifts my hand and places a delicate kiss on my knuckles.

"Everyone is looking," I hiss under my breath and go to yank my hand back, but his fingers tighten momentarily, holding me in place before letting my arm drop.

Both brothers look at someone over my shoulder and grin.

"That's the point," they say in unison.

I start to turn toward where they're looking, but a shrill voice calls my name.

"Miss Hart."

Dread hangs over me like a cloud at the sight of Damon's mother approaching.

Bash leans in, kissing my cheek. "See you, sis."

"Don't you dare abandon me."

He grins just before his mother reaches us. "Don't you know? Escape is what little brothers are best at."

I groan internally. Am I going to be forced to speak with every member of the Everette family tonight? Solemnly, I plaster a polite smile on my face and greet the matron.

"Where are they running off to?" Mrs. Everette is

dressed impeccably, as expected. A light navy dress hovers respectfully over her curves, down to below her knees. Her dangling pearl earrings gleam as she looks after them before turning her razor-sharp attention toward me.

"They didn't say." I fight against the urge to cower from her, but this woman has honed her ability to convey disdain with a simple look, like a blacksmith would a blade.

"No matter. Have you been doing your job, Miss Hart?"

Job? Truthfully, I haven't been doing much other than standing here. "The event is going well. There's not much for me to set up here."

"Now, now. Did our conversation teach you nothing? Damon will not go out of his way to find a wife, so we need to do it for him."

Oh, she couldn't be more wrong on that front.

"That there is Rosalie , eldest daughter of the St. James family."

She discreetly gestures to a young woman whose father is currently speaking with Damon. My heart sinks at the sight of them. She's his perfect counterpart. Poised, elegant, the definition of grace as she delicately lifts her glass to hide her smile.

"She graduated from Yale Law, top of her class," Mrs. Everette continues.

Of course she did...

A sour twist forms in my stomach when Damon smiles at something she says.

By the time I glance back toward his mother, she's appraising me, and I'm clearly failing.

"What do you think, Miss Hart? Do they not look good together?" Her voice is smooth, but there's an edge that's sharp as a knife.

"Yes...they do." I look them over, and acid burns in my throat at being forced to say anything.

"You know you don't belong here."

My attention snaps back to her. "I'm working."

"So I've been told, but it appears you have somehow deluded yourself regarding Damon's affection."

"What?" Cold ice crystallizes my veins and freezes me in place. I'm suddenly sixteen again, surrounded by mean, catty women all dressed in pastels, explaining how, no matter how hard my parents try, we will never belong. My fingers tremble around the wine flute I've been nursing. She's right. I don't belong here.

"I understand you're likely sleeping with my son, but don't misunderstand, he will not stay with you. He will not *love* you. You're just an amusement as he passes his time. Just because you've been allowed to chase at his feet doesn't mean you belong here. Do you understand, Miss Hart?"

There's a razor-sharp sting piercing through my ribs until my chest caves in. My eyes sting, and I desperately blink back tears, not wanting to give her the satisfaction of knowing her words hit exactly where she meant them to.

She doesn't know that I'm already well aware of how much I don't fit into this world. That the lesson was sliced into me years ago.

My chest burns to take a breath, but I'm afraid it'll come out in a sob. I stumble back, needing to create space between us.

The sweet scent of smoke and cologne fills my nose milliseconds before Damon's arm wraps possessively around my waist. His voice is a dark warning when he says, "Watch how you speak to my *wife.*"

Chapter 30

Damon

RAGE BURNS like flames inside of me, and it's only Misty's cool grasp on my wrist that's keeping me sane.

"Apologize."

Mother's staring at Misty, mouth agape, eyes wide in shock, before her expression twists into disgust. "I hope it's temporary."

"You would hope that," I say tightly, every muscle tensing to keep myself in place. She may be my mother, but she's walking a razor-thin line.

I tuck Misty into my side, moving between her and my mother, and lean forward to loom over her. My voice is cold as death when I command, "You will treat her with respect."

Her throat bobs, and she shifts her weight back, putting on her best fake smile. "Yes, of course. I won't say a word."

There's enough condescension in her words that it makes my skin crawl.

"What did you just say?"

"Well, you obviously want to keep her a secret, dear. I didn't realize you were this desperate to fulfill your grandfather's request. I'm sure you have your reasons." She looks Misty up and down. "I imagine if you only want someone to fulfill the required timeline, she's a perfect choice."

Misty flinches as if an invisible hand reached out and slapped her.

I let go of her and move slowly toward the woman who dared hurt her. "You will regret that."

Slim, cool fingers wrap around my wrist and tug me back. Misty's shaking her head at me. She tries to smile, but it wobbles at the corner. "Let it go, Damon. You know she's right."

"Fuck that." I switch our grip so that my fingers are entwined in hers and pull her toward the stage.

She fights my grip, whisper yelling the entire way there. "What do you think you're doing? That's enough. Let me go."

I don't bother answering. It was a mistake to follow her little rule, and I'm going to fix it, whether she likes it or not.

The stage stairs are steep, and I switch my grip to her elbow when she stumbles up them. By the time I get to the microphone, a hush has fallen over the room, and all eyes are on us.

They swing a spotlight, and I pull Misty into my side when she tries to hide behind me. This was inevitable.

The mic's already on when I speak into it. "I want to thank you all for coming tonight. I appreciate your attention. Let me present to you Misty Everette, my wife."

Misty gasps, then glares at me, mouthing the words "I. Am. Going. To. Kill you."

She's so fucking perfect. "Fuck, I love it when you're all stabby. Feel free to try."

Misty is fuming beside me during the car ride home, her nails drumming on the windowsill. But underneath that anger, there are flashes of fear that have the hair standing up on my neck.

After the other night, it's clear something happened to her, something that I'm determined to find out, even if it's just to crush the person who made her feel this way. I reach over to pull her toward me, but she slams the armrest down between us like a wall. "You're a real bastard, you know that?" she says between clenched teeth.

"It needed to happen."

She exhales sharply through her nose, giving her head a small shake. "You would think that. It's not going to affect *you*!"

"You're an Everette now. No one will dare say anything about you."

"Oh really? What about a year from now, after we separate? What do you think they'll say then?"

If her words didn't piss me off so much, I'd love how feisty she's behaving.

"You don't have to worry about that."

"No, *you* don't have to worry about that. Hell, I'm going to have to move to Europe to get away from the fallout."

A muscle twitches in my jaw with the effort to stop myself from explaining that this will never be over. That there is no *after*. There's not a timeline in this universe where she gets away from me.

She's as sweet as ever when she says goodbye to Nicholas, who can't help himself from smirking at me, but she remains cold as ice when I try to speak to her.

I follow her up the stairs, enjoying the flush that crawls up the back of her neck. I move, closing the distance between us, and crowd her against the wall, stopping her ascent.

"Back off." She looks up at me with narrowed green eyes, a dare written over them I can't resist. I crash my mouth into hers and lick at the seams until she opens for me with a moan.

A dam breaks inside her, and her anger burns her from the inside as she scratches her nails along my back. She pours her frustration into me, and I drink in every last drop.

"Fuck," I groan, pushing my hips into her, staggering

my feet on the stairs for balance, and kiss her jaw when her head falls back to rest on the wall.

"You are so fucking sexy right now," I murmur into her neck, then bite the delicate skin. She bucks against me, and I reach down, lifting her by her thighs until she wraps her legs around my waist. Misty buries her fingers into my hair and hauls my mouth to hers, biting my lip hard enough for the taste of iron to fill my mouth. A low groan rumbles in my throat, and she rocks herself against my throbbing cock.

Her movements are rushed, jerky, and sharp, with built-up frustration as she tries to tear my belt open. She's just about to slide her hand around my cock when the door a floor above us opens, and her eyes snap wide.

She instantly drops her legs from around me and goes to sidestep me. I grip her arms, holding her in place. "Don't."

She yanks her arm back. "Let go of me."

I'm forced to stay to the side as a young couple walk down the stairs holding hands, giving Misty time to put space between us. I'd prefer to make them move around me, but something tells me Misty would not like me harassing our neighbors.

The second the couple passes, I take my time stalking her. She doesn't look back when she enters the apartment, but she doesn't close the door either. Whether she wants to admit it or not, she wants me here.

The door to our bedroom slams shut, followed by the soft click of the lock the second I clear the threshold.

I knock softly. "It's not a good idea to run from me, Little Nymph."

"Leave me alone." Her muffled yell comes clear through the door.

"You're in our room," I point out helpfully.

"Sleep on the couch, or better yet, go to your own home."

My jaw ticks, but a slow smile takes over my mouth. When I fuck her again, I'm going to remind her just how much she wants me here.

"Am I supposed to sleep in my suit?"

There's a long pause, shuffling noises coming from the other side of the door, before it clicks open. I barely register her face before she tosses clothes my way and relocks the door.

I drop my forehead to the hollow wood and take a deep breath in. It still smells like her. Fine. If she wants to play this game, I'll play.

I return to the kitchen and pour myself two fingers' worth of whiskey, sipping it slowly, giving her time to form a false sense of security.

My phone buzzes.

> Bash: How pissed is my sister?

> Xander: The way she stormed out of there was impressive.

Bash: Some fucking asshole was talking shit about her. Don't worry. We took care of it.

Xander: Highlight of my night.

Matthias: The two of you made a fucking mess of it. You're lucky I caught the camera feed and wiped it. Next time find somewhere hidden.

Me: What the fuck did they say?

Bash: Nothing anyone will say again.

There's a simmer in my veins, but I know for any of us to survive, I have to trust my brothers. I put down my phone and take another sip of my drink, letting the smooth liquid burn my throat.

I reach into my briefcase, pulling out the small velvet box. My Little Nymph is playing a dangerous game. Five minutes after the lights turn off in her room, I set my glass down and make my way to her. A butter knife makes quick work of the hinges, and it's seconds before I have the door off and set against the wall.

Misty sits up, arms crossed over her chest. She's wearing one of my oversized shirts, which hangs off her shoulder, revealing her tanned skin beneath. But it's the tears streaming down her face that catch my attention, and it's like I've been slammed in the gut.

I crawl over the bed and shift my weight over her, brushing back one of her tears with my thumb before licking it off. "Are these tears from me?"

She shakes her head no.

I meet her eyes, a striking green highlighted by her tears. "Then why?"

"Your mother's right." She looks devastated, and I want to tear the world to pieces to fix it.

"About what?" I ask, swiping away another tear.

"That I don't belong with you? That I'll just ruin everything."

I'm going to fucking kill my mother. "You're not an idiot. Don't act like one."

Misty jerks her face away, but I grip her jaw, dragging her attention back to me. "I don't give a single fuck what anyone else thinks. What do *you* think?"

She looks between my eyes, scanning back and forth between them before the seam between her brows loosens. "I want to be here."

"Good girl."

I sit back, forcing myself to give her some semblance of distance. Her brows pull together as she watches me present her with a small, black velvet box.

She gasps, taking it from me, eyes wide as she traces her finger along the seam.

I cover her hand with mine. "Open it."

As if snapping out of a daze, she lifts the lid on its hinges, and her mouth falls open at the sight of the ten-carat canary diamond in the center.

"I can't take this."

"It's cute that you think you have a choice." My jaw clenches at her rejection. I lift her hand with one of mine and slide the jewelry over her finger. It fits perfectly, as expected since I measured it in her sleep.

For all her feigned resistance, she doesn't try to stop me, instead following the movement in stunned silence.

I lift her knuckles and press my lips against them. "Don't take this off." I lie flat on the bed and pull her side against me, marveling at the sight of my ring circling her finger. There's no mistaking she's mine.

"That sounds impractical."

"I'm not joking."

She just rolls her eyes. I'm addicted to this part of her. The feistiness she only shows me.

She yawns, and her eyes droop, so I kiss her softly for several heartbeats. "Sleep, beautiful."

I run my fingers through her hair, curling the ends until her breathing evens out. I avoid her back, knowing she's not ready to tell me yet, but she will be. And when she does, whoever the fuck hurt her will wish he was dead.

Misty murmurs and turns her face into me, sighing. I kiss her temple.

"Don't lock the door again, wife, or I'll have to fuck some sense into you."

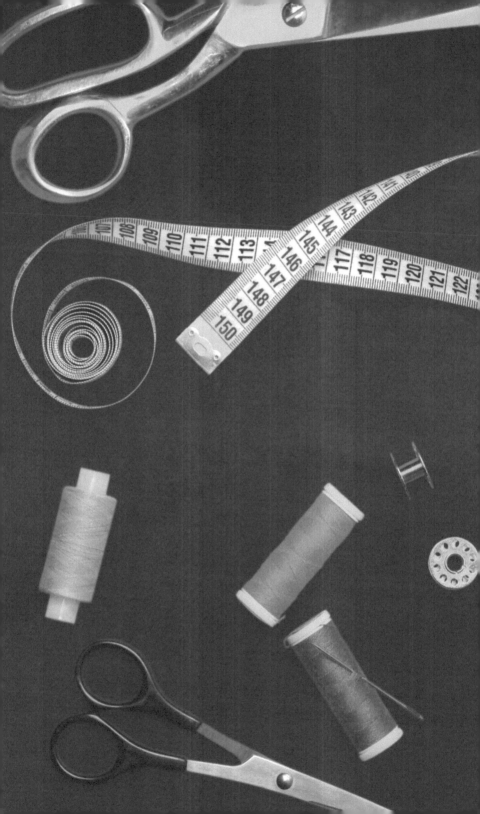

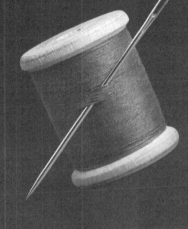

Chapter 31

Misty

SENDER: *Mrs. Everette*

    Subject: Primrose Gala

    Misty,

    Due to the public announcement of your marriage to my son, you will be expected to attend the Primrose gala as his date. Myself and a team of stylists will arrive at your place of residence at 1:00 p.m. tomorrow to prepare you to be properly presented to our society. Your attire will be provided.

    Regards,

    Mrs. Everette

I read Damon's mother's email for the third time before dropping my forehead into my palms and rubbing them over my face. Just what I freaking needed, an unhinged mother-in-law. I may actually murder him for this.

I want to tell her to go screw herself, to take whatever plain dress she has picked out and shove it up her ass, but there's this nagging feeling I can't shake. The one that reminds me that I don't belong, that I never did.

From: *Misty Hart*
To: *Mrs. Everette*
Subject: *Primrose Gala*
See you then,
Misty.

I'm back in my cubicle at the Bruins building. I wouldn't say I'm exactly hiding, but I wouldn't *not* say it either. The idea of arriving at—whichever building Damon's in today—and having to walk past the rows of his no doubt gossiping employees makes my skin itch. It's one thing to be married to him in secret; it's an entire other thing to have everyone know.

Waking up to the *Times* headline being *"Billionaire heir marries young employee"* was enough to make me sick. It's still leaps and bounds better than its less professional rivals that dedicated whole sections on my gold-digging abilities and that they hope he got a prenup...

The fact that they aren't completely off the mark stings even more.

I'm in PR—I know exactly how this is going to play out. By the time we separate, I'll be listed as some kind of gold digger who couldn't even secure any money in the divorce, then be laughed out of the industry. What's the point of getting my visa if I can't work here anyway?

The absolute best-case scenario is they paint it as a love story, and I come out as devastated in the end...at least with that narrative, I'm not an absolute bitch.

I lift the white-gold chain from around my neck, pulling out my ring, and spin the simple band between my fingers. It's warm to the touch from being against my skin, and the emerald cut gleams more than glistens.

I hadn't been ready to put it on this morning—it felt too real to just walk around in public wearing it. Instead, I'd stolen the necklace Damon wore yesterday so I'm not completely breaking Damon's demand that I wear it. *He didn't specify it needed to be on my finger.*

A shiver rolls down my neck, raising goose bumps in its wake at the thrill of pushing him. I shouldn't. I know I shouldn't.

Damon's not the type of guy to push. All I have to do is look at how the other men in his class defer to him to know that he's a man who likes control.

I've spent years being perfect, being the fun girl that you keep around. And it's worked for me. Keeps me safe. I learned the lesson not to play with men in positions of power over me the hard way, and I have the scars to prove it.

So why do I feel so comfortable pushing boundaries with Damon? There's a thrill that goes through me every time I defy him. Like I'm some kind of adrenaline junkie seeing how high I can climb before I crash to the ground.

That's not right, because he'd catch me, and something tells me I'd like every second of the way he'd punish me.

Sidney: You're married!

I rarely get to see Sidney since moving to Boston. She's married to Jaxton Ryder, leading goal scorer in the league. He, Piper, and Lucas grew up together and kind of scooped Sidney and me up into their family, whether we wanted to be or not. Jax managed to get himself traded to the Ottawa Senators when she'd landed her position in parliament.

Me: Temporarily married. More like a marriage of convenience.

Sidney: I know, Piper told me but I thought you were keeping it a secret. The story's all over Canadian news. Canadian girl moves to the U.S and marries a billionaire. Has a nice ring to it.

My hand trembles holding the phone as dread sinks low in my stomach. If she knows, my family knows. Thomas knows. The room grows dark, and blackness takes over my peripheral vision, and I have to force myself to breathe to stop from fainting. There's no way they're going to let this slide.

Me: It was supposed to be a secret. The asshole just couldn't keep his mouth shut.

"Am I the asshole?" Damon's low, rumbly voice comes from directly beside my ear, and my entire body jerks.

"Jesus, you scared me." I hold a hand to my chest, trying to regain some semblance of calm.

His eyes narrow on the ring he gave me, hanging an inch below my palm.

"Do you enjoy disobeying me?" He raises a perfectly arched brow.

I bite my lip to hide my smile, because yeah...I do. "I'm technically wearing it."

He cups the back of my neck before rubbing his thumb over the tight tendon there.

"Tell me, wife. Since you're obviously not bothered by me"—his grip tightens, and his voice turns dark, edged with a warning I don't think is for me—"what made you look so scared?"

"Nothing."

The stubble on his chin scrapes against my temple. "You're a horrible liar."

I huff out a laugh because he's wrong. I'm an excellent liar. I've been hiding every single dark part of me for nearly seven years.

"I received an email from your mother." Deflect, deflect, deflect.

His brows pull together as if he knows exactly what I'm doing. He shifts so that he's leaning against my desk. Damon looks wrong here in his perfectly tailored navy suit, showing off just a hint of stretch across his shoulders.

The contrast between him and the fake wood paneling is a perfect representation of the two of us. We can be in the same space, but we'll never belong. Yet another lesson Thomas's family taught me.

He leans back, watching me. "What did she want?"

I shudder. "She's coming over tomorrow to help me get ready."

His lips twitch into a smile.

"Do you want me to call her off?" His voice is low, serious.

"Hardly. I can handle her."

He eyes me for a long time. "I spoke with her, and she won't speak to you like she did again."

My chest tightens, but I push through it. "Thank you."

"I won't be there tonight. I have to go out of town for a meeting."

I'm curious but don't bother asking. It has nothing to do with me.

As if reading me like an open book, he continues. "The Mercer acquisition has hit a stalemate. If it was anything else, I'd have one of the other reps take care of it."

"You don't have to explain yourself to me."

His head tilts to the side. "Don't I?"

I break eye contact before I can say something stupid like he doesn't have to tell me, but I want him to.

I go with something safe. "Does that mean we won't go to the gala?"

"I wouldn't miss a chance to show you off to the world. I'll be back in plenty of time."

My cheeks flush, and now I'm biting back a smile. This man is entirely too charming when he wants to be.

"Don't look so pleased to be rid of me, Nymph."

He couldn't be further from the truth. I swallow before replying, "Of course. What kind of dutiful wife would I be if I didn't wait by the door for my dear husband."

He tucks a stray strand of my hair behind my ear, dragging his knuckles over my cheekbone. "I don't think *dutiful* is the right word to describe you."

"Oh yeah? How would you describe me?" I regret the words instantly.

He takes my hand and places it on his cock, over his wool-blend pants, then bends down until his lips nearly touch mine, and his breath tingles my skin. "You are a tempting goddess whose sole purpose in life is to test me."

I swallow hard, and his gaze tracks my tongue, wetting my lips. He hasn't touched me since the night I'd pulled away from him, and my body is starting to rebel. I lift so our mouths connect, and a low groan rumbles in his chest before he pulls away.

"This card will buy you whatever you need to be ready for the gala."

"Anything? What if I decide I need a car."

He pulls out his phone and hits a few buttons until mine beeps. "That's the number to our preferred dealer. We've vetted their quality, but you can go wherever you want, of course."

"I was kidding."

"I'm not." He unlatches my necklace and slides my wedding ring off it, carefully returning it to my finger. "Do not take this off."

I roll my eyes because all that did was make me want to wear it on the chain even more. "Of course, Sir."

His eyes turn molten, and his chest rises and falls as if he's holding himself back for several moments before he relaxes. "Lock your door tonight. Matthias will be stationed downstairs if you need anything."

"Your brother? That's not necessary."

"I assure you, it is."

Chapter 32

Damon

"THAT'S the tenth time you've checked your phone," Bash says, kicking his feet up on the leather plane seat in front of him. We still have another half an hour left on this godforsaken flight.

He's not wrong. I've been checking on Misty all morning, but the feed's not working.

I've been texting Matthias to get it fixed, but the last message he sent back told me to fuck off, quickly followed by: She's safe. Relax.

"Your point?" I glare back at Bash. The only reason I brought him with me was to get him out of trouble. He's been splashed all over every gossip site for the last several months. Apparently, he can't get his dick wet without letting every person on the planet know.

He drops his head back against the seat rest, a relaxed smile on his face. "Fuck, Damon, you're stressing me out. I never thought I'd see the day my big brother would be obsessed."

Obsessed doesn't even begin to cover it. Every second I've spent with her is one that ingrains her deeper into my soul. I pull up the feed again and scowl at the black screen. I'm going to fucking kill Matthias.

"Mother's with her, helping her get ready for the gala tonight." I roll my wedding band around my finger, the platinum warm to the touch.

"Oh shit." Bash goes rigid, lifting himself out of his casual pose. "She's a fucking viper, man." Bash has never been close to our mother. She'd all but abandoned us by the time she had Bash, not even a year after Xander. They would have had a stronger bond with their nannies than our parents, but my mother dismissed both women when the boys were six. She didn't want any witnesses to the damage being held hostage had left behind. Nothing could threaten the perfect image of the Everette family she wove. Not even her own sons.

Which left their upbringing to Matthias and me. It's a miracle they're only semi-screwed up.

"Exactly. I didn't anticipate the meeting running late. I'd planned on being there before she arrived." I sent another text to my mother, but still no response. Nerves crawl under my skin, leaving the two of them unattended, especially after the bullshit my mother tried to pull the other night.

"Why don't you call her?"

"I did," I growl and run my hand through my already messy hair.

The overhead speakers crackle before the pilot's voice comes out crisp. "Prepare for landing."

"Thank fuck," I say under my breath and spin my ring again, the surface smooth under my rough touch.

Bash raises a brow at the motion but doesn't say a word when I meet his eyes. Misty is still so fucking skittish around me, and like fuck am I going to leave her to the wolf that is my mother.

"You know this is all temporary, right? Didn't you make some kind of idiotic deal that she just has to put up with you for a year?"

I didn't realize my baby brother had a death wish, but he's pushing my limits.

"She'll learn the truth when she's ready. For now, she needs to believe she can get away."

"It's fucked up that you're planning to basically hold her hostage."

"I never said it wasn't."

He chuckles, his head falling back to its original position. "You know, I'm really looking forward to her kicking your ass. She's got you by the balls, and somehow, you're still delusional enough to think you make the decisions."

He's wrong, of course. I know exactly how much power she holds over me.

My body jerks when we touch down, and I'm already standing before we come to a stop.

"Find your own way home," I tell Bash before I step out into the rain and head directly to my black-on-black Ferrari. I'd messaged Nicholas to have it brought over, knowing I was going to break more than a few laws to get to her.

"Hey! Fucker, I don't have a car."

I get into the driver's side and shout back at him just before the door closes. "Not my problem."

Cherry and blue lights flash behind me, but I don't slow down. Once the officer pulls my plate, he'll know to back off. I curb the car in front of the entrance, feet away from Matthias.

He doesn't comment, just lifts one brow.

"Where is she?" I demand as I swing the door open and head up the stairs.

"Exactly where you left her," he replies, only a foot or two behind me.

"Did you check on her like I asked?" I glare at the doorman when he takes too long.

"I said I would. She's been fine." Matthias is two steps behind me as I rush up the stairs.

"She better be." The swipe pad beeps as I swipe my card over it, and the door swings inward.

It takes several beats before I can process what's happening.

There's a rack full of dresses, all in muted pastels I know Misty would hate. None of the women are visible. Instead, I can just make out their voices in the bathroom.

"Much better." My mother's voice grates on me.

"I'll still need at least another hour to put color back in. This is only the first step," a woman I don't recognize says. They must be the stylist.

My strides eat the distance between me and the open bathroom door when I realize exactly what they mean. My mother and an unknown woman stand next to each other in the cramped space.

But it's Misty that has my attention. She's sitting on the edge of the tub, her eyes like voids as she stares at the wall, muted pale blond hair brushing her shoulders.

"Get the fuck out of here," I roar, my voice vibrating with the anger pulsing through my veins.

"But we're not done—" The stylist's words cut off when my attention falls on her.

"Leave."

She rushes out of the room, not bothering to grab her things. Which is lucky for her because I'm seconds away from tearing everything in here apart.

"Calm down, Damon. We know what we're doing." My mother goes to place her hand on my arm, but I catch her wrist.

Tension rolls through me, and it takes several beats before I let her go. "Get the fuck out of our house."

Her eyes widen on me in shock. "But—"

"Get. Out." My head cocks to the side. "Do not make me say it again."

The only thing saving her is Misty's soft eyes on mine. They've started to glisten, with tears pooling on her lash line.

The front door slams shut, the intruders gone seconds before I kneel in front of my life. I tuck a strand of hair behind her ear, and she flinches.

"I told...I told you I didn't belong." Her voice cracks, and it takes my heart with it.

"I've never wanted you to be anyone other than who you are. I can assure you my mother will pay for this." My teeth grind together as I suck a breath through my nose. Rage beats at my chest, burning to escape and rampage at anyone who hurts my girl like this.

She looks down at the linoleum floor. "I'm not sure why I'm crying. It's not like I didn't know what would be expected of me."

I run a thumb along her cheek, catching a tear. "The only thing I expect from you is to tell her to fuck off."

Her glassy green eyes snap to mine, and she gasps. "I can't just tell your mom to fuck off."

I chuckle and rock back on my heels. "You can do whatever you want to do. You're my wife."

She rolls her eyes, but I grip her jaw, keeping her attention on me. "It won't happen again."

Misty searches my face, then gives a hint of a nod.

I want to wipe away her hesitation. To force her to

see that she's exactly who she's supposed to be, but we have time for that.

She lets out a breath and reaches up to run a strand of baby blonde hair through her fingers. "Funny enough, I've tried to get my hair this light a few times. She actually did a good job at it."

I roll my neck, the tension of the day slowly seeping from me. "You wanted to be blonde?"

"Ha! No. I wanted to go soft lavender, but if there's any yellow in your hair, it turns like a gross, mucky brown."

"Do you have any left?"

Her head tilts. "What?"

I take the strand from her and let it slip through my fingers. "Of the lavender dye. Do you have any left?"

"Yeah, but..." She looks behind me. "You kinda evicted the stylist."

I stand. "I'll do it. Where's the bottle."

Her mouth forms a pretty O shape.

"Misty?"

She gives her head a jerk. "Seriously?"

"I'm always serious."

A laugh huffs out of her. "It'll be messy."

"I like messy." I run my tongue over my teeth as her eyes darken on me.

She takes several deep breaths before replying. "Don't say I didn't warn you."

I smirk. "Consider me properly warned. Now, where's the dye?"

She points to the small vanity I'm blocking. "You'll have to move so I can go through that. There's a few colors in there."

I glance back at the tiny cupboard. Sure enough, the room is so small I'm blocking the entire thing. "Alright, I have to make a call. I'll be right outside."

She stands, and her fingers push against my shoulders until I'm standing in the hall. My chest lightens when she raises a brow, daring me to say anything. That's my girl.

Shock registers through me when she slams the door in my face and I hear it lock.

"Misty?"

"I have to pee. Your freaking mother was here for hours." Her voice is muffled through the door.

I bite my cheek, fighting back a smile. I can't remember the last time I felt this way. If I've ever felt this way.

I pull out my phone and dial Matthias.

"Have you calmed down now that you've seen your wife?"

"Tell security that Mother is barred from future events."

He lets out a whistle. "That's not going to be easy."

"Do I sound like I care? You're fucking lucky it's not you. You said she was fine,"

Silence meets me, and by the time he speaks, his voice has gone cold. "Was she not fine, Damon?"

It's moments like this that remind me just how lethal Matthias is.

"Physically, yes." We both know firsthand it's not the physical that leaves the deepest scars.

"She'll be okay. They'd planned on turning her into one of Mother's perfect society girls."

"You mean miserable," he states, and I can almost hear him run his hand over his face. "I'll see to it myself. I'm looking forward to our mother being told no for a change," he says before the line disconnects.

The door opens, and Misty's standing there in a black robe and holding a basket with a few bottles and bowls inside. "You sure you want to do this?"

I hold out my hand and lift one brow. "Give it here."

She goes to hand it to me but pulls it away at the last second. "You can't wear that!"

I'm still in my Armani suit, but I couldn't give a fuck. "I'm serious. You can't wear that."

The snap of my pants clicks open as I make quick work of divesting my shirt and smirk at the way her cheeks pinken.

"Is this okay, Nymph?

She runs her tongue along her bottom lip and nods, focusing still on my chest.

I clench my fist at the urge to fuck her against the wall and take the basket from her. "Now what?"

"You've never done this?"

"Do I look like someone who dyes other people's hair?"

She chuckles. "No. I can't believe I'm letting you do this. Don't make me look bad."

"You could never look bad."

"Stop it. I'm serious." She's laughing for real now, and it seeps into my chest, wrapping itself around my heart. There's nothing I wouldn't do to keep her laughing like this.

Stepping forward, I crowd her back into the bathroom. "Haven't you realized? I'm very good at what I do."

She just smirks at me. "We'll see."

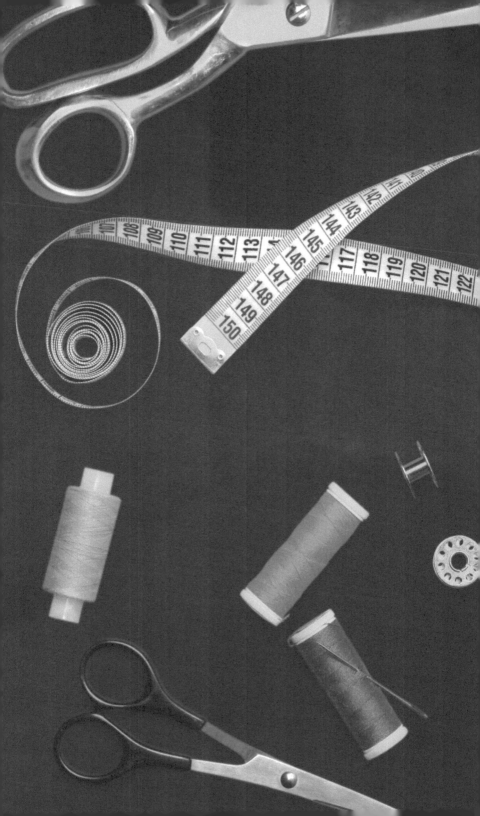

Chapter 33

Misty

EVEN THROUGH THE ROBE, heat burrows into my spine when Damon's chest brushes against me. My fingers curl around the edge of the vanity, and I lean my hips further into it for support as I watch him in the mirror. At first, I thought it was sweet he was willing to color my hair, but now I'm wondering if it's not some form of cruel torture.

The weight of his presence towers over me as he meticulously lifts a strand of my hair and lathers it in lavender lotion. His finger grazes my ear, sending tingles down my neck, and I brace myself to stop my reaction from showing.

Damon's brows are drawn together as he works his way through each piece, taking care to coat it evenly before moving on to the next. Warmth curls in my stomach as I watch him. There's something adorable about how hard he's concentrating.

"Missed a spot," I tease.

There's a quirk to his lips, but he doesn't look away from his task. "No, I didn't."

"You know, you're pretty good at this."

He grips the back of my nape and twists my head down and to the side until I can't see him anymore. "Did you have any doubts?"

I wipe a drop of purple from the white ceramic sink and rinse it down the drain. "Uh, yeah. I'll be honest, this isn't a skill I expected you to have practiced."

"You'd be surprised at all the things I'm good at."

I let out a small moan when his thumb presses into the base of my nape, releasing tension that had been building there.

Finished, he pulls off his gloves, tosses them into the garbage, and leans into me. Lips press into the base of my neck, and his breath brushes against me, heating me to my core. With each moment, the space around us loses focus as my body hones in on him. The scratch of his stubble, the heat of his hands, the scent of sweet smoke that clings to him.

Each of his breaths draws me nearer until he's all I see, know, feel. Until he's captured every molecule of my attention with one simple touch of his lips.

"Now what?"

"Wait twenty-five minutes, then rinse." I turn to face him, and a laugh bursts from my chest. There's a smear of purple over his brow from when he kissed me. "Oh my God."

One dark brow raises in question, and his lips twist into a grin. "What?"

"You've got...you've got dye on you." I reach back, grabbing the wet cloth I'd been using to keep the color from staining my own face, and wipe it off.

"You don't think I'd look good in purple?" he asks, low, playfully.

"I think you'd look good in anything, but I'm not sure even you can pull off a blurred smudge on your forehead."

Damon leaves the room to toss a few things out while I pull my trusty plastic cap over my hair to stop it from making a mess and start tidying up the counter.

"Here." Damon holds out a sandwich.

"You made me a sandwich?"

"I could barely think over your stomach rumbling."

I can feel my cheeks heat, but I take a bite anyway. It's nothing special, peanut butter and jelly, but I moan when the sweet taste of jam bursts into my mouth.

Damon drags his thumb along my bottom lip, catching some of the jelly, then sucks it off. "I've been dying to see that up close."

"Up close?" I let my thoughts drag over his words.

"Do you have a dress?"

"Your mom brought some."

He dismisses that. "Misty, do you have a dress?"

I think about the gown I made last year but never had the opportunity to wear it. It's not practical in the least, more whimsy than black-tie.

I shrug. "It's probably not appropriate."

"Sounds perfect."

As Damon and I enter the grand hall, a hush falls over the crowd. The ballroom is awash in soft lighting emanating from the stunning five-foot-wide chandeliers that sway above us. The floor is filled with women dressed in elegant gowns, their arms linked with men in impeccably tailored suits that could rival Damon's sharp attire.

Their dresses are nothing like the one I chose. If its plunging neckline wasn't enough, the vibrant emerald green that brightens my eyes and complements my hair definitely stands out.

I glance up and catch Damon already watching me. His hair is styled back, not a strand out of place. Nothing like the wild mess it was while we stood together in my bathroom. My brain freezes, trying to reconcile the Damon who belongs in this room full of stuffy people and the one that spent an hour making sure my hair was the perfect shade of lavender.

He leans in, dropping his mouth to my ear. "What's wrong?"

"They're all looking at us," I whisper back.

A low chuckle rumbles from his chest. "Let them."

"I don't belong here."

He pulls back and cups the side of my neck, using his thumb to tilt my head up. "You belong with me."

There's a twist, snap, pop of emotion flooding my chest. The little voice that normally screams that all of this is just temporary is quiet for once. For now, I'm exactly where I'm meant to be.

My lips twist up into a smile, and I pull my shoulders back and face down the judgmental onlookers. "This is going to suck, isn't it?" I ask.

His laugh vibrates my arm, and he gives me a slight nod. "I tried not to come. You're the one that insisted."

"You were supposed to be looking for a wife!" I scoff.

"I already had a wife," he says darkly, the low rumble erupting goosebumps along my shoulders.

"Is it too late to turn back?" I gesture to the exit.

"Unfortunately, there's no getting away for you." He entwines our fingers, giving them a little squeeze before guiding me through the crowd.

We zigzag through the crowd. Damon expertly introduces me as his wife to members of his peers. Each time, it's the same. Hidden under the congratulations of our marriage, the men want to know what it is about me that caught the Everette heir, and the women watch me with envy, delicately dissecting me with their words.

Of course, no one dares to be outwardly rude.

Instead, we play a dangerous game of backhanded compliments and fake smiles.

They expect me to not understand that when they're

welcoming me into the fold, they're actually pointing out that I'm an outsider. But I know exactly what's happening. I've played and lost this game before. They'll tolerate me, but even being married to Damon won't change that I am not one of them.

After what feels like my millionth introduction, Damon's fingertips trace a trail of fire down my spine over the silk fabric, lingering at the curve of my lower back. He nods toward the back of the grand hall, where a live band plays and couples twirl gracefully across the checkered dance floor. I know the dance, the elegant steps drilled into me by my parents, always desperate to fit in with this high-society crowd that we could never truly belong to.

I struggle to breathe as my eyes are glued to the sheer opulence of it all. The place is practically a palace dripping with money, screaming at me that I'm the one that stands out. Suddenly, I wish I'd done what Damon's mother wanted. That I'd kept the soft blonde hair and pastel dresses. My fingers tug at my collar, desperately trying to pull the neckline up.

Damon's lips press against my temple, staying there until my heart rate slows. "Do me the honor and dance with me?"

"You're kidding. We're already drawing attention."

"I assure you, I'm not kidding." He trails his fingers down my neck, running the thin strap between his fingers. "Half those men wrongfully think they can take you from me. I want them to see my wife in my arms. I want them to know you're mine."

The air is pushed from my lungs as he sweeps me into his arms, easily joining us in time with the other dancers. The dance is fast and full of turns, but Damon expertly guides me through it. His sure movements take the lead, making it easy to follow.

His heartbeat pounding against the hand on his chest is the only thing giving away how he's feeling. I gaze up, expecting his expression to be pinched, closed off from the crowd quickly gathering around us, but I'm captured by his piercing gaze. The room shrinks around us as the air grows thick. His deep cologne fills my nose and makes my head grow fuzzy. He sweeps his thumb over the bare skin at the nape of my neck, then runs his knuckles down my spine until they graze the curve of my ass. I shiver. The simple touch has me wanting more. His arm around my waist tugs me closer until there's no room left between us. I rest my head on his chest, eyes closed, trusting him to guide us through the spins and twirls.

An overwhelming feeling of being wanted, accepted, fills my chest. One that I'd never expect to feel in a place like this. But Damon's touch, his breath against my neck, his firm arm banded around my back, allows me to finally exhale. I'm safe in this world, as long as I'm with him. For however long this lasts. The thought has pain piercing my chest at the reminder this is all temporary. That I'm not really his wife, that this is all to fulfill his obligation and to get my visa. An act that I unwillingly started to believe.

I lift my head from his chest, but he squeezes the nape of my neck and says, "Just a little longer. I'm not ready to let you go."

My fingers dig into his tux, wanting it to mean so much more.

Eventually, the song ends, and a familiar face approaches us. He looks like a younger version of Damon, only his cocky smile separating them.

He gives me a playful bow. "May I have the next dance?"

"Watch it, Xander." Damon's voice is sharp with warning.

"Oh, come on, man. I've barely had time with my new sister," Xander replies easily, not worrying about the dark stare Damon's bearing on him.

I need to stop this before it escalates in front of everyone. "I'd love to dance."

Damon's hold tightens, and I smile up at him. "We're married, remember? People expect me to be close with your brothers."

His gaze narrows, searching my face before he lets me go. "I'll be right over there."

"She'll be fine. Relax." Xander is already pulling me toward him, ignoring his older brother's death glare. "Plus, you have business to handle." He looks into the crowd, where three gentlemen stand watching.

Damon finally lets go of my hand. "One dance."

Laughter bubbles in my chest at his possessiveness, even when it's his brother.

I look over my shoulder as Xander leads me further onto the floor. "Don't be jealous."

The side of Damon's mouth quirks up. "You like me jealous."

His words zing through me because he's right.

"You two need to stop looking at each other like that before this party turns into an orgy with the energy you're putting off." Xander spins me, but unlike Damon, he keeps several inches between us, and his hand is respectfully placed on my upper back.

I can feel my cheeks burn, but I ignore his baiting words. "So, are you looking for a wife too?"

A bark of laughter escapes him. "No. Do I seem like someone who wants to be tied down?"

With his mischievous smile and gleaming eyes, he really doesn't. Unease fills my chest, knowing that soon he wouldn't have a choice. "I'm sorry about your grandfather."

His head tilts to the side, still moving in time with the beat. "Why?"

My brows pinch in confusion. "Because he's going to make you get married."

Xander's eyes twinkle with some unshared secret. "Ah, yes. The Everette tradition. How could I forget about that?"

Really, how could he? If it was me, I'd be doing everything I could to find someone before I had to marry.

Unlike Damon, I doubt he'll just coerce someone. All the Everette brothers can't be that insane. "But you'll—"

"You look thirsty. I'll get you some champagne," Xander cuts in before I can press him further. He looks more amused than concerned.

I swallow, my mouth dry, and let him guide me back to the crowd. "Thank you."

"Of course. I'll always take care of my sister."

I don't correct him on the *always*.

Xander disappears into the crowd, and I inhale deeply. I'm flushed from dancing and hungry for air. It's been so long since I've spun like that it's hard to keep my balance. I reach out to steady myself, my hand connecting with a hard bicep.

I snap it back. "Oh, sorry—"

Dread sinks deep into my gut, twisting it into nausea at Thomas's familiar face. "What are you doing here?" My words come out barely above a whisper as fear licks up my spine. But I already know. This is his territory. I'm the one out of place.

"Now, what kind of welcome is that after all of this time? Didn't you miss me?" He smirks, but unlike Xander's playfulness, his cuts like glass.

I'm frozen, staring at his near black eyes before sanity descends on me, and I rip my attention away, turning to escape.

He grips my arm, tugging me toward him. "Where do you think you're going? Don't want to be seen with me? Are you afraid that your new husband will find out what you really are? That you're just some used-up, dirty whore. That not even your parents care about you." His grip tightens painfully. "You couldn't even stay pregnant right."

Pain lances like a knife, slicing through my gut. My lungs scream for me to breathe, but it hurts too much to inhale. With everything he did to me. Erasing who I am, raping me. It's the miscarriage that haunts me. It's the doctors apologizing that I'll likely never get pregnant. It's the absolute devastation of that loss that broke something deep inside. But I'm no longer that scared girl. He can't control me.

"Let go of me," I sneer, enunciating every word.

He releases his grip, but his cold smile holds me in place. "What do you think he'll do? Do you think he'll keep you around once he knows you're broken? You're ignorant, but even you have to know he needs an heir. That the entire reason he married you is to breed you like the bitch you are."

Tears sting my eyes. I know it doesn't matter. That it's never been the plan, but God, does it hurt. "Leave me alone."

"Don't worry. I won't tell him. I'll leave him to find out just what kind of backstabbing slut you are. Just like I did," he whispers harshly, then turns away, giving me his back as if nothing happened.

I stumble back, blinking rapidly, trying desperately to get a grip on myself. Not here. I can't fall apart here.

Not when so many people are looking forward to my inevitable crash.

"Hey. Are you okay?" Xander asks, voice low with concern. He's holding out a champagne flute toward me.

I take it, downing half the glass before replying. "I'm a little overwhelmed with the crowd. Is it hot in here?"

He raises a brow but doesn't question me. "You do look a little flushed. Let's get you back to my brother before he accuses me of making you...uncomfortable."

He clears a path, moving effortlessly through the throng of people. Damon's standing with two older men I don't recognize, their faces drawn in concentration. A Black man in a double-breasted suit, his graying hair the only thing denoting his age, and a thin, prickly looking man whose face is twisted like he tasted something sour.

The second we approach, Damon's attention is on me, a soft smile on his lips before it slips away and concern replaces it.

He separates himself from the men around him and pushes a strand of hair behind my hair. "Do you want to go?"

How does he know what I need? How does he always know?

The men behind him are still deep in conversation, neither paying attention to us. "I'm just a little light-headed from the champagne and dancing. You stay. I'll go with Nicholas."

"No. We go together."

"Damon, we have the...*meeting* tonight," Matthias cuts in, and I can feel Damon go rigid.

He glares at his brother, anger radiating from him. "Take my place."

"I'm sorry, brother, but this time, you need to be there."

"Fuck," Damon growls, and his hands slide up my arms. I clench my teeth to hide the wince when he touches the spot Thomas bruised. "Go straight home. I'll meet you there."

"I'm not a child, you know?"

A muscle ticks in his jaw, and his grip tightens momentarily. "Straight home."

"Yes, Sir." I smile, trying to put him at ease, but I know it doesn't reach my eyes.

He kisses me deeply until my lungs burn and my head grows fuzzy.

I want to stay buried in his chest, wrapped in his arms. Safe.

But my past just came to remind me exactly why that's impossible.

Chapter 34

Damon

Misty's shoulders are folded in, making her already short frame smaller as her eyes dart around the room, looking for some unknown source of unease. I hate myself for dragging her here. I shouldn't have let her leave my side.

I tighten the arm I have banded around her back, gently guiding her gaze back to mine, and lower my forehead to rest on hers. "You really hate it here?"

Her eyes widen before she releases a long breath. "I'm just tired. Between your mom and the crowd, all I can think about is crawling into my bed."

"Our bed."

A pink blush covers her cheeks, but she's back to looking around the hall.

Men are rapidly disappearing from the room, heading to the meeting that's about to start in the Vaults. Everything in me screams not to leave her like this. That whatever she is, it's not fine. I'm about to tell Matthias to fuck off when Misty smiles gently at me and pulls out of my arms.

"Mrs. Everette. Are you ready?" Nicholas's standing beside us, black suit impeccably pressed. If I didn't know the truth, I'd think he was born to this.

"Yup. Let's go." She nods, but there's a false levity to her tone.

There's a look of concern and a silent promise that has the tension in my shoulders easing.

"Take care of my wife."

"You know I will, sir."

My fists clench at my sides as I watch them weave through the crowd, then disappear through the large double doors.

"I'm so fucking ready for this." Bash appears out of nowhere, clapping his hands together. The curl of his lip and the gleam in his eyes are the opposite of Xander's serious expression.

For the first time, I'm more interested in going home than I am in doling out punishment.

Matthias wraps an arm around my shoulders. "Burn off some of that anger before you go back to your wife."

Fuck, he's right. I crack my knuckles as anticipation buzzes in my veins. I'll just have to make it quick.

The Everette hotel is one of the oldest in the city. Where the upstairs is newly renovated, the underlevels have been maintained in their original version.

I follow my brothers down the twisting marble staircase, grooves worn into it from the years of use. The entire place is lit by the soft glow of sconces that line the sides. Noise filters up to us before we reach the bottom, men gossiping in whispered tones as they wait for us to arrive.

"Don't forget this." Bash tosses me my gold mask with a grin as he slides his on.

The three of them transform in front of me into men to be feared. Gone is the playfulness they show each other, morphed into a predatory display of dominance.

They keep their postures relaxed, an illusion to put you at ease, but there's no mistaking the warning underneath.

We'd been raised for this, and when they tried to take it away from us, we destroyed to get it back. Even as boys, we'd been feared. I've made sure to hone that fear, to twist it into power so no one dares come after us again.

The room goes completely silent as my brothers enter one by one. It's dimmer than the stairwell, the lights from the high ceilings casting the members in shadows as we walk down the aisle. Men are lined on both sides, silver masks in place. Their heads are bowed in respect as we make our way up to the front.

An Unsainted I don't recognize stirs, his gaze meeting mine before Anthony grabs his arm and drags him lower. He'd petitioned to introduce his cousin in hopes of him entering the Order of Saints. It's not going well.

I take my spot at the end of the hall, my brothers lined behind me, and stand in front of my throne, daring them to challenge the Everette family.

The silence is broken as two men are dragged in front of us and pushed to their knees. Their faces are bruised and mangled to the point they are nearly unrecognizable. They're both Unsainted members, not protected by a specific family.

I lift a dagger from the nearby table and clean my nails with it as I examine them. They'd been worked over thoroughly, neither of them fully able to see through swollen lids. Their fists are wrapped in gauze, stained a deep brown, and they're hunched low, collapsed in on themselves. Matthias caught them two days ago. Looks like he's been busy.

They flinch simultaneously when I step toward them.

"You've both been charged with being traitors to the Order. You have been found guilty of killing Unsainted," I say in a low voice.

They tremble as I approach closer. My feet stop directly in front of the blond's knees.

I fist his hair and yank his head up to look at me. "Who did you work for?"

"We don't know."

I raise my knife to his eye, the sharp edge cutting the thin lid. "You don't need eyes to answer."

The man still looking at the ground beside us whimpers, and the acrid smell of piss fills the air.

"Tell me who you work for, and I'll make it all stop."

"We don't know. We never saw them. They texted a name, then money was deposited." The bowed man's voice shakes, barely able to get out the words.

I lift the man in front of me by his collar. "Is that true?"

"Y...yes. We don't know."

"What if I ask your family? Your wife? Do you think she'll know?" It's an empty threat, but it does what I want.

The man shakes violently in my arms. "I swear. I swear to God, we don't know."

I hum under my breath. "I believe you."

The man relaxes prematurely right before I slice through his throat, the sharp blade sliding without resistance.

The other tries to scramble away, but his broken body doesn't allow him to flee. "How about you? Do you have any information for me?"

His eyes widen, and his mouth gapes open, searching for anything he can say that would be useful. Unfortunately for him, whoever hired them was smart, and there's nothing left to tell.

"I didn't think so." Blood splatters on my white cuff as the blade does its job.

I turn to the crowd. Someone here is the traitor. "I will hunt you down in whatever crevice you're hiding in. I will find you and gut you like the rat you are. It's only a matter of time."

I wipe the blade on the dead man's shirt and toss it back on the table.

"Clean this up."

I don't bother sticking around. I have a wife to get back to.

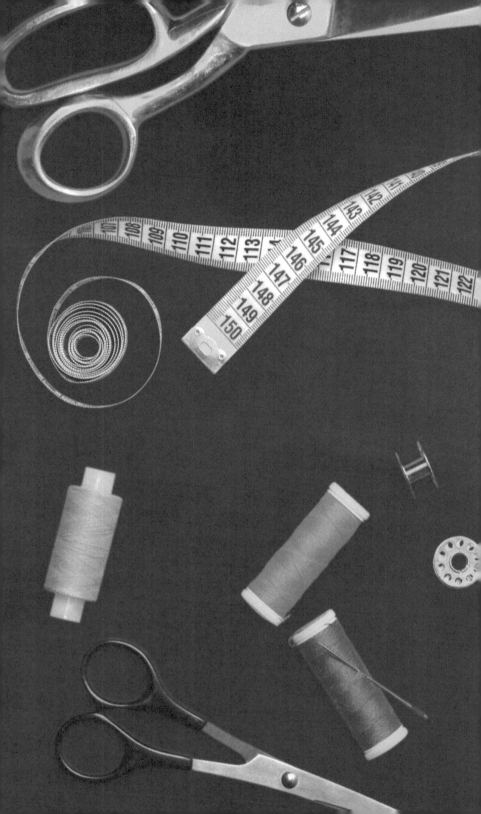

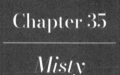

Chapter 35

Misty

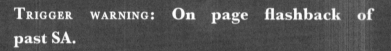

TRIGGER WARNING: **On page flashback of past SA.**

Nicholas opens the door for me and holds his hand to help guide me out. I'm shaking so badly I don't dare take it, instead shifting around my dress in an excuse to get out on my own.

"Thank you for the ride," I manage to say. He tried to chat like usual, but I didn't have it in me. All I want is to get home. To pretend like none of this happened. To hide in the space I built for myself. My heart feels like it's been cracked open, like the most vulnerable part of me is exposed and I need to get away to somewhere I can close that part of me off again.

Nicholas's eyes are warm with concern when he says, "I'll walk you to your apartment."

"I'm fine, I swear. Geez, you're as bad as Damon." I don't give him a chance to argue, already walking toward the door.

The newly installed doorman opens it. He's tall and burly, looks more like a bouncer than someone who opens doors for a living, but it's a layer of safety I desperately need.

He grunts as I thank him and walk through. It kills me to take my time walking up the stairs, tears of frustration already pooling in my eyes, and the bodice of my dress feels like it's slowly suffocating me.

My skin itches and crawls everywhere Thomas touched me. I'm desperate to wipe his filth off and climb directly into the shower, not bothering to remove the dress. I fight to breathe as panic descends on me, my lungs collapsing in on themselves as I scrub my skin raw, but I can still feel the press of his fingers. I can still smell his sour breath. Memories I've been hiding wrap around me, pulling me under. I can't escape as they flood into me, and I crash to my knees on the floor.

"Let's go back to the party before your mother notices we're missing." I push against Thomas's shoulders, trying to put space between us. He's not a massive guy, barely above average, but he doesn't so much as budge.

"Come on, baby. Don't be like that." Hot breath that reeks of booze fans over my neck, making my skin crawl. *"No one will know."*

His fingers skate up my thigh, dragging my knee-length skirt with them, and I frantically grip his wrist to hold it in place.

"I'm not ready." I push at him again, and this time, he leans far enough to face me.

"You're a fucking tease. You know that?" he hisses, grabbing my shoulder with one hand, pinning me against the wall while the other breaks free from my grasp and lifts my skirt above my hips.

He bites his bottom lip, leering. "How can you tell me you don't want it when you look like that?"

"Please, let me go." I dig my fingers into his collared shirt, shoving him, and the pop, clack, ting sound of buttons breaking off fills the air.

"Bitch." Thomas's slap feels more like a punch.

The world rings around me as pain radiates in my cheek, deep into my jaw. His mouth is moving, but I can't make out the words as shock ricochets through me.

"Did you fucking hear me?" His fingers reach into my underwear, his touch revolting.

"Stop," I scream, slamming my fists into his chest.

"You are a fucking tease, Misty. Do you think that I don't know what your parents want? That you've been using me?

"I don't want anything." Bile climbs my throat, and tears burn my eyes.

He tears the seam of my underwear, and they fall to the floor. "Well, I want something from you."

Panic laces my blood, pumping adrenaline through my veins.

I want to scream that this can't be happening, but it is. It's not fair, it's cruel, it's horrendous. But it is happening.

That doesn't mean I have to make it easy on him.

I dig my nails into his neck, pulling him down while slamming my knee into his dick.

Thomas lets out a pained groan and slams me back again, my head connecting hard with the wall. Black rims the corners of my vision, but it's fear that takes over.

"Don't touch me." I slam my forehead and clip his nose, blood splattering on my cheeks.

He lifts his hand to his nose, then stares at the blood.

"You fucking bitch." The remainder of his cocky mask evaporates. He buries his fingers into my hair, the pain pulling a scream from my chest, and tosses me to the ground.

My palms and knees sting with the force of the landing. He already has me by the hips as I try to scramble free. Fingers dig into my hip bone, holding me in place. I kick out and fight against his hold, fight to get away from him. Fight for a different reality.

A sharp point nicks my neck, and I freeze at the pain.

"Do you know what this is?" He strokes it over my nape before slicing easily through the back of my shirt, leaving me instantly bare from my waist up.

No. No. No. Fuck. I'd bought him a butterfly knife for Christmas. It's the only thing he wanted that I could afford. I even had his name engraved into the handle. Now, the blade I picked out is digging into my spine.

"Please," I cry desperately.

"Fuck, I knew you'd beg for it." The sound of his zipper going down breaks something in me. He's barely holding me.

I can't let him do this.

I break free, scrambling forward on the smooth tile. It's milliseconds before his knife digs into my lower back, cutting a deep horizontal gash as he drags me back.

"That wasn't very fucking nice. Look what you made me do." He pushes the knife in deeper, and warm liquid trails over my hip.

My cry catches in my mouth, the pain stealing away my ability to breathe. Something hard pushes at me from behind, and I try. I try so hard to break free, but this time, he digs the knife into my shoulder blade, forcing my head down.

Tears splash down around me as the pain wins the battle against my mind, and the mercy of blackness takes over.

Chapter 36

Damon

"DON'T GET blood in my car, asshole," Matthias says as he parks in front of Misty's apartment.

I rub my palm over the dash, smearing red over the tan leather, and wink. "I'll buy you a new one."

"Fucking cheery, asshole. You're lucky we like her."

My jaw twitches, and I glance his way. "What do you think would happen if you didn't?"

"Fuck. Easy. I was kidding. Sensitive." This time, Matthias's mouth quirks to the side, and all the anger drains out of me.

Misty's doing wonders with him, and she doesn't even know it.

Knowing she's upstairs, laid out asleep, has me climbing out of the car.

The window rolls down behind me. "Take a shower before you give her nightmares."

I look down. Blood splatters my white shirt and hands. Right. Shower first.

The apartment's quiet, the lights turned off when I step inside. She'd looked so exhausted earlier. Matthias was the only reason I didn't follow her home. I don't give a single fuck about my responsibilities, about the fact that they caught two traitors, that I'd be the one to dole out their punishments. I'd leave that all to my brothers if that meant I could take care of my wife.

She'd looked delicate, almost fragile. None of the fire lit up her eyes. I hated it.

The light is off in the bedroom, complete silence emanating from it. I have to fight against the pull to go to her and head to the bathroom instead.

The sound of running water is my first sign that something is wrong.

Nothing prepared me for the sight in front of me when I open the door.

Misty is curled in on herself, fully dressed, body shaking under the spray of water.

My throat closes, making it hard to swallow, as I stumble into the room. I push the shower curtain open further and climb into the tub with her. The water's brutally cold, freezing through my shirt as it rapidly clings to me. I cover her from the spray, using my back as a shield as I adjust the temperature. How long has she been in here?

The tub's small, so I pull her onto my lap, wrapping my arms around her, trying to put heat back into her. She's trembling against my chest, her fingers digging into my shirt.

"You have a fever. I'll call my doctor. Everything's going to be okay." A strand of hair is clinging to her cheek, and I push it off her face.

Her eyes snap up to mine, the pretty green rimmed with red. "No. I'm fine."

"You are so far away from fine."

It's minuscule, but I feel her flinch in my arms in response. It's like ice pouring through my veins, freezing me in place.

I palm her cheeks and search her face. "What is it? Did I do something?"

She shakes her head, but it's the tears pooling over her eyes and streaming down her face that has my world crashing down around me.

"Misty. Tell me what's wrong." My voice is a plea as my hands run over her, looking for any signs of injury. Her dress clings around her thighs. Her breath catches with each inhale—she's fucking crying. She's not fucking fine.

"I can't breathe." Her words are so low I barely hear them, but it's her hands tearing at the bodice of her dress that gives away what she means.

Within seconds, I have her freed from the soaking fabric, the top now hanging down to her waist. She's taking hungry lungfuls of air like she hasn't had one in hours.

I band my hand around her waist, guiding her into

my chest, and kiss the top of her head. Fear clashes with helplessness as I hold her. I hate that I don't know what's wrong, but I refuse to push her further.

I run my hand up and down her back in a calming motion, then freeze as my fingers travel over thick, raised ridges.

There are two deep scars on her back, clean, crisp lines that can only be carved by a knife.

She stills in my arms as I trace over them. This is what she's been hiding. This is what she didn't want me to see.

Rage burns through my veins, turning my vision red. Whoever dared touch her is going to die for that mistake. Misty grows still in my arms, her eyes downcast, and her hands tremble where they're holding on to my shirt.

Pain lances my chest at the terror written all over her. There will be time to track the fucker down later. Right now, all that matters is my girl.

I cup her jaw and guide her face up, dropping my forehead to hers. "I'm here for you. I'll always be here for you."

Her breath hitches, and she pauses for several seconds before speaking. "It was years ago...I should be over it by now."

I had my own personal battles with trauma, and there's one thing I know for sure. "No one gets to decide when or if they'll ever be over it. That's not something anyone should ask from you."

She sniffs. "He was there tonight."

Fuck! My teeth grind hard enough to break, but I don't tighten around her. The last thing I want to become is another person to fear.

"Who was there?"

"Thomas."

I wait, wait for her to be ready or not. The name Thomas isn't much of a lead, but combining it with him being at the party narrows the potential dead men extensively.

"He...he raped me."

I flinch. Muscles spasm throughout my body. The pain in her voice is nearly my undoing. "I will kill him for you."

"His family is scary well-connected."

A rough laugh rumbles in my throat. "I can promise you that won't be a problem."

"I can never tell if you're being serious or not."

"I'm always serious." I brush our lips together before pulling back.

"Is it wrong that I love that?"

"Your darkness matches my darkness." Her eyes soften, and I run my thumb over her bottom lip. "Let me get you out of here."

She sniffs again and nods. "Okay."

Her wet dress hits the linoleum with a splat as I lift her into my arms and carry her into the room. Shuffling through my drawer, I pull out one of my worn T-shirts and lower it over her head. It completely engulfs her, more of a dress than a shirt.

She pushes her hair back off her face and tucks it behind her ears. A hint of pink washes over her cheekbones as she gazes up at me.

"You look perfect." I kiss her forehead. Even after the warm shower, she still feels cold. I pull back the blanket, making a spot for her to climb in. "I'm going to go make you some tea."

The second I'm out of the room, I text Matthias.

> **Me:** There was a guy named Thomas at the party. Find him.

> **Matthias:** Any other information?

> **Me:** He hurt Misty.

> **Matthias:** Give me twenty.

> **Me:** Make it ten.

The water boils, and I drop in the bag of chamomile tea and stir in some honey. I trust Matthias to find the asshole; it's only a matter of time. If I have to haul in every Thomas in attendance and question them individually, so fucking be it.

Misty's sitting up in bed, knees pulled to her chest under the blanket. The collar of her shirt is darkened from her damp hair, and there are goose bumps where the strands touch her neck.

I grab her hair dryer off the vanity, and she gives me a small smile as I approach.

"Are you freaking serious?"

"You're cold."

"I'm tired."

I shift her forward so I can sit behind her, my back pressed against the headboard, both legs on either side of her. "It's a good thing I'm the one doing it, then, isn't it?"

"This is ridiculous—"

Her words are cut off by the whoosh of the dryer. I take my time, deliberately being mindful of tangles. It probably takes twice as long than if she'd done it, but by the time I'm done, she's looking up at me with hooded eyes.

Her tongue sneaks out and wets her bottom lip. "Make me forget, Damon."

Fuck me. Power washes over me. At being the one she asked, at being the one that can take her pain from her.

I flip our positions so I'm over her, elbows bent, and she's cradled beneath me. I take her lips in mine in a slow, delicate kiss, taking my time as I devour her. She moans softly when I make my way down her ear, nipping at her earlobe before traveling lower. "Relax for me, wife."

Her body goes languid in my hands as I travel lower, following the path her pleasured sounds lead me down. I swirl my tongue around her nipple over her shirt until the fabric's wet and it's a solid peak. Misty's fingers dig into my hair, both pushing and pulling me as I kiss down her sternum, lifting the hem of her shirt to expose more of her as I descend between her knees. It's not until her pretty pink pussy's in front of me that I pause to check in with her.

Her gaze is hooded, her teeth sinking into her bottom lip, and her back's arched off the bed, practically begging me for more.

I suck on her thigh, teeth scratching the surface, leaving a mark. Her fingers curl painfully in my hair as she guides me to where she needs me. I bury my nose against her clit, breathing in her sweet smell before licking along her seam. Her hips jerk against me, and I hold them in place as I work my tongue back and forth, bringing her closer to her orgasm with each touch. My cock's rock hard against the bed, begging me to be touched, but all that matters is her pleasure.

Her hips rock into me, begging for more, and I circle two fingers around her entrance. She cries out as I push them deep inside her, curling them against her G-spot.

Her words change to pleas for more, and I give it to her, sucking her clit as I twist my fingers deep inside her until she pulses around my fingers. Her orgasm crashes around her, and I kiss her slowly, delicately, over her skin until she squirms away from me.

"Sensitive." She hums, head lolling to the side. I get off her and drape her limbs over my chest, needing her as close as possible.

Her hand travels down my abs, but I stop it before she can cup my cock through my boxers. "I will fuck you, but not tonight. Go to sleep, Nymph."

I stroke her hair for less than a minute before she's out to this world.

My phone lights up on my table, and I'm careful not to wake her when I reach for it.

My lips pull at the corner at the message.

Matthias: Got him.

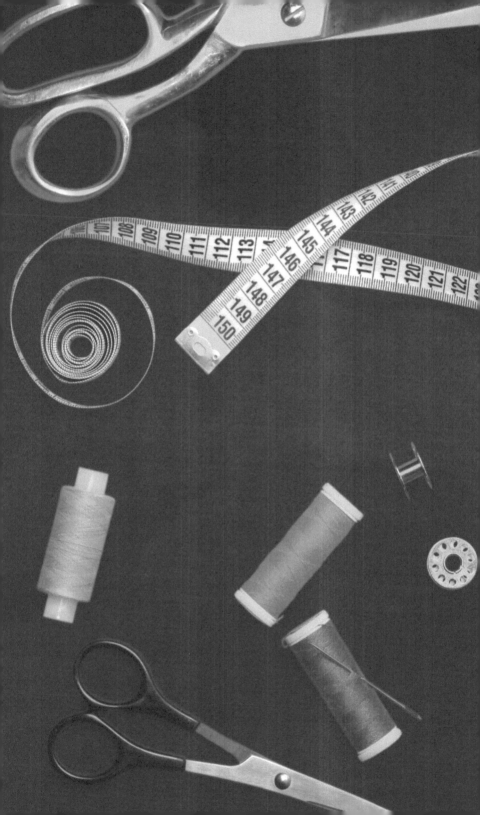

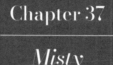
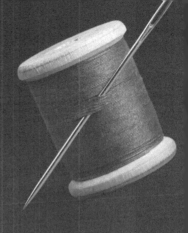

Chapter 37

Misty

I'm woken by the feeling of soft lips kissing along the scar just above my shoulder blade. Heat floods my stomach as the sensations filter into my still-sleepy mind. Damon's large frame is wrapped around me from behind. Tingles run down my spine at the feel of his hard cock notched against my butt, just begging me to push into it. I'm cocooned in his warmth. One of his arms is under my head, and the other hand crosses my chest like a seat belt and cups my breast.

I arch into his touch, and he hums, rolling my nipple between his thumb and forefinger.

"Good morning, Nymph." His low, gravely words brush over my sensitive skin, his mouth still making its way over the visual proof of my past.

I tense, and he pinches my nipple in response. "Relax. I wasn't there to take care of you when it happened. Give me the chance to do it now."

His heart pounds against my back as he waits for my answer, the steady rhythm like a tranquilizer to my nerves.

"You don't think they're gross?" I turn my face toward the pillow to hide my morning breath. God, did I even brush my teeth last night? Memories of Damon waking me up again with his mouth between my legs, until I was crying out with pleasure, have heat rising to my cheeks. He'd come out of the bathroom with a toothbrush in his mouth and another ready for me.

"Do you think my scars are gross?"

I twist my body, turning under him. Up close, I can see the constellation of scars that line his shoulder, chest, and arms. Marks from nicks and cuts delivered over time. His breathing grows rapid as I trace each one, taking my time to ask him about them. There's a small circle just below his collarbone, the skin smoother, almost like glass. "What happened?"

"Picked a fight with the wrong guy. Bastard got me with his cigarette before I could realize what was happening." I flinch, my thumb pressing into the mark as if I can take away the pain that's been long healed over.

"Don't worry, Nymph. He got what he deserved."

My chest expands, a giddiness growing there. I like that entirely too much. I want every single person that hurt him to pay for what they did. I've hidden my scars since they'd been cut into me; now that they're in the open, Damon's mouth caressing them, I'm not ashamed. I'm angry.

There's another circle on his upper shoulder. This one's indented, and the skin around it is jagged. "How about this one?

"Bullet." Damon's voice is strained. There's a wall between us, but his eyes don't leave mine, letting me know if I asked, he'd answer.

I run my finger over the raised line above his nipple, and the pink tip peaks with my touch. "I thought billionaires were coddled, with diamond-encrusted spoons in their mouths."

Goose bumps rise where my thumb brushes the rose-pink underside.

He brushes his fingers through my hair absentmindedly, pushing it off my face. His voice is low, dark when he answers. "Sometimes you need to be a wolf to rule over sheep."

I flatten my tongue over his nipple, twirling it before nipping gently with my teeth. I gaze up at him through my lashes, finally feeling safe again. "Be my wolf?"

"Fuuuck, Misty," he groans, pulling my mouth to his. His kisses aren't soft or gentle. His lips, tongue, and teeth are dominating me. I feel like I'm being hunted down and devoured.

I kiss him back fiercely, my hands digging into his hair, pulling him closer. It's not enough. I want more, I need more. I want him everywhere. I want to be consumed.

He pulls back, breaking the kiss and resting his forehead against mine. His chest heaves, and his heart beats rapidly against my palm.

He nips my lips again like he can't stop himself. His fingers tremble where they hold my arm. "I'm so fucking gone for you."

My heart swells, and my head grows light as his words swirl through me. He doesn't give me a chance to respond, instead lifting my leg over his hip and trailing the tip of his cock through my slit.

He purrs into my throat. "So wet for me already." He pushes in until just the tip enters, my brain short-circuiting. "I think I told you, you'd have to beg for it."

The reminder of our first night in this bed together, the way he'd made my body sing without touching me—I can't go through that again. "Please, Damon. Please."

"Please what, Nymph."

"Please, fuck me."

"Please, fuck me, *what?*"

My eyes flash to his, lust searing away reason, but there's zero chance I'm calling him *Sir* right now.

He chuckles softly and sinks his cock deep inside me. The stretch burns quickly, followed by pleasure.

"I'll give you whatever you want, *wife*. All you have to do is ask." He rocks his hips harder, fully seating himself.

Fullness overwhelms my senses, but he doesn't give me a second to adjust, rocking into me again. He grips the back of my nape, holding me in place, capturing my mouth as he moves in purposeful, controlled motions. His cock reaches the intense spot deep inside me.

Pleasure erupts below my navel, tightening with each of his movements, until the entire world is tied to him, waiting to break open.

He grips my thigh, opening me wider, and I whimper as he sinks impossibly deeper.

"Look at me," he commands and smirks when I listen. "That's it, my Little Nymph. Watch me as I make you come apart."

His gaze is steady on mine, eyes bright and glossy, full of warmth as he takes his time pushing me closer to the edge. He skims his thumb along my cheekbone and murmurs, "Come for me, wife."

I can finally put a name to this feeling: adoration.

Tension pulls into a tight, electric ball, holding me over the edge as he fills me over and over again. He reaches between us, twisting my nipple, and my vision goes blank as my orgasm crashes around me.

I melt into a puddle against the bed, my head limp on his arm, my chest rising and falling in rapid succession as I try to regain some semblance of composure.

"That was—" I pant. "That was amazing." My eyes widen when I shift and his cock's still buried hard inside me. "You didn't come?"

Jeez, what an ego blow.

"Oh, I will," he chuckles, hands moving to grasp me around the hips and flip me facedown under him. "But now I want to fuck you hard and fast until you can't do anything but scream my name."

His words are a promise, punctuated by his cock filling me to the hilt. The new angle, with my forehead to the mattress and my ass in the air, has my eyes rolling back with the increased pressure.

"You're too big," I breathe.

"Look how well your greedy pussy takes my cock." He slams into me again, none of the slow, languid movements of before. He sets a punishing rhythm, and I struggle to inhale between each thrust.

I cry out when he grips both of my thighs under my ass, lifting me higher, reaching impossibly deeper.

"That's it." His hips snap against my ass, his cock filling me completely.

My fingers dig into the mattress, arms trembling as I try to keep myself in place. The sensation is overwhelming, like the universe is stretching and contracting around us, like gravity itself is pulling us together. His strokes turn jagged, a low groan forming in the back of his throat.

"Fuck." He pulls me so I'm on my knees in front of him, my back to his front, and reaches between my thighs, working my clit as he chases his own release.

I'm too full, too fast, too much... I reach back, gripping onto his hair to hold on as the intensity tightens inside of me like a band, only to snap the second his cum fills me, and I cry out.

He guides me to my stomach, bracketing my shoulders with his arms, and kisses along my back, taking extra care with my scars.

"You okay?"

"Mmokay," I mumble, too tired to lift my face from the pillow.

His chest vibrates with his laugh. "I'll take that as a yes."

I nod, eyes closed, senses blurry as he rolls to the side and pulls me into his arms.

"I have a surprise for you, and I'm not sure if you're going to like it or not."

I snuggle into his chest, breathing in his scent. "Does it involve waffles?"

"Fuck, you're adorable, but I think you should hold off on the waffles until after you see it."

"I dunno, Damon. I'm pretty freaking hungry," I grumble.

"I've got Thomas tied up in the basement of Elysium." His arms tighten as if expecting a volatile reaction.

I take a second to let his words settle over me and tip my chin onto his pec so I can read his face. "What are you going to do with him?"

A slow smirk pulls at the corner of his lips. "Whatever you want."

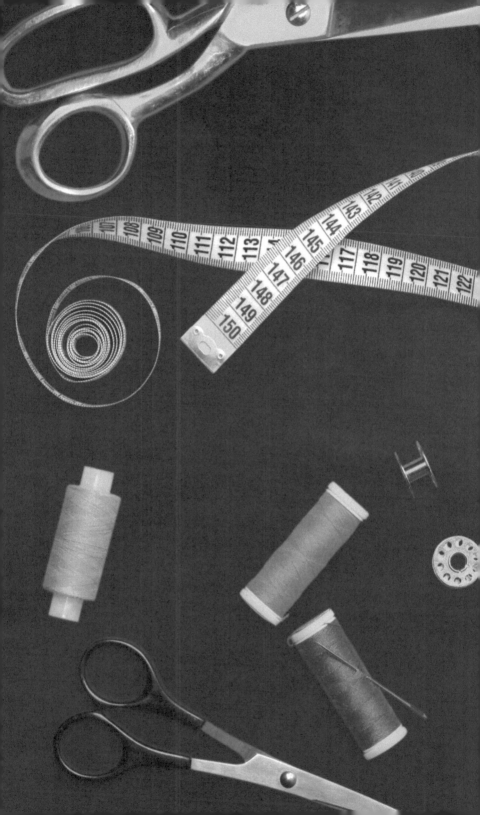

Chapter 38

Misty

DAMON KEPT me in bed most of the day and by the time we pull up to the back of Elysium, the sun's setting, casting the entire area in shadow. Damon grasps my hand before I can get out of the car, his brows pulled low. "Are you sure you want to see this?"

"Not even a little bit." There's a jitteriness to me that's so intense I might actually start crackling with the electricity racing under my skin. My stomach is on its one-hundredth revolution of its mad Ferris wheel between nausea and anticipation. It took Damon over an hour to explain the Order of Saints and the Everette family's role in it. By the end, it was like someone opened a door to an alternate universe. Now, I'm Alice falling down the rabbit hole.

"Anytime you want to go, just tell me. We go. If you want it to stop, I'll stop it." He grimaces. "Unfortunately, it is too late for him to live, but you don't need to have anything to do with that."

Not alive, dead, murdered.

Holy crap! I'm an accessory to kidnapping and murder!

"Am I going to be arrested?"

I can tell he's trying to fight his smile but loses. "I'd like to see the cop that would dare. If that's not comfort enough, we called in our business partners who are particularly skilled in this."

"Skilled in this?" I raise one brow. "Torture?"

"Murder, body disposal, the entire process."

He sounds entirely too chill for the conversation at hand, but there's something about his calmness that has this new reality settling over me.

"What can I expect when we get down there?"

He doesn't belittle my question. "He'll likely be chained, beaten fairly badly, but he'll be conscious."

"Is it going to smell?" I scrunch my nose.

He chokes on a laugh. "Why would it smell?"

"Bodies smell."

"Dead bodies smell. The way Rush likes things set up, he'll have some chemical cleaner there, so it'll likely smell like that."

"And Rush is the torturer guy?" I'm acting way too casual now.

"That's Beck. Rush is more of a handler for the four of them."

"Four?"

"Rush, Beck, Nico, and Raegan. They're from the Gentlemen and Mountsummer."

Damon guides me down the stairs that leads to a hall with several doors. Muffled shouting coming from the first one on the right.

My heart climbs into my throat, and I'm suddenly light-headed. Am I really doing this? Then Damon looks at me, searches my face, and cups my cheeks between his hands.

"You don't have to go in there. You can go about your day knowing he got exactly what was coming to him."

Tempting. Tempting to keep my conscience at least a modicum of clean. Damon's watching me with patience, letting me work this out on my own. But for once, I don't want to overthink it. I don't want to be the perfect girl who does perfect things, that everyone likes.

I'm not that girl, and the man tied up inside that room is who made me this way.

I lift on my toes and press a chaste kiss against Damon's mouth. "My darkness matches your darkness. Right?"

He growls low, tugging me into him, and bites my lower lip hard. "Jesus Christ. You're lucky I don't fuck you right here."

The door swings open behind him. "Are you fucking kidding me?"

Damon eyes the dark-eyed man. He has two guns strapped in a holster around his shoulders, then nods. "Nico."

"Are you seriously trying to fuck your girl while you have someone being tortured?"

A girl with fiery red hair peeks her head around his shoulder. She's in a band T-shirt and short black shorts that show off matching twin guns strapped to her legs. "It's better than that time we did it during the torture."

"Okay, Firecracker. Stop fucking with them." A man wraps his arms around her middle, dwarfing her. His hair is buzzed at the sides, revealing grayscale tattoos that run from his neck all the way down his arms.

She swats him off and holds out her hand to me. "I'm Rae. You ready to torture this asshole?"

I examine her. She's a few inches shorter than me, probably more than a few pounds. But she's not afraid of anyone here; she's not squeamish about what's happening. *She is so fucking cool.*

My hands shake when I take hers, and she gives it an extra squeeze. "Love your hair."

I'd pinned as much of the lavender mass as I could on top of my head. "Thanks. He did it."

I gesture to Damon, who's watching me intently.

"No shit!" Rae claps with genuine excitement.

I can already tell the girls would love her. Just have to hide the guns and torture and stuff.

"I'm sorry to interrupt, Little Thief, but the punk just came to, and I'm not sure how much longer we'll have him. I may have gone a little overboard."

Terror would've overwhelmed me at the sight of the guy, now towering over us, blond hair slicked back, blood splattered over his cheeks, partially covering his multi-colored tattoos. It's the way he's looking at Rae like she hung his literal moon that keeps him from looking scary.

"Are you covered in blood?" The words are out before I can stop them.

There's a dimple in the blond's cheek when he faces me. "You can be, too, if you want."

He winks—freaking winks—before turning back into the room.

Damon's hands hold my upper arms, supporting me. "You know, most people are afraid of them."

I tilt my head back to read his expression. "Should I be afraid?"

"Of Beck? Normally. But you never have to be afraid when you're with me. Nothing bad will ever happen to you."

Lightness fills my chest, like years of weight have been lifted from my shoulders. "Let's see, shall we."

He doesn't let go of my arms when I walk into the room, and I quickly realize why. My knees wobble and knock together at the sight of Thomas. He's in the middle of the space, sitting on a bench, and his arms are strung up with chains to the ceiling.

It's like reality smacks me in the face, and I'm suddenly not sure about any of this anymore.

"Fucking slut. You never could do what you're told." Thomas spits blood out. "Did you tell him how fucking broken you are? How useless you are to him."

Damon tenses behind me, but I'm already closing

the distance between Thomas and me, slamming my palm upward into his nose. I wince at the sickening crunch it makes, but I don't back off.

Beck rolls back on his heels. "Fucking nice." He approaches me, twirling what looks to be a surgeon's blade between his fingers before holding it out to me handle side first. "I hear he gave you some scars. I thought you might like to return the favor."

The metals cool to the touch and weighs more than I expected. "Um...thank you?"

I move around to Thomas's back, who is now thrashing against his chains. I hold the knife awkwardly between us. I don't have the first clue what I'm doing.

"I'll help you." Damon steps into my back, his hand forming around mine.

He brings the knife to Thomas's back but lets me be the one to apply pressure. It's squishy and gross, and I don't like it at all. But I love the way Thomas hisses. How he pleads for me to stop.

In the end, the cut is only a quarter the size he left on me, but I'm filled with an overwhelming sense of satisfaction when he looks up at me with terror.

Maybe he's right. Maybe I am broken. Maybe that's exactly what I'm meant to be.

"Soooo do you want to do the honors, or can I?" Beck asks gleefully.

Rae slaps the back of her hand against his stomach. "Don't freak her out."

Beck leans in, kissing her temple, only for Rush to

kiss the other, and suddenly, their relationship is way more interesting than torturing Thomas.

"Are you guys together?" I ask.

"Yes," Rae replies, eyes slitted as she waits for my reaction.

"Oh my God. You have to meet Mia." I'm too excited to notice the four matching looks of surprise.

Beck leans in and play whispers, "Who's Mia?"

I smile wide with pride. "My friend who has two NHL hockey player boyfriends. I'm sure there's like tips and tricks you guys can talk about."

"She should try it with a third," Nico, who's been silently scowling from the corner, chimes in.

My head jerks back as I look at all of them, and then realization dawns on me.

"You have three hot mafia boyfriends?" I practically squeal the words, and Rae grins.

"Why, are you looking for more?" she asks.

"Back off my wife." Damon's arm crosses my chest possessively.

I glance up, placing a kiss under his chin. "Relax. Just girl talk."

Wet coughing draws my attention back to Thomas, who I magically forgot was here. He's turned a putrid green color as he watches us with narrowed eyes. There's pure hate there, and I know if given the chance, he'd make it so I'd never be safe again.

I hand the blade to Damon. "You do it."

"My pleasure." He stalks toward Thomas, whose eyes are wide with visible terror.

"Please. Don...don't kill me...just let me go." Thomas's voice cracks around the syllables as the distance between the two of them closes.

"You don't want me to kill you?" Damon asks.

"I'll do anything. Whatever you want. You'll never see me again, I swear."

"Okay."

What? The air catches in my lungs. I can't believe Damon would just let him go. I *won't* believe it.

"You just have to do one thing first." Damon slices through the fabric of a struggling Thomas's pants.

"Fuck you. No. Stop—"

Thomas's shouts are morphed into excruciating cries. Nausea crawls up my throat. With Damon's back blocking my line of sight, I can't see exactly what's happening, but from his hand placement and the way Thomas is screaming, I can guess.

Damon stands and looks down at a now limp Thomas. "That wasn't so bad, was it? You want to be free, don't you?"

His only reply is a whimpered plea as Damon's bloody fingers grip his jaw, prying it open before shoving something in.

Thomas chokes and gags until the sharp knife is pressed below his neck, grazing his throat.

"I thought you'd enjoy this? You like putting your dick where it doesn't belong."

I almost feel bad for him. *Almost.*

"Now, chew," Damon commands, voice flat as Thomas thrashes against the grip he has on him and forces his mouth open and closed like a puppet.

The muscles in Thomas's jaw clench as he does before he gags and vomits around his own flesh.

Damon's already out of the way, twisting the handle of the knife in his fingers.

Tears streak down my ex's cheeks. "I did what you said. Now, let me go."

Damon just laughs before bringing the knife back to Thomas's throat. "You really thought I'd let you live? You're lucky I'm going to let you die."

The knife easily cuts through Thomas's skin, and I hold my breath as the iron smell of blood hits my nose, not daring to inhale. The world grows fuzzy and dark around me.

"Fuck. Catch her."

Strong arms circle me, and I'm lifted into the air and pressed into a hard chest.

"I've got you." Damon's familiar cologne scent fills my nose seconds before everything goes black.

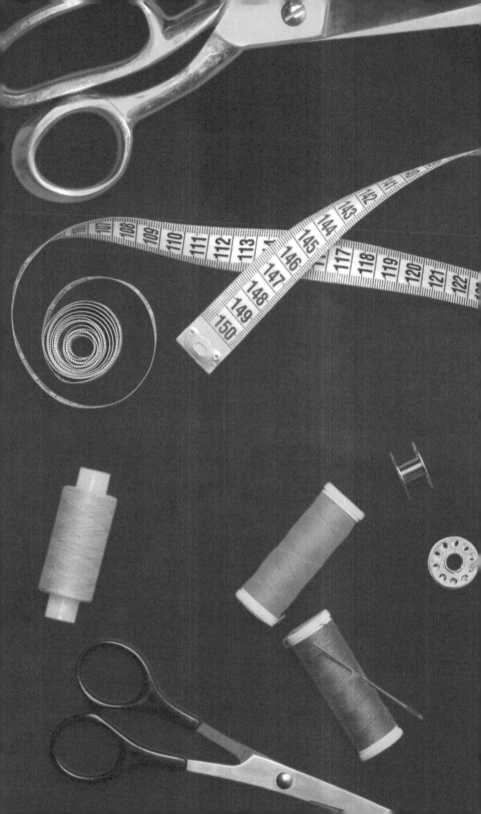

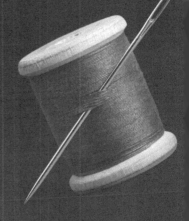

Chapter 39

Misty

THE CRISP ZEST of ginger ale fills my mouth as I take another sip, breathing through my nose. Why did I think I could hang with murderers? I can definitely not hang.

My stomach flips at the thought of all of that blood, and I drop my head between my knees where I'm sitting on one of the large leather lounge chairs in the Everette's private room at Elysium.

"You okay?" Damon asks, rubbing a hand tentatively on my upper back.

No, Damon. I'm not okay. I just participated in my first torture, murder! My hands grow sweaty as I let that settle over me. We'd killed Thomas. Like, if there was ever a guy, he'd be it, but still. I'm just a normal freaking girl.

People joke about killing their ex. In Mia's case, she helped get hers arrested.

We definitely do not murder them.

Well, most of us don't. Rae looked pretty comfortable with the idea. I wonder if Damon will give me her number?

The nausea fades, allowing me to finally look up.

Damon kneels in front of me. His fingers brush a damp piece of hair from my face and tuck it behind my ear. "I'm sorry, I shouldn't have brought you in there."

Honestly, I'm not sure if it was the whole concept of murder so much as it was the overwhelming amount of blood. My stomach rolls at the thought.

I swallow hard. "Does it have to be so messy?"

Damon cocks his head to the side. "Torture? Yes, normally, although there are psychological techniques that are just as effective."

I hold up my hand to stop him. "You know what? Never mind."

The door pad beeps as Matthias enters, a frail older gentleman following closely behind him. His eyes dart skittishly around the room before landing on Damon and immediately looking down at the ground.

"I'm sorry I'm late, Mr. Everette," the man says, lifting the strap of a large leather bag higher on his shoulder.

Damon scowls at him, and I swear the man can feel it because he shifts his weight from side to side. "Dr. Clark. This is Misty Everette, my wife. She's gone through an ordeal tonight and is feeling light-headed."

The doctor looks up, and there's a complete change in him. Now that he understands why he's here in the middle of the night, his confidence has fully returned. I can't help but wonder what other things they've called him out for.

He approaches me, and Damon reluctantly moves a few feet away, his arms crossed over his chest as he watches the doctor work.

"I'm Dr. Clark. So, you're feeling dizzy?" He holds out one of those small pen-like flashlights all medical professionals seem to have and flashes it in my eyes.

"I'm fine, just a bit squeamish from—"

"You don't have to tell me what happened." The doctor cuts me off, glances quickly at my husband, then turns a relatable pale shade of green.

I hold up my can, wanting to put this poor man out of his misery. He looks like if he has to spend a second longer under Damon's stare, he's going to pass out. "Like I said, I'm fine. Just a bit of nausea."

"Misty, you fainted. Let the doctor work," Damon commands, and I raise a defiant brow at him. He matches my expression, and I give up.

I look back at the doctor. "What do you have for me?"

"I'll give you an IV for fluids. That should help," he says with a tentative smile.

"Are you freaking kidding me?" The doctor flinches, and I wince, mouthing, "Sorry," then turn my anger on the man who deserves it. "This is overkill. Let the poor doctor go."

Damon completely ignores my outburst. "Alright. What else?"

The doctor's entire body stiffens at Damon's tone. The man is genuinely terrified, and not for the first time, I wonder what my husband did to earn this type of response. After tonight, I definitely have a better idea. "Food...something to eat will help."

Damon turns his attention on me, his brows pulled together in worry as he searches my face. "What do you feel like eating?"

I shake my head. "Damon, it's like 3:00 a.m. Nothing's open."

"Let me worry about that." He seems entirely too confident in his ability to get what he wants.

"I want a clubhouse and fries from Smitty's Sandwich shop." I smirk. I know for a fact that they aren't open.

"You're going to feel a small pinch," the doctor says a second before stabbing me with a needle.

I flinch at the pain, and Damon prowls forward, his expression dark on the doctor, who is practically trembling in front of me.

"Sorry, I should have expected that." I give the doctor my best comforting smile, and he looks at me like a lifeline.

He hangs a bag of clear liquid on a hook he'd assembled above my head. He adjusts the line that leads to my arm. "Twenty minutes ought to do it."

"You're dismissed. I can handle the rest."

The doctor sighs, and his shoulders relax as he gets up, gathering his things rapidly, then heads to the exit. "Call me whenever you need."

The second the door shuts behind him, I narrow my eyes on Damon. "Did you have to intimidate him? He already came out in the middle of the night!"

"He's on retainer. I assure you, he's paid more than well enough to come out."

Okay, well, that's probably true, but still. "He seemed terrified of you."

"I haven't done anything wrong to this doctor if that's what you're worried about," Damon replies absent-mindedly as he types away at his phone.

"*This* doctor?"

Damon's eyes flick up to mine before returning to his phone. "The last one disappeared after information leaked to the public."

"You are freaking crazy," I gasp.

"You're just figuring that out?"

"You're dangerous." Even as I say the words, they don't taste right.

Damon tucks his phone back into his pocket, closes the distance between us, and gently grazes his thumb along my cheekbone. "Not to you."

"What if I, I don't know...piss you off or something?"

His lip twitches. "I honestly don't see how that's possible."

"Oh yeah? Not even if I hit on one of your brothers?" Why am I doing this? But I know why—some sick part of me likes pushing him as far as I can. Likes the security in somehow knowing he won't snap. Not with me.

His eyes narrow into black slits. "I'll miss them."

A laugh bubbles up in my chest. "You *are* crazy."

He leans in, touching his forehead to mine. "When it comes to you, I'm so much more than crazy."

He's so close each of his breaths fan over my lips, and his sweet scent of cigars and cologne fills my nose. It's like he's pulled the invisible rope tying us together taut, drawing every ounce of my attention. I can't stop myself from tipping my chin up and grazing my mouth against his.

He groans low in his chest, deepening the kiss, stealing all remaining thought.

There's a soft knock on the door, breaking the moment.

"What?" Damon shouts, voice daring whoever interrupted us to enter.

The door opens and Bash walks in, holding a white paper bag with a familiar logo on it. "I have your food, asshat. Do you have any idea what I had to do to get this? You owe me one hundred K."

"Just give me the food." Damon's different around his brothers; the hard edge he wears around anyone else is completely missing. Instead, there's almost a lightness to him.

"Keep your grubby hands off. I did this for my sister, not you." Bash gives me a bright smile that looks entirely too mischievous.

I take the bag from him, careful not to disrupt the IV. Bash's gaze catches on the line, and he turns a cold stare on his older brother.

"What the fuck were you thinking, bringing her there?"

"I was thinking she deserved to have the choice," Damon replies easily.

I take a bite of the clubhouse, the delicious taste of mayo and crispy bacon filling my mouth. I swallow before saying, "He asked. I can tell you, I've been through worse."

Both men's eyes flash to me, brows pulled together. Bash looks like a younger carbon copy.

A muscle ticks in Damon's jaw, and it's several seconds before he says anything. "We killed that bastard way too fast."

Put plainly like that, my throat grows dry. "We killed him."

Damon steps closer, a look of concern pinching his face. "We did."

I search inside myself for any regret and come up empty. "I...I don't feel bad."

Damon kisses the top of my head. "Good."

"I'm going to leave you two lovebirds alone. Take better care of my sister, asshat."

The brothers continue talking, but their voices are fuzzy as my brain twists and turns the words *lovebirds* around. And the way Damon didn't contradict them.

"Put me down!" I screech for the fifth time since Damon lifted me out of the car and cradled me to his chest, carrying me up the stairs.

"We're almost there, Nymph." His chuckle reverberates through my side, and I give up, letting him carry me to our bedroom.

I sigh when he lays me down on the soft mattress. "I had no idea I could miss my bed this much."

"Not a night owl?" he asks, but it's clear from his tone he already knows the answer. He seems to know way more about me than he should.

I go to pull the blanket up, but Damon stops me. He holds out a worn navy T-shirt.

"Arms up."

I sigh and lift my arms, too tired to form a reply. Once I'm safely tucked into bed, he chucks his shirt and pants, then climbs in beside me, pulling me into his side. His chest rises and falls with each breath, and the steady sound of his heartbeat starts to lull me into sleep.

"When I was sixteen, a rival family thought they could take over for mine and tried to wipe us all out."

Damon's voice is barely a whisper, and I draw circles on his chest to show I'm listening.

"They killed my father in front of me, but they took my brothers." His voice is raw, and my heart aches for him.

He spins my wedding ring around my finger, and it takes several moments before he continues. "That's when I killed my first man, and my tenth, and my twentieth. That's when I learned that I needed to be something dark in order to keep my family safe. To keep you safe."

His entire body stiffens.

"I understand if, after tonight, you may not want to be around me, but I will not let you go," he says, voice pitch-black.

I glance up at him. The pink light from the sunrise tints his skin. I suddenly realize I don't want him to, and that one-year timeline ticks in the back of my brain.

"My darkness matches your darkness. If you're broken, then I am too," I say.

The breath leaves his lungs, and he tugs me closer, his arm a rigid band like he's afraid I'll shift away in my sleep.

We stay there, me tracing the intricate lines of his tattoos and him playing with my hair, until his hand stills and his breathing evens out.

The growing light from the window highlights his features. He looks almost boyish in his sleep. Like the weight of the world has been lifted off him.

"Stop staring and go to sleep." His arms tighten, and he tucks my head below his chin, almost immediately letting out a small snore.

I'm in the arms of one of the most feared men, and all I can think of is how freaking adorable he is.

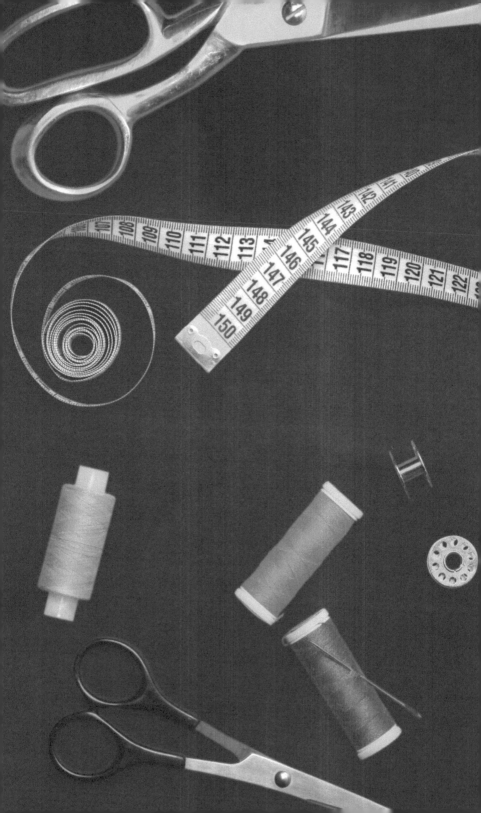

Chapter 40

Misty

SUNLIGHT PRESSES into my closed eyes, forcing me out of sleep. Groggily, I pull myself awake, cracking one eye open. Damon's already watching me, his eyes soft as they dance over my face. His fingers graze over the curve of my waist, sending shivers through me. I'd fallen asleep wrapped in his arms, and from the state of us now, it appears he never let me go.

I wipe my mouth, suddenly mortified.

"You're cute when you drool," he says softly into my hair.

I groan, burying my face into his chest. "You could've just kept that to yourself."

"Where's the fun in that?" His words vibrate against my cheek, and his steady heart beats in my ear. I could stay just like this, wrapped in his arms forever, if he'd let me.

Pushing those thoughts down, I ask, "What time is it?"

"Ten."

"Oh shit." I shoot up, already scrambling to get dressed when he pulls me back into him.

"Where do you think you're going?" he grumbles into the back of my neck, his fingers lifting my shirt over my rib cage.

"It's Monday! I'm late."

He guides me onto my back and climbs over me, placing kisses along my collarbone. "Did you forget I'm your boss? I already let them know we'll be out for the next few days."

"You can't just do that," I scoff.

"I own the company. I can do whatever I want." He travels lower, placing wet, open-mouth kisses down my chest.

I gasp when he sucks my nipple into his mouth, twirling his tongue around the already hardened peak.

"Damon. I can't just skip work."

"That's it, Nymph. Say my name." His teeth graze my nipple, and heat pools between my thighs. He moves to my other nipple, showing it the same amount of attention. I can't stop myself from arching off the bed into his hot touch.

My thighs wrap around his hips, and the hard ridge of his cock nudges the sensitive spot through my panties.

He groans and bites my nipple when I rock my hips

upward, pressing us closer. "Patience. I haven't had my breakfast yet."

His words send a shiver down my spine, goose bumps following after his descent between my thighs. He runs his nose over me and takes a deep breath. "Fuck, wife. I'm going to eat you every morning."

His promise has me dripping, and I thread my fingers through his hair, encouraging him.

He hums in approval and slides my underwear down my thighs, lifting only enough to remove them completely.

His tongue runs up my slit, and there's a low rumble from his throat. Dark eyes meet mine. "I've never tasted anything so sweet. I'm already addicted to you."

Before I can respond, he's lifted my hips higher, angling me so he can dive his tongue into me. I squirm at the sensation, both needing more and overwhelmed.

No matter how many times he touches me, I can't get used to it. Can't get enough.

He replaces his tongue with two fingers, stretching me, and sucks on my clit.

"Damon." I plead for something I don't understand.

He sucks harder, adding a third finger, driving me higher over the edge. My body is crackling with tension as every muscle tightens in preparation. Damon bites my clit gently, sending the waves of my orgasm over me, pulling me under with each ripple of pleasure.

When I collapse onto the bed, body languid, he watches me with slitted eyes, licking me again.

"Sensitive...too sensitive." I jolt, gripping his hair to pull him up, but he doesn't move.

He chuckles as he tortures me. "I'll make you come again."

"You can't."

"Don't underestimate me, wife." His tongue delves into me, then slowly ascends to my clit before doing it again.

"I've never come this close together before." Even as I say it, my clit begins to throb under his touch.

A sound of pure satisfaction rumbles through him. "Good girl."

He's slow, soft, purposeful, never stopping his assault.

It's only when I'm moaning that he increases his tempo, listening to my every sound.

I feel hollow, needy, like my entire body is going to combust if I don't have him inside me. "Fuck me, Damon."

He groans and slips his fingers back inside me, coating them in my wetness before pulling out and circling my back hole. I shift, but he holds my hips firmly in place with one hand as he applies more pressure.

"No one's had you here?" He circles his fingers until I'm coated and wet.

"No," I breathe, my body completely frozen.

"I'm going to fuck this hole, and you're going to love it, but you'll have to wait. I'm going to take my time with you, when I do." His words shoot fire through me, and I come apart as he presses deeper, breaching the rim slightly. I tremble in his arms at the force, my head fuzzy.

Damon's cock notches to my entrance, and I reach between us to guide him in. He captures both my hands and pins them over my head, keeping me in place.

"Patience, needy girl." He swirls his cock, coating it, then sinks into me painfully slowly, filling me inch by inch.

The pressure is all-consuming, taking over all of my senses.

Damon groans when he's fully seated, pausing only for a second before pulling back and burying himself into my pussy.

"Your pussy's made for me. Squeezing me so good." His gaze is locked with mine, soft and attentive as he strokes me from within. If I didn't know better, I'd say there's adoration there. A possessiveness that makes me feel owned.

He drops his forehead to mine, cock still moving slowly, and his ragged breaths tickle my lips. "You're made for me."

He captures my mouth in a demanding kiss, sweeping his tongue over the back of my teeth, pushing it deeper until he's tasted every inch. His hips rock faster, the head of his cock hitting me in the perfect spot each time.

A new kind of tension builds, a deeper, more primal feeling as he works me over and over until he's pounding into me, chasing his own release. I'm so close, my hips coming up to meet his.

He grips my jaw, holding my face. "I want to see you come on my cock. I want you to know exactly who's owning this perfect pussy."

He lets go of my jaw, but I don't dare look away as he presses his thumb to my clit. I'm lost to his control, his body directing mine.

"Come for me, Misty," he commands, and I break apart as his hot cum fills me.

"Jesus Christ," I whisper, unable to breathe deep enough to talk.

Damon brushes the hair out of my face and kisses my forehead. "You're mine now, Nymph. There's no turning back."

I almost believe him.

By the time I'm out of the shower, Damon's standing over my stove with a frying pan in his hand. My mouth waters at the sight of him. He didn't bother getting dressed. Instead, he left himself on display in nothing but a pair of black boxer briefs. I bite my lip as my gaze travels over his back, watching the muscles shift as he works, then catch on the perfect curve of his ass.

I make a low sound, and Damon turns to me with a knowing smirk. It's so relaxed and playful it steals my breath away.

"I like you watching me."

My cheeks grow hot, and his smile only widens.

Damon slides a pancake onto a plate and turns off the stove before covering them with maple syrup. He takes a seat at the dining table, placing the plate in front of him. "Come here."

I take a tentative step toward him, and he raises his brow in challenge. I huff out a breath and close the distance between us, only to have him pull me down onto his lap.

"This is unnecessary," I grumble, pretending that I don't love the easy affection.

"I assure you, it's completely necessary." He nuzzles the side of my neck. "Now, eat."

I cut a piece with my fork and place it on my tongue, moaning deep in my throat as the sweet syrup coats my taste buds. "Oh my God. Is this real Canadian syrup?"

"I had it brought over last night."

I can't even wrap my head around how much something like that would've cost.

He reaches for my hand not holding the fork and twirls my wedding ring between his fingers. "This looks good on you," he says, then slips his fingers between mine.

The moment's so intimate I can't help but meet his eyes, needing to see if he feels the way I do. His gray gaze meets mine, a small curve to his lips.

I've never wished to be able to read minds more than I do right now.

375

His phone buzzes, breaking the moment, and he reaches across the table to grab it without letting me go.

"What do you want?" His gruff greeting doesn't seem to bother whoever's talking on the other end.

"How did they find out?" Damon barks into the phone.

I stiffen, and he kisses my temple. "Family meeting at Massimo's restaurant at five."

"Make it happen."

He ends the call and trails his fingers up and down my spine. "I can already tell you're worried."

"Did someone find out about Thomas?" I'm almost afraid to ask.

"Yes, his cousin did. We've had a truce with that family for over a decade."

It's hard to swallow. "I'm sorry. This is all my fault."

Damon grips my chin. "Listen to me clearly. It's not your fault. Thomas was going to die whether you were involved or not."

"If I hadn't told you—"

"You really think I wouldn't have flipped the world over to find out what happened after seeing your scars? You're an Everette. We take care of each other, and no one fucks with us."

"So, is there going to be some kind of turf war?"

Damon lets out a breathy laugh. "We showed them long ago what happens when someone decides to go against us. And that was when we were still boys. No one would dare risk it again."

"So what happens?"

"Meet with my brothers. Show a united front, then we'll set up a meeting with Anthony Ricci."

"Isn't that dangerous?"

He tilts his head, a darkness taking over his eyes. "Yes, for him."

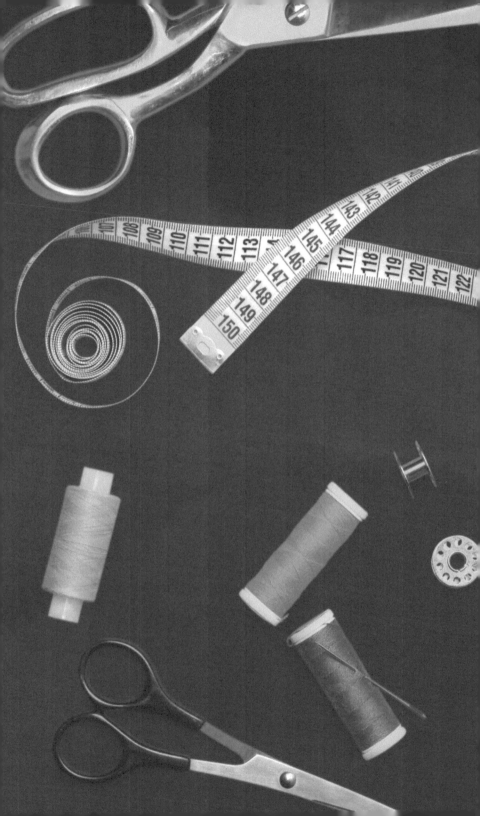

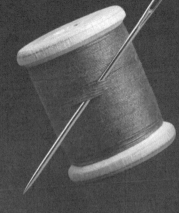

Chapter 41

Misty

"You're a fucking asshole," Xander says the second we sit down at the table with them.

I move closer to Damon, who wraps an arm around me and replies, "It needed to be done quickly."

"You don't think we wouldn't want to be involved? She's our fucking sister."

Wait? He's not mad that we got caught. Is he mad that he didn't get invited?

Damon tugs me closer, and I rest my head against him like we weren't having a casual chat about murder. "You were out of town."

"I would have come back if I'd known."

"It's so sweet that you care about our sis." Bash cuts into the brothers bickering. He motions toward me. "How are you feeling? Late-night snack do the trick?"

"Fucking Bash was there?" Xander practically

explodes, and Damon leans over the table, the tension in the room crackling.

I pipe up, trying to break the moment. "I'm honestly not sure I could've handled one more person."

"See? Relax," Bash says and waves down the server with a wink. She has pretty brown hair swept up into a ponytail, and from the way she's looking back at him, she's definitely interested.

She goes around the table, taking our orders. It's not lost on me that there are no prices on the menus, and it's mostly written in Italian.

Damon whispers into my ear. "I'm getting chicken with risotto. Does that sound good?"

"Perfect." Grateful for his help, I lean in and kiss the edge of his jaw.

Xander lets out a low whistle, and heat flushes my neck, settling into my cheeks, embarrassed by my impromptu public display of affection. I'm not ashamed, but this is definitely not the environment to be climbing all over my husband.

I go to move away, but Damon holds me with one hand and kisses my temple. "Let them be jealous."

The server is staring at the two of us, eyes wide and mouth slightly parted.

"We will have the risi e tochi."

She clears her throat. "Great choice."

"And for you?" She's looking right at Matthias, but he's staring off across the restaurant, eyes narrowed.

There's an unmistakable chill coming off him, and I'll be forever grateful that I'm not the one he's looking at.

"He'll have the same as me." Bash answers for him, looking concerned. "And a bottle of red."

"Of course. I'll bring the house's finest."

Once she's gone, I'm able to follow Matthias's line of sight, and it becomes clear what's caught his attention. There's a stunning woman in deep conversation with the man across from her. The low light bounces off her light brown hair, giving it an almost halo-like appearance, and she's wearing a dress perfectly tailored to mold her body. They're definitely on a date, and from the way they're leaning toward each other, it's going well.

Damon spots what we're looking at. "That's Scarlet Laurent. Her family was associated with the Order of Saints."

I don't like the sound of that. "What happened to her family?"

Matthias doesn't look at me when he answers. "We did."

The things Damon told me about the Everette brothers flash through my mind, but I struggle to find an ounce of pity. If her family was wrapped up in the failed takeover, then they got exactly what they deserved. Damon will always believe his hands are stained black, but looking at him with his family, I know he did what needed to be done. He not only stopped the coup but made it clear to everyone the risk of trying it again.

The woman laughs, and the muscle in Matthias's cheek twitches as he grinds his teeth together. It makes a faint sound, and I'm honestly worried he's going to break one. He gets up from the table and takes five steps toward them before turning around and walking out of the restaurant.

The woman looks up as if she felt his stare, but when she doesn't see anyone, her attention goes back to the man in front of her.

"Is he going to be okay?" I ask, looking between the guys.

It's Damon who answers. Bash and Xander whisper quietly, in their own little world.

"She was involved when the boys were kidnapped. We know she wasn't a part of their plan, but Matthias hasn't spoken to her since."

The server comes around, pouring our drinks, and I take a sip of the tart liquid. "He's not acting like someone not interested."

"None of us knows exactly what Matthias went through during his time confined. We do know he came out despising her, but when we pushed, he shut us down."

"Speaking of cranky Everettes," Bash cuts in. "When are you going to let our mother out? She's well past cantankerous."

Xander chokes on a laugh. "More like a raging bitch."

The last time I saw the Everette matriarch, she'd been doing everything in her power to make me feel small. She'd seen me as the outsider I am and wanted to be sure I knew it.

Damon leans over the table, his tone leaving no room for questioning. "She can come out when she learns to apologize properly."

"Fuck, I want to be your wife. Doesn't need to be incest or anything. Like we don't need to fuck, but seriously, can you protect me like that?" Bash says, causing Xander to spit out his wine.

Damon raises a brow. "Behave."

Both boys swallow, suddenly looking significantly younger than their early twenties. Heat burns at my cheeks at what Bash had implied.

Shame makes me correct him. "You are aware that the marriage is temporary, right? I assumed you'd know."

My fingers dig into the fabric of my skirt to hide the fact that they're shaking, and Damon gives me a reassuring squeeze and scowls at his brothers.

His brothers laugh in shocked surprise.

"We know exactly how this is going to play out." Bash winks. "Sister."

Chapter 42

Damon

"Sir, if you could sign here, here and here." The head of accounting points toward the papers on my desk. He's flagged where I need to sign with yellow flags.

Normally, I'd take the time to read the document front to back, but I can't take my eyes off Misty sitting in the cubicle on the other side of my office window. Her hair is curled into soft lavender waves, and it brushes over her shoulders every time she moves. She tucks her hair behind her ear, revealing the long column of her neck, and my mouth waters at the desire to mark her.

Before I left, I made sure she was covered in them, using my mouth and teeth to leave a visible trace on her that no man could mistake for anything other than what it is. A claim.

She runs a pen over her bottom lip, and my cock instantly hardens. It's been three fucking days since I've seen my wife, and now being so close without touching her is torture.

I spent the entire plane ride home from Montana picturing her laid out in bed waiting for me, but she'd already left for work by the time I reached our apartment.

I know for a fact that I'd cut her workload down to revolve around me, but I'm not surprised Misty filled her schedule against my wishes.

I'd been like a lost puppy when I arrived at the office, only to find out she was in a meeting. Every second that delayed me from feeling her soft skin, hearing her greedy moans, and tasting her on my tongue was pure agony.

"Sir?" The head of accounting clears his throat.

I take my eyes off her and sign the papers, not bothering to read a single word. I am a drowning man, and every glimpse of her is a sip of air.

"Is that all?" I hand him back the papers.

"Y...yes. I'll get these sent off right away."

He leaves without another word from me, and I cuss low when Misty's no longer at her desk. I scan the room, but there's no sign of her fuchsia dress.

Just as I stand to go find her, my phone rings. "Fucking Christ."

I sit back down and answer the phone. "What."

There's a deep laugh.

"Is that the way you treat your new business partner?" Maverick replies.

"I was just with you," I grumble, so done with today

already. We met through a mutual acquaintance years ago who thought, since we were both influential families with four brothers, we'd get along.

They couldn't have been more wrong at first. The Blackwoods don't bother coming out to the city, instead spending their time on the ranch, but when some shit went down last summer, we'd grown closer. A fucking suit bastard tried to run them out of town. I guess you could say we bonded over ruining that man's life.

"There's a few things I want to go over while they're fresh."

"The contract is nonnegotiable." I drop my head, giving in to the fact that I can't chase my wife every minute of every day.

"I fucking know that. I wrote it. Now, shut up and listen for once in your goddamn life."

Prickles run along my spine as I bristle at his tone, but I've been around him long enough to know it's not personal. "I'm tired. Make it quick."

"Stayed out late with the boys, did you? I thought you were married?"

"I am married," I cut in, not liking what he implied.

"Sorry, didn't mean to piss you off there. Point made."

He continues to talk, but I stop listening, my eyes riveted on Misty stepping into my office. She locks the door behind her and hits the automatic privacy blinds.

"I have to g—"

Misty stops me with a shake of her head. It's the

mischievous smile that has me obeying. I think I'd do anything she told me to so long as she smiled at me like that.

She walks around my desk, and I immediately reach for her, needing to feel her under my palm, but she slaps my hand away and raises a brow. Message loud and clear.

She rolls my chair back a few inches and comes to stand between my thighs. I grip my phone in one hand and the edge of the desk in the other to keep myself from touching her. Misty's playing, and I want to see what she's up to. I want to encourage her to take whatever she wants.

"Did you hear me?"

Fuck, what did he say? "You wanted to know about the term?"

"Yes..."

Luckiest guess of my life. Misty places both hands on my thighs, nails digging through my deep gray pants, then lowers herself to her knees.

I groan, eyes hot on her as she looks up at me with round, playful eyes.

"You sick or something?"

Her hands stop moving, and she looks at the phone, mouthing, "Talk."

"Yes, something is getting to me."

She smiles and works my button open with her delicate fingers. I clench my fist when she pulls my cock out and runs her tongue up the length before taking the head into her mouth. Warm, wet perfection as she takes me deeper, working me expertly into the back of her throat. She pulls up and swirls her tongue around the tip before taking me all the way in.

Every muscle in my body clenches as she works me over. I can feel my release building in my tightening balls, and I grunt through clenched teeth.

"Fuck, you really are sick. Go home and get that sweet wife of yours to take care of you."

My wife grips my balls, tugging lightly as she works my cock. I groan low, so fucking close to coming. "Good idea."

I hang up, gripping her hair in my hand and pushing her down, forcing her to take more of me. She gives a pleased moan that's nearly my undoing.

"You take my cock so well. Look at your pretty lips sucking me down."

She grips my base and works me simultaneously with her mouth.

Tension builds to a peak, and I run my thumb along her throat. "You're going to swallow every last drop."

She nods and takes me impossibly deeper, her moan vibrating through me, setting off my release. She swallows my cum as it pours down her throat, not releasing me until she's taken every last drop.

It's dripping from the edge of her lips when she pulls back, and I sweep it with my thumb, then press it between her teeth. She takes care to clean it off before releasing it.

"You are going to be the death of me, wife."

She just smirks. "I've been dying to do that."

I growl and swipe my things off my desk, lifting her and placing her facedown against the hardwood. Her perfect ass is in the air, and I don't waste time pushing the hem of her skirt above her hips, revealing a lace thong that matches her dress.

I spread her legs wider and trace the seam, the fabric darker where she's soaked through it, and slide them down her thighs before pocketing them.

I kneel behind her and get a good look. Her pretty pink pussy's gleaming, practically begging for my touch.

Misty starts to twitch as I stare at her, uncomfortable with being on display this long. I bite her bare ass hard enough to leave a mark, and she squeals in shock.

"Do not move. You tortured me. Now, it's my turn."

She freezes, but goose bumps rise below my palms. "Good girl."

I lean in and trace her seam with my tongue, gripping her ass to spread her wider. Her taste fills my mouth, going right to my head, and my touch turns ravenous. I fuck her with my tongue until she's whimpering and grinding against my desk, chasing her release.

"Don't stop," she whines as I pull back and stand behind her.

"The only place you're coming is on my cock." I line up my cock and fill her in one thrust. We both moan as I stretch her wide around me. I place a kiss where I know her scar is beneath the thin fabric of her dress. "*Fuck. You're so tight.*"

I pump into her, slowly building my rhythm, not giving a single shit who hears us. I want to make her scream my name, beg me over and over for her release. Only then will I give it to her.

But I know she wouldn't like that, so I put that in the back of my mind for at home and reach around her hip, circling her clit with my fingertips.

She arches off the desk, pushing into me as her cries turn ragged. "Yes. God yes. That feels good."

I bite her shoulder and fuck her harder. "I like when you call me God."

"Fuck," she hisses, her pussy pulsing around me as she orgasms, dragging me over the edge with her. My second release hits me just as hard as the first, and I have to set both palms on the table on either side of her to keep myself stable.

I push the hair that's sticking to her face behind her ear and kiss her temple.

"I missed you." She whispers it tentatively, and it's like she reached into my chest and gripped my heart.

I turn her so she's sitting facing me and capture her mouth, wanting to taste her words, then drop my forehead to hers. I never want to be apart from her again. "Next time, you come with me."

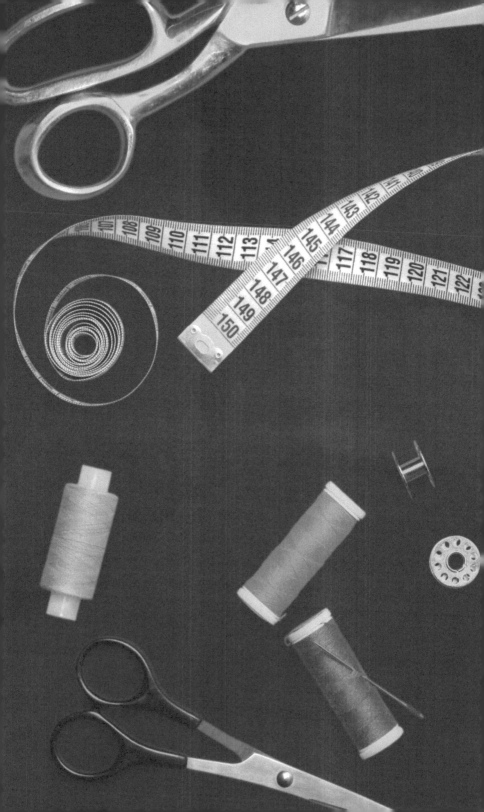

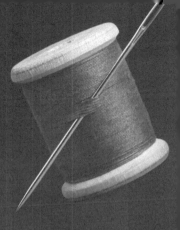

Chapter 43

Misty

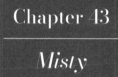

"Dɪᴅ ʏᴏᴜ ᴡᴀɴᴛ ᴀ—" Whatever I was about to ask evaporates from my mind when I spot Damon standing in front of the mirror in my small bathroom. His hair's slicked back, wet from his shower, and I follow a rivulet as it makes its way down the curves and valleys of his chest and disappears into the towel slung low around his hips.

My cheeks heat as I slowly make my way back up, taking in every detail of his tanned, cut body. His muscles twitch under my gaze, and he leans into me when I reach out to touch him.

"If you keep looking at me like that, I'm never getting out of here."

The reminder of him leaving has the muscles in my back tightening, and I cross my arms in front of me. "What if I said I didn't want you to go?"

Matthias called an hour ago to let us know he'd set

up a meeting with the Ricci family tonight. Everything in me screamed to not let him go. That there's no way it's not dangerous. Damon, on the other hand, doesn't seem worried at all.

He moves toward me, cupping my face between both palms. "It's adorable when you worry about me, but I promise I'll be fine. No one would dare start anything in the Vaults."

I let out a breath and lean against the doorway, not exactly happy about this whole thing. I didn't like that he was even having to do this because of me, no matter how pleased I am that he'd gone a little crazy after seeing my scars. 'Cause let's face it, that's hot.

Damon kisses between my brows before turning back to the sink and using a round bristle brush to lather shaving cream and apply it to his face. The sweet smell of sandalwood fills my nose, and I can't help but move in closer.

I follow his hand as he drags the blade of his razer down in a perfect line along his cheeks. I have no idea what's overcome me, but I'm suddenly asking, "Can I shave you?"

Damon smiles, the cream on his face making him look funny as he says, "Is this an attempt to slit my throat with a blade?"

"I...I don't know. Forget it." My neck and cheeks heat with embarrassment, and I take a step toward the exit.

Damon wraps his hand around my waist, stilling me as he holds out the razor. "Have you done this before?"

"No." I bite my lip because I'm starting to question this entire idea.

"Okay." He sits on the edge of the tub, spreading his knees, then gestures me between them.

I bite my lip as the edge of his towel spreads, revealing more of his thighs, but not quite high enough to see what I want.

"Eyes up here, Little Nymph." Damon's smirking at me, and I blush again.

I huff. "This is totally not my fault. If I was just in a towel, you know you'd be looking."

Damon's eyes go dark, and he catches the bottom of my dress, tugging me closer. There's a gleam to his eyes that I don't quite make out until it's too late.

White lather is spread across my exposed chest, my low neckline providing plenty of real estate for his assault. I squeal and tug his ears backward, trying to break free, but both his arms are wrapped around me, locking me in place.

He laughs, full and deep, and the smile he lands on me takes my breath away. His normally cloudy gray eyes are crystal clear, capturing all the light in the room as he looks up at me. My heart swells in my chest, my lungs struggling to fill against my tight rib cage. I think I'd do anything to have him look at me like this again.

Damon cups the back of my neck and pulls my lips to his. I don't even care that the taste of shaving cream fills my mouth or that it covers my cheeks. Not when he's kissing me so gently, owning me to my very soul.

He doesn't let go until he's explored every inch of my mouth, and still, his eyes don't leave mine.

"You are beautiful." His voice is reverent. He grabs the towel from the bar and proceeds to wipe off my cheeks, down my neck, and over the swells of my cleavage.

His touch makes my body come alive, and the realization that I love Damon slams into me. I thought I'd been smart enough to protect my heart, but this man's been smashing down any wall I put between us. I don't say the words. Can't say them. Not when all of this will end, but that doesn't stop my heart from aching.

"You going to start, or are you just going to keep staring? I'm okay with both," Damon says smugly.

I roll my eyes and hold the razor to his cheek, not nearly as confident now that I'm about to start. His hand covers mine, and he slowly guides the blade to his skin, dragging it downward, showing me how to do it.

He lets go of me, and we're silent as I concentrate, taking care not to nick him. His breaths fan over my fingers as I make my way around his mouth in short, controlled strokes. The air feels thick around us, tension building with each second he trusts his face in my hands. Shit. I need to get a hold of myself.

I push distracting thoughts about him aside, switching them with the upcoming auction for Mia's charity. I'd demanded being able to keep planning it, even after Damon had pulled an overbearing move and changed my job to his personal PR. He'd agreed to his brother and him participating in the auction, and at the time, I'd been thrilled, but now I'm less than happy to have someone else bid on a date for my husband.

The razor scratches a bit too hard, and Damon's eyes slit open, peering up at me with one raised brow.

I let out a breath. "So I was thinking. Since we're publicly married now. I don't think you should be bid on at Mia's gala."

"You'll be the one that wins. Just bid whatever it takes."

I make a displeased sound in response, still not happy about the bidding itself.

He hums in the back of his throat. "You're cute when you're jealous."

I hold the razor up like a threat, and he just laughs.

He strokes his thumb over my jaw. "Always be like this with me."

My legs go weak, and I place a hand on his shoulder for balance. Trying to play it off like he's not absolutely destroying me with his words, I play along. "You're obsessed with me, aren't you?"

He pulls my face to his, his lips rubbing against mine. "Something like that."

Chapter 44

Damon

My brothers are already in our suite when I arrive at the club. All three of them are dressed in all-black suits, none of their playfulness on display.

"Are you ready for this?" Matthias asks.

"Do you think Anthony will cause problems?"

Matthias runs his hand through his hair. "I doubt it. I looked into him, and he wasn't close with his cousin. Seems like he was doing a family favor bringing him here."

I nod. "Good, I'd hate to have to kill him."

Xander smiles. "You know we're down for a war for our sister."

I look between my brothers, none of them contradicting him.

We head down the stairs into the large open room below. This time, only Anthony Ricci is waiting for us.

As the heir to his family seat, he's been well trained in this game we're playing.

My brothers filter in after me, flanking my sides in a show of power. "Anthony, to what do I owe the honor?"

"You killed my cousin," Anthony responds, but his posture doesn't change, still as relaxed as when we walked in.

I tilt my head. I know for a fact we didn't leave evidence behind. He could be bluffing. "Did I?"

Anthony tucks his hand into his pockets and looks me over. "I just wanted to tell you that I'm not looking for Thomas anymore. We were never close, and to be honest, he was always an asshole."

Tension eases from my muscles as he corroborates Matthias's sources. Thomas would be a stupid man to go to war for, but you never know when pride will blind someone. Especially someone who was born with a gold spoon in their mouth and has probably never been told *no* in their lives.

"Asshole? Smart choice not to go looking for him," I warn. I'm careful not to admit to killing him. It's one thing to brush off suspicion and another to let a full-blown confession slide. I know better than anyone that in this world, a slight against your family is one you can't ignore.

Anthony lowers his gaze in respect. "The Ricci family stands firmly beneath you. I truly appreciate you meeting with me today."

Something in his tone makes me uneasy, but I can't

expect him to be pleased in this situation. "You are dismissed."

"Congratulations on your recent marriage. A very unconventional pairing," Anthony responds.

Electricity flickers in my veins at the thinly veiled insult. "Be careful speaking about my wife, or you may end up finding your cousin."

His face blanches, and he swallows. "Thanks again for meeting me."

I watch as he practically flees up the stairs, and we don't speak until I hear the door slam after him.

I look to Matthias. "Watch him. That was too easy."

"Already on it."

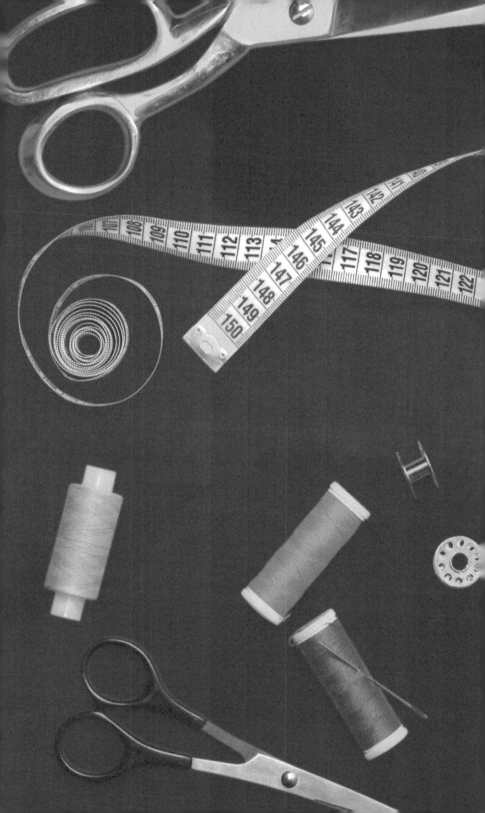

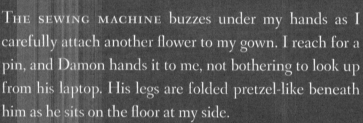

Chapter 15

Misty

THE SEWING MACHINE buzzes under my hands as I carefully attach another flower to my gown. I reach for a pin, and Damon hands it to me, not bothering to look up from his laptop. His legs are folded pretzel-like beneath him as he sits on the floor at my side.

"You know, you really don't have to do this," I say, taking the pin from him.

He's wearing sweatpants and a hoodie, his casual appearance almost as attractive as his suits. All I want to do is curl up in his lap and let his warmth seep into my bones.

"You wouldn't let me buy you a dress" is his only response.

"That's because I like to make them." The buzz of the machine stops as I move the fabric.

"I know." Damon grins and hands me another flower. "Hence the helping."

A warm, fuzzy feeling fills my chest that I try to capture and put in a box to take out and look at after. After he stops looking at me that way, after all of this is over.

If I'd known love would hurt this badly, I'd have done a better job at avoiding it. Not that he'd given me a choice. I swear, he'd come at my defenses in a strategized attack. I didn't stand a chance.

I change the topic to something that's been rolling in my mind. "The girl in the restaurant. The one Matthias couldn't stop staring at. Have you ever tried to intervene there?"

Damon hums, then cracks his neck, kicking out his long legs in front of him. "We did once. It's been obvious for years there's something between them. Even if it's hate. We thought if we stuck them together, maybe they'd sort it out."

Curiosity at an all-time high, I ask, "What happened?"

"Mother invited her over to spend the weekend with us. She'd been on her own for a year, and all of the families had done their best to include her."

"And it didn't go well?"

"Not at all. Matthias disappeared for over two weeks. No one could get a hold of him. He didn't talk to us for a month when he finally showed back up. That's the last time I've tried to interfere. Some things are better left alone."

I'm wrapped in warm arms and pulled off my feet the second I walk into the small diner, the smell of grease and fries instantly filling my nose.

"I freaking missed you." Sidney gives me a tight squeeze before letting me go. We'd all gone to the same university, but she'd been more Piper's friend than mine. Over the years though, Piper, Mia, Sidney, and I had formed a close friendship, even with the distance between us.

"When did you get in?" I ask and pull out a chair, taking a seat at the table with the other girls.

"Just a few hours ago. We went to Mia's place to drop off our stuff first. Then, you know, the boys had to bond for a bit."

Mia hums. "They are freaking adorable when they get like that."

"Whatever, I'm pretty sure it was just the four of them giving each other crap on who had better stats this season," Piper chimes in between sips of a large strawberry milkshake.

I eye it appreciatively. I'm definitely getting one of those. Somehow, all three of these girls landed professional hockey players who, as it turns out, are absolutely obsessed with them.

We order and chat, catching up on everyone's day to day. Even though Mia, Piper, and I live in the same city, I don't see them nearly enough.

Once the food arrives, I take a bite of my burger, the juicy taste filling my mouth.

Piper sets down her cup with a loud clack and looks right at me. "Did you know you're practically glowing? Looks like everything's going well with that husband of yours."

I choke on my burger, taking large gulps of water to try to wash it down. "I took your advice and learned to enjoy the time."

Mia claps her hands together. "Hallelujah. It's about time." She looks me over. "There's something more, isn't there? Piper's right— you've got this lightness to you I've never seen before."

It's not like I can explain Damon helping me kill my rapist ex really helped alleviate my past trauma. I take another bite, running through anything I can to explain the change in me. There's a truth that I'd rather keep to myself, but I know there's no chance I'm hiding it. I'd been privileged to see the ups and downs of their relationships. It's only fair they see some of mine.

I shrug. "I like him."

Sidney gives me a warm smile. "Honey, you more than like him."

I can feel my cheeks heat and take a deep breath. "I love him."

The girls all make pleased sounds, but they cut off when they see my face. I blink back the burn in my eyes. It's not like I didn't know this is how it would all go down.

I swallow hard, and my voice cracks when I say, "Remember, it's only for a year."

Sidney's grin grows impossibly wider. "Tell me you learned from my mistake."

She's definitely referring to her leaving Jax because she had to. Thank God that man was head over heels and didn't let her go.

I shrug, doing my best to appear unaffected. "A deal's a deal."

"Wait." Piper leans towards me. "Wasn't it your rule?"

My brows scrunch together as I process that. "What?"

"You both had rules, right? Wasn't that yours?" Piper says, her smile growing wider.

Some of the tension releases in my chest, and the tempting feeling of hope replaces it.

Mia places her hand over mine. "He never mentioned a timeline, did he?"

"No," I breathe, a floating feeling building inside of me.

"You have to tell him," Sidney adds.

Tell him? Tell him what? That I don't want this to end? That I'm in love with him?

"What if he doesn't feel the same?"

"Girl, what if he does?" is Mia's reply.

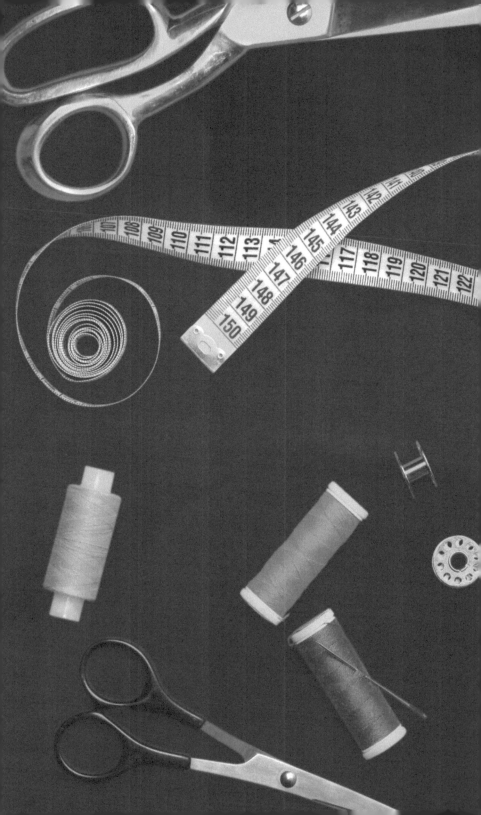

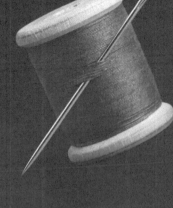

Chapter 46

Misty

"I'm sorry. Just a few more minutes!" I shout through the closed door as I slip on my gown, careful that my hair doesn't get stuck in the zipper. I kicked Damon out of the room, knowing I already take forever to get ready, and I'm still at least fifteen minutes behind.

Groaning when the zipper snags, I give it another sharp tug, but it doesn't budge. Over the years, I've become a master of doing this on my own, but the top of this dress is basically a corset.

I give up, knowing if I keep trying, I'll ruin the dress and make my way to Damon. "Can you help me with this?"

He straightens from where he's leaning on the island the second I come into the room. His lips curve into a grin as he looks at me appreciatively. "You look beautiful, wife."

He's dressed in another perfectly tailored black suit,

crisp white shirt, and black tie, his hair styled back in waves. He looks like he just stepped out of a freaking Tom Ford magazine.

I ignore the fluttering in my chest and spin, revealing my back. "The corset's a little snug."

Within seconds, he's behind me, but instead of zipping me up, Damon places light kisses along the scar below my shoulder blade. After years of never showing anyone the permanent marks Thomas left on me, I'm starting to grow used to Damon's casual touches. He doesn't miss an opportunity to caress the raised skin in tender touches. Every time, it feels like something more. Something deeper. Not like he's trying to make them disappear, more like he's trying to heal that part of me.

He kisses the curve between my neck and my shoulder, the scent of his smooth cologne filling my nose. "Have I told you you're beautiful tonight?"

I laugh under my breath. "Yes, you just did."

His fingers spread over my stomach, pulling me taut to his chest as his lips graze my ear. "Then why do I feel the need to tell you again?"

Shivers travel down my spine, and I can't help but tip my head to the side, giving him more access. Damon instantly takes advantage, placing open mouth kisses to my neck. I jerk away the second his teeth graze my skin.

"No you don't! I'm not going to a charity event with a freaking hickey."

He bites his lip, and the playful, unashamed look he gives me nearly has me undone. His knuckles graze along my back as he zips me up, placing a gentle kiss behind my ear when it's done. "All done."

I'm frozen in his arms, not wanting to break this moment. Tonight, I'm going to tell him the truth. Tonight, I'm going to admit I love him, and I'm low-key terrified he's going to laugh in my face.

The audacity to think someone like him could love someone like me.

But he'd helped me stop hiding, so I'm not going to hide from him.

I twist in his arms, arms pressed against his chest between us, and run my fingers along his lapel. Without meeting his gaze, I say, "Sorry I took so long."

He guides my chin up, forcing me to meet his piercing gaze. He searches mine, and his brows pull together, not liking what he finds. "Misty. Listen to me. I am not a patient man. But I'd wait forever if it meant you're by my side. Now, let me see that dress I nearly lost my limbs making."

I huff out a laugh. "I told you that you didn't need to help."

"And I told you that I did. Now, give me a spin." He takes my fingers, lifts them above my head, and guides me into a twirl with the hand that's on my waist.

The pale pink, nearly nude chiffon skirts fan out around me. The vibrant embroidered flowers we'd painstakingly sewed on make it look like something made in a fairy tale.

Damon stops the spin, pulling me tightly against

him, his thumb running along the boning seams of the corset inches below my sternum. He drops his head to mine. "Do we have to go?"

Giddiness takes over, and I laugh. "Yes, we have to go to the event I've been planning all year."

He runs his nose along mine, nearly brushing our lips. "I can't just donate a bunch of money?"

My head feels dizzy with just how tempting this man is. "I'll let you do anything you want to me tonight if we go now."

"Anything?" His voice is a dark, low rumble, promises written in just the one word.

Heat flares between my thighs, and my breaths grow shallow. I'm making a deal with the devil, and I don't want to stop. I push at his chest. "Yes, but we leave now."

He groans his approval and lifts me from the ground, one hand at my back and the other beneath my knees.

"Wait! My shoes." He moves closer to the island as he walks out, slowing down just enough for me to grab my shoes and purse, causing a laugh to bubble up from my chest.

It's a twenty-minute ride to the venue, and by the time we're pulling up, every nerve in my body is bouncing with anxiety. This is my first solo project, one where I coordinated all of the different trades to make it come to life. Of course, I depended heavily on the caterer, event planner, and decorator, but in the end, I'm the one responsible for it all. I don't realize I'm picking at my nails until Damon covers my hand with his own.

"It's going to be perfect."

"How do you know that?"

"Because you did it," he says plainly, like there's no other option.

"What if it doesn't though? Then everyone will know it was me." I look down at the second button on his shirt. "It could look bad on you."

"Look at me." I tentatively raise my head. "I do not give a single fuck about what anyone else thinks. The people that matter. Our family. Your friends. They know how hard you worked. The ceiling could fall down, and they'll still be impressed."

The final link chaining me to my past shatters with his words. For my entire childhood, I'd been taught that I always had to be perfect, that I'd be rejected if I showed an ounce of my true self. Here's this man who not only accepts my shortcomings but seems to like me even more because of them.

The car slows to a stop.

"Do you have the black card?" Damon asks, and I hold up my purse. He kisses the corner of my mouth, where a frown starts to form. "You are adorable when you're jealous. Win that date for me and I'll take you anywhere you want."

I roll my eyes. "What if it's like a million dollars?"

He lifts a brow at me. "That's it? That's all you think I'm worth."

I bite the corner of my lip. "I can spend anything?"

"Anything you want, Misty. I can assure you, we can

afford it." He gets out of the car and walks around to my side before I can process the *we* in that statement.

The castle-like venue was a perfect choice, with its soaring architecture and intricate stone details, all bathed in the dreamy glow of the fairy lights. It is the Midsummer Night's Dream theme come to life, a fairy-tale setting that transports us to a realm of magic and enchantment.

I take a deep breath. The air is filled with the scent of fresh flowers, a mix of blooming roses and jasmine, enhancing the fairy-like atmosphere of the venue.

Damon leans in, placing a barely there kiss to my temple. "I told you, it's perfect."

I let him guide me through the large oak double doors and into the ballroom, and my breath catches. I'd been in this venue countless times now, but nothing prepared me for seeing it all come together. Round tables adorned in gold tablecloths are placed so they can all see the large stage at the front. Moss and flowers line the grand pillars, leading your eye up. Fabric panels hang from the ceiling, mixed with twinkle lights, making it look like the night sky.

The event sold out months ago, no doubt in part to Damon encouraging his buddies to participate. Now that I understand more of his world, I've realized it was probably less encouraged and more demanded. At eight thousand dollars a table, I really don't care if Damon held them at gunpoint. I'm ecstatic we've raised so much money before the auction has even started.

Damon wraps his arm around my waist and points out a few people in the crowd. "Over there, that's Nikolai Volkov and his two sisters. He recently became a Saint."

One of the women is wearing a flaming red dress, almost in spite of everyone else. I instantly like her.

"Anthony Ricci and his father are over there." Damon gestures with his chin, and I grow still. I know Damon said that all was fine between their families, but the entire thing felt too easy.

My gaze roams over what are now becoming familiar faces and lands on Scarlet Laurent. She's with the same man as when we saw them at the restaurant, but this time, his brows are pulled low over his eyes, and it's almost as if he's towering down on her.

"Damon." I tug on his sleeve to point them out, but they've disappeared before he can see.

"Fuck, I like it when you call me that." His breath on my neck has me warming from within.

I pull away to glare playfully at him. "We're in public."

He shrugs. "Some people like that sort of thing."

"I need to know what has you blushing like that," Piper says cheerfully from beside me.

"Hey, you look nice tonight," Lucas says.

Damon's grip tightens on me, even though Lucas is basically draped around Piper.

The couple is dressed in theme, Lucas in a deep

green suit, and she's wearing a pale blue gown that shimmers when she moves.

"You two look adorable."

Piper beams at me. "We wanted to look the part."

"And you succeeded, Pipsqueak." Jax is next to show up, unsurprisingly looking dashing in his navy suit. Sidney follows close behind him, dressed the most on theme with crystals embroidered in her dress, making it look like it was made with starlight.

She smirks at me. "I read some fantasy books for inspiration. You like it?"

Jax kisses her head. "Love it, Trouble."

Damon greets my friends with a pleasant smile I know he's working hard to keep in place. "Thank you all for coming. I know that it means a lot to Misty."

He completely skips that the entire event revolves around Mia's charity, and it doesn't go unnoticed. I'm met with cheeky smiles, and I roll my eyes back at them.

"If you'll excuse me, I have guests I need to greet. Please look after my wife." Damon squeezes my waist before disappearing into the crowd.

"Was it just me, or did he add an extra boost of possessiveness at the end there," Sidney asks, earning snickers from all of them.

"Drop it," I demand, only making them laugh harder.

"What's so funny?" Mia walks up with Alex and River close behind her.

"Just that Misty over here has Damon whipped."

"Ha ha."

Mia winks at me. "Oh, come on. You like it." She looks around. "This is truly amazing. I seriously can't thank you enough."

"Honestly, I'm just grateful you let me plan it."

River and Alex had given me the equivalent of an endless budget to play with, and that's not something you normally trust with a junior member of a team.

"No one could do it better," River replies.

The sound of the mic tapping draws our attention, and the auctioneer looks out to the crowd. "Ladies and gentlemen, please take your seats. The main event is about to begin."

"I'll see you guys after." I wave at my friends and make my way through the throng of people. As Damon's wife, I'm required to sit at the Everette table. Dread forms a pit in my stomach at the thought of seeing Damon's mother again. I'm not looking forward to the look of pure disdain.

Bash is the only one sitting when I arrive, Damon standing behind my chair and pulling it out for me. He pulls me into his arms for a quick kiss. "I'm up first. Bid high, make me look good."

I huff out a laugh, the thought of him being up for auction no longer bothering me now that I have the go-ahead to drop an obscene amount of money. It's all for a good cause, making it even better.

Xander gives my shoulder a quick squeeze as he follows after his older brother. "I'm right after him.

Please don't bid on me. I'd like to leave here with my legs intact."

I bite the corner of my lip, not positive he's joking.

"That leaves just you and me, kiddo," Bash says, handing me a glass of champagne.

"How old are you again?"

"Twenty-two. Don't worry, I've made sure to tease the fuck out of Damon for your five-year age gap. Basically a cradle robber." Bash's tone is joking, but that doesn't stop me from punching him in the arm.

"Hey, now. I'm delicate."

I snort into my glass of champagne, not bothering to answer that bit of nonsense. The hair stands up on my arms, and prickles form at the back of my neck as the bidding on Damon starts. There are six bidders to start. I confidently raise my paddle after each one while the number goes up and up. There's a woman at the back, just as easily keeping up with me, and she's looking at my husband like a treat. My teeth clench together as I raise my paddle again.

"I don't know why you look jealous. He's not going to cheat on his wife," Bash says, handing me another glass of champagne. I didn't even notice I finished the first one.

"It doesn't help that he only married me to secure his inheritance." Even though things feel like they've changed now, that thought still stings.

Bash chokes, and it takes him several seconds to

recover before he looks at me with wide eyes. "You still believe that? I just thought by now you'd know."

"Know what?" I'm still only half paying attention, not wanting to miss a bid.

"That yes, every heir was married, but they'd never been made to. Pure coincidence. Damon basically dragged our grandfather out to make the announcement so he'd be able to marry you."

"What?" My face snaps to his. "That doesn't even make sense. He already had leverage with my visa."

"Maybe he didn't think you'd go for it and wanted to lock it down. The man's been basically obsessed with you since the moment you met. You know with the cameras, stalking, and all of that."

"Cameras?" My voice is raised at a high pitch, but I can't seem to care. The world goes blurry, and there's a tingling in my stomach. It is the exact opposite reaction I should be having to that little revelation. Freaking traitorous body.

Bash winces. "I probably wasn't supposed to say that. But you're my sister now, and family doesn't keep secrets. Please tell me you know the whole sleeping-in-the-same-bed rule is bullshit too?"

I just blink at him, and he shakes his head.

"Seriously? How did you even believe that?"

My mouth falls open and closed, not being able to think of a single excuse. My stomach twists with nausea as embarrassment floods me.

I glare at Damon across the room, and he's already watching me.

"Asshole." I mouth the word clearly, and the way his eyes widen lets me know he got the message.

I place the paddle fully on the table and cross my arms. Damon's brows pull low as another bid goes through, but this time, it remains uncontested. If he wants to lie to me, let him deal with the consequences. His eyes narrow as the woman at the back is called the winner.

"Fuck, sis, you're playing with fire."

"I haven't even started yet."

Xander goes up next, and I raise my paddle high, loving the way Damon glares at me. He's supposed to be speaking with the woman who won, but all of his attention is on me.

I bid again, and Xander looks worriedly between me and his brother and sighs in acceptance. By now, Damon's seething, but all I do is bid higher, this time calling out two million, winning the auction in a second.

Damon breaks away from the woman and prowls toward me. I skitter out of my seat, not willing to be caught so soon.

Bash catches my arm just as I'm about to leave. "You know I can't let you leave. He's already going to kill one of his brothers tonight. Please don't make it two."

"You're telling me you won't protect your only sister?" I give him wide doe eyes, and he lets go of me.

"That's just cruel."

"I'll make it up to you," I call over my shoulder and escape through an emergency exit. I breathe a sigh of relief when there's an Uber just down the street, and I run to meet up with it before Damon catches up.

I'm panting by the time I get into the car and duck my head to not be seen. If the driver thinks it's weird, he doesn't comment.

"Where to, miss?"

"The Holiday Inn on Seventieth." It's a midrange hotel, one that I can afford on my own. "First, stop at a gas station. If he wants me, he's going to have to come find me."

Chapter 47

Damon

I've lost track of Misty as I push through the crowd, trying to get to her. The little minx is going to pay for that. But something in the way she looked at me let me know she wasn't the only one in trouble. Unease settles in my bones at just what that could mean. Somehow, I'd pissed my wife off, and I can't fucking have that. The things between us are too new, and she'd spent her entire life hiding herself. A rock settles in my stomach at the idea of her closing herself off to me again.

I need to get to her before she starts to spiral in her own head whatever lies she's telling herself.

My fist clenches when Bash isn't at our table. The man had one job, and he let her fucking go. He might be my younger brother, but I'm not above beating the shit out of him.

It only takes a second to spot him with Jax Ryder and the rest of Misty's friends.

I eat up the distance between us, casting a shadow over the table, and smile at the way my brother's face blanches at the sight of me.

I come up behind Jax, who's thanking Bash for letting him borrow his jet. I ignore the fact that Bash doesn't have a jet, which means he's been lending out mine.

The entire table goes silent when I circle around and grip Bash's shoulder. "What did you say to her to piss her off?"

My voice is full of warning to not fuck with me right now as I haul him out of his chair. I don't need her friends overhearing us.

Once we're out of earshot, I let him go, a low growl forming in my throat. "You were supposed to be watching her."

He glares right back, but I don't miss the minuscule step back he takes. "You shouldn't have lied to her, asshole."

Every muscle in my body freezes. "What did you tell her?"

"Everything." He raises his chin in challenge, as if daring me to deny it.

He grunts, folding in on himself when my fist lands on his stomach. He takes a second to recover before grinning at me. "That girl was made for you."

"I fucking know that."

Xander steps up to us tentatively, careful not to get too close.

I point at him. "And you. You're a fucking dead man."

He tilts his head. "Shouldn't you be finding your wife instead of threatening me?"

Fuck. Tension builds in my spine as I push past them. I'll deal with their insolence later. A part of me can't help but be proud that they're sticking up for her, no matter how much it pisses me off.

I exit the building. There are several groups of people out front, chatting while they smoke. But there's no hint of my pixie out here, no sign of where she's gone.

A wicked smile pulls at the corner of my mouth. She has no idea how much I love the chase.

Run, little mouse. Then, I pull up her tracker.

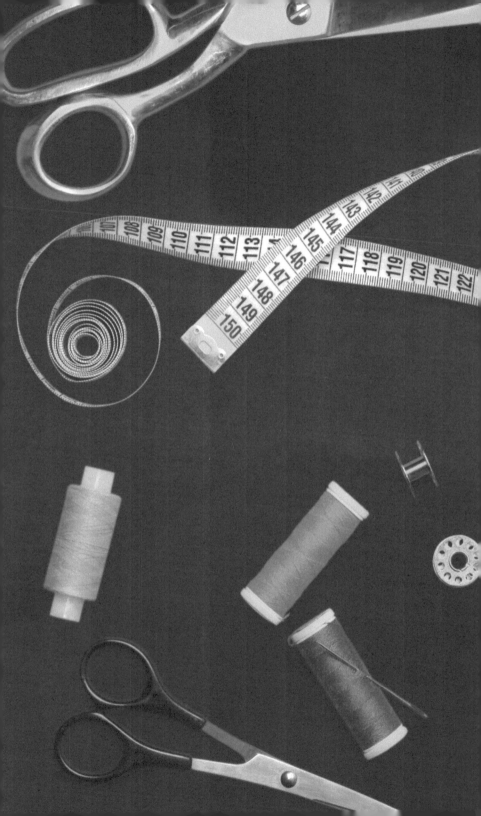

Chapter 48

Misty

MY UBER PULLS UP to the front of the hotel, and I pay
him in cash. There's something that feels entirely wrong
with spending Damon's money while running from him.
Not that I think he'd care—hell, he'd probably encourage
it. All the easier to track me. Not that he needs any help
with that.

The lobby's lights are dimmed, giving it a nighttime
mood, with a fake fireplace on one side and an unattended laminated wood counter on the other.

There's a little card that says, *ring the bell for
assistance.* My fingers hesitate over it, everything in me
screaming that no matter what the card says, it's rude to
ring this bell. What if they're in the bathroom or something? There's a large clock ticking away, and my heart
beats faster with every shift of the long hand. Just this
once.

I give the bell a light tap.

A young guy, early twenties, comes out of the back room. His collared shirt is wrinkled, and his hair looks like it hasn't been washed this week.

"Welcome to the Holiday Inn. Are you checking in?" he asks in a tone that says he's said this phrase a million times before.

I shift my weight back on my heels and wince. "I actually don't have a reservation."

He glances up from his computer screen, giving me the side-eye clear as day. "We're normally booked up."

"Can you please check?" I fight back the urge to point out his own word. *Normally.* Not always.

His fingers fly over the keys, and he says in a bored tone, "You're in luck. We have a king suite open."

My fingers tighten on the strap of my purse. I only took out a few hundred cash. "How much is that?"

"One-fifty for the night, plus a hundred dollars for the incidentals fees." At my raised brows, he adds, "That's paid back tomorrow, so long as there's no damage."

Okay, okay, that's good. I can cover that. I pull out my purse and start laying my cash on the table.

He takes my ID and looks a little too long at it, his brows pulling together. "Your name sounds familiar. You famous or something?"

Shit. I act as casually as possible. "Would I be staying here if I was famous?"

He shrugs, going back to the computer, seemingly appeased by my answer. Which is funny because the answer is actually, yes, yes I would.

Time's ticking away as I stand here out in the open.

"One card or two?" the clerk asks, pulling me out of my thoughts.

"What?" It takes a second for me to process his words. "One, please. There won't be anyone else."

I wouldn't normally offer up that information, but putting one more barrier in front of Damon is worth it.

"Okay, room 505. Wi-Fi password is your last name plus your room number. Have a good stay." He gives me a bored smile before disappearing again.

By the time I get to my room, my breaths are coming out in shallow pants as my heart pounds its way out of my chest. I'm playing a dangerous game here. On one hand, I can only imagine what he'll do to me when he finds me. Warmth grows between my thighs, and I sit on the edge of my bed, reaching down to remove my heels. On the other, what if he doesn't come?

And if I'm being completely honest with myself, that's the real reason my pulse is racing out of control. I ran, and I want him to chase me. During the Uber ride, I went back and forth on what Bash admitted to me. Damon's a big fat liar. Or a big ripped liar or whatever. *Do not think of his naked body at a time like this...*

He's a manipulative, egotistical stalker...

And I have to admit, after years of never feeling

confident enough to show my true self, I love it. I love that he went as far as he could. Love that he knows even the tiniest details about me.

He forced his own grandfather to participate in an intricate ruse, for Christ's sake.

The cameras, the stalking, the one-freaking-bed rule.

All of them are crossing a line, but I can't find a single part within me that cares.

I want him crazy. Obsessed. Possessive.

I want to push every one of his controls until he breaks.

I want him to *find me.*

Unzipping my dress, I inhale deeply as the corset loosens around my ribs. Pretty, but not practical in any sense of the word. I chew on my bottom lip while assessing the situation. Crawling into bed without my dress on is just asking for problems later, but I can't help the thrill that travels down my spine at what that'll be. I let the dress hit the floor, and then, after a few seconds of deliberation, I push down my panties and unclip my bra.

He deserves a prize after going through all that work, after all.

The comforter is heavier than I expected, and I tuck myself deeper within. A quick glance at the clock tells me it's been at least forty minutes since I left. There's an ache growing in my stomach as the minutes tick by.

What if he doesn't come? What if it was all just a game, and now I found out it's over?

I turn over my phone, not a single missed call.

What have I done?

Chapter 49

Damon

My body aches with anticipation, every second feeling like an eternity as I wait for my chance to get my hands on Misty. I pace the hotel room, running my fingers through my hair, and let out a deep breath. The two-hour wait for her to fall asleep nearly kills me, but I know it will be worth it.

I sink onto the cheap fake-leather headboard, my heart racing with excitement. It had been a simple task to bribe the clerk downstairs to open up the room next to hers. A quick call to the previous tenant, offering them a larger room due to "electrical issues," had them out of here in minutes.

But waiting has never been my strong suit, and these past few hours have been torture. The walls are paper-thin, amplifying every tiny movement she makes. It's taken her hours to finally settle down enough to fall asleep. At one point, I could have sworn I heard her crying, and I nearly blew my cover just to go check on her.

But now, as I watch the numbers on my phone change from twenty-nine to thirty, a slow smile spreads across my lips. She's almost mine again. The thought fills me with both excitement and guilt, but I push it aside as I focus on the thrill of getting what I want. The anticipation is almost unbearable, but it only makes the end result that much sweeter.

My girl wants to play a game of chase, and I am more than willing to oblige. But this time, she will learn what it truly means to be mine. No matter how far she runs or how hard she tries to escape, I will always find her and bring her back to me.

It won't be long until she realizes that no matter how much she pushes me away, I will always come after her.

Unlike the front doors, the interconnecting doors between rooms have a standard dead bolt. It takes seconds to pick it and swing the door open quietly, careful not to wake her before I'm ready.

The light from the window casts a halo around her face, illuminating the soft angles. I stop at the head of her bed, fingers grazing over her cheeks, and frown at the residue from tears.

Soon, she'll learn that no matter how far she pushes me, I'll always come after her.

I graze my lips against hers, and warmth builds in

my chest when she shifts toward me. Even in her sleep, this girl is mine.

With a deep breath, I slowly slide the covers off her body and reveal only bare skin beneath. *Fuck.* I pop my trouser button and slide them down my hips, fisting my hard cock.

I undress slowly, savoring the opportunity to admire every inch of her body. Her breasts are pressed together, and my fist tightens as I vividly picture my cock stroking between them. She's on her side, one leg out straight and the other bent in front of her for balance. I walk around the foot of the bed to where her thighs split, and her pretty pink pussy is on display for me. Careful not to wake her, I climb up the bed and graze my nose up her slit, breathing in her scent.

My cock aches to drive into her, but I want her to be dripping for my cock.

Climbing the remainder of the way, I bury my chin into her neck and nestle my length between the seam of her ass. I exhale sharply as she pushes back into me, chasing my touch.

I take my time teasing her, tracing my fingers up and down her body before gently rolling her nipple between my thumb and index until she's arching subconsciously into my touch. I check her again, her breathing still even, before continuing lower. Her legs shift open as I trail a path down her stomach and dip them between her thighs.

"Fuck, baby. You're already ready for me." Wetness

coats my fingers, and I suck them into my mouth, groaning at the taste of her.

I shift so the head of my dick is nestled between her thighs before slowly pushing in. My muscles strain with restraint, but I don't want her waking until I'm fully seated.

She stirs with every inch, slight moans coming from her lips, but she's still out. I kiss just behind her ear as I move deeper. She's taken me to the hilt. "Are you dreaming about me, Nymph?"

I rock my cock in again, feeling the way her greedy pussy tightens, begging for more. I grip her hip, holding her in place, and snap my hips forward.

"What?" She gasps, body stiffening before trying to pull away. "What are you doing?"

"Caught you." I nip at the back of her neck, rocking my cock into her in languid motions, soothing her.

She moans as I stretch her wider, forgetting she's supposed to be fighting it.

"I didn't think you were coming." Her voice sounds small, and I can't fucking have that.

I twist her chin to face me, brushing my lips over hers, and promise, "I'll always come."

She gasps out with each snapping thrust as I fuck some sense into her. Without pulling out, I shift back so she can turn her shoulder toward me and grip her neck to hold her in place as I devour her mouth.

I break the kiss only to suck and bite her neck. "I'm going to mark every inch of you."

"Do it," she pleads, having no idea what she's doing to me.

I grip her neck and devour her mouth, my tongue pushing deep, eating up every one of her moans. I spread her legs wider, hooking the top one over mine, and press in further. "That's it. You're taking me so well."

"Too deep." She rocks back, taking more. "Damon, you're too deep."

I tighten my grip around her neck and watch as her eyes lose focus. "You ran from me, and now you're going to fucking take what I give you. I'm going to imprint this cock into your pussy so hard that it'll ruin you for anyone but me."

I loosen my grip, only tight enough to hold her lips to mine, and cant my hips, hitting even deeper.

She gasps, parts cry, moan, and plea.

I shift so that I'm hitting that sensitive spot inside her with each thrust, loving the way she turns wild in my arms.

"Too much," she gasps.

"Just breathe. That's it. Feel how good my cock feels inside you." Her pussy squeezes around me, drawing a groan. "You're so fucking tight."

Her words lose meaning as I take her even harder until the only sounds escaping her mouth are incoherent pleas.

She starts to pulse around my cock, her first orgasm building within her. I shift my hand between her thighs and press down on her clit. She explodes around me, her head slamming into my collarbone with the force of her orgasm.

I stroke my fingers over her breasts, marveling at the goose bumps that follow their wake. "Who owns you, Misty?"

She's trembling in my arms when she twists to brush her mouth against mine. "You do."

Her eyes widen as I drive back into her at a brutal pace. She grips my hair, holding on to me as I fuck myself into her.

I groan into her neck with each thrust as her pussy imprints around me. Wanting to go further, I flip our position so I'm on my back and she's riding me, facing away. I let her set the pace while she adjusts and watch the delicious sight of my cock disappearing with each of her downward motions.

Once she's rocking smoothly, I curl up, grabbing her wrists and tugging them behind her. Misty gasps when I push her forward so she's unbalanced and the only thing holding her up is my grip.

I show no mercy as I pound into her from below, forcing her to take every inch of me. By the time the night's over, I'm going to own every part of her, every sound, every fucking gasp.

She tightens down hard on my cock, and my eyes roll back in my head. Her pussy's perfectly made for me, wrapped tight around my length.

My balls tighten as my orgasm grows closer, but I need her to come again first. I lift so I'm on my knees and she's upright, back against my chest, as I continue to grind into her. Her hands go immediately around my neck, holding herself up as I pinch her nipples between my fingers. She flinches from the pain but moans as the pleasure takes over. I pinch her again, and this time, she bucks against me in response.

My lips graze her ear. "That's my girl."

She presses back, desperate to take more of me as she chases her orgasm. Her breathing grows ragged, her body tight as I push her over the cliff, my cum filling her with my own release.

She's gasping for breath when I pull her down beside me, my chest to her back and my leg thrown over hers.

She squirms when I don't pull out, instead pushing my rapidly softening cock deeper. I run my teeth along the shell of her ear. "I can't stand the idea of your pussy being empty without me."

Misty's breath catches, and a shiver rolls through her, but she no longer tries to push away.

I lean back, looking between us, then kiss the nape of her neck. "You look so pretty warming my cock."

She squeezes around me, and I groan low in my throat. If she keeps this up, I'll be fucking her again sooner than planned.

I stroke her hair off her face and kiss her temple. "Get some rest. I'll wake you up when it's time to go again."

"Again?"

"You didn't think you'd get away without a punishment, did you? I'm going to keep making you come until you beg me to stop. Until I've wrung every last ounce of pleasure out of you. Then I'm going to make you come again."

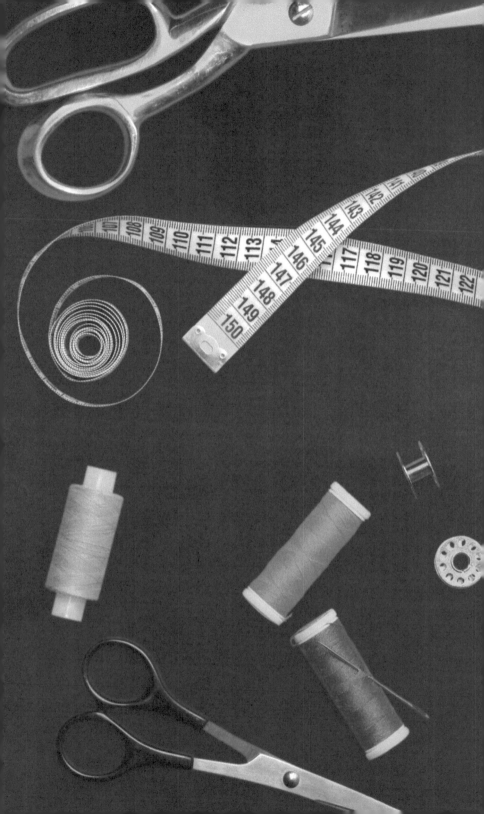

Chapter 50

Misty

THE SENSATION OF A WARM, wet mouth running along my slit coaxes me out of sleep. Damon's clear, gray eyes look up at me under heavy lashes as he swirls his tongue around my clit. He's taking his time, licking every inch of me before sucking gently on my still-sensitive nerves.

"You taste so fucking good." He hums in the back of his throat.

Opening his mouth, he lets a trail of spit run down his tongue, dripping onto his fingers, then slides them into me. My hips jerk from the bed, and he presses them down, not giving me space to shift away as he patiently builds tension in my body. A storm stirs inside me, the waves growing as they sweep through me, sending shivers rolling down my spine at each peak.

He doesn't rush me as he licks, sucks, and fucks his fingers into me, knowing exactly what to do to turn the shifting waves until they're crashing around me.

443

"Damon," I gasp as my orgasm overtakes me, sucking me under the water as I buck into his arm.

He grins at me from between my thighs, giving me one last lick before crawling up my body and dropping his forehead to mine. "I want you waking up screaming my name every night."

"That doesn't seem practica—"

Damon cuts me off, kissing my taste into my mouth until I'm limp and pliable beneath him.

"Perfect." His eyes are soft as they gleam above me, and my heart clenches at the possible meaning behind them.

Before I can say anything, he flips me onto my chest, my forehead to the bed, and raises my hips into the air. I suck in a breath as the head of his cock notches to my entrance and seats itself into me. The stretch burns—even after multiple rounds, it's a lot to adjust to. But that burn quickly turns to pleasure. The pleasure speaks to my body in its own language, demanding a response. I push back, taking more of him with each thrust. I have no hope of coming again, but that doesn't mean I don't want this. That I don't want to feel it when he fills me up.

There's a slap sound every time we come together as Damon pounds himself relentlessly into me. His movements grow jagged as he grows closer to his release, but he doesn't let up, instead resting his chest on my back.

The new angle has me crying out his name as he pounds into the perfect spot.

"There it is," he murmurs in my ear as he pushes me harder.

My fist clenches into the sheets, and my toes curl as I hover on the impossible verge of another orgasm. "So...so close." I clench my teeth as all my muscles tighten painfully, crying for the release that's out of reach. Each of Damon's thrusts holds me over the edge; all I need to do is tip over. I growl in frustration, and he chuckles, his chest vibrating against my back.

"Breathe." Damon runs a hand down my back and gives my ass a squeeze. "I've got you."

I think I'm going to murder him when his finger slides along my entrance and pushes inside with his cock.

"No, no, no, no," I say frantically as he stretches me wider.

"Just breathe, Misty."

The sensation draws every ounce of my attention, overwhelming my senses until it pushes me blind off the edge of my orgasm.

I can't breathe as I spasm, Damon holding me up as his hips snap at a frantic pace. He grunts with his orgasm, the hot liquid pooling inside of me.

He's gentle as he pulls out, and then we collapse to the bed. I jolt when his fingers sink into me again and scramble away from him, holding a pillow like a shield between us.

"I can't."

Damon grins playfully. "What did I say you had to do for me to stop?"

"You can't be serious."

He rips the pillow from my hands and tugs me under him, chuckling under his breath as he trails a hand up my leg. "I'm so fucking serious."

"Fine." I grip his wrist, stopping its ascent. "Please. Please, I can't take any more."

He tilts his head to the side. "Are you going to run from me again?"

My answers stick in my throat because I can't promise that I won't freak out. I can't promise that I'll suddenly get over my fear of rejection just because he asks.

Damon runs his thumb along my jaw, his gray gaze warm on mine, and grins. "Go ahead and run. There's nowhere you can hide that I can't find. You can trust me to chase you. So, go ahead and run. Besides, I think it's cute you think you can get away from me."

I can't stop the broken, damaged, insecure part of me from saying, "It's not like our deal is permanent."

Damon reels back like I slapped him. "The fuck it's not. You married me."

I bite my bottom lip, testing a little more. "We can get divorced?"

His laughter shakes my entire body as he struggles to breathe. There are tears in the corner of his eyes, he's laughing so hard as he pins me beneath him. I hiss, mouth falling open as he slides his hard cock into me.

He cups my cheeks, tracing his thumbs along my temples, and smiles at me. "Good luck finding a lawyer or judge that will release you from me. You've been mine since the second you signed those papers."

I grip his legs with mine to keep him from distracting me. There's one thing left. The secret I held from him. The one I didn't think would matter. "You might not mean that once I tell you this."

He frowns, kissing between my brows. "Not possible."

"After what Thomas did, there was an infection. I was pregnant, and...I lost the baby." I swallow hard at the look in his eyes and shield myself for the next part. "I can't have your kids, Damon."

He searches my face, the crease between his brows slowly smoothing out. "Okay, so we won't have kids."

"Don't you want kids?"

"Sure, but only if it was with you."

"But...but you're the heir. You're supposed to carry on the lineage and all of that."

That earns me another laugh. "I have three brothers. I'm sure one of them can handle it."

The swell in my heart is nearly overwhelming.

"I love you." My words rush out before I can stop them.

Damon growls into my neck, sending shivers through me, and lowers until his weight is pressing me into the mattress. "I've been dying to hear those words come out of your mouth since the first time I saw you and couldn't stop myself from pissing you off. I should punish you for making me wait so long." He bites my neck, and his breath comes out hot against my ear as he says, "I've loved you longer."

Damon thrusts forward, his cock hitting a new angle, and the air is pushed from my lungs as I realize exactly what he has planned for my punishment.

It's hours later, my head resting on his chest, too tired to move. "How did you find me?"

He twists my bracelet. "I never lost you."

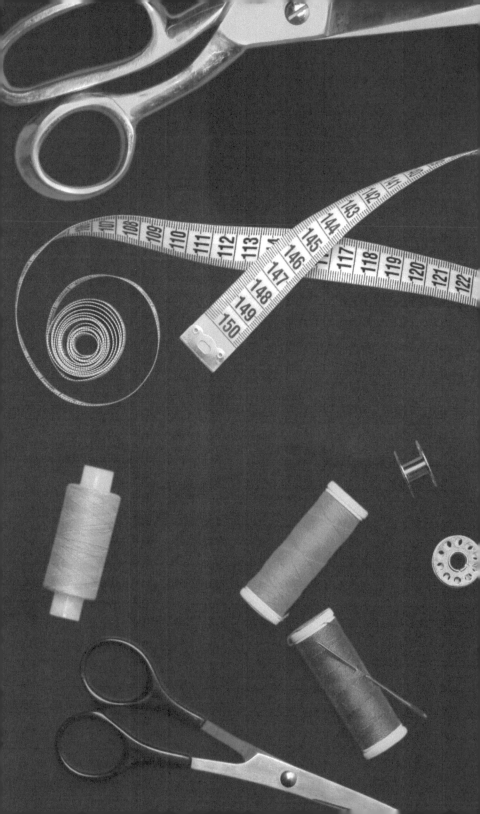

Chapter 51

Misty

I HIT the snooze button on my alarm when it buzzes on my nightstand and let Damon pull me back under the fluffy covers. I bury my face into the fabric, but the bright sunlight streaming in my window tells me it's not the first time I hit it. We've been holed up in our apartment for two days since Damon found me at the hotel, fucked my literal brains out, and brought me home.

I turn into his chest, running my finger along the lines of his tattoos, and just breathe him in. "I need to see her."

"Cancel," he mumbles into his pillow, arm not loosening. He's being adorably defiant.

Laughing, I attempt to peel his arm from around me. "Let go. Sidney's leaving today. I have to go."

I squeal with laughter as his fingers dig playfully into my side, tickling my bare sensitive skin.

"Mercy. Mercy!" I squirm away from him, but he

451

just rolls me under him and brackets my head with his forearms.

I stiffen. "Wait. Are there cameras in here?"

Damon runs his nose along mine. "Not yet."

"Is it weird that I sorta love that you've been watching me?"

His hair is mussed to perfection, giving him that bed head look others take patience and the perfect amount of dry wax to achieve. I cup his face and run my thumb between his brow, arching out to his temple. He looks a decade younger, like all of that pain and stress he's been carrying around is wiped away. I meet his twinkling eyes, and he raises one brow at me.

"You're staring again."

I'd be embarrassed if he wasn't staring right back, eyes scanning over my face like he's memorizing every detail. I want to tell him that I'm not going anywhere, that he caught me and now he's stuck with me forever. That I'm going to spend my entire life doing my best to annoy him until he drops his hard shell for good. At least around me. Instead of saying any of that, I lean up and press my mouth to his, pushing all my feelings into that single kiss. He takes over kissing me slowly, his mouth softer than I'd ever imagined.

He breaks the kiss, resting his forehead on mine, and touches our noses together. "I love you."

His grip tightens slightly. "Misty Everette, will you marry me again? This time, with your friends, my family, and hundreds of other guests. I know you won't let me buy you one, so I want to help you make the perfect dress. One so long we need four people to hold the train. I want to scream in front of a crowd that I love you with every ounce of my being and that I am the lucky fucker who gets to keep you."

I bite back my smirk, bubbles of giddiness popping in my chest. I hum as if there's any possible answer but yes. "Will your mom be invited?"

His mouth grows closer to mine, his eyes narrow. "Only if she apologizes to your satisfaction."

I brush his hair back from his face. "What if I don't want a big wedding and I just want it to be my friends and your brothers?"

He lowers, lips brushing mine. "I'll give you anything you want, Nymph. Just ask."

"I love you." I lift up to kiss him, and he pulls back.

"And?" He gives me a look that says he'll happily wait all day.

"And I'd be honored to marry you. Again."

He captures my mouth in a kiss so tender it steals my breath away. His hands map out my body, taking their time to worship every inch of me. My alarm goes off again, but I'm too lost to his touch to care.

Forty-five minutes later, I'm still wrapped in his arms. I'm cocooned in a place I never want to leave, but I know if I don't get up now, there's no leaving this bed today.

I place a chaste kiss on his chest and push up. "I have to get up. I'm already going to be late."

"Fine." he huffs, rolling onto his back. "I've been putting off checking in with Matthias." He twists my bracelet around my wrist. "I'll see you later.

I run my finger along the smooth metal that's brought me comfort, fiddling with it countless times. "Is this really a tracker?"

I should be disgusted—hell, terrified—but all I am is elated. "Of course it is. You know, you're basically a walking red flag."

He smirks. "You love that about me."

Fuck it. "I really do."

I sent the girls a group chat message saying I was running late, giving me enough time to shower and put myself into some semblance of put together. I chose a light green sundress that lands just below my knees and twisted my hair up in a claw clip, too exhausted to pull off anything else.

The group chat immediately blew up with a dozen lewd comments about Damon and me disappearing off the face of the Earth for the last few days.

The sun beams warmth down on me as I walk toward the cafe where I'm meeting the girls. There's an overwhelming lightness filling my chest, an almost giddy happiness overtaking my every sense. Everything feels perfect in the world.

Sometimes it's hard to spot the pretty in a city, but

the birds are chirping, and the leaves are turning to a rusty red, giving a hint of the fall to come. Soon, it'll be sweater weather, filled with pumpkin spice lattes and Ugg boots. I cannot wait to see Damon's face when I pull out my Snuggie covered in cat faces.

There's a lady up the sidewalk from me. She can't be more than a few years older. Her clothes fit her perfectly, the seams crisp and pressed, making her stand out like a sore thumb in this neighborhood. And by the way she's looking at her phone, then up and down the street, she's clearly out of her comfort zone.

"Do you know where you're going?" I give her my friendliest smile, knowing people do not trust strangers out here, and just hope that my being another woman will help ease that anxiety.

She's wearing her own smile, but it's tight, curved too high to the right, like there's something wrong to it. Like it wants to be three times the size, but she's holding it back.

"Yeah, sorry, I think I got off the bus at the wrong stop."

I give her outfit another glance over, spotting her Hermès purse, and tension grows in my spine. This is not the type of lady that takes the bus.

"Oh, that totally sucks. Which route did you take? The D1 or V2?" I ask, knowing damn well neither of these exist—Boston doesn't use letters for their routes.

A thin line forms between her brows. "Definitely the D1. Was that not right?"

Unease settles over my shoulders, and I take a tentative step back. The stranger catches the movement and shakes her head.

"No use doing that. You're not going anywhere, Misty."

Tires squeal from around the corner, a van pulling up to the curb, its large side door sliding open to reveal a man I've never seen before holding a gun right at my face.

Every survival episode has taught me not to get into the vehicle. That nothing good comes at the second location, so I do what feels insane and run.

I only make it three strides before a firm arm bands around my stomach, the force knocking my breath away. I heave to get air into my lungs just as a cloth is wrapped over my mouth.

The world goes black.

My body rocks like it's riding a wave, the motion making my mouth fill with saliva as I try to hold down my already twisting stomach. The screech of brakes cuts through my blinding headache. The world slowly filters in around me, but nothing that's happening makes any sense. The last thing I remember is walking to meet up with the girls.

No...the last thing I remember is a too-wide smile and deep black hair. Fuck.

Fear crashes through me, and I struggle to keep my breathing even. The last thing I need right now is for them to figure out I'm not asleep.

I push through the pain in my head and try to get my bearings. I'm lying on something hard, but it's not cold like metal. More like metal covered in some kind of scratchy fabric. Tears sting the back of my eyes, realizing I'm in the back of the van.

"Wake up," a deep voice says and punctuates it with a kick to my sternum.

The air knocks from my lungs, and I gag as I try to inhale, coughing until acid fills my mouth.

"You're awake. Good," the man says, using his foot to roll me onto my back. There are no windows in the back, so the only light filters through the windshield, giving everything a muted gray tone.

"Fuck you." I spit the bile pooling in my mouth in his direction, earning me another kick.

He waits until I recover to speak again. "Do you remember me?"

I scan his face, searching for recognition in every detail, and the realization hits me harder than any kick ever could. Anthony Ricci looks down at me with hate in his eyes, like I'm a disgusting bug that he can't wait to crush.

"You didn't think he'd tell me? Thomas was my favorite cousin, after all. Of course he told me all about his whore of an ex, who'd walk around like a fucking tease." Anthony smiles, and it's the most sadistic thing

I've ever seen. There's a pride emanating from him that makes my stomach flip. "He taught you a lesson, didn't he? He taught you all about what happens to little unimportant sluts that go around being a tease. Tell me, how did you end up with Damon? Hmm? Did you spread those pretty legs for him? Did you give it up like the fucking whore you are?"

I open my mouth to call him an asshole, to tell him to fuck off and his cousin deserved everything he got, but nothing comes out.

"Nothing to say? Fear will do that to you. Awful, isn't it? When you're helpless?"

I grip my bracelet, the only thing grounding me. They won't have noticed I'm missing yet, so all I have to do is stay alive. Damon's coming. He promised.

Delicate fingers grasp my wrist and try to pull it toward them. I grip it tight to my chest, holding it to me with my other hand.

The lost girl from the street gives me a sweet, sickening smile. Any hope I had that she'd call the police is washed away by the realization she'd set me up.

Her nails dig into my wrist, and warm liquid drips down my fist, but I don't let go, knowing this is my last lifeline.

Cool metal is pressed into my forehead, drawing my attention, and my eyes focus on a black gun handle, a thick finger wrapped around the trigger. "Give her your fucking hand."

My chin quivers as I loosen my grip, letting her pull

my arm toward her. She immediately tries to remove my bracelet. I grunt when the metal ridge is stopped by my bones.

The woman's fingers are replaced by male hands, and I hiss out in pain when he tries to rip it off.

"It slides on, but it doesn't slide off, asshole." Serves him fucking right.

But the way his smile grows tells me I've made a terrible mistake. He holds my wrist so my pinky is against the van floor and my thumb is in the air.

"No!" I rip my hand back, freeing it for a split second, but there's no time for relief. He shoves my hand back into place, his strength at least doubling my own.

He moves so that I'm forced to look at his face. "I want you to know I'm going to enjoy this."

His boot comes down on my wrist, filling the van with a sickening crunch as the thin bones crack. My vision goes white with the pain, my scream caught in my throat as he does it again.

Tears pour down my cheeks, and I beg him to stop.

My limbs convulse as I try to drag my injured hand against my chest, but Anthony doesn't let go. Instead, he slides the bracelet I've loved over my damaged hand.

I scream at the excruciating pain as the metal finally clears my fingers.

He releases his hold, concentrating on the bracelet.

I use my good arm to move as far away from him as the tight space will allow, holding my broken wrist instinctively to my chest.

He turns it in his fingers. "This is a precise piece of technology. Expertly hidden from the unknowing eye. I'll admit, I probably wouldn't have figured it out if it wasn't for the fact..." He grins at me. "That the Ricci family is the one that created it."

The van slows, and my body rocks when it comes to a stop, pain lancing down my arm with the unexpected motion.

He hands the bracelet to the woman. "Make sure it keeps moving. We want him chasing after it instead of looking for us."

She smiles at him, and it's clear she's in love. That she'll do anything this sicko tells her. All hope is crushed when the sliding door shuts behind her.

The line that ties me to Damon, effectively cut. My teeth rattle against each other.

Anthony grips my chin, holding another cloth to my face.

"He can look all he wants, but he won't find you. No one will."

Chapter 52

Damon

BASH PULLS a bright yellow pillow from underneath him where he crashed on the couch and kicked his feet up onto the table next to Xander. "Cute pillow."

The two of them take up the entire thing, their arms forced to hang over the sides. This is the first time my brothers have been over, and they're going to have to get used to it.

Matthias leans against the wall, arms crossed over his chest as a muscle ticks in his jaw.

"What's the update?" I hand him a glass of whiskey, settling next to him.

"You mean since you fell off the face of the Earth, chasing after your girl?" Xander says, a mischievous smirk taking over his face.

I take a long drink, the whiskey burning the back of my throat. "You could always leave."

"Geez, I was only teasing."

The sharp click of Matthias's ring against his glass brings our attention back to him. "Three Unsainted wives have shown up dead. This time, they were mutilated first."

"What the fuck? I thought they backed off." Bash gets up from the couch.

"Sit the fuck down," I say, voice steady against his frantic posture. "Explain."

Matthias hands me his phone. Sure enough, there are three dead bodies, all cut open from sternum to pelvis. All women.

"All three of them missed their check-in a week ago. They didn't show up again until last night." His back teeth grind together, and he takes another long drink before continuing. "They were left on the steps of the Vaults."

"Jesus Christ," Xander says, whistling under his breath.

This told us two things. They were definitely members of the Order Of Saints, and they were challenging us directly. That's not completely true though. You can't challenge someone if you don't show your face.

"I don't get the secrecy though. Why bait us, then hide?" I examine the photos again, looking for anything that would give away which family it is.

Matthias grunts his disapproval, never one to back down. "They're smart enough to know they can't challenge us directly. That the other Saints won't risk it."

I swipe through the photos again, this time seeing the fourth. With only three dead, I wasn't expecting the extra photos. My blood runs cold as I process what I'm seeing and flip to the next photo. The same two cuts sliced into the woman's back.

"You look like you've seen a ghost."

The ringing in my ears is too loud for me to make out which brother said it. The cuts are a perfect replica of Misty's. I drop my brother's phone as I scramble for mine, immediately pulling up her tracker. She's moving fast, to the other end of the city. Away from where she was meeting her friends.

My phone buzzes with a number I don't recognize. I hit speakerphone for my brothers to hear. Piper's familiar voice fills the room. "I got your number from Lucas. Is Misty there?"

A shudder crawls up my spine. "Is she here?"

"What?" Bash asks tightly.

"What do you mean is she here." It's fear not anger that laces her voice, and reality comes crashing down on me.

Piper's voice turns pleading. "Please tell me you know where she is. She didn't show up, and at first, we thought you just distracted her again. But then she wasn't answering her phone...her phone went to voicemail."

Ice burns my veins, and my fist trembles at my side as I process what this means. What the cuts on the victims' backs signify.

"They fucking took her." I'm out the door, running down the stairs and to my car, not waiting a single second.

A hand grips my arm, hauling me back, and Matthias shakes me. "They're baiting you."

"I fucking know that. They can take me. Fucking torture me. Cut off my skin while I'm still fucking screaming, so long as they give her back. Now, let me the fuck go."

Matthias looks to the side, his grip tightening. "I can't do that, brother."

He barely dodges my blow as I step in to attack him, all senses gone, leaving me in a vicious state of bloodlust.

"I will fucking kill you and anyone that stands in my way of getting her back. I will set the world on fire to smoke those fuckers out. I don't think you understand just how far I'm willing to go. How much I'm willing to sacrifice for her."

"Just wait. We'll come with you," Xander says from behind me, his arms binding mine to my side to stop me from lashing out.

My throat grows thick, and my voice cracks around the vowels. "You don't understand. I told her I'd always find her. I promised I'd come for her. Let. Me. Go!"

Xander drops his arm, but Matthias still holds on to my shirt. "Keep your fucking phone on. We'll head to the house, stock up on whatever we'll need, and follow you to the location. Do not go in without us."

I'm already backing away, breaking his hold on me. "Damon. Do you hear me? Don't go in without us. You will fucking die."

I get into my car and reply as I'm shutting my door. "Then I'll kill them as a ghost."

I've nearly caught up with the blinking dot on the tracker app when it stops, and the dot moves from the road and into an outdoor mall courtyard. Fuck. I pull my car onto the sidewalk, not giving a single shit that I nearly hit two people. When the man starts yelling and gets in my face, slowing me down, I push my keys into his chest. "It's your lucky fucking day. Take it."

Now that he's staring at the car instead of me, he's easy to get around. The second I'm free from him, I run, eating up the feet between me and Misty. My eyes scan the open area, searching for any signs of her lavender hair. She'd worn it up today in a cute little yellow clip.

The muscles tighten in my neck as I look at the app again. She should be right here. I turn, searching each person's face, scanning for anything that might be out of place.

My gaze lands on a woman, midtwenties, who looks just a little too well put together. I've spent my entire life surrounded by women like this, and they wouldn't be caught dead here. I track her, keeping my distance as she moves through the crowd.

She's sketchy, eyes darting around the courtyard as she watches for people following her, for me. She's not trained, though, and never looks directly behind her. I'm surprised when she lines up at the bus stop. It doesn't make sense that she'd be hiding Misty there.

It's not until I see the glimmer of metal she slips into an older lady's pocket that I realize what's happening. The second the bus pulls away, the tracker starts moving again down the road.

"Fuck," I want nothing more than to rip her fucking head off and spit down her neck. There's only one way they got that bracelet off, and it fucking shatters me to think of it.

I push the air from my lungs, fighting every instinct I have screaming at me to attack the woman. But without the bracelet, she's my only link between me and my wife.

Several minutes later, a bright red car pulls to the side, and she gets in. I curse that I gave my fucking car away, not that I could follow her in it anyway. I walk straight into the road, in front of a mid-class Chevy car. The driver wails on his horn when he slams to a stop, narrowly missing me. I press both hands against his hood for balance, then walk around to his window.

"I've got a dash cam. Insurance scams won't work with me." He's looking at the camera mounted to his visor when I open his door.

"Do you know who I am?"

His brows pull together in confusion, wasting

precious seconds before his eyes go wide. "You're an Everette."

"That's right. So you know this is real." I unclasp my watch, handing it to him. "It's worth at least five times your car. Now, get out of the fucking vehicle."

He undoes his seat belt, and I grab him by the shoulder, hauling him the rest of the way out. I'm already in the car and racing the way the woman disappeared. My pulse is rushing in my ears as I look down the busy streets, my chest caving in on itself with each moment I don't see it.

A car revs up ahead, and I spot the red roof, relief flooding through me as I follow her toward an upper-class residential area, red brick row houses with black roofs. I park several cars behind as she gets out and makes her way into the dwelling. I don't follow the car, spotting the Uber logo. I get out and walk across the street to get a better view. Rushing in hot right away will only make it more likely that they'll kill her.

My ribs crack in my chest, and I push the thought down before it can incapacitate me.

The woman walks in front of the window, her ear to the phone. Thank God for the rich's vanity, never missing out on the opportunity to show off. I watch as she pours herself a glass of wine, laughing as she walks around her living room. The realization that Misty's not here presses on my chest until each breath is a struggle.

Matthias answers my call immediately.

"They took the bracelet off of her and used it as a

fucking decoy. I've been chasing the wrong person for the last hour."

He's silent for several seconds, knowing exactly what it entailed to remove that bracelet. "Do you still have eyes on the perp?"

"Of course I fucking do. It's a woman. She's at home. I don't think Misty's here."

"Fuck." I can almost hear him thinking through the phone. "Fuck."

"That's all you got? What the fuck am I supposed to do," I demand.

"Stay there. Watch her. Hope she meets up with the person that has Misty."

"Hope? You want me to fucking stay here and *hope?*" I yell down the line, pushing every bit of anger through it.

"There's nothing else you can do."

My heart bleeds as it fills with anguish.

Misty won't survive on hope. And it's my fault.

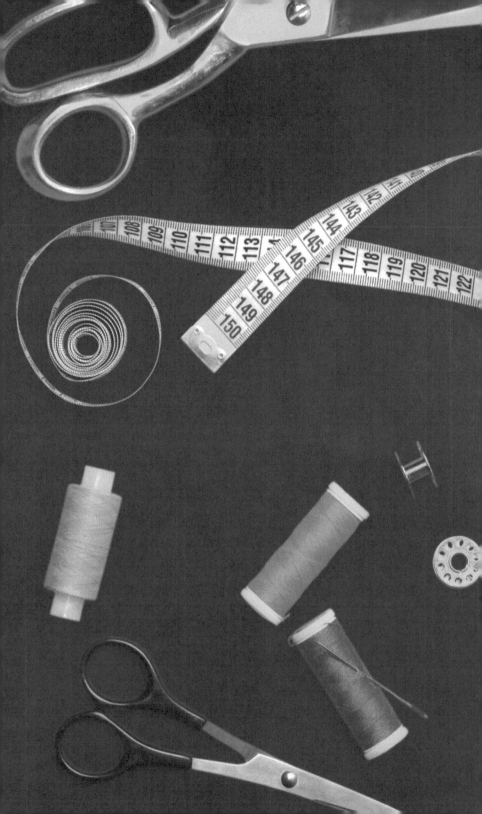

Chapter 53

Misty

THUMP, thump, thump. Each heartbeat feels like a hammer to my wrist, breaking the small bones apart from the inside out. The pain radiates up my arm in an ever-expanding distance, like sharp shards slicing through my veins. The world is fuzzy every time I wake up, floating in and out of consciousness. My uninjured arm cradles my broken one to my chest instinctively, and I thank God that they didn't tie me up. My teeth chatter from the chilling cold that seeps from the concrete floor into my bare thighs, the fabric of my dress too short and too thin to provide any form of insulation.

Throbbing agony constricts my thoughts, and I force myself to breathe through it. This is the most lucid I've been; I can't let myself pass out again. Breathing slowly, I take stock of the world around me. If I have any chance of surviving this, I can't give up now.

473

Damon's coming for me. He'll find me. He'll always find me.

I just have to keep myself alive.

My heart skips when minuscule movements show that my wrists and ankles aren't bound, and a small hint of hope needles away in my chest.

With my eyes covered, I stretch my other senses out, reaching for anything I can find. The sound of feet shuffling and men's voices speaking in sharp tones to each other. Their voices echo in the room; mixed with their distance, it makes their words hard to make out.

Metal on metal screeches from my right, finishing off with a blunt bang, and the cool breeze that's been raising the hairs on my arms is cut off.

Echoes, large doors, concrete floors. My guess is they're keeping me in some kind of warehouse.

There's a muffled sound from the far end, and I turn my head slightly to hear it. That's when I feel it. The cool steel encircling my neck.

I gasp, my eyes burning as the realization crashes into me. They didn't tie my hands and feet because they've leashed me here like a dog.

"Look who's awake." Anthony's mouth is twisted in a mockery of a smile as he removes the fabric from my eyes. "Welcome back."

The throbbing pain in my wrist is replaced by pure terror as he stands, legs straddling mine, and leans down. My stomach turns, and acid climbs up my throat as he brushes his fingers against my cheek, pushing my hair back.

"You look pretty rough." He kneels over me, grabbing a bottle of water from the ground beside us. "Can't have you die just yet."

The plastic rim presses into my lips, and he grips my jaw until I open my mouth.

"Good. Need to keep you nice and fresh, at least until that little husband of yours gets here."

I spit the water into his face the second the bottle's removed. The sharp slap against my cheek rings in my skull. "Fucking bitch. Look what you made me do." He pries my clenched teeth open and pours the liquid into my mouth, not stopping when it overflows my lips and my throat starts to gurgle.

I lurch to the side, coughing up water the second he releases me. My eyes burn with tears as I struggle to breathe.

He'll find me. He'll always find me.

I repeat it over and over. Knowing he'll come is the only thing that keeps me from falling apart.

"That's fucking disgusting." Anthony stands to get away from my mess. "I'll give you something to choke on. Thomas said it's the one thing you were good at." His fingers go to his belt, and panic compresses my chest.

"You're doing all of this for Thomas?" I rush the words out, anything to stall for time.

Anthony laughs. "Fuck no. That Unsainted little

bitch did have his use though. We've been searching for Damon's weakness for years. A way to lure him out of his protection." He grips my hair, tilting my head back. I clench my teeth together hard enough to crack. "You see, the Saints won't follow me until he's dead, but once I drag his carcass into the Vaults, they'll see. They'll see who the real Lord is."

"He'll fucking kill you," I hiss.

He tilts his head and looks entirely too pleased. "That's why you're here. Bait. I've been watching him, and when it comes to you, he has no control. The best part is all I have to do is wait, and he'll wrap himself into my trap for me."

He unzips his pants. "Now, be the little slut you are and—"

"Boss." A man in tactical gear approaches from behind. He's got some kind of rifle draped over his shoulder, two guns at his hips, and what looks like freaking grenades around his belt. "Everyone is in position."

"Remind the men they're not to kill Damon. He's mine," Anthony commands.

My fear morphs, changes as I take in the scene. They know Damon will come for me. They're planning on it. My heart aches, and I bite back the sobs at being the reason they catch him. For the first time tonight, I beg the universe for him not to find me.

The woman from earlier walks in, eyeing Anthony's and my positions. "Job's done."

Anthony gives her a warm smile, and she's an idiot if she can't see it for the manipulation that it is. "He followed you?"

The woman wraps her arms around his chest and grins. "He's here."

Chapter 54

Damon

My EYES never leave the black Chevy Impala with tinted windows and a dented back bumper as I trail it through the maze of warehouses in the industrial district. The moon casts an eerie glow over the rows of massive cranes that loom over the ocean, ready to unload hundreds of containers stacked six high on each ship.

The leather stitching on my steering wheel frays under my grip as I force myself to keep distance between us. The cover of night, compounded with my lights turned off, helps keep me out of sight. I'm just hoping whoever's driving is a regular fucking person because anyone trained would have already spotted me.

The Impala pulls up to a large mechanical gate, guarded by two men fully loaded with assault gear. It screeches as it opens, allowing the one car in before closing again. But it's the glowing sign plastered on the side of the warehouse that has my sanity coming apart. Ricci Technology.

"I'm going to kill that asshole," I growl, fully prepared to crash through that fucking gate.

"We're five minutes away. Fucking wait!" Matthias yells through the car speakers.

"I don't give a shit. My wife is in there."

"Well, we fucking do. You don't have to do this alone. You saved us. Now let us help save your girl."

I pull over several hundred feet back and tuck my car behind a shipping container.

"You better fucking hurry."

"We're three minutes out" is his only reply.

I scan the area, and there's a constant stream of men walking behind the gate. I double-check my Glock's magazine. The seventeen bullets won't be enough. Matthias is right—I'm going to die the second I walk past those gates. Maybe that's the entire fucking plan. I click the magazine back in place and get out of the borrowed car.

No, my Little Nymph's getting out of here. I promised her I'd keep her safe, and I'll die keeping that promise, but not like some asshole without a plan.

A black SUV pulls up behind me, and my brothers step out, their doors clicking quietly closed. All three of them are decked out in tactical gear.

Bash comes up to me and slaps me on the back. "Fucking asshole. You had me worried you'd steal all the fun."

"Your sister is hurt in there, and you call this fucking fun?"

He stiffens, his eyes lowering before meeting mine. "Hurting anyone that hurts our family will always be fun. Now, let's get you geared up."

I grab my own set of clothes from the tailgate, stripping out of my Armani suit in preference for the black-on-black tactical gear.

My brothers surround me as Matthias pulls up the satellite feed.

"Fucking Christ," Xander says under his breath, and I grab his shoulder.

"You don't need to be here."

He shrugs me off, completely ignoring me.

"Quite the welcome party." Bash chuckles. "You think they're expecting us?"

It's worse than I thought. There are six men at the gate, another forty more walking patrols around the building. There are a few bright spots coming from the darker areas, signaling there are even more men hidden there. But it's the two gunners on the roof that have the hair on the back of my neck standing up. These aren't some rich pups dressed up, not with the kind of gear they're packing. Somehow, the Ricci bastard put together his own mercenary army.

Bash whistles low under his breath. "Getting around those will be fucking tricky."

Matthias starts handing out weapons from the back of the truck. Two silencers and a knife. We now have thirty-four rounds each, and I like those odds significantly better.

I check both guns over thoroughly before holstering them. Running all possibilities through my head, I pick the one we're least likely to get killed in.

"We go over the walls and pick off the patrols one by one before they realize we're here. The more dead men, the better odds we have of getting Misty out of there. There's no way we're taking down those gunners. Get close to the building out of their line of sight. Then we just need to worry about who's left on the ground."

Matthias puts his hand on Xander's arm when he cocks his gun. "Even with the silencers, it's too quiet out here to use the guns." Matthias holds up his knife, glinting in the low light. "We're doing this up close and personal for as long as we can. The second they see you, open fire."

"Use the containers and crates as barriers." I meet my brothers' eyes. "Don't get pinned between them and the gunners. Got it?"

Bash smirks at us. "Be quiet, up close and personal, kill as many as you can, and don't get mowed down by machine guns. Yeah, I think we got it."

Xander holsters his gun and grabs one of the extendable ladders. It's compact, only one foot high when closed, but it'll go up twenty feet. He tucks it under his arm. "I don't understand how people don't remember ladders fucking exist. Bash and I will take the left. You two take the right."

"Wait." Matthias hands each of us a microphone to tuck into our ears. "Keep the line clear unless you need help."

"Yes, sir," Bash says loudly into his mic.

We all wince, feedback screeching.

Bash grabs his ladder. "What? I was just testing it."

I look at my brothers all geared up and ready to go against the worst odds fucking possible. "Don't fucking die."

"Aw, he does love us," Bash says, leaning into Xander, who smiles as he pushes him off. "Let's go fucking kill these bastards and get our sister back."

Matthias sets up his ladder first and grabs my shoulder. "I know you want to get to your girl, but we need to level the numbers first. If you go in there now, you'll have forty men up your ass with automatic weapons."

"I wouldn't leave you anyway. Never have."

I step out of his grasp and head another twenty feet down before setting myself up. The cinder block walls, stacked fifteen feet high, provide the perfect cover. The silence is deafening as I crest the top, scanning the area. A slow smile pulls at my lips as a patrol steps directly below me. I'm going to enjoy this.

My knife's in my hand when I drop down behind him, the force of the drop rattling through my bones. Before he can turn, I slice across his throat, warm liquid immediately covering my hand. The man looks back at me, rage turning to fear as he gurgles, drowning in his own blood.

I pull him close, whispering into his ear. "You picked the wrong family to fuck with."

The wall casts a shadow perfect for hiding his body. There are steps coming from the right, and I duck behind a crate just in time for another patrol to show up. The dim light catches the raised scar on his face. This isn't his first fight, but it doesn't matter because he's going down anyway.

I reach down, grabbing a broken piece of wood from the pallet, and toss it to the side, drawing his attention. By the time he realizes what's happening, it's too late. I grab his shoulder and jab my knife upward into his throat, severing the major arteries. He grabs my hips on his way down, ripping at my holsters with his nearly dead fingers. I don't have time to get it back from him as three more men approach. I stalk around the crates, coming up behind them, taking them out one at a time.

My heart pounds in my chest as I look at the blood staining my hands and sleeves. I led my brothers into a fucking bloodbath. Even if we do walk out of here, what kind of damage will they be left with?

"Four motherfuckers." Bash's voice crackles through the mic.

Xander laughs. "That's it? I'm at seven. The bastards are everywhere. Easy picking."

A second later. "Eight and nine. You're fucking slow."

"Shut the fuck up," Matthias says, then adds, "Fifteen."

A smirk curls at my lips. They'll be fine. Twisted, but fine. I cut a path through the patrols while my brothers one-up each other in kill count. We're cutting down almost too easy.

Five shots in quick succession come from where Bash and Xander are, and I'm already running toward them before I've processed it.

"Bash. Bash!" Xander's voice grows desperate, and I move faster, not even bothering to hide myself. We'd killed at least forty of the fifty men, thinning them out significantly.

"Fucking answer me." Xander's voice cracks. We're all close, but the two of them have something special.

"Hold your fucking horses, man. I had to finish killing him. The bastard shot me in the fucking arm."

Relief crashes through me, and I lean against the crates for support, sucking in breaths to try to regain some semblance of control. "Xander, get to Bash."

"Already on my way."

"Aw, were you worried about me?"

"Guns out, boys. Hide-and-seek is over," Matthias cuts them off, punctuated by gunshots through the comms.

I reach for my gun and remember that scar face ripped them off just as large spotlights light up the entire area. Fuck. I shift around a crate, hiding myself from the gunners.

They open up fire at Xander and Bash, who I can

now see clearly. They're tucked behind a forklift now peppered with holes.

The second gun moves to the middle, right on top of Matthias. "Fuck, I'm pinned."

There's a ten-foot kill zone between me and the building. I grab the dead patrolman's foot and pull him toward me, prying the gun from his tight fist. "I'm crossing it. Don't fucking die."

"I'll cover you. On the count of three."

Each count has my blood pounding harder. *I'm coming, Misty.*

Matthias opens fire, and I race toward the wall, wood cutting my exposed skin as the crates disintegrate under machine gun fire around me. A bullet just nicks my arm before I can press my back against the safety of the wall.

"Lucky bastard," Bash says, his voice more strained than I want to hear. I need to hurry the fuck up. All three of them are pinned, and it won't take long for men to round them.

I look over at Matthias as he pulls a rifle from a dead guard. Looking calm as ever, he calls over to me and gestures with his head to Xander and Bash. "Just get your fucking girl. I've got them."

The steel warehouse door opens as I approach, three men rushing out of it. Their bodies collapse on top of each as I fire off rounds. The last one out is kind enough to prop the door open for me with his foot, and I climb over him into the open space.

"You finally made it. Took you long enough. I started to think I brought in too many men," Anthony says from where he stands on the other side of the warehouse, Misty kneeling at his feet.

Her arms are a fucking mess, and her cheek's bruised black. Anthony steps on a chain, and Misty jerks with the action. Rage burns my chest at the sight of her tied to the wall with a fucking metal collar like a dog. He's going to fucking regret that.

I shoot the two guards surrounding Anthony with five perfect headshots before pointing it at him and pulling the trigger. The hollow click has dread filling my stomach.

"You're so predictable. I'm almost disappointed. It's so easy to catch the great Damon Everette." Anthony points his gun at me.

Misty's sob pulls my attention. Visible tremors shake her body, and tears flood down her cheeks. I try to fill my eyes with the words I can't say. *It's okay. I'm getting you out.*

"I will fucking kill you," I promise him, rage burning through my veins.

"Will you though? You're not armed. And you're oh so easy to break." Anthony shifts the gun from my head, and the loud crack of a bullet echoes in the room as he pulls the trigger.

The world goes quiet and compresses around me as her eyes widen with fear, but I can't feel the pain from being shot. Something is screaming at the back of my brain, telling me to snap out of it, but I just look at her, wishing I could tell her, *I'm sorry that I can't keep my promise, but my brothers will get you out of here.*

Misty's green gaze meets mine, searching my face, eyes tracking back and forth as if she's trying to imprint it into her mind.

I do the same, happy that the last thing I'll see is her. Why are her cheeks so white? My chest tightens, the air so thick I can't fill my lungs as Misty's dress turns from green to a deep brown. A tremor rolls through her, and she falls forward and coughs. She mouths, "I love you." Bright red liquid bubbles over her lips.

No. This can't be happening. I run, catching her just before she collapses. Sound seeps back in, nearly deafening as reality pushes against me. My hands frantically search her body for the wound until they hover over the hole in her stomach. My hands shake as I press hard on it, desperately adding more fabric, but blood pools around my hand. I rip off my shirt, pushing it into the wound, and the already black fabric goes glossy.

Soft fingers cup my jaw and bring me back to piercing green eyes.

I cup her cheek and brush away the tears.

"You are not leaving me."

Her lips lift slightly in the corner as she looks me over, her fingers trailing over the lines in my face.

"You. Are. Not. Leaving. Me," I command, but she doesn't stop her touch, tracing every contour with less and less pressure.

"Misty." Her head slips back, and I catch it in my palm, refusing to let her look away. "You are not leaving. Okay?"

She nods, tracing her thumb over my eyebrow, each of her breaths a soft rasp.

A gun cracks, and the burn of a bullet pierces my shoulder. I set Misty down softly. "Wait for me."

Another bullet slices through my side, but I don't leave her until she nods.

"I'll be right back. I promise." I stroke a red-stained strand of hair from her face, then get up.

My vision tunnels on Anthony, standing in front of me, feet wide. His gun jerks with shots, but all I can see is red. My nostrils flare, and my lips curl back as I charge him, the loud ringing of his gun and the tearing of my flesh barely registering to me.

I catch Anthony's wrist, squeezing hard enough the delicate bones break beneath my grip, and tackle him to the ground, breaking his hold on the gun.

He cries out as all the blood drains from his face, and spit covers his lips as he speaks. "You should be dead."

I smile, all sharp teeth and bad intentions. "There's one thing you never considered, asshole. Men who are prepared to die are unpredictable."

His eyes go wide when I grip the sides of his head, then bash the back into the ground. I'm losing mobility, my body's turning to ice from loss of blood, but I'm going to kill the bastard.

I slam Anthony's head over and over until the back crushes in and blood pours out of his mouth.

It's the lack of sound that draws me back to Misty.

My stomach twists painfully as I rush back to her. She's cold. So cold. "I'm here. I'm fucking here. Wake up, baby. Please, baby, wake up." Her head rolls to the side, completely limp. "I'm so fucking sorry." A sob racks through me as I shake her hard. "Don't leave me."

I try again, but my arms won't listen, my body betraying me. I collapse beside her, staring at her lavender hair, covered in blood.

My brothers' voices filter in, calling for help, pressing on my wounds. It's too late. It's too late. I don't want to be saved.

I force my hand to move, brushing over Misty's cheek. "Don't worry, Little Nymph. I'm coming to find you. Even death can't stop me."

Chapter 55

Damon

A BRIGHT LIGHT shines in one of my eyes, then the other. "Call the OR and tell them we have a trauma coming in."

It's like I'm ten feet underwater, trying to listen in. "He's hemorrhaging!"

Alarms start going off, loud beeping piercing the surface of my fog. A woman presses down on my chest, pain searing beneath her hand.

"Stay with us." The pain dissipates, replaced by ice so cold I go completely numb. "Shit! He's bleeding out. We're losing him."

Lavender hair and clear green eyes are the last things I see before the blackness pulls me under.

———

Muffled voices filter in, pulling me toward them.

"We almost lost him." Matthias.

"He's going to be pissed when he wakes up." Xander.

A voice I don't recognize cuts in. "You can't be in here."

The noise grows quiet, and I'm sucked deep into a fog.

———

"How are we going to tell him?" Matthias says, and I fight to the surface. Is he talking about me?

"There was so much blood." Bash.

"Misty..." Another voice I don't recognize—it fades off at the end, and I desperately reach for consciousness. I grasp the rope hanging in front of me, dragging myself upward. I need to know what he says next.

Clear green eyes, red hair. That's not right...her hair's purple. A memory slips to the forefront of holding her in my arms. There's blood on my hands, on her lips, soaking through her shirt.

I promised her I'd keep her safe. Promised I'd stay with her.

I stop fighting, welcoming the dark. I'm coming, Misty.

Beeping erupts from the machines around me, and there's someone directing others, but I let go of the rope I'm holding and fall.

Light sears the back of my eyelids, and my throat burns.

"Water," I breathe, barely above a whisper. Everything hurts. I peel my eyes open, but I'm frozen in place. My arms are too heavy to lift.

"If you ever fucking do that to me again," Matthias' fist digs into my shirt.

I blink, trying to process what's happening. I'm not supposed to be here. Where am I supposed to be?

Realization dawns on me, bringing clarity, and the pain of living past her is worse than the bullet wounds. "Asshole. Why didn't you let me die?"

"Let you fucking die? *Let. You. Die!*" He stumbles back a step, rubbing his palms over his face before raking them through his hair, pulling on the ends. "How can you ask that?"

"I'm supposed to be with her. Let me go." My voice cracks around the words, more plea than statement.

Matthias searches my face, then huffs out a breath. "I don't think she'd like that."

"What?" My brows pull together, trying to process what he just said.

"Quiet, or you'll wake her." Bash comes into the room, holding two coffees.

Wake her? Wake who? I'm still fuzzy from whatever painkiller they have me on, but there's a dangerous hope bubbling in my chest. I force my head to turn, and my ribs constrict around my chest, my heart aching.

Lavender fills my vision...Misty. She's asleep on a bed, pressed against mine. Her small hand reaches toward me even in her dreams.

She's alive. She's alive. She's alive.

How is it possible? I watched her die.

My eyes burn, and tears overflow as I take her in. She's bruised, and her skin has a pale yellow tint, but she's here.

Pain radiates through my shoulder, but nothing can stop me from tucking the stray pieces of hair behind her ear. I never thought I'd be able to do it again.

Her lids slip open, and her stunning green gaze meets mine, a faint smile on her lips. "Welcome back."

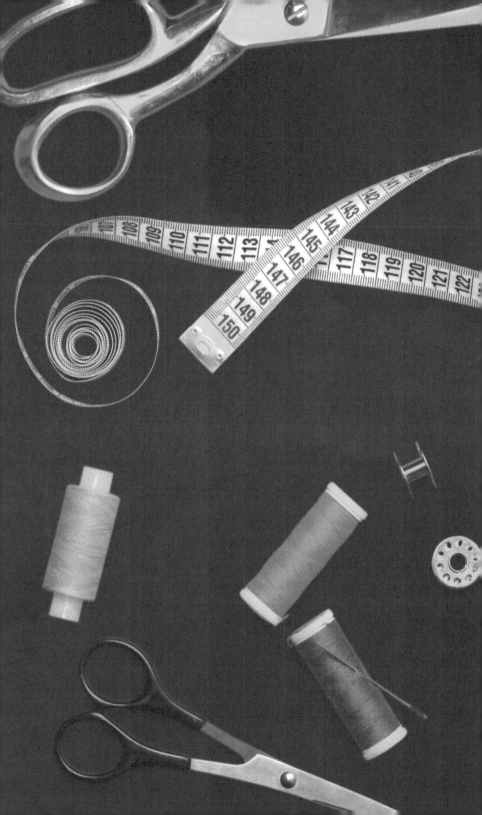

Chapter 56

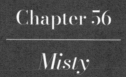

Misty

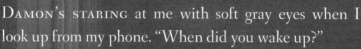

DAMON'S STARING at me with soft gray eyes when I look up from my phone. "When did you wake up?"

"A few minutes ago. What time is it?" he asks, voice groggy. It's been a rough few days, but now that we're closing in on a week at the hospital, we're mostly on the mend. The hospital staff were not happy about us both staying in the same room, beds pressed against each other, but considering Damon donated enough money to fund a new wing, they stayed quiet about it.

"Ten." I roll to my good side and brush a stray strand of hair off Damon's face, revealing the impression from his pillow on his cheek. I can't help but smile.

"What?" He lifts my injured hand, wrapped in a fluorescent green cast, and kisses my knuckles.

"I just can't get over how adorable you are—" I say, laughing as he lifts me toward him, careful not to hurt either of us, and adjusts me on his bed beside him.

He buries his nose into my neck, stubble scrapping the delicate skin, and his voice rumbles against me. "Adorable, am I?"

"Would you prefer burly? Mean? Scary?"

He raises an unimpressed brow.

"How about gorgeous, hot, sexy?"

He kisses along my jaw before resting his forehead on mine. "We need to get out of this hospital, or the nurses are going to get a show when I fuck you right here."

I laugh. "I don't know if you realized this, but you have several gunshot wounds healing right now." I trace fingers over the gauze wrapped around his shoulder where a bullet had pierced clean through. He'd been lucky. The tactical vest he'd been wearing blocked the shot that should have pierced his heart, leaving him with a six-inch bruise over his chest, but it did nothing to stop the next one from embedding itself into his thigh.

His expression grows serious. "How are you feeling?"

"Better." And it's not a lie. Turns out the location of my gunshot wound isn't that painful once the initial hole scabbed over. Something about how internal organs don't signal pain the same way. Or...they've just given me really good painkillers.

I huff out a breath. "Still probably too strenuous to have sex yet."

A crooked smile twists his lips. "You don't have to move—"

"Knock it off, you two. I did not spend all that time trying to keep you alive just to have you fuck it up now," Bash says cheerfully from the doorway. Xander and Matthias follow after him. There wasn't a single time I woke up in those first few days that at least one of the Everette brothers wasn't present. It made my heart twist that I couldn't tell my friends, but there was no way I was explaining all of this to Piper.

Matthias crosses his arms and lets out a long sigh. "You scared the shit out of us. The two of you are going to be the literal death of me."

"Oh, come on. Barely a scratch." I raise my wrist, my fingers a green that rivals my cast, and all four boys wince.

"We should've killed them slower" is Matthias's only reply.

Bash spreads his hands out, lifting one and then the other. "I have good news and bad news. What do you want first?"

I groan, not sure I can handle bad news, and Damon strokes his fingers along my arm.

Slow breath in, slow breath out. "Let's go with the bad first."

Bash winces. "The Ricci family went into hiding before we could get to them. Looks like Anthony tipped them off that there might be trouble coming their way."

"*Fuck,*" Damon says, and he looks like he's ready to explode when Bash cuts him off.

There's a glint in his eyes when he says, "I'm happy

to report no one made it out of that warehouse with their life."

"Well, that's good." I start to relax when a new worry slams into me. "My parents might sit tight for a while, but they'll cause trouble."

"I'd like to see them try, Little Nymph."

Damon's words calm a part deep inside me. *Safe.* Even after everything that's happened, he makes me feel safe.

Bash claps his hands together. "Alright, enough of that. We're breaking you out of here."

My eyes widen. "I'm not sure busting out of anywhere is a great idea for either of us right now."

Xander grips Bash's shoulder. "What he means to say is now that you are no longer on the brink of dying. We've got the go-ahead to transfer you home. A doctor and a nurse are all set up to keep you pumped full of painkillers and whatever else they do."

Matthias rubs his hand over his face and rakes his fingers through his hair. "Although, after what we just walked in on, it might be better not to leave the two of you alone."

"I'd never hurt her." There's no playfulness in Damon's voice, and his three younger brothers seem to sense the danger.

"Yeah, we know. I'm just going to wait outside for the doctor," Bash says as he flees out of the room, Xander close on his heels.

Matthias is the only one brave enough to stay. "You better fucking not," he says before walking out.

I expect Damon to laugh, be mad, something when I look at him, but I didn't expect the way his eyes soften with sadness.

"All of this happened because of me."

"That's not true—"

"I shouldn't be another one of your captors." He spins my wedding ring, looking entirely too serious.

The monitor beeps as my heart rate climbs. "Hey, now—"

"But you are mine, Little Nymph. And I'm never letting go."

I lift up so that my lips brush against his, ignoring the soreness in my stomach. "I love you."

"I've loved you longer." He smiles against me. "We need to get you another tracker."

Epilogue

Damon

PRIDE FILLS my chest as I look at my Little Nymph approaching my front door. She still looks intimidated by the pretentious building, but there's a rigidness to her shoulders, and her head's held high.

Between her newly colored pastel green hair and her knee-length floral dress, she looks like she sprouted from the forest.

She's everything this world hates and everything I want.

I'd have been happy to never come back here, but there was a wild glint in her eyes when she suggested it's the perfect spot to meet my mother.

Misty looks back at me, holding her hand out. "You ready?"

"Always." I reach for it, entwining our fingers, and tug her chest into mine.

She stumbles into me, and I steady her with an arm, skin meeting skin when I wrap it around her lower back.

I run my thumb along her scar, tracing its ridges back and forth, and marvel at the way she erupts with goose bumps. She feels delicate in my arms, but she's strong. Stronger than I'll ever be, and I'm so fucking in love with her.

I kiss her on her temple and graze the shell of her ear with my lips. "I love you."

She pulls back, smiling wide. "I love you too." Her smile turns into a wicked smirk that makes me want to drag her back home to worship her. "Now, let's go harass your mother."

My body goes rigid, but if Misty notices, she doesn't say anything, instead moving toward the door. My mother better be on her best fucking behavior.

The house has always been cold, but seeing it through Misty's eyes has me hating it. I'd let my mother renovate it prior to me moving in. It's all muted tones and cold stone. It lacks the life and warmth that our apartment has.

My Little Nymph's eyes are wide as she takes the room in. There are two grand staircases flanking the entrance, leading up to the second floor, framing a ginor-mous chandelier that's made to look like it has a thou-sand candles on it.

She points up at it. "I kinda like that."

"You have excellent taste. That's a Mernier piece." My mother's tone grates on my ears. It still holds an edge of haughtiness I'm not sure will ever disappear, but she'll have to learn to fake it when speaking with my wife.

"It's a little gaudy, but I like over-the-top things." Misty shrugs as if she didn't just directly insult my mother, and her confidence has my cock growing hard.

A muscle ticks in my mother's cheek as she weighs the situation. She looks at where my fingers are firmly curled around Misty's hip, then back to me.

I raise a brow, letting her know that I won't come to her defense. That I will never pick her over my wife.

She lets out a slow breath and plasters on a fake smile. "Dear, I think I owe you an apology."

Misty cocks her head to the side, making her appear at complete ease, but she leans into me for support. "Do you? What for?"

My mother stiffens, not expecting to be questioned. She glances at me again, then back. "I was terribly rude to you."

"Oh yes, I remember. What was it? You said that I was chasing at Damon's feet, but not to misunderstand. He could never love me, and I didn't belong with him. Am I remembering that correctly?"

The blood drains from my mother's face. "You must forgive me. I was under the weather that day. Of course you are the perfect wife to my Damon."

Misty looks her up and down before tucking herself

into my side. "Of course. You're Damon's family, which makes us family, right?"

"Right." I kiss the top of her head, resting my chin there. "Didn't you say you had somewhere you needed to be, Mother?"

Sharp eyes meet mine, but she bows her head slightly. "Yes, afternoon tea. I will see you both later."

Unlikely. She may have apologized, but I have no plans on letting her be anywhere near my Little Nymph.

When the door closes, Misty collapses back into me, a sigh escaping her lips. "She's exhausting."

I spin her in my arms and capture her mouth with mine. "I know the perfect way to help you relax." I look around. "But not here."

Misty:

"Where are you taking me?" I ask Damon as he leads me down ancient marble stairs. When he said we were visiting the Everette hotel, this was not what I expected. I run my finger along the cold stone wall, marveling at the intricate details carved in. My ankle rolls on the uneven step, and I stumble forward with a sharp cry, and Damon catches me easily.

"Are you okay?" He immediately scoops me into his arms, making the rest of the descent.

I rotate my ankle, and there's no lingering pain.

"Yeah, I'm fine." When he doesn't put me down, I add, "I've had worse."

If I expected that to help the situation, I was extremely wrong. Damon's brows lower, pinching together in the middle and making a thin line between them. "Not funny."

"Oh, come on. It's a little funny." I reach up and run my thumb over the line until it smooths out.

Whatever I was going to say next is cut off when my gaze adjusts to the low light and focuses on the room around us. I twist to look at Damon and lower my voice to a whisper. "This is the Vaults?"

"I thought you'd be curious."

"I mean, I'm insanely curious." Who wouldn't be. My husband is supposedly the head of some super top secret, billionaire-only cult thing, and there are no women allowed.

As he moves through the space, his footsteps echo off the walls of cold marble. The room seems to stretch on forever, disappearing into the shadows and making it impossible to gauge how big it is. Every surface is impeccably clean, without even a speck of dust or a hint of musty air. It's clear that despite its age, this place has been meticulously maintained. There's a design laid into the floor that looks like a stonework runner that leads all the way up to a raised platform with giant thrones.

"So this is where you meet and stuff?" I ask, eyes still dancing from one thing to another.

His low chuckle rumbles against my side. "And stuff. You're not impressed by this at all, are you?"

"I mean...it's a bunch of guys wearing masks doing ceremonies and stuff. I'm pretty sure you don't allow women because they'd call it lame." My words break off in a laugh as his fingers tickle my sides.

"You're going to pay for that." He sets me on the throne and moves to the side so I can get a better look at the room.

There's an underlying thrum of power that courses through me just sitting here that undermines my last comment. The weight of centuries lives here, and it's so palpable I can almost touch it. What does it feel like to sit here when it's full of men in silver masks, all bowing to him?

I look at Damon, who's watching me, and I'm suddenly intimidated by the whole thing. He's always been this rich, influential guy, but this is so much more. And who am I?

"Don't do that." Damon cuts through my rambling thoughts, crouching down to place a kiss on my temple.

"Do what?"

"Overthink this."

I huff out a laugh. "How am I not supposed to overthink this? You command a freaking secret society, and I make dresses and plan press conferences. We are not the same."

Damon moves around me, dropping between my thighs.

"I may be their Lord, but you are my queen." He bows and places a kiss along the exposed skin just below my skirt. "Whatever power I have is yours to wield. Ask for anything, and I will give it to you."

An inkling flies in and out of my mind, and I bite my cheek, too nervous to say it.

"Out with it," he murmurs, his tongue hot on my thigh.

My heart beats like a drum, and I swallow before saying, "I've always wanted you to beg on your knees."

He lets out a low, satisfied growl and nips my leg before looking up through his lashes. "I'll happily beg for you." His hands encircle the tops of my thighs. "Please, Misty."

A shiver rolls down my spine, and my stomach grows taut. "Please what?"

"Please let me taste you." He runs his tongue along my skin below my skirt, leaving no room for confusion.

"What, here?" I squeak, trying to get up, but he holds me in place.

"I can think of no better place to bow to you than on your throne," he says as he slips my underwear down, leaving me bare.

Heat floods my core at his words, and my skin flushes, my apprehension burning away. I give it one last protest. "What if someone comes in?"

"Then they'll get to watch me worship you like the queen you are." With that, he pushes my skirt up until it bunches around my hips and spreads my thighs wide.

I squirm, embarrassed to be exposed like this, but his fingers tighten.

"Don't. Let me look at you." His thumb brushes along my seam, and my eyes roll back.

"So fucking wet already." He hums in the back of his throat and repeats the motion, and this time, my hips curl to deepen his touch. All modesty is lost when he lifts my legs, tilting me back for better access, and runs his tongue from back to front, licking his lips when he meets my gaze.

"You taste fucking delicious." His mouth is back on me, stroking, sucking, biting until I'm a writhing mess in his arms.

"Damon," I cry, fingers digging into his hair as I try to hold on to my sanity.

"I've got you." He slips one finger in and then another, hooking them inside of me to hit the perfect spot.

My teeth clench as he orchestrates the pleasure in my body to build over and over itself until I'm lost to the noise of my orgasm breaking me apart.

Panting, I grip one hand around the chair arm, and the other stays in his hair as he gently traces my clit with his tongue. I twist against his touch. "Sensitive."

He just smiles and sucks it between his lips, drawing a gasp from mine.

There's an aching hollowness that only he can fill growing inside me. I grip his hair, pulling him back so his dark gaze meets mine. "Damon, I need you to fuck me."

That earns me a smile as he lifts from his knees. "Anything you want."

A thrill rolls through me at the promise in his eyes. "I think I could get used to this you-obeying-me thing."

"Is that right?" Damon says, then flips me so I'm facing the back of the throne, my knees firmly on the seat.

His fingers trail up the back of my thighs, flipping my skirt up, and he groans low in his throat.

"Fuck," he hisses right before his teeth sink into the soft flesh of my ass.

I cry out, but he just chuckles and licks the sore spot until pleasure replaces the pain.

The hard head of his cock circles my entrance, and my mouth falls open as he slowly fills me, drawing out each second until he's buried deep within me.

There is a burning, tingling sensation as my body adjusts to his with each thrust, until I'm pushing back into him, encouraging him to move faster.

He groans, his fingers tracing where he's entering me. "I wish you could see how well your pussy takes me."

"Damon." I breathe his name, struggling to speak as his rhythm turns punishing.

His fingers wrap around my throat, applying gentle pressure as his chest rests on my back, guiding me to lean into him.

"You feel so fucking good I can't be gentle with you."

"Fuck me, Damon."

He chuckles low against my neck and obeys, fucking me harder as his grip tightens around my neck until my head grows fuzzy.

"That's it. Take me just like that." He pounds into me as his hand reaches around, pressing down on my clit, instantly pushing me over the edge of my orgasm.

He doesn't stop as it crashes through me, until his own hot cum fills me.

Damon pants against my neck, lips grazing the sensitive skin, and says, "I don't fucking deserve you, but I'm going to make you happy that you love me every day for the rest of your life."

Continue with Matthias's book: A Twisted Arrangement

The Everette Brothers

Bash: Matthias you going to fill us in on you and Scar?

Xander: Yeah, what's going on there anyway.?

Matthias: Fuck off.

Damon: Leave the guy alone. Just read their book: A Twisted Arrangement

Matthias: ...

Xander: Have you checked out Wilder Ones - Jessa Wilder Reader Group? Heard she's really active in there.

Bash: Misty is literally named after one of her readers.

Xander: Wish I won the giveaway.

Damon: You're already in the book...

Bash: Still cool though

Matthias: There's lots of sneak peeks and early access.

Bash: He speaks!

Damon: While we wait for the next book I'm going to read The Gentlemen.

Bash: Right?! Fucking curious about those sickheads.

Xander: Nothing to do with Rae being a total badass?

Bash: She'd literally kill me. I for one wouldn't want to deprive you of this pretty face.

Matthias: Travesty

Bash: You know if you enjoyed this book you should consider giving it a review.

Xander: Definitely helps motivate J to keep us alive.

Bash: Shudder

Damon: She's not going to kill us.

Matthias: You sure about that?

Xander: Okay, okay. So just make sure you review. Alright??

Damon: See you soon.

Thank you!

The biggest thank you to Nicole, Jen, Brittany, and Eden. I couldn't have done it without your feedback.

Thank you to Sandra, for putting up with me and repeatedly saving my butt with my last minute editing requests. (I promise I'll get better.)

Thank you to Sam and Val for coming in at the end and helping to save my sanity.

Thank you to C. R Jane for being my inspiration. Also for forcing me to be more positive. You've saved me from many spirals.

I always forget people when I write these. Just know that I appreciate every single person who's been with me on this journey. You have made this a life changing experience.

Xoxoxo

Jessa

Also by

Rule Number Five

Book 1 in the Rule Breaker Series

<u>READ NOW</u>

I had my whole life planned out... until I met a hockey player obsessed with breaking all of my rules.

My 5 simple rules for hooking up keep me from being distracted. And now I'm so close to landing my dream internship. Nothing is going to make me break them.

Even a protective hockey player with clear grey eyes, a sharp jaw, and a body that makes my breath catch.

Until Jax wins a bet and one kiss has me breaking them all.

TROPES:

· Slowburn
· He Falls First

· Friends with benefits
· Jealousy
· Mutual pining

Rules Of The Game
Book 2 in the Rule Breaker Series
READ NOW

He's the star hockey player, my brother's best friend and the boy I've been in love with since I was 7.

The problem? He wants nothing to do with me.

Then why does he sneak into my room when I have a nightmare?

Gets jealous when I go on a date?

And has a tattoo of my birthday on his ribs.

Lucas Knight's a lot of things. He's possessive, jealous and overprotective. And he just might be in love with me.

Angst filled, heartbreaking and kick your feet in the air giddy inducing.

TROPES:

* Brother's Best Friend

* Secret Pen Pal

* Jealousy

* Mutual pining

* You're going to suffer, but you're going to be happy about it.

The Gentlemen Series
READ NOW

She's a kickass thief and the heads of her rival gang, Beck, Nico, and Rush need her help.

Whychoose, Multi-POV, Badass Heroine, Tons of funny banter, All over 20 years old, Forced Proximity

By Jessa Wilder & Kate King

The Blissful Omegaverse Series

<u>READ NOW</u>

In a world where Omegas are cherished, Alphas are revered, and Betas are forgotten I wouldn't have changed a thing.

Growing up in foster care, my friends and I took care of each other. Ares, Killian, Rafe, and Nox, were my everything: my first loves, my only family, my pack. Until the same night they told me we'd be together forever, I presented as an Omega, and everything changed. By Jessa Wilder & Kate King

Stalk Me

Follow Jessa on:
Tik Tok:
Jwilderauthor

Instagram:
Jessawilderauthor

Website:
jessawilder.com

Made in United States
Troutdale, OR
12/08/2024

26109675R00322